THE
BLINDFOLD TEST

BARRY SCHECHTER

MELVILLEHOUSE
BROOKLYN, NEW YORK

THE BLINDFOLD TEST

Melville House Publishing
145 Plymouth Street
Brooklyn, NY 11201

www.mhpbooks.com

ISBN: 978-1-933633-74-9

First Melville House Printing: April 2009

Book design: Kelly Blair

Library of Congress Cataloging-in-Publication Data

Schechter, Barry.
The blindfold test : a novel/Barry Schechter.
    p. cm.
ISBN 978-1-933633-74-9 (alk. paper)
1. Political satire. I. Title.
PS3619.C339B65 2009
813'.6--dc22
                   2009009760

In memory of my parents,

Allan Schechter, December 28, 1912–February 14, 2007

and

Edith Schechter, December 10, 1916–September 29, 2008

ONE

"Not only *that*," Fran was saying. "You're unobservant."

Parker closed his eyes. His left temple, an electric bass, and the pale orange spot behind his eyelids throbbed in unison. "The tablecloth is red, green, and black—a plaid gingham."

"You don't know what gingham *is*."

"You have three gray hairs above your forehead," he continued, "just to the left of the part. Your glass is two-thirds full, and you haven't touched it for fifteen minutes. Your teeth are clenched. The cocktail napkin you're shredding had a cartoon of two Mexicans tipping sombreros at a busty woman on a mule. I couldn't read the caption upside down by candlelight, but it was in nine-point California type and ended with an exclamation point. The mule was beige."

"California type? You're bluffing. What else?"

"You're wearing black wool stockings—probably stopped shaving your legs again—a blue denim skirt, a white blouse, and a defense perimeter of sweaters and vests. Oh, and new shoes, brown with low heels."

"Had 'em for years. I'm wearing one sweater and one vest. Have you missed anything important?"

"Ummm. It's 1985."

"You've observed what year it is, and it's only October—spectacular. What are you missing?"

Parker opened his eyes and, brushing back the tablecloth, theatrically checked his fly.

"Cute," she snapped, eyes narrowed, twin blips of candle flame at the centers. "Haven't you noticed the guy in the booth behind you across the aisle? Oh God, don't turn around."

"Okay, I won't. What should we talk about now?"

"What I hate most is you've just given up," she said. "You have your book and a Ph.D. from Cornell. So why are you teaching Freshman Comp at Skokie Valley Community College?"

"Nobody was giving me tenure, remember? You know how long it's been since I was called back after an interview? I used to have a joke about how long it's been. I've forgotten the joke. That's how long it's been."

"I can imagine what you're like at interviews." Slouching in her seat, she ran her thumb along an imaginary drooping mustache. "'I know I won't get the job and you've called me here for your own amusement, so get it over with.' Jeff, your luck will change if you'll give it a chance. It's statistically inevitable."

"Not necessarily. It's statistically inevitable that some people be unlucky all the time. If you flip three billion coins for eternity, seven hundred thirty-three will come up tails forever."

"Is that true? What's your source?" She was staring past his shoulder.

"I don't know. Modern science. By any chance are you staring at a bald guy wearing mirror sunglasses, a trenchcoat with the collar turned up, and a slightly askew fake beard?"

She leaned forward. "He was at the restaurant this evening and in the lobby of the Biograph. If you noticed, why haven't you said anything?"

"He probably thinks he's on a mission, right? He thinks we're part of it but he's not sure. Keep staring at him and you're going to be part of his mission. Why don't you come home with me, Fran?"

She was gathering up the shreds of her napkin and rolling them into a ball. Fran had long, dark hair, light green eyes and cheekbones Parker had once compared to small blunt instruments. "Considering our history, is that a good idea?"

"Considering our history is *never* a good idea."

She propped her chin on her hand. "Tell you what, Jeffrey. Why don't I give you a ride home, and—Goddamnit!"—her eyes had shifted to the right again—"I'll ask him what he wants."

Fran had spent most of her twenty-seven years in Schuyler, Minnesota, pop. 5,000, and her notion of a homicidal maniac was still based, no doubt, on rude salesclerks and people who talked at the movies. Parker grabbed her wrist as she rose out of the booth.

She looked imperiously at his hand on her wrist. "Jeff..."

"All right," he said, "charge!"

Dropping two fives on the table, he came up behind her where she was standing over the heavily disguised man and saying, "Mission accomplished. Report back to headquarters at once."

"Beg pardon?" Lights from the nearby video games swarmed in his mirror lenses. "You with the convention, ma'am?"

She said, "Haven't I seen you someplace before—like the Biograph and the Twenty Three-Fifty Pub?"

"I get it. Lady, you must've seen *three* guys wearin' beards, shades, and trenchcoats. Guess you didn't hear about the convention. It was on all the news shows, Bob Greene did a column on us. My name's Hank Monroe, Junior." His lips distended into what might, in a less disguised man, have been a smile.

"I'm Jeff, this is Fran. We were just leaving, but nice meeting you."

"Hold it, Jeff. Fran here asked me a question. There're about a hundred of us: We're Vietnam vets, and we dress like this so people will know about our little hassle with the V.A. See, the Vet's got a limit on how many facial reconstructions they'll pay for. After that, if you can breathe through it, and swallow with it, and make noises with it, it's a face. They ain't payin' to make us pretty. We call ourselves the Legion of Faceless Men, and we dress like this 'cause you wish we'd stay underground and incognito. We don't get some action soon, the beards, the make-up, the shades—it's all comin' off. You better get some pretty shoes that day, Fran, 'cause you're gonna spend a lotta time lookin' *down*! Ever wonder what a Claymore mine can do t' your face? Take *my* face. Please. Ain't much of it left—most of what you see here's made from this stuff like Silly Putty. You could poke a hole in it, I wouldn't even feel it. Go on, Fran, give it a shot!"

It seemed to Parker that the man was going for spectacle rather than perfect realism. But Fran looked spooked; she backed into their waitress, who just managed to steady a tray of drinks.

"I'm sorry," Fran pleaded to the waitress, Parker, and the heavily disguised man. "God I...." Putting an arm round her shoulders, Parker started for the door.

"It's okay, lady," said Hank Monroe, Jr.

She stiffened when a shrill male voice yelled, "What's the *problem*, buddy?" At the bar a crowd had gathered round a massive neck in a DePaul sweatshirt and a clenched little man shouting "What—what's the problem?"

He was steering her through the crowd near the door when some-body tapped his shoulder; the waitress handed him his jacket.

"Oh, right, thanks!"

"Unobservant?" Fran murmured as he guided her out the door.

The crawl sign on Halsted Federal read 1:05...58°...ASK ABOUT TAX DEFERRED IRA. They crossed the street to Fran's blue Omni.

"You couldn't be too upset if you're still keeping score," Parker said.

She was looking at the dim blue neon of a darkened Chinese res-taurant. "Okay Joy," she read in a cracked voice. Through willpower or sheer decorum she could hold a tear beaded in each eye without shed-ding it.

He hugged her, her hair blasting around them. "I've missed you."

"Me too."

"You haven't said anything about my leather jacket." He zipped it up, hoping the chance to make fun of him might lift her spirits. "My mom found it in her basement. Got it nineteen years ago when I was sixteen. How about it: Peter Fonda in *The Wild Angels*?"

"Hmm. The Glum Angels," she said tracing his lips with her finger. She put his collar up. "Would you mind taking the El, Jeff? I'd like to go home and scream for a while. Do you hate me?"

"We'll see. Why should you let that guy—do you really think we saw *three* of them, and they're all bald? Faceless men's convention, come on! The last American casualties would have been *how* many years ago? Silly Putty, come on."

"I didn't say I *believed* him, I just—"

"And he *was* following us."

She tucked her hair behind her ears. "Um...why?"

"I don't know, some kind of nutball performance art. I think he gets off on reactions like yours. Anyway, I doubt there's anything wrong with his face."

"There's a place for you in the Reagan administration. You could review disability benefits."

"What happened to you back there? You had me on the ropes in the argument. Then you face down the madman like he's some harmless neighbor playing his music too loud. You were magnificent! And then you buckled. You know why his story blindsided you? It's growing up in Schuyler. I've always thought it left you with an insufficient sense of horrible possibility."

She laughed. "What a nice way of saying I'm naïve." She turned her profile to him as she sometimes did when she needed to think. Her tremendous length of straight dark hair seemed to have its own weather, roiling and rippling. He liked to watch her think. Sometimes in light like this, he'd stare into the deeps of her cheekbones and wonder what was going on in there.

She turned back to face him. "Has it occurred to you that I might be upset *because* he was making it up? He picks us out at random, follows us around in disguise—just so he can tell that story? How do you know I wasn't shaken up by that? By *not* believing him." God, she was resourceful! "Doesn't it disturb you at all that you can be a good person minding your own business and suddenly you're picked out?"

"I'm just trying to understand you. Clearly you weren't afraid of him. I don't think you'd get so upset unless you believed his story... But no need to make excuses—you're compassionate. Now that I'm thinking about it, it's not so implausible. He didn't say it *was* Silly Putty. It's a prosthetic substance with some surgical property that's somehow *like* Silly Putty. They're doing amazing things with artificial skin."

She gave him a soft punch in the arm. "Don't patronize me. And stop using Schuyler to explain me. I haven't lived there for five years. We had maniacs in Schuyler. The maniacs were nicer, that's all."

"Tell you what. We'll go back there, I'll pull his beard off. If there's nothing wrong with his face, you go home with me."

"That's the least romantic proposition I've ever had. Look, in spite of everything it was good to see you again. If you decide you don't hate me, call me tomorrow." She gave him a quick kiss and ducked into her car.

* * *

He won the argument by himself on the northbound El. He decided, first of all, that he wasn't unobservant, or at least not insensitive. True, he'd left stores without his bags; he once put the lit end of a cigarette in his mouth; and Fran liked to recall the barbecue where he started mixing piña coladas with no lid on the blender—oblivious, she claimed, to the flies gathering on his eyebrows. But even when he'd escorted her into a lamppost, he was listening all the while to what she said.

Fran's encounter with their stalker had reaffirmed Parker's belief in selective observation. He liked to remind her that a third of all homicides result from unnecessary eye contact. The statistic, which he'd made up, had occurred to him seven years ago at about 3 a.m. in the New York subway. He'd been in New York that August to accept a job at City College that was suddenly withdrawn in a flurry of apologies and budget statistics. The friends he stayed with had to work the next morning, so on his last night in town he sat alone through three sets at the Blue Note and two more drinks at a bar next door, then caught the subway at West Fourth Street. He was depressed, fairly drunk, and sweating so much that during a stop the peeling of his shirtfront from his skin was audible. He was closing his eyes when someone yelled "Commies!" Across the aisle a blotchy man in a fishing hat was jabbering to himself in the window. None of his other sounds seemed to be language, and the explosion of graffiti above his head might have served for a thought balloon. There were four other people in the car, all pointing, mouthing, giggling, screaming. The words, shipwrecked, were incantations: Jesus, cancer, twat, shit, brainwaves, butt-fuck, commies. He'd heard that thousands of psychotics lived in the subway, attracted by something more mysterious than freedom from vagrancy. He was thinking that people like these must ride the subway during the day, particles in a larger chaos, when he noticed he'd missed his changeover at 59th. On the train back, two out of five passengers were talking to themselves, and a man in a Hawaiian shirt stood glaring at him. The Broadway Local platform at 59th was patrolled by a huge bag lady in a quaking red dress. Her terrifying bass voice boomed gibberish in liturgical rhythms. When two lanky teenagers came over and told her to shut the fuck up, she inhaled, a wolf about to blow down their house. The fury she released threw them back cringing. At that moment she caught Parker looking at her: Here was the man who tore up her petitions unread; who filled her brain with fumes; who kept her ovaries in a little green jar. She was swelling up, massing above Parker's bench; he was too exhausted for any defense but to slouch lower. Whatever insulated him against noises, smells, and indignities seemed to have peeled away and skittered off with the gum wrappers. The Number 1 train slammed in just as she puffed to full size; he ducked under her outspread arms through the doors. Since then, he still believed he'd help anyone in trouble, but in the presence of solo dialogue, spittled enthusiasm, and elbows nudging the air, he was actively unobservant. He unobserved.

But what if he were unobservant in a less voluntary sense? Another Alfred Levitt? When Parker was a grad student at Cornell, Levitt held the McDowell Chair in Literary Criticism. He was a plump, stately man in his mid-fifties with white hair that could fill pillows. Everyone agreed he was kind and witty, and no one doubted his eminence in the field. Nonetheless he was snubbed by the faculty and held at more than a respectful distance by his students. When word got out that he felt unwelcome at Cornell, Harvard and Yale extended offers, then withdrew them. They'd just, uh, changed their minds, and they didn't want to talk about it, okay? Everyone else in the department knew the reason, but who'd dare tell Levitt (who, unfortunately, had never married)? It had nothing to do with factions or personalities. It was just that when Levitt spoke he'd pause every three or four words—"interstices of the expressible," "the actualized ideal"—to gag and snort down snot. As one of his teaching assistants put it, a five-pound ball of snot circulated perpetually through his body.

After years of layoffs, non-renewals, and rejections, Parker dreaded he was missing some snotball of his own. There had to be something about him that everyone else could see—that turned whatever he said or did ridiculous, contemptible, or ineffectual. He sometimes imagined it perched on his head: a foul-mouthed parrot or a striped propeller beanie. At any rate, he wasn't unattractive if you counted "off-beat good looks": tall and thin, with a long, bony face, a drooping mustache, dark irreparably messed-up hair, and a characteristic expression that Fran called sardonic bewilderment—as if, she liked to say, he'd suddenly forgotten something witty. It occurred to him with genuine horror that at this moment he was dressed like Peter Fonda in *Wild Angels*. He looked around, but no one on the El was staring at him: A couple were necking and a few people read the papers, but most, like Parker, studied the imaginary partition two inches in front of their faces.

The problem didn't seem to be his teaching; according to Fran he was simply lazy and unambitious. It was true that even the idea for his dissertation had come to him as a joke. Someone at a department party had complained that if free verse was like playing tennis without a net, contemporary poets were playing without the ball. "In that case," Parker had observed, "good sportsmanship is everything." *Form and Responsibility* had elevated good sportsmanship to an aesthetic doctrine. It argued that since the personality of the poet had replaced myth and conventional form as organizing principles, aesthetic failures could usually be traced to failures of character. He barely had time to decide whether he believed any of this when he found himself praised at twenty-five as "the vanguard of a new moral criticism" (*PMLA*). It was also true that most of his writing in the years since had consisted of freelance reviews for *Down Beat* and *Film Comment*; but even so, he had nearly enough literary criticism for a second manuscript.

By Fran's standard, though, he was unambitious. She'd have her law degree from Chicago next year, and their friends agreed that some day she'd be practically a nuclear power. He was convinced she'd have stuck with him in a more palpable crisis. If he had cancer, she could have drawn on her resources for heroism, but she was unequipped to see him through mediocrity. "Have you tried A, B, and C?" she would ask. "Then what about D and E?" They'd broken up ten months ago, shortly after a party where Fran introduced him as "the former Parker" (intending, she claimed, Jeffrey Parker, author of *Form and Responsibility*).

Two couples with spiky green hair and purple-ringed eyes stopped in the aisle next to Parker and stared. Perhaps it was a form of conceptual art: By simply outnumbering him, they made him the odd one.

"Like, your hair's on fire?" said the kid nearest Parker. Despite his effort to maintain his snide demeanor, he looked anxious and bewildered.

"I'm hip," Parker said.

The kids traded exasperated looks till one of the girls rattled in her purse and handed Parker her mirror-compact. "Look!" she demanded.

Even before he held it up he could smell singed hair. It wasn't too bad—a tiny wisp of smoke, a few red pinpoints glowing at the ends of stray hairs. He slapped it out.

Handing back the mirror he asked if they'd seen what happened. They shrugged, mumbled, backed off.

"Did anyone see what happened?" Parker called out to the other passengers. But he was facing a wall of newsprint and eyeglaze.

* * *

He lived in a dirty maroon court building near the Granville El; its window frames and ledges had recently been painted an unconvincingly jaunty green. There were two letters in his box. Someone wanted to interview him for *The American Scholar*, but judging by her tone, he suspected an academic "Where Are They Now?" The second, from the Soviet embassy, contained forms.

Passing through the lobby, he remembered that Fran called it an Egyptian burial chamber: archways, echoes, and a huge stone table at the center. He'd come downstairs once and found her lying on the table with her eyes closed and her arms crossed over her chest.

On the second floor he paused before turning the key. He had opened his door on other nights to find the apartment ransacked or flooded with raw sewage or—the result, apparently, of an electrical fire—reduced to the struts and wires behind a movie set. But the card-table furniture, cheap stereo, bare bulbs, and bald velveteen couch that made up his remaining living-room furnishings would hardly tempt crime or even bad luck.

Discarding himself on the couch, he considered that most of his mental life these days was divided between dread and whimsy. His whimsies distracted him from his nameless fears and therefore increased proportionately. One consequence was the forms from the Soviets. *Down Beat* magazine ran a regular feature called "The *Down Beat* Blindfold Test": A jazz musician would listen to unidentified albums and record his moment-by-moment responses. When Yuri Andropov became the leader of the Soviet Union, the press was filled with gossip about his Americanized tastes in literature, interior decoration, Scotch, and jazz. Parker had attached a memo to one of his *Down Beat* reviews suggesting that he or one of the regular staffers fly to Moscow and give Andropov the blindfold test. Everyone had something to gain, he'd argued: publicity for *Down Beat*; propaganda for the Soviets; and—considering that diplomatic breakthroughs are often achieved through anonymous go-betweens—a possible negotiating channel for the Reagan administration. Parker wasn't terribly serious about any of this, but he was intrigued by how plausible a case could be made for it. When Art Lange at *Down Beat* laughed him off, he'd written to the embassy on his own. ("The name of the feature," he'd reassured the Soviets, "is strictly figurative. At no time would the Chairman literally be blindfolded.") He'd written three years and two Chairmen ago, and this was the first response.

The envelope was postmarked on September 10th; today was October 25th. If he cared to, he could probably construct a conspiracy theory involving the delayed letter, the man in spy drag, Yuri Andropov, and the *Down Beat* Blindfold Test. But at the moment the only inference he could draw from their seeming connectedness was that he needed to go to bed.

He was awakened by the doorbell. It had to be a junkie or a neighborhood gang, but he wondered if Fran was in the lobby impersonating a prim corpse. Not *these* days, and not—he turned the clock face-up—at 4:06. The intercom and the buzzer in his apartment didn't work; there was nothing to gain from going downstairs but the novelty of being mugged in his pajamas. He drifted off thinking about his conspiracy theory. He couldn't quite piece the facts together, but he beaded them in a row, and they resonated faintly like wind chimes.

TWO

Jim Gazeekas was slumped on a chair in Parker's office. "Right," Jim nodded as Parker explained the grade on his last assignment, "no thesis, mm-hmm." There was something suave about Jim's apathy—a gracious host nodding and murmuring at guests who never leave.

The assignment—"Analyze a bad book, play, movie, or television program"—had produced some of the best writing this semester, confirming Parker's observation that these kids were intimidated by excellence. His most popular assignment was "Rewrite the following paragraph as verbosely and redundantly as possible," and he'd once proposed a Comp course based entirely on mandatory bad writing: "Write an essay in which no verb or pronoun agrees with its antecedent (since accidental agreements will be severely penalized, reread Chapter 3)"; "Write an essay with no discernible principle of organization (to avoid stray topic sentences and thesis statements, reread Chapter 1)"; "Write an essay using the phrase 'in today's society' at least nine times. Each essay will be read aloud in class. Attendance required!"

"So, what's your point here, Jim?"

Jim stared out the window over the parking lot as if his point gleamed off car-tops and hoods. It was the kind of October day when all the cars looked new, and Skokie seemed hoisted into the stratosphere. A day—Parker's mind was wandering—that substantiated the nonexistent word he'd found in a student essay: opulescence. In honor of the morning's opulescence, Parker had dressed in the navy-blue blazer, old-school tie, white duck pants, white spats, and straw boater he'd worn in a college production of *The Importance of Being Earnest.* The outfit's nostalgia and goofiness cheered him up for the first hour; since then he'd done a double-take each time he realized he was still wearing it (except the hat). Wouldn't it take less work to just be sad?

"I thought *that* was my thesis," said Jim, pointing.

"A thesis is the controlling idea of your paper—not a two-sentence digression."

"Anyway, that's what I meant."

"We've had this discussion before. You never manage to write what you mean."

Jim's shrug implied "Sue me." The doorway behind him framed a segment of the cream-colored hallway; a skinny man in a green corduroy jacket sat down on the bench against the wall.

Parker said, "What if everyone used language that way, Jim? Suppose—you still work at Klein's Men's Store, right? Suppose someone walked up to you at the counter and said, 'Your money or your life'? When he's picked up by the police he claims to have meant 'Let me see something in a double-breasted tweed.' Shouldn't we hold him responsible for what he actually said?"

"If everyone used language that way,' said the man on the bench, "we'd know exactly what he meant."

Parker thought he recognized that Brooklyn accent with its undertone of "Nyah! Nyah!" and the haze of red frizz floating above the head. Now, who always looked like he'd just been beaten up: clothes mussed, nose pushed slightly to the side, eyes still dithering from the impact? "Steve! Steve Dobbs!" Parker boomed, and even before the words were out he was disappointed. It was one of those moments when he was glad to see an old school friend before recalling an instant later that they hadn't been friends. During their freshman year at Northwestern, he and Dobbs had lived on the same floor of Foster House, known the same people, smoked dope in the same rooms, and exchanged a hundred words at most. He couldn't even remember why they hadn't been better friends. He remembered Dobbs mostly for his demeanor—abrupt bursts of mannerism alternating with clenched rigidity, like a squirrel on a tree trunk. About ten years ago he'd heard the astounding news that Dobbs—who seemed born, even bred to fail—was running a successful nightclub in Lincoln Park, and a few years later that the club was defunct and the natural order of things restored. Like many other failures, Parker wished to believe in the natural order of things.

When Jim left the office Dobbs seated himself with his left ankle on his right knee and, hunching forward, clamped his hands tightly round the other knee. He maintained that posture of a Ronco utensil that wouldn't quite open or retract as they discussed the careers, marriages, and metamorphoses of various friends. Why was he here?

Dobbs was saying, "I ran into Henriquez a few weeks ago. Can't believe that guy's got enough brain cells left to be a commodities broker. He told me you were working here. I used to hear rumors you were teaching at Princeton."

Early in his career Parker had taught there for a semester. Despite superlative student evaluations and peer reviews, he was fired after his first semester. His lawyer from the union never got anywhere. The Dean of Faculty wouldn't meet Parker's eye—even his letters had read like shame-faced mumbling.

"I'd've liked to stay," he replied to Dobbs, "but Skokie Valley Community College made a better offer."

Dobbs reached back and shut the door. "I suppose you used to hear the rumors at Northwestern that I was a narc."

"Uh, no," Parker said truthfully.

"Well, anyway, I was a narc. More police Red Squad than Narcotics, really; and more a freelance operative/informant status than official Red Squad. Don't look at me like that. It's not what it seems."

"I don't even know what it seems," Parker said.

"Look, Jeff, you must be wondering why I'm here. I have some news for you. I'd like to come right out with it, but I know from experience that without some groundwork people don't even disbelieve it. It just dead-ends somewhere behind the eyes. Give me ten minutes."

Parker suspected that Dobbs had been "born again." Still—he glanced at the pile of papers—this might be his best shot today at an interesting experience.

Exchanging legs in the same convoluted posture, Dobbs said, "I started working with the Chicago Police Red Squad because I cut a deal after my second drug bust. But I figured the infiltration didn't all have to be one way. Why shouldn't one of *us* infiltrate *them*?"

"Who are we?" Parker asked.

"The Left," said Dobbs, exasperated. "I keep forgetting the only conviction our generation still holds is hatred of polyester."

"I'm just trying to follow your story," Parker said. "Wait a minute. Didn't you used to carry around shopping bags full of—"

"Yeah. 'Abbie Hoffman: Activist or FBI Agent?' The FBI wrote that stuff. They were always starting their own leftist splinter groups. Anyway, I was going to be a journalism major; why not write it all up for *Ramparts*: burglaries, illegal wiretaps, police provocateurs, the letters to employers and landlords, the right-wing paramilitary groups they encouraged to break up meetings and beat people up. The cops *liked* me, Jeff. They bragged about what they were doing. They were paternalistic because they saw me as a confused, fucked-up kid. I *was* a confused, fucked-up kid. A cover always works best when it's your real identity."

"But then it's not a cover, right?"

Dobbs sighed. "I guess you can't expect an outsider to grasp all the subtleties of covert operations. Anyway, there were personal problems and I had to leave school. Just personal problems, okay?"

"I didn't say anything."

"I worked at an ad agency for a while, and one day I got a call from one of my right-wing paramilitary acquaintances. He said I was a smart kid and all I needed was a break. Said he was looking for someone to manage a bar he was opening, with maybe a junior partnership in the future. Now personally he's a nice guy, but politically he's a troll. On the other hand, I'd already worked with him politically (though for what I considered perfectly valid reasons), so it would have been senseless and hypocritical to turn down a perfectly good business offer. Well, one thing led to another—did you hear about the nightclub?"

"Yes, I was sorry to hear it closed. Listen, Steve, I hate to be rude but I have papers to grade. Let's have a drink some day."

"I'm getting to my point. It took me a while but I became a journalist after all. I took my savings from the bar and started *The Exhibitionist*."

"*You* publish *The Exhibitionist*?" Parker laughed. "My compliments to the author of 'Hitler's Brain Found in Bus Station.'"

"I'll pass it on. There's sort of a follow-up in this month's issue: 'Win Hitler's Brain!' The Federal Trade Commission's giving us shit."

"Here I've been feeling sorry for you when you could probably buy this whole place including all the cars in the lot and our combined salaries. I guess it wasn't *too* painful to give up serious journalism."

"I *am* a serious journalist."

"Right."

"No, I mean it," Dobbs said with so little trace of levity that Parker replied, "Maybe I'm thinking of another magazine. You're a paranoid-conspiratorial version of the tabloids I read in check-out lines, right?"

"I'll have you know," said Dobbs, deadpan, "that beginning next month you'll be able to read *The Exhibitionist* in checkout lines, too... I suppose you think all the stories are made up."

"No, Steve, I think they're all true."

"In either case you'd be a fool. How'd they let you teach at Princeton if you can't make essential distinctions?"

"I dunno, I always erase the board after class," Parker said. "You're saying that some of the stories are true?"

"About ten percent."

"Don't the other ninety percent damage your, uh, journalistic credibility?"

"I should hope so," Dobbs enunciated in the tone of an adult instructing a slow child. "How else could I get away with publishing the truth in America?" He let the "k" sound catch in his throat.

"I see. And where do you get these stories?"

"Oh, my Sixties contacts and their contacts; disaffected intelligence agents; sometimes—what's the opposite of disaffected?—affected agents."

"You mean, from the agencies themselves?"

"Sure. They know that most serious journalists and anyone involved in Western or Soviet-bloc intelligence reads *The Exhibitionist.* Their stories are disinformation, of course, but all disinformation is based on a kernel of truth. The cognoscenti can pick it out. The mainstream press works pretty much the same way."

"Can you give me one example of a completely true story in *The Exhibitionist* ?"

"Matter of fact I'm here about a story we're running in January. The other night you met a man who calls himself Hank Monroe, Junior...."

It was as if Parker had walked smack into the man himself, the non-face with its mirror lenses filled with his own gaping. He gripped his Styrofoam cup with both hands and gulped the dregs of his coffee. "He told us there was something wrong with his face."

"He's a quick thinker alright. The Charlie Parker of the lie. He just wanted to get your attention; didn't think you'd have the balls to confront him. Your girlfriend, though..."

"Who is this guy?"

"You might say he works for the government—depending on how you define 'works' and 'government' and 'the.'"

Parker threw open his top drawer, brushed away memos and paper clips, and dropped the envelope from the Soviets onto his desk. "Why do I have the feeling it's somehow connected with this? It came Saturday."

Dobbs turned the envelope around. "Uh, the postmark is September 10, 1982."

"I didn't notice the year. Naturally there was no reason to think—I, uh..."

"Not very observant, are you? Don't feel *too* stupid. It happens to a lot of the victims. They develop what I call a protective obtuseness."

Parker said, "Epistemology aside, do you know why this letter came three years late?"

"I suppose Hank Monroe, Junior took it out of your box and kept it for three years."

"Oh, well."

"Speaking of protective obtuseness, do you think you'd notice if some person—or persons—had been following you for fourteen years? Suppose this person—or persons—unobtrusive, nondescript—were there on the El every morning; at restaurants; even other cities. Would you assume that you're being followed, that coincidence in the English novel has a basis in reality, or just that you've seen a familiar face? Or would you be so wrapped up in what you're thinking or think you're seeing, you wouldn't even notice?"

"I'd assume," Parker insisted with a trace of petulance, "that there's no reason whatever for anyone to have been following me for fourteen years."

"You'd be absolutely right, of course. It's thinking like that that makes their work so easy."

Parker stood up. "Well, Steve, don't think it's been edifying, but I have papers to grade."

Dobbs remained seated. Reaching into his inside pocket, he produced a brown leather notebook. "I think it's time you heard *The Exhibitionist*'s lead story for January. You might not believe what I tell you, but keep it handy. Like a concealed weapon, which, incidentally, I'd also advise. But first, just so you don't dismiss it out of hand—" He flipped several pages. "On April 4, 1982, you made your daily stop at the talking Coke machine outside the Granville El. Before it dropped your Coke, the machine said, clearly and distinctly, 'Parker, you asshole, wake up!' You didn't skip a beat; just picked up your Coke and somnambulated away."

Parker sat down.

"It's like remembering a dream, isn't it?"

Parker nodded. "I don't remember mentioning it to any of my friends."

"I haven't been talking to your friends," Dobbs muttered as he flipped pages. "Two weeks ago you broke out in a rash. Red sores, white pustules, itched like hell, went away in twenty-four hours. That was a mild contact poison. I'd advise you to buy a new box of detergent every time you do your laundry."

The least implausible scenario was that Dobbs was part of this, whatever *this* was.

Dobbs was saying, "August 15, 1971. According to the front page of your home-delivered *Sun-Times* Mickey Rooney's died. You've always been a Rooney fan so you mention it to your friends at work. No one's seen the story. It's not in the later editions. When you get home and check the paper, the story's not there."

"I thought—" Parker gave up. "I don't know what I thought."

"You probably didn't allow yourself to think about it at all. Protective obtuseness."

Parker had barricaded himself behind a raised eyebrow and a bemused smirk, implying, he hoped, that he'd fathomed the joke clear to its punch line and found it only mildly amusing.

"Ever hear of COINTELPRO, Jeff?"

Like a man who determines to stop thrashing and float on his back till rescue arrives, Parker calmed down. He rested his eyes on the reassuring bulk of *Two Hundred Years of American Rhetoric* by Clyde C. Thurnball. In the lot a girl in a billowing orange dress flared out of a green Camaro.

"Ever hear of COINTELPRO, Jeff? The FBI dirty-tricks program?"

"Sounds familiar."

"J. Edgar Hoover started the program in 1956. It was supposed to 'neutralize and disrupt activists and their organizations.' A lot of it involved the sort of thing the Red Squad did later in the Sixties: break-ins, illegal wiretaps, burglaries, poison-pen letters. But Hoover was always urging his people to be innovative and 'forward-thinking,' and sometimes they were almost whimsical. They tried to start a gang war between the Mafia and the American Communist Party. They must've spent hundreds of man-hours trying to get a scoutmaster in East Orange, New Jersey drummed out of the corps. But some of this stuff—well, for example, Hoover was worried about 'the rise of a Negro messiah'; the FBI bugged Martin Luther King's hotel rooms and wrote him a letter implying that unless he committed suicide they'd leak the tapes to the press. Then there was that actress who was sleeping with a Black Panther; apparently they drove *her* to suicide. Don't look at me like that. This all came out in the Seventies: some of it when the FBI office in Media, Pennsylvania, was burglarized, more when William Saxbe became Attorney General and when Carl Stern at NBC sued under the Freedom of Information Act. In 1978 the House Select Committee..."

"I heard the news stories," Parker said. "But if you expect me to believe that the FBI singled *me* out for harassment, I don't buy it. I handed out leaflets, attended some demonstrations, wrote a few anti-war columns for *The Daily Northwestern*. Besides, they called that stuff off in the Seventies, right? So what are you saying, Steve? The FBI is talking to me through a Coke machine? J. Edgar Hoover wanted me to think Mickey Rooney was dead?"

Backhanding away these remarks, Dobbs continued, "In May, 1968, Hoover initiated 'COINTELPRO—New Left.' As usual he reminded his mischief-makers to be sure their gags were 'forward-thinking' and untraceable. Field offices were ordered to assign 'an experienced, imaginative special agent' to the program. And some of the new tactics *were* pretty imaginative. For example, they used to selectively leak real FBI documents 'to enhance the paranoia endemic in these circles,' as Hoover put it, and 'to get the point across that there is an FBI agent behind every mailbox.' But, for the most part, the brightest agents were discontented with ideological work, and COINTELPRO was causing morale problems. On the other hand, the agents who worked in political intelligence by choice tended to be unimaginative hacks; unless you think every mollusc contains a pearl you wouldn't expect much 'forward-thinking' from these guys.

"Well, someone came up with an approach that guaranteed both 'forward-thinking' and deniability. He called it the Breather Program. He figured that if COINTELPRO relied entirely on FBI hacks, their dirty tricks would become as identifiable as their blue suits and pointy shoes. So, why not go to the real experts—crackpots, cranks, psychotic practical jokers? The kind of people who—for example, have you noticed that if you call a radio talk show, they won't let you give your address or phone number on the air? It's because everyone in public life gets crank calls and hate mail. The weather girl, Bozo, everyone. There are people out there who, if they know you exist, hate you. If they know where to find you, you'll be lucky to get off with hate mail filled with squiggly obscenities in every shade of the Crayola Rainbow Assortment, and coated, maybe, with dried blood and semen."

"All right, all right, I get it."

"I seriously doubt that you do. But imagine how unpalatable life could be if one of these people were paid to think about you all the time."

Parker imagined the furious subway bag lady sitting at a desk in an empty room, thinking about him. "You mean, just *think* about me?"

"And act out whatever he's thought. Kinda like a National Endowment for the Arts for maniacs. And it was all deniable: The FBI could pay one of these people in cash, turn him loose, and leave the rest to his autistic license. He's got nothing else to do but hate you. If he's caught and claims to be working for the FBI, who'll believe him?

"Until then, COINTELPRO had targeted high-profile types: movement leaders, outspoken celebrities. But 'to enhance the paranoia endemic in these circles,' the Breather Program went after nonentities. Most of the college kids involved in demonstrations had no strong ideological commitment; if the rumor went out that your life could be ruined just for marching a few blocks, you might get started buying three-piece suits."

"Wait a minute. I thought this was all supposed to be untraceable."

"It would be untraceable to the press: They wouldn't dare print a story like this without solid evidence. On the other hand, it would be unmistakable to the victims, who were already hallucinating all those FBI agents behind mailboxes. But before the program had time to work the kinks out—or in—all COINTELPRO activities were canceled on April 28th, 1971—a month after the first press leaks and three days after Hale Boggs denounced COINTELPRO on the floor of the Senate. Course, that didn't do *you* much good."

Parker, who realized by now that the more he expressed his bewilderment, the further Dobbs perpetuated it, remained silent. He didn't think there was much to learn from people's eyes, but, for what it was worth, Dobbs's were the median brown and neither glinting nor void. They darted a good deal, not, it seemed, evading Parker, but rather tracking the hairpin turns of Dobbs's thought.

"In November, 1970—five months before COINTELPRO was called off—Hank Monroe, Junior was discovered by the program's talent scouts. Monroe, Junior was behind a notorious series of crank calls in Bismarck, North Dakota. He'd phone women and tell them he was with the Health Department. Claimed there was an epidemic of 'folicosis' in the neighborhood, and to avoid infection—I'll bet he was real imaginative describing the symptoms—to avoid infection they were supposed to shave their heads and leave the hair in a bag on the doorstep. Believe it or not, about four dozen women shaved their heads. They'd've never caught him, except he went around and collected the bags.

"The Bureau saw to it that all charges were dropped, and Monroe, Junior was recruited for the Breather Program. I don't know what he did between November and January—just that he went through four victims in a row, and so satisfactorily the Bureau decided to use him in a sort of honors Breather Program. He'd be given an unlimited expense account—the money could be laundered through one of the trusts or foundations they used for sensitive projects; funny word, 'sensitive'—and assigned to one person on a long-term basis. What could be scarier to the Bureau's enemies than the prospect of a customized, personal demon?"

Dobbs had propped the notebook on the higher of his crossed legs and poised a ballpoint over it. "Any comments for our readers?" His ironic tone might have alluded to his imitation of a serious journalist or—more likely, considering his slant on things—his imitation of a mock journalist.

Out the window, leaves rose in a spiral over the lot; Parker dropped a grammar book on a twitching pile of essays. "Let's see that notebook, Steve."

It came spinning edge over edge; Parker caught it one-handed, and the assurance of his gesture calmed him. Dobbs's handwriting had been squashed kicking and screaming into its confines. Even where a distinct group of letters could be made out among scrunched verticals and imploded loops, it was usually an unfamiliar acronym or abbreviation. The entry for 12-14-84 read "V.D."

"It's a covert operations term, 'venereal disinformation' He pays women to almost go to bed with you."

Rather than sit there looking stupid, Parker continued the oral exam, reading a phrase aloud and eliciting Dobbs's evasive or laconic response. By this means he learned that as of two nights ago every book in his apartment was missing its last page; that the charges against him in a letter routinely circulated to tenure and hiring committees were so outrageous they were never discussed at the meetings, and Parker was rejected on the handiest pretext; that on the night of August 3, 1971, Hank Monroe, Jr.—at a momentary creative ebb—snuck up behind Parker on Sherman Avenue and brained him with a lead pipe.

Fingering the scar at the back of his head. Parker said, "I don't suppose you'd reveal your sources."

"Sorry, journalistic ethics." Shrug, upturned palms.

"Where can I find this guy?"

"I don't know."

In the pause that followed, Dobbs recrossed his legs several times and kept scratching a spot beneath his jacket. A car started; a girl's voice in the hall said "Two weeks from Thursday."

Parker said, "So this guy's like a Japanese soldier in the jungle who doesn't know the war is over."

"That's one possibility. Personally I think he's still getting paid by the FBI. At any rate, he hasn't held an aboveground job for ten years. Maybe he knows enough to blackmail the Bureau. Maybe the Bureau's curious about what he'll do next—maybe it even has a sense of humor. I favor the 'No One's in Charge' theory. Obviously covert operations weren't spelled out in the FBI budget. They'd sort of burrow their way between line-items. In the case of a long-term operation, there might be an automatic disbursement mechanism to shield it from reviews and audits. What I'm saying is, the checks might still be going out to Hank Monroe, Junior, and no one in charge knows it. Mind tossing that notebook?"

Parker thought of keeping it—for what, evidence?—then tossed it. Resuming his newshound pose, Dobbs said, "You look skeptical. Any comments for our readers?"

Parker told Dobbs's readers that he couldn't explain everything he'd heard today; he couldn't explain magic tricks either, but he didn't change his belief system every time Doug Henning made an elephant disappear. He urged readers of *The Exhibitionist* not to succumb to paranoia merely because it explained a few puzzling facts; we might as well go blind so we can learn Braille. ("I think this is called whistling in a graveyard," Dobbs said over his notebook. "Don't let me stop you if it helps.") Parker inhaled. On the other hand, if there was anything to this conspiracy, Dobbs here had to be pretty chummy with the conspirators to learn of it in such detail. ("Not necessarily," Dobbs muttered, eyes on his writing. "I might have found out through the Freedom of Information Act." "And? Did you?" "Well, no.") Parker reminded his audience that the FBI used to leak its dirty tricks to the victims in order to crank up their paranoia. Wasn't it plausible that Dobbs was here on just such an errand? But why assume that the FBI was funding whimsical maniacs and surly Coke machines? Why not assume that Dobbs was Hank Monroe, Jr.? It could have been anyone the other night beneath the beard, the sunglasses, and a latex bald-wig. Anyone could have produced that John Wayne someday-this-will-all-be-beef drawl. Parker speculated that sometime about 1970 Dobbs had flipped out—or, at the very least, acquired a political sophistication capable of embracing contradictory ideas and opposed sides. Perhaps he'd begun to confuse his identity with the cover he used when he spied on the Left or the cover he used when he told himself he was spying on the police. And what would be the effect on such a subtle mind if it ingested large amounts of LSD, Machiavelli, dialectical materialism, moral omnivorism, undercover police procedure, and *The National Enquirer*? Wasn't it likely to finesse itself into insanity? Some time about then Parker must have looked at him sideways and become part of his mission. Parker apologized to readers of *The Exhibitionist* for not taking his own advice about paranoia, but he was sure they were used to reconciling contradictions, so he'd leave that task to them. Finally—and this was strictly off the record—he wasn't about to let Dobbs leave this office until he produced some ID and a verifiable address where, in case of further trouble, he could be beaten up on the doorstep.

It was hard to tell whether threats made Dobbs nervous—as it was hard to tell whether they made him skinny or redheaded. When he stopped writing and looked up, he was grinning. He stretched, the open notebook dangling from his hand, and resumed his usual posture (crowded, it seemed to Parker, as if the air were inhabited). "I love it. Write up your version, we'll run it alongside ours. Just remember, even people with real enemies can be paranoid." After amiably tolerating an ID check, a comparison of his ID with his phone book listing, and Parker's calls to a mutual friend and the editorial offices of *The Exhibitionist*, Dobbs said, "As to beating me up, maybe I'm biased. But I suppose you've considered the possibility that I'm the only one who can help you?"

"It's crossed my mind, unfortunately." Parker divided his papers among three manila envelopes and dropped the envelopes, his grade book, and *Two Hundred Years of American Rhetoric* into his briefcase. He massaged the back of his neck. "Boy, conspiratorial thinking is hard work. It feels like someone's yanking my brain by the vertebrae."

Dobbs nodded sympathetically. "Your nervous system's bucking the new order. Hang in there."

"Okay. Explain this. If so much effort has gone into ruining my life, why is it my life isn't *that bad*? Whole neighborhoods in Chicago are more miserable, and *they're* better off than two-thirds of the world. Monroe, Junior must be in the lowest percentile of demons. I could easily have ended up like this"—he gestured vaguely—"through the unassisted course of events and my own lack of character."

"That's the beauty of it. A good practical joke always looks like 'the unassisted course of events.' Anyway, he's in it for the long run: If you die or go nuts, the Punch-and-Judy show's over. What I think he had planned for you was a gradual, stately downward arc. Course, he hadn't counted on your defenses. All that work, and his only audience is an obtuse Job.

Watch out, I think he's bored."

"I have a class," said Parker, fastening his briefcase. A scattershot of leaves gusted against the window. "What now? I go teach the uses of the semicolon and forget the whole thing, right?"

Dobbs stood up. "Hang in there. We've got sworn affidavits, a memo initialed by the assistant director. We're gonna nail these fuckers. In the meantime, buy a handgun. You'll feel better even if you never use it. For walking around, there's a legal weapon called the Taser—looks like a flashlight, shoots little hooks on wires. Fifty thousand volts, non-lethal."

They stepped into the hallway, where classes were letting out. Parker said, "People are always telling me to avoid self-pity and take responsibility for my own life. I guess that's out, huh?"

"Pious American bullshit," said Dobbs, leaning against the wall to let people by. "Your troubles *are* someone else's fault. I'd say self-pity's perfectly justified in your case. We've got to start mapping a strategy. Why don't you come over for dinner on Sunday? You can meet my wife, verify my address again. What's that look? You're wondering about the Dobbses, do they spend a quiet evening tearing up the furniture looking for bugs? See for yourself. Bring Fran."

"I'll have to check my appointments. Wait a minute, you've been working on this story for a long time, right? You said that when you ran into Henriquez a few weeks ago he told you I was working here. You must have already known that. Every detail of everything you say disintegrates on inspection, right? You said this guy *calls himself* Hank Monroe, Junior.... "

Coming out of the office next door, Professor John Connor Murray did a stylized double-take. "Young Parker, you're wearing spats! What became of *Form and Responsibility?*"

"Let me know about dinner," said Dobbs, backing into the crowd. "In the meantime, keep checking IDs. Use your peripheral vision. And wake up as much as you can, okay?"

THREE

The world without blinders looked just the same. Parker started down the hallway, blinking at the cream-colored walls, the numbered doors, and the usual faces as if an earthquake had just bounced its rubble back into perfect order. He walked into his classroom, rested an elbow casually on the podium, and wondered how his students would react if in the next few seconds he proved to be completely insane. No doubt they'd stare at him dutifully for the full fifty minutes. But like a patient in shock who automatically recites his name and social security number for the admitting clerk, he taught two classes in a row on dependent and independent clauses. When it was all over, his beeline for the door was blocked by a paper held in his face. His first impulse was to charge through it like a bull through a cape. But the weirdness of things didn't obligate him to go crazy; it was no less appropriate to help Joe Sapperstein with his transitions and ask him where he learned so much about bass fishing.

The same logic got him through the El ride home: It was no less appropriate to give your seat to an old woman, stand clear of the doors, and read the *New York Times* folded lengthwise than to charge into the crowd, briefcase flailing. The train car was the model that resembles a hospital waiting room—fluorescent panels, tan and salmon seats—and, like people expecting the worst, its passengers stared out the windows or deep into empty space. He realized that he did see some of these faces every day. Nothing sinister there—he always caught the train at this time. There'd be no way to tell if he was being followed until he reached his stop—short, that is, of shoving his way from car to car or ducking in and out of the doors. He doubted if he'd learn anything that way, and the people wedged against him looked aggravated enough already. Nonetheless he found himself returning the stares of people who were merely staring back. Should he be looking for people who stuck out, or who blended in? The sore thumb of the bunch—with real bruises—waved to him from the other end of the car. Ziploc, as he was known around Skokie Valley College, was a short, peppy man in his fifties with tortoiseshell glasses, broken teeth, and, regardless of the season, a dark-blue stocking cap and a brown jacket whose fake-fur collar seemed to have been ripped out in handfuls. As always he was carrying the "jumbo" Ziploc bag containing the "sandwich" Ziploc bags that housed his collection. In the course of five or six El rides, he'd given Parker the complete lecture series, pointing out the dead seahorse, the network of tiny brass rods, the piece of string dyed two colors, and the pale slushy substance Parker had taken for applesauce but which Ziploc referred to as "the unidentified gelatinous mass." He seemed to read a good deal, dropping references to psychology, physics, and the Bible, but his ideas passed through something like the crusher in an auto graveyard and emerged indistinguishable and impenetrable. Still, there was something infectious about his scholarly enthusiasm. It wasn't clear why he'd begun hanging around Skokie Valley College, but he'd achieved colorful character status there, invited to seders and Thanksgiving dinners and interviewed for the *Bulletin*, where his decimated smile flashed above the caption, "If you think about it, all modern physics is in the Five Books of Moses."

But if anyone here qualified as a suspicious character, it was the man who looked too much like a professor. He was standing about twenty feet away—briefcase, slightly baggy flannel pants, patched tweed jacket, school tie, and summing it all up, an empty Dunhill briar pipe like the tag on a stuffed animal. His features came from the same warehouse of clichés: his face craggy, his jaw jutting, his nose Roman, his hair sandy, and of course his brow high. In short, he'd stepped out of a Norman Rockwell poster of the professions, leaving a slightly baggy void between the Butcher and the Baker. The get-up seemed intended not to make him look like a professor but to flaunt itself as a disguise—much like Hank Monroe, Jr.'s beard, shades, and trenchcoat. Or maybe the guy taught at Skokie Valley and needed a self-deprecating joke to cheer himself up. For pretty much the same reason Parker was wearing white spats (he'd stuffed the straw hat in his briefcase shortly after he put it on). But wasn't it implausible that he'd see two such outlandish people every day in the same place? Yes. But if he connected all implausible events to each other and himself, where would that lead? To reading the *National Enquirer* like the Kabbalah. To viewing everything through a thicket of quotation marks.

He gripped a pole as the train lurched. 1) Buy a gun. If that was too scary, a Taser. It seemed the best way to go on with life as usual—just keep it handy in case he needed it. 2) Ask the super about people going in and out of the apartment, maybe pretending to be friends or repairmen and asking for a passkey. 3) Pressure Dobbs for more information. 4) Was it worth seeing a private detective? He'd be lucky to afford a day's service. The phrase "private detective" intensified his sense of unreality. 5) See a legal-aid lawyer about using the Freedom of Information Act. The only person he knew who'd sent for his FBI file was his friend John Standell, and all he'd gotten for his trouble were fourteen pages of deletions and one extant sentence: "Like many of his generation, Mr. Standell believes in 'doing his own thing.'" 6) Come to think of it, John would be in a position to help. He hadn't seen John for over a year; they'd both grown uncomfortable with the etiquette that required John to diminish his achievements and Parker to magnify the glimmer of his distant prospects (more to avoid embarrassing his friend than himself). Like other friends who seemed genuinely pained by Parker's failure, John had crossed streets and reversed direction to avoid him and therefore could be trusted.

He was already thinking that none of this activity would amount to more than beadwork for the nervous. But reduced to essentials it was a simple task. All he needed was an address. He reminded himself that if the story he'd heard was true, he'd been given the chance of his life: Whatever had been sitting on his chest all these years had taken a shape he could wrestle with. Maybe he was still numb, but Parker wasn't out to kill anyone; he didn't quite believe in the "potential" life his demon had ruined, and though he tried to imagine the "real" Parker—posed him under a tree on Harvard Common—the image blurred into its tweedy caricature at the other end of the car.

At the other end of the car the "professor" and Ziploc were talking quietly. The "professor" gestured tersely with his pipe, and Ziploc spoke with none of the usual enthusiasm that nearly picked him up and threw him. They'd stopped talking and were staring directly at Parker—but of course he'd been staring at them. He scrunched and excused himself forward, and just as he stepped into view, Ziploc turned the voltage back up, arms flailing, eyes, mouth and brows aboil. "Eh, Parker! How ya doin'!"

"Got something for you, Zip," said Parker reaching into his briefcase. Ziploc's real name was Jack Gretsky but, like a true celebrity who knew the common currency of fame, notoriety, and condescension, he preferred the nickname. He had two black eyes today, and the fluorescent light revealed further darkness beneath his stubble. Last month Parker had chased away some teenagers who'd surrounded Ziploc on the Howard El platform—doubly infuriated, apparently, by a didactic lunatic. From his briefcase Parker produced a sheet filled with bar graphs, vectors, asterisks, spirals, pie charts, and dotted lines—one of the mailbox stuffers with which Jan Cohen, his department chairman, kept the staff apprised of breakthroughs in the science of Composition. Parker had thrown them out until he'd begun saving them for Ziploc.

"Chomsky'll wanna see this, yeah." For the past few months Ziploc had been sending 9 x 14 envelopes bursting with his incoherent "researches" to the M.I.T. linguist Noam Chomsky—put up to it, Parker was certain, by a smartass on the Skokie Valley faculty—and his one reply was displayed in the jumbo bag: "Have received your manuscript. N.C."

While Ziploc studied the chart with a raptness that would have puzzled even Jan Cohen, Parker smiled blandly at the man who looked too much like a professor. "Haven't I seen you at Skokie Valley?"

"...loosely affiliated...interdepartmental...the general, not the particular...the journals...." Most of the man's words were lost behind train noise, the pipe in his teeth, and a voice both well-modulated and indistinct, like a radio heard in sleep. Parker wondered if the man was talking gibberish just to spook him. But when the train stopped at McCormick, he took out the pipe and said clearly and distinctly, "How do you stand it?"

Parker stared. The "professor" was around forty, his face lined to accommodate a bemused smile and raised or knitted brows. Having spent most of his life in classrooms, Parker was convinced that people who were actually thinking didn't knit their brows. The man had made a career as some sort of fraud.

"I mean," the professor said, "how do you stand teaching at Skokie Valley? I have more training than the average surgeon and make considerably less than the average grape-picker, which means I get less monetary return on my education than the average Trappist monk—with none of the spiritual compensations."

So there was nothing sinister or mysterious about him after all. Just another Skokie Valley whiner. Whining was the faculty's social glue, playing the same role as that filled at other institutions by bridge, racquetball, or gossip. Parker, who'd done his share, was always ashamed to hear how it sounded. When he'd started there four years ago, he and John Connor Murray were the only Ph.Ds in the department, most of the staff consisting of graduate students from other schools and middle-aged women returning to work. But these days the place was infested with snide, ironic Ph.Ds, nothing better to do with their excess brilliance than crack allusive jokes and stuff the mailboxes with charts—sometimes parodies of Jan Cohen's—comparing their lot to that of Burger King fry cooks or streetcorner windshield polishers. Like most of the others, Parker used to have three or four other part-time jobs, but these had suddenly and mysteriously been withdrawn. His demon seemed content, though, to let him stay on at Skokie Valley.

Ziploc placed a hand on Parker's shoulder. "Perfessor High Muck-a-Muck Parker here use to teach at Princeton."

"Then what are we doing here?" asked Parker's colleague.

Parker said, "You're the victim of demographics, the new materialism, the decline of interest in the liberal arts, and the relaxation of mandatory faculty retirement. *I'm* the victim of a conspiracy." They both laughed.

By now he was nearly certain he saw this man on both trains every day, regardless of which car he rode or how he changed his schedule. And the same face was coming into focus in bars, theater lobbies, ballparks, crowds in the street. Or was he mistaking the cliché's familiarity for the man's?

"Here's where I get off," said the professor, and with a minimalist Ivy League wave to Parker and Ziploc, he nudged his way out the doors.

Ziploc placed a finger in the center of Parker's chest. "Three-point-seven! I can look at some somebody and tell what percent of their brain they're usin'. That guy there, forty-seven-point-nine. See, you thought I was makin' this up. That baby there, a hunerd percent. That's right, babies have very *intense* brains."

Parker searched the windows for anything familiar or reassuring. The sun was going down, splattering through the passing trees, and in the clearings he focused on power lines, golden arches, traffic, dead neon, the blue peaked roof of a Big Boy drive-in. This, he supposed, was what he meant by the real world: predictable, self-explanatory, mildly irritating, and, except in emergencies, conveniently ignored.

Ziploc was well into his monologue, setting forth his ideas with the gusto of a juggler tossing up more and more objects even as they crashed in a miscellaneous din. Wasn't he an ideal recruit for a "Breather Program"? He was telling the story of a man in Sauganash Park who walked around with an empty leash till in three days he'd produced a "hypothetical dog" through "dynamic optimism."

The day's absurdities were beating Parker down; as a charm to restore normalcy he yelled, "So, Zip, how about those Bears!"

Ziploc recoiled as if slapped and, as the train pulled into Skokie Boulevard, turned and shoved his way out. "Sorry, Zip," Parker yelled as the doors closed. Applied to a real human being, Dobbs's theory seemed pernicious, a demonology of victims.

His two most obvious suspects at large, Parker scanned the remaining faces. There was more to being observant, surely, than singling out weird people. The people encircling him—kids in Niles West jackets, a couple of men in three-piece suits, shoppers with bags from Old Orchard, a woman with a baby in a stroller—looked completely, but not suspiciously, plausible. Of course if the story he'd heard were true, he might be the world's least qualified judge of plausibility. Come to think of it, what was he looking for? By the time he changed trains at Howard, he'd given up looking around, and he rode to Granville with the *Times* blurring in his face.

He walked out of the station ahead of the crowd, round-shouldered against the chill. The sunset and the orange streetlights seeped into the dingy buildings. He passed the Liquorama and some boarded stores and, glancing back, turned left on Winthrop. It didn't look like he was being followed; how else would it look if he was? But the sense of danger was general and the hostility of passersby impartial. Broken glass flared the length of the sidewalk, and as always he'd no idea where it came from. He asked himself why he hadn't moved after the burglaries, fires, floods of raw sewage, etc. and decided 1) he couldn't afford to, 2) he'd been no "luckier" elsewhere, 3) since things had gone awry routinely for most of his adult life, he'd barely had a standard by which to judge himself unlucky—having no more sense of the norm than would, say, a crash-test dummy.

He passed through the entrance without stopping for his mail, clacked and reverberated through the lobby, took the steps two at a time, and, turning the key as quietly as he could, threw open the door and hit the lights. Everything precisely as he'd left it: bare bulbs, white walls, card-table and chairs, books, couch, stereo, the usual stains. He felt like a kid who turns the light on a second after the monsters have turned back to toys and furniture.

According to Dobbs, the last page was missing from all his books. Okay. He walked to the bookcase and removed *The Pound Era* by Hugh Kenner. He'd used a copy in the library a few days ago, same paperback edition, and recalled that there'd been no additional pages—flyleaves, notes on the author or the typeface—after the index. And the last entry in the index is..."Zukofsky, Louis!" He exhaled, equally relieved and ashamed to see it.

Parker didn't consider himself gullible. Unobservant, maybe—but how had he come to this? He thought back to his session with Dobbs and tried to retrace the arc from irritation to fear to slack-jawed belief. It had little to do with Dobbs's encyclopedic knowledge of his pains and humiliations, or the man's flair for arranging inexplicable facts into consistent, coherent absurdities. But there was something reassuring in the notion of a personal demon: The next best thing to a savior, it absolved you of screwing up.

The book was still in his hand; he was about to reshelve it when he turned to the last page of text. The last sentence began

His mind on Carpaccio, on cats and stones, on butterflies ("gasping," "milkweed the sustenance"), on the conversation

and dead-ended. The following page had been removed without a tatter.

The phone rang. He turned on the light in the bedroom and, now that he was observing, looked with new interest at the charred floor-boards, the hole his last burglar had inexplicably punched in the wall, and the half-dozen russet blotches over the headboard of his bed which Helen Garrity in Biology assured him could not have been five-inch cockroaches. He picked up the receiver, then the cradle, and trailing the cord back into the living room croaked hello.

"Hiii!" Fran's breezy small-town-folks tone.

"Oh, hi." He set the cradle down and pulled out *The Education of Henry Adams*—yup!—tossed it on the floor and tried *The Selected Poems of Louis Zukofsky*—mm-hmm!

"Hello, Jeff? Is this a bad time?"

"No...uh, no. That's okay." Kneeling down, he reached into the crack between the case and the wall where books sometimes fell off the top and removed a dusty copy of *The Blue Hammer* by Ross MacDonald. "Actually," he said, "someone's razored the last page out of all my books."

"You're weird."

He wondered how long it would take—how many people?—to meticulously remove one page each from 3,000 books. They'd've used garbage bags, probably still in the trash bin. Upstairs the nightly thuds were beginning. It had started about three months ago, a sound like a concrete block being dropped over and over, lasting anywhere from a few minutes to all night. For the first time he considered the possibility that someone *was* dropping a concrete block over and over. Maybe several people working in shifts. Parker had quickly grown used to the noise as he did to most irritations. If this was the Breather Project, what a chintzy, measly conspiracy—less a hell or purgatory than an extended fraternity hell week. As far as he knew, he'd never seen "R. Braff." What if he went up there and knocked on the door?

He heard himself "mm-hmm, mm-hmm" during Fran's pauses. She was saying, "The spice dealer has all these confused flour beetles in his saffron and he sues the shipper." In the bathroom he pulled out *The Inimitable Jeeves* from behind the radiator. Right. In the bedroom again he took down the box his mother had sent over. Pez dispenser, fielder's mitt, ray gun: *The Boy Scout Handbook* was missing its last page. Fran was saying, "I argued that the trucking company's liable for the confused flour beetles."

"What? What do you mean, 'confused beetles'? How can they tell the difference between a confused beetle and one who's got his shit together?"

"It's a type of beetle. Though they do look confused. They stagger around in spirals, a fact not unrelated, I suspect, to their being two or three times as prolific as other beetles. Anyway, this is boring."

"No, really I..."

"Do you want to go dancing, or what?"

Parker didn't read much into this. She was hurt—well, surprised—that he hadn't called. Frances Anne Girard was a politician's daughter, and her instinct was to win people over. Once she'd done that, she had no idea what to do with them.

"It's Monday night," he said.

"I have a new system. I do everything I please, and then I can study without distraction."

"Does it work?"

"No-o-o," they groaned in unison, drawing the vowel out plaintively. "But I'm caught up anyway," she added.

In the living room he turned out the lights and sat on the floor next to the windows, catching a whiff from last month's flood of raw sewage. His windows faced a sort of courtyard around the graveled lower roof; the neighbors' shades were all down, most of the windows lit.

She was waiting him out, her breathing punctuated by the thuds upstairs. This wasn't the moment to realize he was still in love. It wouldn't do him any more good than knowing he was insane. For hours he'd been turning over something Dobbs had said. Even if someone were trying to ruin his life, why keep him under surveillance? Suppose—he couldn't rule out any premise on the grounds of mere absurdity—suppose they wanted to be sure he didn't look too damn happy? Then living well is the best revenge!

"What's this 'fun' people keep raving about?" he asked.

"Don't ask me, I'm a law student."

He was just thinking his demon had been content to let them stay together for three years. "Meet me at that place near Rosemont at 8:30. We're going to look into this matter of 'fun.'"

"Seems to me we never had much fun *there*...."

"Then that's where we'll take our stand. We're going to have fun if it kills us."

"Alright," she said, "we'll circle the wagons and have fun. See you there."

He wasn't ready to go upstairs just yet, so he pushed the phone into one of the squares of light and dialed John Standell. Peggy answered and when she recognized his voice yelled, "John, guess who this is! Jeffrey Parker! John! Get off the damn couch! He'll call you tomorrow," she said to Parker. "So, how've you been?"

"Oh, let's stretch a bit and say fine. Still teaching?"

"I'll be on maternity leave in five weeks...Oh, John was supposed to call you...."

"That's terrific, Peg! Slap John on the back for me. Boy or a girl?"

"We want to be surprised. Though if it's a boy or a girl, how surprised could we be? So, Parker, why have you been avoiding us? We actually cleaned the house! You used to be the only one uncritical enough to invite over."

"Unobservant."

"I was being polite. Of course now that it's clean, all that work would be wasted on *you*. Just kidding. Want to come over for dinner some time this week? Say, Thursday?"

He was timing the thuds. They recurred at intervals of precisely five seconds.

"I'm looking forward to it," Parker said, "but ask John to call me tomorrow. I need his professional advice."

"Let me guess. You think your phone's tapped."

"That's part of it, yeah."

"All of John's friends get around to asking about their phones. It's a status symbol to be bugged. I hope you won't take this the wrong way,

Jeff, but you're not important enough for anyone to bother. Anyway, *we* like you. But John will ask if you hear strange noises on the line, you'll say yes, and he'll tell you a good tap doesn't make any noise."

"Actually, I don't hear any noises."

"Well, dear, that can mean one of two things."

"I'm impervious to sarcasm. Congratulations again, and see you Thursday. And when John comes to, ask him to call me. Oh, guess who I saw today? Steve Dobbs."

"John, he's been talking to Steve Dobbs! . . . You must know Dobbs is crazy," she said to Parker.

"Crazy enough to razor the last page out of all my books?"

She laughed. "No, and I don't think he'd short-sheet your bed, either. It's what he says, not what he does."

"Then if he came to me with some weird story, I should disregard it."

"Now that's the problem with Steve: It's probably true."

"Parker, ya knucklehead!" John had taken the phone. "Stay away from Dobbs!"

"I'm fine, thank you. Congratulations, pal!"

"Thanks. Listen, ya jerk. We used to have an answering machine on this phone just so we wouldn't have to talk to Dobbs. Last time I saw Steve he was sitting here with his mouth full of lasagna saying, 'Boy, I'd hate to be the Chilean military attaché; he'll be dead by the end of the week'"—John's imitation sounded more like Bugs Bunny—"and I'm thinkin' 'Jeez, I *don't* want to know this stuff.' You know what Dobbs and the magazine are? A cult. Ever read *The Paranoid Style in American Politics* by Richard Hofstadter?"

"Thanks for letting me get a word in: No."

"Then remember the *Twilight Zone* episode about the napkin holder that tells your fortune? William Shatner keeps dropping in pennies because he's addicted to bad news? All these people hang around Dobbs and send him money because they need their hit of bad news. Then they go through the made-up stories in the magazine and look for codes. Anyway, do what you want, but if you show up Thursday looking like a zombie, we won't let ya in. Gotta go. Bye!"

Parker stood and listened to the noise upstairs. The block, if that's what it was, sounded hollow: One two three four, BLOINK! On a whim he walked to the kitchenette and from the cupboard took down a heavy Pyrex quart measure: It might put his neighbor off-balance to ask for a cup of sugar, and the measure could be used as a weapon.

He stepped out the door into the haze of frying foods on the landing. One two three four, BLOINK! continued without variation above a dissonance of TVs and the vibrating bass of a stereo. He practiced grips on the cup as he climbed the brownish carpeted steps. Outside his neighbor's door the noise sounded more than ever like a hollow concrete block. He reminded himself that everyone did things the neighbors found peculiar—one of his college roommates made noises like Curly during sex—and he'd read of a sculptor who, attempting to incorporate chance with choice, would carve an outline in stone and keep dropping the thing till the pattern more or less broke free. He knocked. Three four, BLOINK! He knocked again, louder. Four, BLOINK!

"Hey!" Parker shouted, giving the door three sound kicks. He wondered if some of his other neighbors might come out, then recalled his eight burglaries. BLOINK! He gave the door eight rattling kicks, flinging up plaster, and just to be sure his point wasn't lost for subtlety, added, "Hey, asshole! Shut the fuck up!"

The noise stopped.

Parker knocked again, discreetly. "Hello? This is your neighbor from downstairs. I wonder if I might have a word with you."

No answer. He waited about a minute; not a peep.

Funny, he thought, if that was all it took.

* * *

Like most commercial property in Parker's neighborhood, Ciao!, as it was called now, was frequently boarded up. The club's new name acknowledged a history of bankrupt owners and defunct fads and was assembled in blue neon from previous names. The new owners had shown the good sense not to redecorate but simply to dim the lights. There was light enough at the bar, though, for Parker to clear a wide berth by reading the *Exhibitionist*. The tabloid was inducing a headache with its bludgeoning exclamation points and underexposed photos of treetop assassins, aerial configurations, the missing, the presumed dead.

"Blazer...white duck pants...ohmygod, spats! Off to prep school, Jeff?" Fran's hair brushed against his cheek as she leaned over his shoulder and turned up the front page. "Hmm!"

Every time he noticed the spats, Parker winced. It was like discovering that the funny hat you'd worn at a party was still on your head days later. "You can wear anything to this place, and if you wait long enough, it—whoa!"

She was modeling her ankle-length black dress—shoulder pads, dolman sleeves—and had turned on her heel and gathered up her hair to show off the plunging back.

"The adequate compliments have been wasted elsewhere," he said as she took the next stool. "I'll just gape stupidly if you don't mind. What, there's more?"

She'd drawn back her hair to expose a flat turquoise earring in the shape of a cow, a smile line curving all the way up the side of its head.

"Now that's what I call a shit-eating grin," he said fingering it. "Kind of a Cubist perspective."

"There's nothing wrong with the cows' perspective. They're content."

"One of my students told me about a new fad at rural colleges. Three or four students sneak up alongside a cow while their accomplice distracts it. 'Hi Flossy, nice weather! Good for the clover!'" He knew he sounded like an idiot, but fear, confusion, and lust had coalesced into giddiness. "'Say, Flossy, is that a new bell you're wearing?'—then bam! the cow's lying on its side, perplexed."

She was forming a moral objection—eyes narrowed, lips compressed—when she suddenly visualized the image. "That's *terrible!*" she laughed. She flipped the tie out of his jacket. "Poor Parker! If I took you out to the country, you'd just think of the cows getting mugged. You're going to be a tough customer for fun. Wait. Let's see how observant you are tonight. What's notable about the people here? Don't look. Look at me."

"Pleasure." He stared at the freckles around her nose, the tip of cleavage and the outline of her breasts, the green eyes rolled at the acoustic ceiling, the black pump wiggling at he end of her toe.

She looked at him now with genuine concern. "You don't know, do you?"

"I just want to put you on notice that I hate this, but okay, I walked in. I opened my paper. I ordered a gin and tonic. That's the trouble: First I was looking at my paper, now I'm looking at you. Let's see. Demographics: The crowd is half Loyola students, half blacks and Hispanics from the neighborhood. All right, I give up."

"I'll tell you in a minute. Let me see your back."

"This is getting tedious," he said. "What's going on?" As she examined his back he watched their reflections behind the dimly glittering bottles, his eyes and cheeks scooped out by darkness, her pale neck and face afloat.

"There's a tear in your jacket. Oh. It goes all the way through your shirt."

He arched his spine as he felt her fingertip on his bare back.

"Look."

He swiveled to face her. Her fingertip held a droplet of blood. "Just one drop of blood," she said. "You're lucky. Whatever it was just grazed you."

Suppressing a shudder he tried to look lucky. "I must've brushed against something."

His first impulse was to get the hell out, but would they be any safer outside? Might as well stick to the game plan, he thought—fun if it kills us!

He turned to look around. A man in huge sunglasses was lurching toward them; Parker thought of the faceless man. The blindered man stumbled closer—white ice-cream suit, slicked-back black hair, arms extended like a sleepwalker's or a zombie's.

The outstretched hands were about to touch Fran's chest. "Whoa!" Parker yelled, grabbing the man's wrist. The man raised his sunglasses with his free hand, nodded apologetically, and joined a crowd of similarly-attired men at the end of the bar. Except for Parker, all the men in the place wore white icecream suits and huge sunglasses. The women wore dark glasses, sack dresses, and beehive hairdos.

Fran ordered a glass of rosé and asked what was up. The bartender, a business major from Loyola, looked disdainfully amused as he told them that this was the "Mondo" look, based on those Italian films of the '50s and '60s where everyone wore sunglasses and flouted bourgeoisie values and danced the Twist with abandon and smoked cigarettes and stepped into fountains with their clothes on; but mainly the dark glasses and the dim room were an excuse to grope strangers. From the sparseness of the crowd stumbling about the dance floor, it didn't seem to be catching on.

Fran was willing her drink not to spill.

"I didn't know the place had gotten this sleazy," Parker said. "Should we go?"

She set down her drink. "No, we'll have plenty of room." She was pulling him toward the dance floor. "Besides, I'm with Mad Dog Parker."

"Damn right," he said. "In the land of the blind, the unobservant man is king."

The sound system was booming a sprightly Italian version of "Let's Twist Again." They found an isolated spot, and she clasped hands behind her head, swayed her hips, and pouted like Anita Ekberg—all very poised and ironic, but it was turning him on. His own dance, nonetheless, resembled the mime trapped in a phone booth. Occasionally other dancers came blundering over, but a touch on the shoulders steered them back on course. Now she was circling him backwards in a high-stepping folk dance. Parker knew two smart moves, the dip— he snatched her out of orbit and draped her over an arm—and the spin—he twirled her out, reeled her in—but he felt called upon for more, and next thing he knew he had her round his shoulders in an airplane spin. He was trying to remember how professional ice skaters keep from getting dizzy when the ruckus began. At first he thought it was derisive applause, but there was shoving at the door. He was pondering how to set her down without falling or dropping her, when the knot of people round the entrance broke, and a man came running toward them.

It was Ziploc. The bartender and the bouncer hustled him out, and by the time Parker had set down Fran and shoved through the people coming back in, the street was empty except for two zonked teenagers on the hood of a car. He asked if they'd seen the guy who just came out; they ignored him and when the question was repeated made a sound between snickering and gagging.

"Gone to a neutral corner, Jeff? It's cold out here." Fran pointed to her breath. "What's that by your shoe?"

He bent down and picked it up off the sidewalk, a gray plastic badge with a crude replica of the FBI seal. Ziploc must have been flashing it when they threw him out. No sane adult of normal intelligence would mistake it for anything but a toy—just the sort of thing the FBI might have handed out to its Breathers.

* * *

Their first evening together they were having dinner at her apartment when she'd looked up from her plate, straightened her back, and held her head perfectly still. She'd sat that way for half a minute, and he'd been ready to employ the Heimlich maneuver. Sirens, she'd explained (he'd barely heard them); at home when you heard a siren someone you knew was in trouble.

Now he recognized that expression as he turned on the lights in his apartment. Staring with her at the bare bulbs and walls, he realized the place looked considerably bleaker than when she'd seen it last, and he dreaded her asking how he'd come to this. But she recovered her poise and, turning on the lamp by the couch, said, "There's too much glare. Do we need all those lights?"

As he adjusted the lights, put on a record, and brought out a bottle and two glasses, he wondered if this was a good idea. Now that the enemy had more or less revealed himself, there'd be no further need for subtlety: the goons could just break down the door.

"To your brilliant career," he said when he'd filled their glasses. He glanced past the circumference of lamplight to where the door would be.

"To"—she had to think a moment—"your next book." They clinked glasses. "What do you mean, someone's razored the last page out of all your books?"

"If it were any more literal, I could drop it in your lap." And before he thought better of it, he added, "Why don't you pick out a book and see for yourself?"

She looked over at the black slab of the bookcase, raised an eyebrow at Parker, and sipped her wine.

"You're determined not to be fooled," he said. "William James said there are two ways to be fooled: dupery through hope—in other words, gullibility—and dupery through fear: refusing to believe the truth for fear of being duped." He was still a bit unhinged; why was he talking like this?

"Let's hear your story, Parker. After all this buildup, it better be good."

"I'm not trying to tease you, but I'm sorry I brought it up. I don't want to draw you into this. Look, it's not so much a story as a hateful little theme you can't get out of your head, like an irritating jingle or the image of everyone on the bus naked. It's not even a new fact, just a highly unsettling way of looking at the things you already know, like the theory, say, that every object in the universe is expanding at the same rate, or, wait, is that true?"

She was sitting with her back stiff, her head still, the glass poised on the way to her lips. "You say it's not about facts, but if every book in your apartment is missing its last page, isn't *that* a fact?" She was determined to discuss the matter reasonably. "I have no idea what you're talking about, Jeff, but I'm worried about you. Is this dupery through fear?"

Parker desperately wanted to change the subject. A novelist he knew marveled that two people ever bridged the gulf between sitting in a room talking with all their clothes on and making love. With Parker and Fran the gulf was particularly awesome, a dump of hurt feelings and old grudges. He'd always thought she dumped him because she was ambitious and knew she could do better; she'd claimed it was because he was obtuse, unobservant, inattentive, barely there, and constantly missing . . . whatever it was he was missing. In addition to which, at this moment she probably thought he was nuts. Parker told her all this and suggested an abrupt transition.

"You're taking an awful lot for granted." She was turning the stem of the glass between her fingers. "Though I guess I can't claim I'm here for the artworks." She gestured toward the obscurity where the blank walls would be. "What do you mean, grudges?"

"There's no way out of this," he said, "but an abrupt transition."

"If that's critical jargon for jumping me, I think not."

The doorbell rang.

"Ignore that." He took the glass out of her hand and set it with his own next to the lamp. "No, what I had in mind is more like a badly edited movie, maybe with reels out of sequence: a bit of exposition, then cut to the middle of a slow, deep kiss. I say 'the middle' since right at the moment beginning seems out of the question. Imagine you went out for popcorn during the boring part."

"Would it work?" She made her eyes bulge.

"Well, it violates the laws of time and space, but I think if I just interrupted myself in the middle of a sentence—," and here they were in a great gulp of tongues, lips, and teeth, barely unclinching to stumble two-backed and four-legged to the darkened bedroom. The doorbell rang again as they fell onto the bed, and the conceit that they were about to be killed flung him into a snarl of zippers and straps. "What—what is it?" she gasped.

"Ignore that man behind the curtain," he whispered and, kissing her breasts and belly, permitted the conspiracy to grind on without him.

* * *

"Here's a hoot: *The Exhibitionist* has a health column." Fran was wearing his blue work shirt, her highly aerobicized legs—propped on the card table and crossed at the ankles—supporting the magazine while she toweled her hair. She looked over her feet at Parker in the kitchenette. "You don't have to do this, you know."

He was dicing up everything in sight for their omelet. "Those other law students scarfing down doughnuts'll be no match for a first-rate legal mind with a hearty breakfast under its—what? belt?" He halved a green pepper and cut the seeds out over the sink. "So far we have onion, mushroom, cheddar, muenster, tomato, green pepper—find a sledgehammer and a bigger pan and I *will* add the kitchen sink."

"I think there's plenty already." She was looking down at the magazine. "Listen to this, from the 'Healthbeat' column. 'Edie Kruger was fifty-five, happily married, a recent grandmother, and co-owner of a small art gallery in Evanston, Illinois; she had no history of mental illness at 10 p.m., January 28, 1983 when, driving home alone on Sheridan Road, she heard a voice say, "Edie Kruger Project. Testing, one, two, three"—a male tenor voice with the Western drawl and the bored, dispassionate tone of an airline pilot or a police dispatcher. The radio was off, the windows rolled up; she threw the car into park and, running into the street, hailed a passing driver. To Edie's embarrassment, her car proved to be empty.'"

"Summarize, condense." He angled the cutting board over the bowl of egg and pushed the dicings with the flat of his knife.

"'The voice recurred with increasing frequency and volume, often drowning out all other voices....seemed to be reading rather than speaking: joke books, labels on cans, lifetime Major League RBIs.' Poor Edie doesn't even know what RBIs are."

Maybe it was Fran or protective obtuseness, but Parker thought the worst was over. What if the "faceless man," and the drop of blood, and the burning hair, and Ziploc's appearance at the disco were the parting shot: His demon had got bored—or retired on his unlimited expense account—and had revealed his presence just to keep Parker flinching in his absence.

"Yadda yadda yadda, 'minister'...yadda yadda yadda, 'therapy.' 'In the past, treatment for conditions like Edie's included lobotomy, leucotomy, electric or insulin shock, tranquilizers, psychotropic drugs, and, these measures failing, as they usually did, long term "warehousing" in a mental institution. But, fortunately for Edie, Dr. Paul "Pinto" Cantrell had broken with what he called "the sham and shamanism of the past."'"

Prying a spatula under the omelet, he flipped it over intact. Last year Parker had shared his apartment with a huge pinkish-white rat. An odd reverie for one of his happier mornings, but, anyway, for months he never saw the thing. He knew it by its teeth marks, the turds it left under the sink, and an occasional, peripheral pinkish-white blur. But one evening he was propped up in bed watching *Magnum, P.I.* when, big man on campus, it settled on its haunches three feet from Parker. It was the size of a terrier—bigger—the twitching of its whiskers, so cute in mice, convulsive and sickening at that scale. And now that he was getting it full blast, Parker had recognized the musty zoo smell that for months had insinuated itself into everything. There were no heavy objects within reach, and he wasn't eager to set bare feet on the floor, so they'd stared at each other all through *Magnum* and on into *Simon and Simon.* Then, having made its statement, it got up and sauntered out of the room. He never saw it again. This morning Parker was inclined to believe that the faceless man, having made his point, whatever it was, would now go the way of the rat.

"Yadda, yadda, yadda, 'ex-Green Beret'...yadda, 'Golden Gloves'... yadda yadda, 'Chairman of Psychiatry, University of Chicago.' Okay, this Doctor Cantrell practices 'a tough, no-nonsense brand of humanistic interpersonal psychiatry.' He doesn't take his patients' stories—'their so-called delusions'—as symptoms, but as 'propositions to be verified or disproved.' 'Other psychiatrists would have put Edie on Chlorpromazine.' Not Doctor Cantrell. '"Nothing else has worked. Let's give Edie the benefit of the doubt."' He moves into the Krugers' home with 'sensitive electronic equipment, including an omnidirectional frequency finder and a broadcast spectrum scanner.' It's three in the morning, he's doing push-ups to stay awake, when Edie shows up at the door in her robe and curlers, 'her face slick with tears.' The voice is back. Okay, he picks up the signal on his equipment and now he's got the Krugers, still in their bathrobes, packed into his 'souped-up Ford Gran Torino.' They're doing ninety on Lake Shore Drive. He turns to the husband, Donald, 'a paunchy Korea vet,' says 'the police can't help us. We may have to kick ass.' Yadda yadda yadda...'apartment building over a nude dance bar on Rush Street.' They're ringing doorbells, banging on doors...they've found the apartment, they've kicked down the door....'Two fiftyish men in their undershirts, badly in need of sleep and a shave' at the kitchen table.... crumpled beer cans...cigarette butts...bare bulb on a cord. One of the guys is writing in a logbook, the other one's reading *Facts on File* into a microphone...."

Sneaking up, he pressed a hand between her thighs and grabbed the tabloid with the other. "No reading at the table." In the kitchenette he stuffed the paper in the garbage and, picking up their plates, said, "If you're devoted to that sort of journalism, we're invited to dinner with the editor." She was over at the bookcase. "Since you insist"—he set their plates on the table—"it's the last page of the *text*."

When she came back her smile was straining to assimilate the joke. "Why don't you tell me what's going on?"

And so for the next ten minutes he told her.

And here was that old four-alarm look. "One thing I'm sure of: You wouldn't cut pages out of your books."

"Well, anyway," he said through his last mouthful of toast and eggs, "I have the feeling it's over. You really should try that omelet. I mean, sure, there's danger, but that's why you see the dentist once a year or get rid of those old newspapers in the basement or wear orange in moose season: You take sensible precautions and forget it. You think I have my head in the sand? I'd say I'm *observing* the sand. Hey, if I'm not worried, why should you be? If you're not going to eat that omelet, I will."

FOUR

John Connor Murray was darting his huge head in and out of the doorway of Parker's classroom in a display of not wanting to attract attention.
Word was out that Parker's course, "Topics in Business Writing: The Letter of Complaint," was the nearest thing on campus to a pep rally.

"Come on in, Jack.... This is Professor Murray," Parker told his class.

With his white beard, washed-out eyes, and baby-pink skin, Jack resembled a soft-boiled John Huston. As always he was nattily dressed,
though the white boutonniere in his navy-blue blazer seemed freakishly
large. "Don't let me cramp your style, Parker. Stun us with your elo-
quence. Go on—stun!" The slur in his speech was not altogether convincing, nor his stagger as he maneuvered round the crowded seminar
table to a chair against the wall. Jack believed that his troubles in academia were due not to his drinking but to a reputation for inconsistency
and unpredictability; therefore he cultivated a slightly blurred manner,
maintainable drunk or sober.

Parker smiled at the woman across the table, her notes bunching up between crabbed fingers. "Whenever you're ready, Mrs. Slansky."

The course *had* been fun the first two weeks, especially the free-form grumbling that generated material for the letters. The good humor of these sessions had depended on everyone recognizing at some level that self-pity is funny. But then Mrs. Slansky had shown up. Adele Slansky was an old friend of Parker's mom. He saw her every three or four years and recalled her as barely changing over the decades from the bland, plump, pleasant presence of his childhood—the makeup just grew thicker and more pungent. But suddenly large pieces of her had fallen away; the vacated left side of her face dangled in folds.

As she began to speak, Parker glared down embarrassed titters and condescending smiles. These weren't mean people; it was just hard to keep a straight face while she trembled and bit her lip over the price of strawberries or people who say "Where is it at?" instead of "Where is it?" Today it was the movies.

Parker's mind strayed as she talked her way into a snit. He'd have loved to upstage her and the rest of these Job wannabes with the story of his personal demon. Skokie Valley was one of the rare places where he might be believed—believed, though, like a framed man in prison: "The same thing happened to us!"

He didn't confuse victims with heroes, but he couldn't help feeling that having a personal demon was a sort of distinction. In a way, it redeemed his life. What had seemed like rounds of daydreaming, watching TV, and doodling in the margins of his stalled manuscript became a secret history of stoicism and resistance. And so he couldn't help feeling... threatened? mocked? by the resemblance of his conspiracy to Mrs. Slansky's. *Her* demons tended to resemble employees in the service industry. They smiled obsequiously and jotted on little pads while flaying her by the millimeter.

He broke off his meditations and tried to catch up with her story. It went something like this:

Sunday she'd gone to the matinee at the Oakton. Ten minutes or so into the movie the screen went nearly black. At first she thought it was a night scene, but there was the sun like a dead bulb. She squinted and tried to follow the story through the dialogue—it might as well have been recited by shapes on the ocean floor!—hoping the projectionist would wake up or that some braver person would complain. But the Oakton is a second- or third-run house, and by the time a movie gets there its audience has usually seen it, decided to wait for the video, or lost interest entirely. When she looked around, Mrs. Slansky discovered that she was alone except for a couple noisily inhaling each other in the back row. She went out to the candy counter and asked the girl to speak to the projectionist. The girl was sorry; only the manager could do that. Fine, where was the manager? The manager was busy and could not be disturbed. The girl went back to dusting the counter as if the agitated woman shifting from foot to foot in front of her were no more solid than the dim blobs on the screen. Mrs. Slansky spent most of her time writing letters of complaint because the two forces that governed her emotional life— lacerating, unfocused anger and fear of making a scene—canceled each other out. But now she walked to the manager's office and pounded on the door and kept pounding till a chair squeaked and an eye appeared in the peephole. "Come in! Come in!" the manager beamed, pleased to be confronting someone who couldn't beat him up. Would she sit down? He was never too busy for feedback from the public. She told him how the screen had gone dark, and at first she'd thought it was the movie or "just me," but then she'd thought, well, in her opinion, maybe the problem was here in the theater. He sucked the smile back into his chubby face: What, exactly, did she mean by *the problem*? Well, she thought maybe—in her opinion?—the picture could be brighter? Ah! He nodded vigorously.

The problem, of course, was the modern cinema. Bergman! Fellini! All that symbolism! He didn't understand it himself, but they'd both have to try to be open-minded. The ridiculous things he was saying seemed a form of bullying: I don't *have* to convince you, you're powerless! Mrs. Slansky pointed out that this wasn't Bergman or Fellini, it was James Bond, and surely—. He begged her pardon for mentioning it, but he couldn't help noticing that she wore cataract glasses. Why didn't she see her doctor about the latest advances in laser surgery? Mrs. Slansky's pulse climbed up behind her eyes and ears as she forced herself to look at this man and tell him that she'd heard Roger Ebert on the Roy Leonard show, and he'd said that movie projectors have a whatchamacallit that controls the brightness, and since this thing costs thousands of dollars to replace, some cheapskate theater owners keep it turned down. He was standing over her now, one of those ugly men who take revenge by *turning up* their ugliness, honing it into an offensive weapon—his plaid jacket, aftershave, and bristling orange toupee a two-by-four to the senses. He told her that unless she left at once he'd call the police, his face expanding and contracting with her pulse as if something inside it were punching its way out. No, she wasn't going anyplace till she got her money back, and if she were thrown out bodily she'd go kicking and screaming, and how would that look? He sat down, smiled. Hmm. Maybe that no-good projectionist *was* playing with the brightness. He'd send in an usher to be absolutely sure the picture was A-OK. A few minutes later Mrs. Slansky and the usher stood watching the screen as two segments of darkness grappled or embraced. The kid said it looked fine to him.

From moment to moment Mrs. Slansky existed in delicate chemical, metabolic, and neurological balance: she took A for high blood pressure, B to counteract an allergic reaction to the A, C for her nerves, and D when the C made her sluggish; and the whole house of cards depended on her remaining calm. The doctors had taught her breathing exercises and transcendental meditation and progressive relaxation, but right at the moment, she informed the usher, her control systems were dribbling away. There was no telling what would happen in the next few minutes. A stroke? A fit? Maybe just one of those muscle spasms that made her curl up on the floor and scream. She felt nothing but scientific curiosity, she told the usher, and an eagerness to get it over with. Perhaps he'd like to stand there with her and wait. He said he'd talk to the projectionist right away.

A few minutes later the screen brightened and James Bond, in black jumpsuit and red backpack, stood facing a vault-like door in the side of a mountain, while inside, men in green jumpsuits stared at control panels and TV monitors and marched on catwalks over cavernous spaces. Then the screen went blank, the lights came on, the lovers sat up stunned and disheveled. The manager stood grinning in the lobby. He asked Mrs. Slansky if she'd enjoyed the movie. She sat down on the lobby's one chair and gripped the armrests, blue veins bulging in the backs of her hands. She wasn't leaving till she got her money back. And what, he asked in nearly plausible bewilderment, was bothering her now? She felt foolish even answering, but she told him. Ah. Hmm. Well. Was she claiming that the movie had ended too soon? That could mean one of two things. 1) She was guessing how the movie should end on the basis of all the other Bond films. But shouldn't we allow the filmmakers the freedom to try something new? Why waste the public's time and the studio's money—money that could back the work of sensitive young talents—on the thousand-first shootout in the cold vaults of technology? By fading out as it did, the movie left all that to our *imagination*. (Mrs. Slansky gripped the armrests, terrified and exhilarated at being completely out of control.) Or 2) that Mrs. Slansky knew the movie was longer because *she'd already seen it*—in which case wasn't it selfish to force a near-bankrupt movie house to remain open and incur unnecessary expenses? His tone turned pleading (she wasn't sure if this was just a new way of making fun of her). He pointed out that the Oakton was the last independent theater in the north suburbs; when it closed there'd be nothing left but those big impersonal chains. Did she think Mr. Cineplex would take the time to chat with his customers? *Was* there a Mr. Cineplex? Who knows! But he, Mr. —, was the last of the owner-managers, and he did everything he could to keep the place going—bought stale candy from other theaters, got discounts on bad prints, turned down the whatchamacallit—but he couldn't do it alone; he needed the cooperation of his patrons, and surely someone of her years must care about *tradition!* She was gripping the armrests, locking her feet round the chair legs, when it hit her. Something about the man's appearance—something beyond his meanness and ugliness—had been making her nervous, and suddenly she knew what it was. His toupee was on backwards. By the time she recovered from her embarrassment and disorientation, the counter girl and the usher had escorted her out the door.

* * *

She shuffled her notes, looked up, flinched.

At first Parker had taken her complaints as substitutes for her real problems, but lately he'd come to see them as allegories in which a rude waitress or sales clerk embodied the annihilating force of the universe. Was this the sort of person a Breather Program might recruit? What story would they tell her? Would it sound like the one *he* believed?

"Comments?"

Chairs creaked, the tree in the window wriggled out of its leaves.

"You certainly have a complaint here"—Parker avoided her magnified eyes—"but I'm not sure a letter would do any good. Where would you write?"

"I thought maybe Walter Jacobson? I could tell him, you know, how strongly I feel about this. What do you think, dear?"

Parker had only been teaching the class five weeks, but already it was clear that television news was a common element in revenge fantasies. The enemy clubbed by microphones, scalded by lights, head scrunched into his collar, hat pressed to his face.

"Amanda?"

Amanda contemplated diving into a splotch of light on the tabletop. "In the first place, it's your word against the manager's. In the second place—I hate to say this, but I don't think it's an important enough story for the news."

Parker quickly changed the subject. "Here's a test for your rebuttal skills," he said to the class. "Who'd like to state the manager's case. Does he have a case?"

"His case goes something like this." John Connor Murray folded his hands across his gut, inhaled, paused. "Die, bitch!'"

Mrs. Slansky gave a startled yelp of a laugh.

"I don't know if I'd call that a case," Parker said.

"Doesn't it seem to you, Parker, that too much gets written about the banality of evil? What about the *wistfulness* of evil? Most evil people are third-rate like the rest of us—big plans, but the ship sailed without 'em. I see this theater manager as a potential Gacy, a Caligula, a Hitler, who never got his break. So he sits in that office nursing his regrets, and when an occasional Mrs. Slansky turns up...'What thy hand findeth to do, do with all thy might,' you see what I'm saying? All he did was cheat you out of a few dollars, madam, but it's the closest he can get to making you dig your grave and jump in."

"He's right, you know," Mrs. Slansky beamed.

Parker, the only one in the room with a genuine personal demon, found their sense of conviction galling.

Feeling the need to hold out a shred of hope, he said, "Why don't you write to the Better Business Bureau? They'll make a permanent record of your complaint."

He wasn't sure why that was a good thing, but Mrs. Slansky smiled, apparently relishing the thought that her complaint would outlive her.

* * *

After class he pursued the leads from Dobbs's visit with little enthusiasm. It occurred to him that he resented his new knowledge almost as much as the dirty tricks—that until Dobbs came along he'd adapted to his world as perfectly as any pale blind thing on the ocean floor.

He was sneakily relieved, therefore, when no one at the *Bismarck Register* had anything on the shave-your-head caller, when Ziploc didn't turn up at his usual hangouts, when the private investigators who'd quote fees over the phone were beyond his means, and when his calls to Dobbs (so eager to tug his sleeve the other day!) failed to get past the secretary. Resisting the impulse to let things slide, he called back and told her that he accepted Dobbs's dinner invitation, and he'd be over at seven on the third. At the Legal Aid office on Dempster a kid in a blue bow tie told him he might speed up his Freedom of Information Act request by telling the FBI why they might have a file on him—which, if no file existed, might prompt the Bureau to start one. He left with a copy of "How to Use the Federal FOI Act" in his briefcase and boarded the Skokie Swift, having so far achieved perfect equilibrium between his duty to investigate and his dread of learning anything.

His final lead of the day was the super in his building. Jim was never too busy to stand in his doorway chatting amiably; Parker was convinced the man hated him. The nearest thing to an outright display of hostility had come last month when, inspecting the latest damage to Parker's apartment—the sudden appearance of a two-inch-wide crack across the ceiling and down two walls—he'd grinned slyly at Parker and observed that these things didn't happen to other people.

Parker liked him anyway and found their small-talk relaxing. Jim was a short squat man with a round face, a flattop crewcut, a faint Southern accent, and a habit of gazing into the distance for his next cliché. He polished his glasses with his shirttail and asked Parker if he thought the Bears could go all the way.

Parker said the Bears looked good this year if McMahon stayed healthy blah blah blah, wondering if a bribe were necessary for information as it had lately been for repairs. He didn't blame Jim a bit: While Parker had been oblivious to the conspiracy, the super must have felt like its victim.

Parker decided to force the money on him up front. Otherwise Jim might feel obliged to say money wasn't necessary and not feel obliged to be helpful.

"Jim, I'd like to give you money for some information. Of course," he said over Jim's gesture of refusal, "you'd tell me anything you know for free. But, wait, this is strictly for my peace of mind. See, I really need this information, and if I go upstairs without it I don't want to wonder if there was something I didn't do to get it. Now you look insulted."

Actually Jim looked confused and suspicious. He knew he was being conned or made fun of but despaired of seeing how.

"I'll give you the money now."

Jim held out his palm. "You want to throw your money away, Jeff, put it right there." He accepted the bill fatalistically.

"I was wondering if you ever see strangers going in or out of my apartment."

"No." Jim stared back self-righteously. "You want your money back?"

"No, that's all right," Parker sighed. "Just keep an eye out."

Jim was closing the door. "Night, Jeff, I hope you—say, you don't mean the repairmen?"

"What?"

"I was changing the bulb in your hallway maybe ten minutes ago when they came by. They said they were TV repairmen. They had a key so I figured—Hey! Your briefcase!"

Parker was running up the steps. "Call the police!"

"Don't be stupid, wait for the police! Hey!"

* * *

He rounded the corner of the apartment court, nearly broke his key in the entrance door, and skidded to a halt when he'd crossed the lobby. Not a sound at the bottom of the steps but the chipper murmurings of TVs. He sprinted the flight to his door, trusting his next move to momentum. He still had no plan when, half-hoping the door would stop on its chain, he turned the key and pushed; it banged open, just missing two men in grey-green coveralls coming out. He sidestepped the wide chest of the first—at eye level with "Bob" stitched in red over the breast pocket—then shoved the second back inside and following slammed the door. The man dropped his tool kit and charged him head down; Parker brought up a fist to the nose. Having nothing to guide him but the movies, he shook the dazed man by the front of his coveralls. "What do you people want?" The nose flung droplets of blood; the thin lips parted to emit a choking sound. The man was having some sort of fit; no, he was snickering. Goofing, he let himself droop in Parker's grip. "What do you want!" Parker screamed into the sallow, pockmarked, moronic face. As Parker shook him the arms flailed like a puppet's, a primary-yellow toupee worked loose from the skull and slid off. A few seconds of shaking dead weight and Parker was exhausted. He let the man drop; as Parker kneeled down—might as well try banging the guy's head on the floor for a while!—the guy hit him in the forehead with a wrench. It didn't hit full force but it doubled him up on his side, a high-pitched tone drilling his ears. He opened one eye; the toupee was nuzzled against his face.

The lock turned and the big man stood in the doorway looking mildly impatient. "So?"

"So nothin'," said his partner. He wiped his nose with the back of his hand, picked up his tool kit, snatched his toupee out of Parker's face, and stepped out. The big man shrugged at Parker and followed.

Gathering up his entire body and balancing it atop his feet, Parker made it out the door. He leaned woozily over the landing rail and called, "What do you people want?"

The big man looked up. He had curly brown hair, pudgy avuncular features, and the build of an out-of-shape wrestler.

"Your TV was working."

"I never called...what?"

"I said it was *working*. You call if it's *not* working, but you wouldn't call *us*."

"Oh." A drop of blood landed in Parker's open mouth. He thought all that might sound perfectly reasonable if not for his skull compacting around his brain.

"We adjusted the horizontal output transformer so the picture'll go into a roll for ten seconds at twenty second intervals. *Now* it's *not* working, see?"

Despairmen. The notion seemed absurd, but maybe it was his head injury. He thought he vaguely recollected having heard of such a service on "All Things Considered." It made sense, he supposed. If an appliance didn't work you had it repaired; on the other hand, if it *worked*... no, wait.

"What are you guys? Gremlins?"

"Hey, Frank," the big man called to his partner somewhere in the lobby, "he says we're gremlins!" He turned back to Parker. "So? We're gremlins."

"You people waste a lot of time and effort creating minor nuisances," Parker said. "It'll take more than a horizontal output transformer to get to me." Big talk, he realized, from someone who had to look at his shoes to verify that he was standing up.

* * *

"Ouch! That's some goose egg you got!" Jim stared past the door chain and Parker's shoulder into the apartment. "What happened?"

Parker unlocked the door and returned the ice compress to his forehead. "I surprised two—two burglars. The police were here; I don't understand why they tell you not to touch anything when they never take fingerprints. Etiquette?"

"That bump looks nasty. You want, I could run you over to Edgewater Hospital."

"I don't know. Give me a minute."

"You asked about people getting in here. I just remembered one guy—I figured you knew 'im cause he had a key, but after the TV guys... God *damn*! Jim halted in front of the television—Parker had succumbed to curiosity and turned it on just as he'd knocked—watching the picture rotate like clothes in a dryer. "Must be your horizontal output transformer."

Parker covered his eyes with the rag; a perky yellow blob in the darkness beat time to his migraine. "Would you mind shutting that off?" He peeped out. "What did he look like?"

"'Bout your height, light-brown hair—like a professor."

"Briefcase? Pipe?"

"Yeah. The kind professors smoke in the movies. It wasn't lit."

"Just a minute." Parker went to the desk and sketched several kinds of pipes on his legal pad. He didn't draw people well enough to do the man on the train.

He showed Jim the pipe lineup. "Which one?"

Jim put a finger on the briar. "There."

"Say, Jim, can you draw?"

"My niece in third grade draws better. I was good in machine shop, that's it."

"What was the man wearing?"

"Tweed jacket with those things on the elbows like professors wear."

"Patches."

"Yeah! Elbow patches."

"This is important. I don't want to influence you. Just relax—that's it, sit down—describe him again in your own words."

Running a hand over his crewcut, Jim slid down the couch. "'Bout forty, your height, light-brown hair, briar pipe, tweed jacket, elbow patches. Oh, he had blue eyes, creases around the eyes. Had those lines on his forehead. Like you guys get from thinking too much." He chuckled to himself.

"Weight?"

"I dunno. Two-ten."

"What about dates? Times?"

"I can't say. Two, three times the past six months." He stood up. "If you don't want a ride to the hospital, I gotta get back."

"Thanks, I'll be fine."

Parker let him out, changed the ice cubes in his compress, took three Extra Strength Excedrin, and dialed the receptionist at Skokie Valley Community College. "Barb, it's Jeff. Maybe you can help me. I keep running into a guy on the faculty whose name I should know by now, and I'm too embarrassed to ask."

"Describe the nonentity, I'll see what I can do."

"Briar pipe, elbow patches, complete Oxford drag. Like an extra in *Lucky Jim*."

"Got it!" She lowered her voice. "At the desk we call him Ward Cleaver. His name's Ken Fletcher. Need a number? Address?"

"I'd say we've got his number. Just needed the name." His finger stopped on the listing in the faculty directory. "Thanks a lot. Take care, Barb."

He brought the phone book and the *Tribune* classifieds to his desk and rolled a sheet into the typewriter.

* * *

The fluorescent lights at the currency exchange pierced into his squint. The clerk had plenty to gawk at as she handed over the money order— the bump on Parker's forehead, the face beneath it tugged between a grimace and a shit-eating grin.

At the counter he sealed the money orders in two envelopes. The first contained a classified ad for the *Tribune* listing a two-year-old Corvette for $5,000, giving Fletcher's name and address, and welcoming late calls and drop-ins. The second contained a classified for a fringe porn magazine (months ago he'd written down the address of the loathsome publication to try to put a stop to their unsolicited "complimentary copies") in which "Fletcher" advertised the vilest predilection Parker could dream up with a headache. He'd tried to overestimate the ad rate.

That would do for starters.

He was humming as he crossed Granville to the mailbox. An Evanston Express slam-banged overhead, windows strobing. Suppose—he had the box open, the envelopes at his fingertips as he tried to separate Jim's description from his own promptings—suppose this wasn't the guy. Impossible. He let the envelopes fall and the box clank shut. Where Granville ended, a moon like an oncoming headlight streamed over the lake.

Back in his apartment he mixed a gin-and-tonic and, singing the tune he'd been humming, dialed Fran.

"Hello?"

"O! Oklahoma! where the wind comes sweepin' off the—"

"I'm glad to hear you so ebullient, but I can't talk. Can I call back?" Her someone-else-in-the-room tone.

"Studying?"

"Checking up on me?" Teasing, but with an edge of irritation.

"Just showing an interest in your life, my darling. Sensitive, remember?" He pressed an ice cube to his forehead, then plunked it back in his drink.

"You sound bummed. Is everything okay?"

"Everything's fine here. *You* sound bummed, if a woman so elegant—"

"How would I sound if I had to get off and you were protracting the conversation?"

"Ah!"

"Can I call late?" she asked.

"Of course."

"If I don't call tonight I'll call tomorrow. Bye!"

He flicked the lemon into the wastebasket. Obviously she hadn't gone the ten months of their breakup without seeing anyone, but her accounts of the period reminded him of a cropped photo: "I had dinner at Le Perroquet." At any rate, he'd been reluctant to ask.

He knew he was overinterpreting. That after scrutinizing everything the past few days, his judgment was having a little meltdown.

Fortunately there was always the conspiracy to fall back on. Might as well get off another ad before Fletcher moved and changed his number. He carried his drink to the typewriter and inserted a sheet. He'd make this one a challenge: an ad for *Popular Mechanics*. Once he'd've spent the evening gnawing every nuance of Fran's remarks. Nothing like a personal demon to put these trivialities in perspective. He typed: "Attention Geniuses! Venture capitalist wishes to back perpetual motion device...."

* * *

John Connor Murray was reenacting the history of envy, betrayal, and academic politics that had plummeted him from the Ivy League through state universities, urban junior colleges, no-name community colleges and spottily accredited business colleges to the thud at the end of the fall, Skokie Valley Community College. Always the plotters—Lionel Trilling, Harold Bloom, Mark Van Doren, et al—spoke with lisps and squeaky voices while the gaping mouth and huge bulging watery eyes of their victim mimed O!

Parker barely noticed anymore when heads throughout the cafeteria turned toward his colleague's bellowing. He used to assume that resentment expressed with such verve and theatricality couldn't be entirely heartfelt, but Jack was an exuberant hater. Parker had hoped to get Jack's unique perspective on his personal demon—hoped at least that Jack, if anyone, would accept his story without reservation (Fran's acceptance seeming more like suspended disbelief). But he'd barely gotten started when Jack had yelled "Those bastards!" and without further transition launched into this umpteenth rave-out against Trilling and Co., as if the same cabal had put the itching powder in Parker's talc.

Parker, irritated that *his* conspiracy had been given short shrift, said, "I don't suppose your troubles had anything to do with roughing up speakers at the MLA." Everyone knew there'd been an incident at a Modern Language Association convention in the mid-Seventies, but the true story was as encrusted in legend as Beowulf's. "I've never heard your version, Jack. What happened?"

Interrupted in mid-rant, Jack looked a bit punch-drunk. He raised an eyebrow at the meatloaf on his fork as if at a sudden, unpleasant surprise, then returned his attention to Parker. "First of all, lad, it was *one* conference, *one* speaker. I can never remember his name—damn! French, one of the Jacques. Lacan? Derrida? Or was it Roland Bar-thes? Anyway, a practitioner of meta-something-or-other. You know the racket. He'd gone *beyond* something—language, intelligibility—that hamstrings ossified chumps like you and me. A meta-guy might say—for example!—that the world is cube-shaped. If you're unfortunate enough to be on the same panel, what can you say? That the world is spherical, slightly pear-shaped, that it's been photographed from space?" Jack made his voice quaver to demonstrate the ineffectuality of this response. "The audience will groan because the round-world view has been around for centuries, it's hackneyed, and this meta-guy has gone *beyond* it. Well, it's time for me to respond, and Jacques—damn! Who was that little faggot? White hair? Bow tie?—he's grin-ning, all set to put me and the entire humanistic tradition in a historical context. So how do you stand up for the truth without seeming prissy or reactionary? I opted for the old Jacques-there's-a-spot-on-your-tie ploy: Decked 'im, chair and all."

He narrowed his eyes at Parker and did his W.C. Fields double-take. "Young Parker, there's a Band-Aid on your forehead! I guess those big ideas just *bust out* like Minerva from Zeus's brow!"

"Actually, someone hit me with a wrench."

"You *do* have enemies." Jack leaned forward and lowered his voice. "You need protection. When Janet gets here, I'll ask for my gun back."

•

"Absolutely not. Don't bring up the gun."

"If the opposition has a wrench, lad, you'll need stopping power. Close textual analysis might stun 'im momentarily, but..."

As Jan Cohen seated herself next to Parker, Jack rose and, leaning across the table, attempted to cast a shadow. "Janet, you have something that belongs to me, and I want it back, now."

Last month in the cafeteria Jack and Parker had been discussing the decline of intellectual life in America when Jack had underscored a point by flourishing that same gun and drawing a bead on an imaginary Lionel Trilling. A few minutes later they were staring at the carpet in Jan's office while she locked the gun in a drawer and lectured them on their responsibilities. "I understand that Jack has his problems," she'd said to Parker, "but I expected more from you."

The department chairperson was a short, thin woman in her fifties—her hoop earrings, large pink-tinted glasses, and shoulder-length gray hair an attempt to soften the gnarl of smile- and frown-lines that gave her a look of haggard irony. After imperturbably chewing and swallowing a forkful of pot roast, she said, "Stop *looming*, Jack. You look ridiculous. Tell me what the problem is and we'll see if we can work it out. I'm sure whatever it is we can handle it without firing a shot." She was willing to indulge or humor her Ph.D.s, but she could afford to be adamant. She knew this sputtering, looming man had no place else to go.

"Do I have your permission to go to the bathroom, Janet? I mean, I don't need a hall pass, do I?" Jack came round the table on the side away from Jan and whispered, "Keep her busy!" No doubt he planned to bullshit his way past the secretary and pry or pick open the drawer.

Parker tried to grab his arm, but Jack had forgotten his stagger and was darting sure-footedly through the crowd. Parker was about to chase after him when a perfectly modulated voice said "Mind if I join you?"

and here was Ken Fletcher in all the crags, tweeds, and patches that so overemphatically declared his profession.

"Not at all," Parker said. "This is Janet Cohen, the chair of the English department. Jan, this is—I don't think I caught your name last time."

"Ken Fletcher." He set down his tray, grasped her hand across the table, and sat down. He did look like Ward Cleaver with shoulder pads. Parker tried to imagine the reality behind the props: Nothing came to mind but a paper doll. He decked it out in a fake beard, bald wig, mirror sunglasses. No, probably not the demon himself—a minion, an imp.

"And you're...?"

"Jeffrey Parker."

Jan tapped her forehead and asked Parker what happened.

"I surprised two burglars in my apartment." Parker watched for Fletcher's reaction, then asked himself what he'd expected. That the man would flinch? Spill his coffee? Turn twitchy and shifty-eyed? He'd slightly deepened the usual knit in his brow to indicate a concern appropriate to someone he barely knew.

"Did you have a doctor look at that?"

"I'm fine, Jan."

"You can feel fine with a concussion—"

"So, Ken, what do you teach?"

"Psychology." Fletcher's mildly puzzled expression made Parker wonder if his own smile was pasted on straight.

"Kenneth Fletcher." Jan perked up. "You're the visiting professor from the U of C."

"'Visiting professor' is an inflated term for what I'm doing. Bill Shackney asked me to teach his 101 section. I knew Bill in grad school."

"That's odd," Parker said, his smile twitching at the edges. "On the train you were complaining about living on your Skokie Valley salary."

A minimal wince narrowed the eyelids and tugged at the mouth. "I apologize for that. I mentioned the U of C to the first two people I met here, and they've snubbed me ever since."

"So you took on the protective coloration of Skokie Valley. Sour-grape color, I suppose."

Fletcher chuckled politely.

"What area of psychology?" Jan asked.

"Societal dysfunction and the psychic mechanisms for ameliorating it. What I call the culture-shock absorbers." The man's enthusiasm overwhelmed his Ivy League bearing, breaking up the rounded gestures and cadences. Parker tuned out after a few seconds but observing academic etiquette smiled and nodded bravely into the rush of jargon. He found Fletcher's enthusiasm troubling. Would a sadist playing games with his victim let down his guard this way? Once again Parker asked himself if he could possibly have the wrong man. Jack would have settled the matter directly: Walk into the man's office, shove a gun in his face, and *ask* him.

Jack!

Across the cafeteria Jack flashed a double thumbs-up and patted his blazer pocket as he swaggered towards the table.

Parker rose and snatched up his briefcase. "Sorry, I just...bye!"

He intercepted Jack halfway across the room and putting an arm round his shoulder steered him toward the exit. "Let's go to my office."

"Wait! Wait! Wait! I keep asking our chairperson, 'Janet, when was the last time you got fucked?—rounded off to the nearest decade?' and she never deigns to answer. I'll bet we get an answer today." His shoes skidded on the linoleum as Parker heaved him into the corridor.

They'd nearly made it to Parker's office when Jack reached into his pocket. "You know, I'll bet if we asked Bill Stein to make a paper hat out of his Wall Street Journal and wear it, he'd be a sport. Hey, Bill!"

Bill halted, turned, and spotting Jack raised his folded paper in greeting. He started back down the corridor toward Jack and Parker, leaning away from the weight of his briefcase.

Parker unlocked his office, hustled Jack inside, and slammed the door, nearly in Bill's face.

He seated himself rigidly behind the desk. "All right, let's see it." He'd have to take it, if only to get it away from Jack. "Wait. Is it loaded?"

"Of course it's loaded. It isn't a MasterCard. You can't tell your attacker you left your bullets at home."

"What about paperwork?"

"Look. You can go on procrastinating or you can start protecting yourself right now."

Jack placed the small blue-black automatic on the desk. Grinning, perched on the edge of the desk, he seemed to be enjoying Parker's discomfort. For a good minute there was no sound but rasping leaves and Jack's emphatic breathing.

"The safety's on. Go on, you baby, pick it up."

Parker went on staring. It hadn't scared him in the cafeteria or even at the Billy Goat the night Jack demonstrated his quick draw. But on his own desk blotter, next to the phone, the stapler, and a pile of student essays, it was startling and weirdly funny, as if painted into its surroundings by Magritte.

* * *

The note in the Standells' front door pane told him to let himself in. When he opened the door, John's voice said, "Congratulations. You have just activated the world's most sophisticated security system. You have one minute."

"John? Peg?" The living room was socked in under the usual drifts of newspapers, schematic diagrams, loose change, circuit boards. John and Peg still lived in the bungalow they'd inherited from her mom, never bothering to replace the black-and-white TV or the Philco "hi-fi," or do anything about the dour, stolid furniture but strip off the plastic covers. Their energy was devoted entirely to their work; they grew rich as indifferently as they acquired newspapers and dustballs.

Parker cleared a spot on the couch—a bag of cat litter spilled from the middle of the pile—and sat down. He picked up a black metal cube topped with rows of blue LED. bulbs and, pressing a button at the side, set two furious blips pursuing each other in loop-the-loops.

"You have forty-five seconds." John's voice was coming from the hi-fi.

"Worried, Parker?" Peggy—a vivacious pug-nosed blonde with bangs and round wire-rims—walked in and gathered a double armload of newspapers against her full-blown maternity dress. "We cleaned up two weeks ago but somehow it didn't take. Hey, good to see you!"

"You have thirty seconds."

Parker stood up. "Let me take those," he said opening his arms.

She turned her back on him and started toward the kitchen. "Sit down. John wants you to experience the world's most sophisticated security system."

"You have twenty seconds."

"This better not involve electric shocks," Parker yelled. "Yo, John!"

"Ten nine eight seven six five four three two one...The world's most sophisticated security system is now operational."

"And...? What's so devilishly clever is that nothing seems to be happening. Wait, I think I hear the alarm bell: the sound of a one-hand clapper."

"You want to hear your ears ring, chump?" John was coming down the steps. He wore black pants and his usual plain white shirt—one of three dozen he'd bought by lot at AMVETS in 1975 and worn every day since. He finessed most of his life with the same perversity and efficiency. His all-purpose guileless smile, for example, allowed him to seem charming while saying whatever he pleased; people sometimes walked away from John at parties with their own smiles slowly dissolving. Not that John's was insincere. There'd been plenty to smile about since the year he quit grad school, married Peg, and transmuted an old hobby into Security Systems, Inc. His nickname, Wonder Boy, had nothing to do with his success: He resembled the kid in the old Wonder Bread commercial who grows from age four to twelve in time-lapse photography. If that boy—blond, blue-eyed, farmboy-wholesome—had shot all the way up to thirty-five and acquired a sense of irony, he might have been John.

He punched Parker's shoulder, rocked back on his heels, grinned. Parker thought he knew the source of John's discomfort. Like other old friends, he seemed to fear blurting out phrases like "miserable hopeless pathetic failure" in the course of conversation. The evening should go well, Parker thought, once they cleared the initial obstacles—"how are you?" for example.

"I don't *know* what happens next," John said. "I'm still working on the warning. See if you can help punch it up—something menacing."

"Give specific, enigmatic directions. Like, 'Place all metallic objects on the table in front of you.' 'Stand between the yellow lines with your arms at your sides.' 'If you are wearing wool socks, remove them.' I don't know, John. This sounds like another yelling briefcase." The yelling briefcase was one of John's rare failures. He'd designed it for clients fed up with ordinary briefcase alarms, which, far from rousing passersby to chase the crook, prompted them to jump out of his way as if from an ambulance or a fire truck. By the time the noise drew a cop, the case had usually been picked clean and discarded. But the yelling briefcase, snatched from its owner, secreted a quick-bonding glue through the handle while a high-decibel recording slurred all races, religions, and ethnicities. The first prototype to be stolen did incite a public-spirited mob to subdue the thief but was stomped to bits in the process. John's contention that it's more honorable to have your goods stomped to bits than stolen failed to persuade clients intent on avoiding both.

John said, "My problem is, I want a battle of wits, but you don't see a lot of masterminds out there." Peg came in and put his hand on her belly.

"How 'bout it, Parker? Can you believe me as a father?"

"I've lost the capacity for disbelief. Seriously, you'll be a good father."

When they sat down to dinner, Parker said, "I saw Steve Dobbs last week."

Peg was refilling his wineglass. "We don't discuss Steve Dobbs at the dinner table."

John said, "Last time Steve was here he claimed the government was testing space-based laser weapons on bums outside the Pacific Garden Mission. He showed us pictures—stiffs with, like, these small-diameter holes burnt in the tops of their heads."

"Thank you, John." Peg raised her glass. "*Bon appetit.*"

"Oh jeez, you didn't *believe* him? They were fakes, ya knucklehead."

She turned back to Parker. "How's Fran?"

"We broke up ten months ago."

She squeezed his arm. "I'm sorry."

"No, wait. We've just started seeing each other again."

She inhaled, awaiting further qualifications. He decided not to mention his vague anxieties about Fran—doubted he could articulate let alone justify them.

"I like Fran," she said. "She's the only one who tries to bring me out of my shell."

"I've never thought of you as someone who needed to be brought out."

"That's what makes it so charming!"

John said, "I think Fran's mad at me. I accused her once of being 'merely perfect.' Tell her it was just a joke."

"You don't tease Fran about being perfect—it's like teasing a hunchback about his hump. I feel guilty talking like this. I know, Peg. Let's talk about politics. We can gang up on John."

"Oh, let's! I still can't get him to vote. John's position, as far as I can make it out, is that he won't vote till a true socialist comes along who's willing to seize our business."

"That's right," John said smugly.

Parker laughed. "We might as well give up. It's impossible to argue with a man who embraces the absurdities of his position."

John said, "If everyone embraced a few absurdities, there'd be fewer absurdities running around loose."

Parker glanced to his left and caught Peg staring at him, her face wrenched into eye-popping, nostril-flaring hatred. Dropping his eyes, he halved the slice of lasagna he'd just cut and edged off the stringy cheese. It had to have been, if not an outright hallucination, then the light on her glasses, a kick from the baby. But he vividly recalled the vein in her forehead, the furiously compacted mouth, nose, and chin. Could he joke about it? What's wrong, Peg? Just now you looked like a head in a David Cronenberg movie the instant before it explodes. Better not try. He reminded himself that he was having a little meltdown, recalling the huge subtext he'd read into Fran's "I can't talk now." Bringing the tiny, perfectly square slice to his mouth, he decided that if he wanted to avoid a padded cell for the next few days, he'd better practice psychotic's etiquette: 1) Keep your voice down. 2) Don't stand in the middle of the street. 3) Don't grab or touch people, particularly strangers. 4) Cultivate a neutral expression.

He heard himself mm-hmm mm-hmm while John argued that the choice of a Democrat or a Republican made no dent in the real power structure. Could John blather on like this while his wife was having a fit of rage?

He looked up and discovered Peg's face—if it had changed at all— uncrumpled and smoothed back to normal.

When they'd finished eating, she abruptly had a headache and went upstairs.

* * *

"So, buddy"—John propped his feet next to the six-pack and the bowl of chips on the coffee table between them—"why haven't we seen more of you?"

Parker couldn't let it pass. "Maybe because you've seen me first." He tugged a can out of its plastic ring and snapped it open. "Six months ago on State Street you saw me just long enough to cross to the other side. I'm not mad, maybe you were in a hurry, but you and Peg are acting like *I've* been snubbing *you.*"

"You mean, like, eight months ago you're coming out of the Berg-hoff, I say Jeff long time no see, you pass by me like I'm Scrooge watching his past life. You mean we're snubbing you like that."

"Oh..........What was my expression?"

"The usual—self-absorbed, puzzled, sort of amused. Peg says the idea for the Walkman came from observing you on the street."

"John, I'm sorry. All this time I thought you've been avoiding me out of pity."

"Does that sound like me?"

"So you've been avoiding me because you thought *I* was avoiding *you*, and I've...Wait a minute. Dobbs said there was some sort of rumor."

It was the first time Parker had seen John embarrassed. His face, locked in a squinting grimace, resembled an astronaut's at takeoff.

After waiting half a minute Parker said, "You're not going to tell me what it is, are you?"

"No."

"But you believe it."

"I never really believed it. Now that I'm sitting here looking at you I'm sure it couldn't be true."

"How come Peggy invited me to dinner? Will you stop making that face?"

John took a long gulp of beer and said, "She thought she'd confront you, we'd have it out, and we'd all be friends again. She wimped out."

"How come you never confronted me with any of this before? Probably because it was so outrageous you were ashamed to admit you could believe it. I guess it was easier to just go on believing it."

"Jeez, I'm sorry. It's just that the details were right. It's, like, if you *had* said and done those things, it would've been exactly that way."

"Don't try to justify yourself on grounds of literary criticism. Whatever I'm charged with must be pretty despicable, judging by the look Peg gave me. I suppose everyone else hates me too?"

"Yup."

"I thought *they* were avoiding me out of pity, too. What a relief. They just hate me."

"You underestimated us.....How do you suppose rumors like that get started?"

"I *know* how it got started."

But John had already picked up the phone off the floor, set it on the coffee table, and begun dialing. "Let's find out."

"If you're trying to avoid talking to me I could just leave."

John hung up. "I believe in the Big Bang theory of jokes and rumors. One instant nothing, then boom! it's everyplace...Tell you what. Why don't you just kill me and we'll call it even? You could use that." He pointed to the lump in Parker's jacket pocket.

"Oh. I didn't think it was that noticeable." Parker handed him the gun and he took aim at a standing lamp across the room.

"You don't seem surprised that I'm carrying a gun," Parker said.

"Yeah, well, you've been talking to Dobbs."

"*Now* are you ready to hear what he told me?"

John was ready once he'd brought out another six-pack and more junk food and retracted his features into a perfect deadpan. "I hate Dobbs's stories. You feel stupid whether you believe him or not."

"Dupery through hope or dupery through fear."

"There ya go! I'll just sit here and not react."

John remained impassive throughout the story, though at one point ("he pays women to almost go to bed with me") a handful of Cheetos froze in front of his open mouth. When Parker had finished, he asked John what he thought of Dobbs's story.

"It's like the stories in the magazine—it could be true, or half-true, or false but with a grain of truth. It could be completely made-up but symbolically or mythologically or—I don't know—cryptographically true. I'd keep the gun handy."

"Do you think Dobbs could be behind all this?"

"Nah. Too passive-aggressive...So, Parker, what's your day like? Safes dropping from upper stories? Electric shocks from the toaster? Pets strangled on the doorstep? Guys in trenchcoats lunging out of alleys?"

"Yeah, basically. Just one guy in a trenchcoat and he didn't quite lunge. Sabotage, yes. My car was in the shop forty-one times in a year before I gave up. Pets: Three dogs died on me in two years. Don't smirk. If you don't have any enemies that you know of and your dog gets run over, you don't immediately wonder if there was a contract on 'im. It's one of the conventions of sanity that you allow plenty of room for coincidence in your misfortunes."

"What about room for plausibility?"

"Compared to what?"

"I see."

"It's supposed to be a sign of maturity that you don't go around asking 'why me'? I thought I was being an adult. Dobbs calls it 'protective obtuseness.'"

John was working to remain expressionless.

Parker said, "Will you help me or not?"

"I'll check your place for bugs. What else?"

"I'd like to catch the people who are breaking into my apartment."

"No booby traps, they could sue us. Though I'll tell you what. I'm testing a prototype that marks the intruder with an indelible stink. By indelible I mean, like, three days, but it's overwhelming. We mount it on the ceiling like a sprinkler system. It won't stink up your apartment; the smell comes with skin contact, like DMSO, the cancer drug? A recorded message tells him he can get the solvent—the antidote—at McDermott Security; they're a rent-a-cop firm we work with. That way he won't come after *you*. Just in case he manages to get rid of the smell on his own—a real good chemist might be able to figure it out—there's a bonus. You think your intruder might be following you: You'll be able to spot him in a crowd because he'll get a bath of infrared-like dye. It's invisible without a viewer. Same technique banks use to catch embezzlers. Wait a minute." John went upstairs and returned wearing oversize sunglasses. "Just pop these on and spot the bad guys."

Parker laughed appreciatively. "Rose-colored glasses! Nice touch. What about Hank Monroe, Junior? Did you ever run across that kind of psychotic practical joker?"

"I deal with thieves and corporate spies. I don't think a lot of career criminals go into practical joking. You know, I don't think I understand practical jokes. I've played a few, but I'm not sure I could tell you what the kick is."

"Besides sadism? I think it's aesthetic. Literary. In most practical jokes that go on for an extended time there's something like a narrative structure—usually a basic progression. Loud-louder-loudest. Big-bigger-biggest, and so forth. Some theme pushed gradually to the point of absurdity. Will you take those things off?"

"Nervous, Parker?" John removed the glasses and set them on the coffee table.

"The high point of most practical jokes is the same as in tragedy—the recognition scene, when the victim sees he's been had. For instance, when I was a teaching assistant at Cornell, some of the other TAs started moving a guy's desk a few feet every day, just to see if he'd notice when he came in. I think he noticed but he wanted to deny them their recognition scene. One morning his desk and chair had reached the hallway; so he sat there in the hallway grading papers and keeping appointments with his students. There was some talk of continuing the joke, moving the desk a little farther every day till it left the building and eventually the campus, but he'd broken their spirit. The next day the desk was back in place. You know what? I think protective obtuseness was my strongest weapon."

"For you, maybe. I'd carry something like this to its conclusion." John stood up. "I'll have to kick you out and go to bed...Think you were followed? Move over." He leaned over the couch and pried up one of the blinds.

"I don't think you'll see the man in the trenchcoat leaning against a lamp post with his collar up, if that's what you're l looking for."

"The man under the lamp post has glasses, a stocking cap, a cruddy brown jacket. He's holding something. Looks like a Ziploc bag."

* * *

When Ziploc saw them crossing the street, he went into his gesticulating dance. "Parker! How ya doin'!" He was theatrically ugly under the sodium vapor lamp, his bruises garish, his manic face seething with leaf shadows. He pointed at John. "This man has *brain* power! Mister, do you mind if I ask a personal question? Do you eat fish? Fish is *brain* food, as I'm sure you know."

John placed an arm round his shoulder and asked him what he thought he was doing.

"Moving the exterior limbs in a dynamic fashion!" Ziploc shuffled from foot to foot, glancing sidelong at John's rose-colored glasses and ambiguous grin.

Parker placed his arm round the other shoulder, crossing John's arm, and they all stood facing the darkened white frame houses across the street. "C'mon, Zip. What are you doing?"

Ziploc continued staring across the street. "Thinkin'."

"Thinking! What about?"

"You! I'm a consultant about you!"

A rectangle of light enclosed them; John turned and waved to an undershirted man squinting through his front-door pane; the light went out.

Parker said, "These days everyone's a consultant. Can you be more specific?"

"Okay, say I have a dream. You're fightin' these giant turtles! Turtles, you know, are a big archetype. Think I'm kiddin'? Read Jung! So these turtles keep comin', and you're sockin' 'em! Then I write it down and people come and take away the notes. Sometimes they're standing over the bed when I wake up."

John pinched his cheek. "I see. You've decided you're a character. Well it isn't that easy. You don't get to decide you're a character—I'll decide if you're a character."

"I think I get this." Parker faced John over Ziploc's head. "Dobbs said my demon wanted his jokes to look like random occurrences. Well, randomness is harder to fake than you might think. That makes Ziploc the perfect consultant. Whose thought processes are closer to blind chance? No offense, Zip."

"It's okay with me!"

"Socked any turtles lately?" John asked Parker.

"No, I guess the Breather people can't use the material raw. It has to be edited, interpreted, explicated."

John rubbed his chin. "Has anything happened that's *like* turtles?"

"Well, no. But I have the feeling a lot of events in my life originated right here, under this stocking cap." He patted Ziploc's head. "Tell me, Zip. We're friends, right?"

"You and me? Suuure!"

"Suppose I told you someone was using your ideas to hurt me."

Ziploc tilted his head, widening and narrowing his eyes as if Parker had gone out of focus.

"What if I made some...some of my own suggestions? Could you put them in your reports?"

"Sure! Whattaya need?"

John said, "I don't believe this, Parker. You're making a wish. Oh, Jeez!"

"John—shut up." Parker turned back to Ziploc. "Here's what I want. I want this to stop."

"This?" Ziploc's gesture took in the houses, the parked cars, the streetlights, the leaves crackling above their heads. The contents of the Ziploc bag rattled and glimmered as he waved his hand.

"I mean, I want you to leave me alone."

Ziploc shuffled his feet, opened and closed his mouth.

"No point hurting his feelings," John said. "Go for what you can get—money, fame, power. How about world peace?"

"Can I actually make a wish?"

"That's the point I'm tryin' to stress!" Ziploc yelled. "Whattaya need?"

Parker was stumped. It had been years since he'd entertained the possibility that he might get something he wanted; he therefore had no idea what he wanted. "Wait—let me think."

He wondered what his wish would look like by the time it passed through Ziploc's mind, got edited, interpreted, and explicated, and came back at him.

John removed the sunglasses and stared at Parker. "Tell me you're kidding." He turned to Ziploc. "While we're waiting, who do you work for and where can we find them?"

"There."

A white Continental with blacked-out windows pulled up to the curb. Parker had his gun out. The electric window on the passenger side cracked open, and a knuckle rapped on the glass. "Bulletproof." Parker recognized the voice of the big despairman.

"I'll keep it out anyway, if you don't mind."

"No problem." A gun barrel slid through the opening. "Just in case you've seen too many movies and you want to shoot out the tires."

"Shut up!" Ziploc yelled. "He's makin' a wish!"

"Don't tell," said the despairman, "or it won't come true."

Ziploc opened the back door. "You think about that wish. I'll get back to ya!"

FIVE

When Fletcher said "anomic stress formation," he nearly sang. He didn't break eye contact or pause a beat when a lunch tray hit the floor with a reverberant smash and clatter. "Directly, not inversely, see?" He leaned farther across the table toward Parker. "Everyone else had it backwards."

Parker's mind floated above his body. It skimmed the fluorescent lights and the ceiling tiles, surveyed the chunky earth-colored specials of the day, buzzed the tops of heads, and skated across the green and beige floor squares, skirting the crowd gathering where he'd heard the crash. It was attempting to follow a pair of tanned calves in a blue denim skirt beyond Parker's line of sight, when he reminded himself that everything about one's enemy is interesting—well, significant.

He found himself involuntarily wadding a napkin as the spoon poised near Fletcher's mouth dribbled onto a tweed sleeve. Parker kept watching the spoon; every few seconds it made a run at the mouth and was shunted aside by a stampede of jargon.

If the man hadn't been plotting to ruin his life, Parker would have thought he knew the type—a collection of academic quirks Parker ordinarily found touching. The brow-furrowing poses and Mr. Chips tweeds belonged to a man who, despite all honors, degrees, and appointments, feels like an impostor (no, wait. Fletcher *was* an impostor).

But when he spoke of...whatever it was he was talking about, Fletcher lost the manner. His face was molten with enthusiasm, as if he might force his thoughts through the eyes, brow, and nostrils. As always, Parker was touched by the social innocence and childlike zest of the truly hopeless bore.

The *Tribune* ad would run in three days, the others within a few weeks. How would Fletcher hold up?

Following Parker's eyes, Fletcher paused in midsentence, contemplated his spoon, and swallowed his soup. "When I did that at home my wife used to quote the Japanese proverb: 'Eat first, poetry later.' The kids picked it up: 'Eat, daddy! Poetry later!'"

Parker rearranged the crumbs on his plate. He didn't kid himself that the ads were a prank—they were psychological warfare—but he'd seen no other way to break Fletcher down. Simple intimidation wouldn't work; the people controlling Fletcher could surely be scarier than he could. But he hadn't considered the possibility that he might also be attacking a wife and kids. Perhaps it had been convenient to assume that Fletcher was too self-absorbed to have a family.

"How old are your kids?"

"Greg's twelve, Jennifer's nine. They live with their mom."

Trying not to show his relief, Parker said the first thing that came to mind. "Your ex-wife, she's Japanese?"

Fletcher knitted his brow. "Why, no. What an odd question."

"Japanese proverb?" Parker shrugged. "I'm babbling. A brain impulse got lost between synapses, is that what happens? You'll have to tell me some other time; I'm late for a class." He gripped his briefcase and stood up.

There was a second crash. "Hey, faggot! Kinda old for trick-or-treat!"

Throughout the cafeteria people rose from their chairs. The crowd was backing away as Parker approached the din. Through the opening a seated man, his face encrusted with purplish-black blisters, grinned at Parker: bald, trenchcoat, mirror lenses, the grin like a flare in the charred face. The man's foot was extended into the aisle, where it had generated a collage of puddles, splatters, smashed plates and glass. From the amount of mess, he must have tripped more than one person. A kid in a green sweatshirt, apparently the most recent victim, crunched over shards as he backed into Parker; he was holding the man's beard.

"Damn, it's hard to get your attention, buddy." (That inauthentic cowboy drawl had run through Parker's head for days.) "Siddown!" Hank Monroe, Jr. pointed at the chair facing his. Three lunches, barely touched, sat abandoned on the table.

Reflected in the mirror shades, Parker closed his mouth. He'd just remembered the gun in his briefcase. The kid put the beard in his hand and backed farther off. Parker stepped up to the table, his reflections in the shades expanding as if he were diving in.

"Lose this?" he said. The beard was made of a wiry synthetic; having touched the adhesive, Parker had to shake the thing loose. He sat down, set his case on the table, and released the flap.

Leaving his beard on the table between them, Monroe, Jr. beamed at the crowd. "It ain't trick-or-treat, folks. I'm ugly 'cause I served my country. What's *your* excuse?" He threw an arm across the back of his chair. "Ever hear the saying, judge a man by his enemies? Well I'm proud to have Jeff Parker here for my enemy. I threw the book at 'im—beatings, sores, pus, dead dogs—guy's an iceman. I mean, he's got this look he don't even know it's happening. What's his secret?" A few people giggled.

Fletcher pushed up to the front of the crowd. "Shall I call the police?"

Parker's hand found the gun in his briefcase. "No." Leaving the gun inside, he rested his forearm on the case.

"His secret," Monroe, Jr. orated, master of ceremonies at a celebrity roast, "—and I don't want to hear you pissants laugh—secret's that he's pure of heart. I know, you're thinkin', pure of heart, sure, how many divisions does the pope have? I use to think that way myself and he whomped me. I'm a proud man but I gotta say it: He whomped me."

Bob Linder, one of Parker's Comp students, yelled, "Way to go, Jeff!"

Parker stood up. "Why don't we discuss our business in my office?"

"Yeah, buddy, let's you an me talk about old times." Monroe, Jr. was Parker's height and a good deal wider. "Always a pleasure talkin' to young people," he said to the crowd. "I hope you kids'll let this be a lesson."

They were given a wide berth through the hallway.

"Damn!" Monroe, Jr. halted. "I nearly forgot this previous engagement. But listen, buddy, we'll have lunch. You take care now, I'll—"

Finding no one else looking, Parker flashed the gun and stuffed it in his sport-coat pocket, pressing the barrel against the cloth. "Don't move."

"I don't want to hurt your feelings, Jeff, but I think I know you, and that gun and fifty cents'll get you a cup of coffee."

Parker noted that he hadn't moved.

A girl approaching them made a quick lateral. "Man thinks he's ringmaster 'cause he got a gun!" Monroe, Jr. yelled after her. "Big fuckin' deal! You want me to maybe...reach for the sky?" He put up his arms, rose up on tiptoe, and grinned hideously.

Parker decided not to make threats—just point the gun and give instructions. "Put your arms down," he said, appropriating the stern, patient tone he took with his problem students. "Step over to that door...good." He took his key ring out of his pocket. "Catch." He tossed it over. "Now unlock it."

His broad back to Parker, Monroe, Jr. paused to study the index card on the door.

"I said unlock it. Don't try locking yourself in."

Turning the key, Monroe, Jr. glanced over his shoulder. "And miss the show? I wanta see what you do you gotta *use* that thing."

Grabbing the keys back from Monroe, Jr. and closing and locking the door behind them, Parker gestured to the chair in front of his desk. He had the gun out when Karen Feinstein waved from the parking lot. "Wait—get the blinds." He flinched when they crashed shut. "Hold it. Don't sit down yet—take your coat off."

In his denim workshirt Monroe, Jr. was barrel-chested and pot-bellied, his skin undamaged from the top of his neck to the graying red hairs in his open collar. "A man should have clear objectives when he points a gun. Looks to me like you're floundering, buddy."

Parker felt slightly giddy hearing himself say "Up against the wall!"

The search produced a wallet, a key ring, a pack of gum and a soiled plaid handkerchief. He set these with the coat on the desk behind him. "Sit down," he said, backing around the desk toward his chair. Monroe, Jr. made himself at home, folding his hands across his belly, stretching his legs, crossing his feet at the ankles. Parker switched on the desk lamp and, twisting its neck, lit up the purplish-black scars.

"Oh please, please! I confess!"

"Shut up." Parker squinted into the glare off the mirror lenses. "Take those off."

The eyes facing Parker were small, gray, bloodshot, and lusterless. "I hate when people call 'em 'beady'."

"That stuff on your face...it's some kind of makeup."

"What it is, is polyurethane, gelatin, and epoxy. Only took you twenty minutes to see what you been lookin' at. That's lightning for you, boy."

"You figured I'd be the one to pull your beard off today. The accent—that's fake, too?"

"It's only fake if I'm tryin' to sound real." He tapped an endpiece of his sunglasses against his teeth.

Parker said, "Start peeling the stuff off your face—wait." He opened the bottom drawer and felt around till he found the duct tape. He always had some around. By the time he'd given up on his car, it was held together mostly by duct tape. He tossed the roll to Monroe, Jr. "Bind your right wrist to the armrest."

"It'll take me longer to get this stuff off one-handed."

"No. It'll just hurt more."

Monroe, Jr. bound his wrist in five turns and let the roll dangle. He took some glop between his thumb and forefinger and drew it out like bubblegum, the side of his face expanding as if it too were about to rip free. "Hope you won't shoot a man for a little constructive criticism, but it seems to me you're takin' this 'ruined-your-life' business way too hard."

The man was killing time, but Parker couldn't resist. "How should I take it?"

"Know what? Check the *in*surance tables for a man your age, weight, and occupation. Bet you ain't been sicker or hurt more or generally unluckier than most. Look at it this way: If all the bad things that happen to you happen on purpose, then the bad things that woulda happened by accident *can't happen*." He tugged at another patch and it worked loose with a slurping, sucking noise. "I know, you had all this *potential*, and I fucked it up. Well, how many potential guys do you see in this room?

Ain't nobody in this world but us actual guys— time you faced it, amigo."
He tugged the piece till it came away in gooey strands. "Quit passin' the
buck. Blame it all on me, and you're lettin' me control your life. Blame it
on yourself, and I still control your life, come to think of it, but I *respect* a
man who takes responsibility."

He delivered this monologue with such self-delighted, sprightly mal-
ice, Parker found himself laughing.

An unhealthy baby face was emerging—round, bald, pale, chubby,
pug-nosed, thin-lipped, and jug-eared. The laugh lines round the dull
gray eyes and famished lips made Parker think of a man who'd died
laughing. Parker stared, assuring himself that this was no allegorical
figure—just a man who sat up late eating Twinkies, thinking up mean
things to do.

Monroe, Jr. was picking the last shreds off his cheeks. "Trouble with
you, amigo, you're like everyone else these days. Everything me! me! me!
My enemies! *My* screwed-up life! *My* conspiracy! Maybe you wouldn't be
so miser'ble if you thought about other people. Get married! Have kids!
Do volunteer work! Help the homeless! You're gonna die all alone in a
room fulla soup cans, and I suppose that's my fault, too." With a moist
resounding rip a bald wig peeled away from his identically bald skull.

Parker didn't bother to ask. He stepped out from behind his desk,
picked up the duct tape roll still attached to Monroe, Jr.'s wrist, and
played it out till the man's chest and limbs were cocooned to his chair.

"I feel snug as a bug in a rug!" Monroe, Jr. declared as Parker returned to his seat.

Parker said, "How about dropping the fake—sorry, the unreal accent. What would you sound like if someone woke you up at three in the
morning?"

"I dunno. Surprise me."

"Tell you what. Be real for thirty seconds. What could happen?"

Monroe, Jr., ran his tongue over a shred of epoxy at the corner of his mouth.

The wallet—it looked expensive; eel skin?—contained one hundred eighty-seven dollars, an accordion fold stuffed with IDs, and no photographs.

Parker read from the business card he'd found in the billfold: "'Tolerance Management, Inc.' What's that?"

"Beats the hell outta me!"

Intrigued, Parker took down the phone number and the State Street address. He brushed the trenchcoat off his desk and spread out the IDs. "I've never seen anyone grinning so fulsomely on an Illinois driver's license," he observed.

"You'd be amazed what the physical act of smiling does for your whole outlook. Come on—try it!"

"What's this?" Parker had just noticed credit cards, Illinois driver's licenses, and social security cards under two other names—Roy Kleemont and Don Ray Smith—each with a separate address. "What's your real name?"

"You're the boss. State your preference."

When he'd finished copying names, addresses, phone numbers, and Social Security numbers, Parker took aim with both hands. "Here's my problem. I can't let you go. Give me some information—something verifiable, something...incriminating—and I'll turn you over to the police. Otherwise...." He didn't want to state the threat flatly, doubted he could sound convincing.

He'd been trying to keep his hands steady, but now he let them shake. He'd be more of a threat acting like what he was—a nervous man with a gun.

He seemed to be having an effect; Monroe, Jr.'s grin shriveled over his teeth.

Parker cleared his throat. "Let's start with an easy one. Why are you doing all this?"

Blank-faced and silent, Monroe, Jr. seemed even more unreachable. The Cheshire cat had disappeared, leaving not even its grin.

Parker picked up the phone. "If we're both lucky we won't have to carry this farce to its conclusion." He punched a number.

"*The Exhibitionist!*" Dobbs's secretaries always voiced the greeting with exaggerated formality.

"Steve Dobbs, please."

"Mr. Dobbs is in a meeting. May I—"

"This is Jeffrey Parker. I have Hank Monroe, Junior in my office. That's M-O-N-R-O-E. Junior. I think he'll want to speak to me *now*!"

Monroe, Jr. grinned. "That's the ticket, amigo!"

"Jeff! Still coming for dinner Sunday?"

Parker was distracted by the irrelevant thought that John Standell was right—Steve *did* sound like Bugs Bunny.

"You might have to set a place for Hank Monroe, Junior," Parker said.

"What'd he do? Drop by for a visit?"

"That's exactly what he did. Listen. Get—"

"Why?"

"I forgot to ask." Monroe, Jr. was straining against the tape; Parker motioned with the gun for him to keep still. "Why are you here?"

"I dunno, thought we'd shoot the shit."

"You were right the other day," Parker said to Dobbs, "he must be bored. Listen. Put together all your evidence and get over here. I'll phone the police." It occurred to Parker that he'd have to get rid of Jack's gun before the police arrived.

"He's so bored he'll wait around for the police?"

"I'm not giving him a choice."

"Of course," said Dobbs, clipped and officious, "I can't be a party to kidnapping."

"I'm holding him for the *police*. Get the hell over here."

A damp breeze rattled the blinds; rain popped and ticked at the window.

"Evidence—yeah. I have to tell you, Jeff, the evidence is kind of— kinda speculative."

"What does that mean?"

Seeing Parker's distress, the bound man contrived a sympathetic shrug, causing tape to bunch up at his shoulders. Parker waved the gun at him.

Dobbs said, "The evidence at this stage requires a grasp of subtleties, a capacity for synoptic thought. The police are so damn linear, I'm not sure—"

"You mean you've got zip."

"I wouldn't put it that strongly, but—well, yeah."

"What about the documents? The FBI memos and all that?"

"Yeah, the memos. We don't have the memos per se."

"What now?"

"Let him go. I doubt he'll press charges for kidnapping."

"Any other helpful suggestions?"

"There's always torture. I'm speaking theoretically, of course, but the systematic application of heat and cold to the soles of the feet is said to be highly effective. Get some ice cubes, some matches and cigarettes, a cigar's even better, then—"

"You know what, Steve? You're a psychotic Walter Mitty."

"I won't take that personally. I understand you're disappointed and you're lashing out. See you Sunday. Bye!"

Parker slammed down the phone.

Monroe, Jr. said, "Hey, you done your best; ain't *your* fault your best ain't worth shit."

Parker was ready to concede the point. The duct tape was a bonehead idea, reducing his options to torture or murder. All right, get rid of the tape, beat the truth out of him in a fair fight.

Then he had a better idea. "Let's phone the police after all. It's a felony to carry a forged driver's license. And I'll bet if you use three names you have some other reasons for avoiding the police. What's the rush—another previous engagement?"

Monroe, Jr. was writhing against the tape, aiming his bald head forward like a lineman about to blitz. Wisps of glop adhered to the crown of his skull.

Parker stepped out from behind the desk and stood over him. "I really must insist that you sit still. I might not shoot you, but I wouldn't mind knocking you cold. That's better. My, your wit seems to desert you under pressure. How about some morsel from the old cracker barrel?"

There was a knock at the door and before Parker had his finger to his lips a key turned in the lock.

"Come ii-in!" Monroe, Jr. sang. Behind him the door cracked open and slammed shut.

No one answered Parker's dry-throated "Who's there!" but the dark spot under the door hadn't moved.

He flattened himself against the wall to the left of the door, where he'd be hidden behind it if it opened. Would the despairmen have knocked?

"Jeffrey, I'm coming in." It was Jan Cohen's voice, sounding more tired and exasperated than scared. The door still hadn't opened. "You're not going to shoot me, are you?"

Parker stepped away from the wall. "Why don't you come back later, Jan?"

"Why don't we contain this while we still can?" she said through the door. "Or do you relish seeing your neighbors on the ten o'clock news observing that you were a quiet loner?"

Parker laughed.

"At least," she said, "your sense of the absurd hasn't deserted you. That if nothing else should keep you from prolonging this one more minute."

"You don't understand what's happening here."

"Oh, I'm sure it's Tiddlywinks!" This clearly wasn't the tone she'd intended, and she immediately tried another. "Why don't you open the door, hand me the gun, and *tell* me what's happening?"

It was Jan or the SWAT team. "Don't get scared, Jan. I'm going to open the door and hand you the gun."

His back to the door and Parker, Monroe, Jr. yelled, "Look out, lady! He's takin' aim! Just kidding."

"Jan?" Parker called through the door. "Are you still out there? I'm holding the gun by the barrel, I'm turning the knob."

She faced him in the doorway, brittle with willed courage. She was dressed up today—white pearls, cobalt-blue suit—as if to bolster the stiff-backed formality with which she accepted the gun. With her free hand she hurriedly lowered the big red-tinted glasses propped on her head.

Parker stepped aside to let her in and closed the door. "I'm the second faculty member you've disarmed. You're gaining a rep as the Wyatt Earp of Skokie. You look spiffy, Jan—what's the occasion?"

His attempt at small talk seemed only to intensify her distress and confusion. "The fund-raiser's this evening," she said tonelessly. "Aren't you...?" It dawned on her that she was pointing the gun at him; she dropped it into her handbag. She stepped in front of the chair to look at the bound man, and whatever look he returned caused her nostrils to flare in distaste.

"I came here for Jack's gun," she said to Parker. "This morning I found out he picked the lock on my desk drawer and took it back. He told me he gave it to you, and I was hoping to stop you from doing something idiotic and getting yourself killed—I'm too late for the first, obviously. I'm sorry, but I'll have to call the police."

Since Parker hadn't managed to get rid of the gun, he was hoping to keep the police out of this so he wouldn't be arrested along with his captive. Was it worth the effort to make up a story for Jan? A bullshit story would only insult her intelligence—the truth even more so. Might as well go out with a funny exit line:

"Janet, I promise this will never happen again."

It failed to break the ice.

She stepped around the desk and picked up the phone.

"Hang up the phone, okay? Will you at least hear me out?"

She hung up and folded her arms, warning him by the set of her mouth and the thrust of her chin that bullshit would bounce off.

But he'd just realized that b.s. could work even if she didn't believe it.

"My friend here suffers from Post-Vietnam Stress Syndrome."

Stepping in front of the chair, Parker glanced at Monroe, Jr., who looked as bewildered as Jan. "I was helping him work through his POW experience."

She lifted her glasses as she sometimes did to underscore a sarcastic remark, then decided, apparently, that it would be lost on him. She picked up the phone.

"Don't waste your time, Jan. It doesn't matter whether you believe me. As long as my friend and I refuse to press charges, this isn't a matter for the police." Then why make up a story at all? Oh, well.

Monroe, Jr. took his cue. "It's like he said, lady. It was like bein' back in Nam."

An enraged beep-tone was pealing from the receiver; she depressed the cradle with her index finger. "What about the gun?"

"I took it," Parker said, "to keep it away from Jack— same as you."

"Whatever trouble you're in, let the police handle it."

"Could we lie about the gun? No? Then thank you for your good intentions."

She hung up, watching Parker as if an undertow had dragged him beyond the possibility of help, a speck shrinking toward the horizon.

"Anyway, it worked like a charm," said Monroe, Jr., chipper. "You cured me, amigo. Thanks! Why don't you get this stuff off me and I'll be on my way."

When it was clear that Jan wasn't about to leave, Parker began unraveling tape. "I suppose I'm fired?"

Checkmated, she hadn't moved from behind the desk. "See me in my office on Monday. I hope you'll trust me enough to let me help you."

"Damn!" Monroe, Jr. guffawed. "What do you have to do around here to *get* fired! Know what, buddy? I feel fit as a fiddle! I think we're onto somethin' with this duct tape. I say we franchise it—chain o' spas, maybe, how 'bout it?"

Yawning and stretching he rose from the skein at his feet, a fat untransformable larva.

* * *

When he was alone, Parker raised the blinds and inhaled till his head cleared. The rain had nearly wound down, plinking and gurgling. A silvery dimness trembled on cars in the lot.

He snatched a sheet of paper about to flit off the desk— the items he'd copied from Monroe, Jr.'s wallet.

He punched the first number.

A bright receptionist voice recited "Tolerance Management! Can I help you?"

"I hope so. I have a few questions about the Breather Program."

"One moment, please!"

A string version of "The Greatest Love of All" filled the pause before a terse male voice demanded, "Who is this?"

"Is this the number for the Breather Program?"

"That would be Jeffrey Parker!" The voice sounded glad he'd called.

"Never mind who—yeah," Parker said. "Who are *you*?"

"We have a great deal to discuss. Why don't you come down to the office? Would 4:30 Monday suit you?"

"Four-thirty. Okay, uh—" Parker hung up. He'd just decided to propose to Fran. His first chance would be Sunday, after their evening with the Dobbses. They'd leave early; he'd have champagne waiting at his apartment; it wasn't too late to put something on the walls. He wasn't sure she'd accept, but there was dupery through hope or dupery through fear, right?

In his new mood he imagined a time when he'd think back on Hank Monroe, Jr. as a ghastly but benign apparition who, like the Ghost of Christmas Future, had shocked him into wisdom: "You're gonna die all alone in a room fulla soup cans!" Parker drummed the desktop, slapping a bass line to a new gust of rain. What was tolerance management?

* * *

Nodding off, Fran put her head on his shoulder. He stroked her cheek and replaced his hand on the wheel. Even with the wipers on high, he could barely reconstruct Lake Shore Drive out of gleaming, seething dots.

She mumbled something under the din.

"What?"

"It's my fault," she said through her hair.

He was driving her car because she'd started putting away margaritas as dinner with the Dobbses turned ugly. "Don't be ridiculous. Steve's a nervous, prickly guy; the strain of trying to make friends finally got to him. Consider it a world record that you got him to relax for a couple of hours."

"Getting people to relax is my...my what?" she wondered.

"Your forte? your lot in life? your fate?" A lightning-burst tripped flashbulbs on the pelted cars.

"Calling. I'm a politician's daughter."

"Do you kiss babies?"

"No," she murmured, her boozy breath warm in his ear, "but I *hold* babies. The babies play with my hair." He let her drift off.

The evening had started out well, despite his warnings that it was more likely to be interesting than pleasant. Their forebodings had caused them to have a laughing fit at the stone gargoyles over the entrance—the building was a Gold Coast landmark—and at the doorman, whose glower reminded them that in the real world Dobbs was the wealthy, respectable citizen and they the suspicious characters.

But they'd begun to relax as Steve, his wife, Barbara, and their two-year-old, Courtney, guided them on a tour of the condo, Fran playing peek-a-boo with Courtney and nudging Parker to indicate cathedral ceilings, Persian carpets, a Ralph Lauren dining-room set, an Eckhart couch like a soft mauve UFO with legs. When it became apparent that Barb savored these displays of pleasure, they gawked brazenly. Sharp-witted, short, slight, and dimly blond, Barb worked as a loan officer at the Harris Bank. From the eager rapidity of her speech and gestures, Parker gathered that they didn't get much company. He'd wondered how a wife might respond to Dobbs's nuttier ideas—wide-eyed endorsement or eye-rolling stoicism. It was more like tolerant amusement. Passing a David Hockney lithograph, she quipped, "We speculate in paranoia and invest in Realism." But Dobbs was a charming host for about two hours, cracking them up with bawdy, tenuously plausible political gossip, laughing in turn at Fran's anecdotes about her father's days in the Minnesota state senate, and teaching Courtney to make a troll face.

After dinner Parker asked to speak to him alone. Steve led him down the hall to his study, closed the door, and, grim-faced, asked Parker if he'd swear to keep a secret. Parker braced himself: Okay. Dobbs told Parker that he hated his study. Before Parker could recover from his confusion and get out his questions, Dobbs launched into a preemptive monologue about how Barb had wanted to have the room refurnished for his surprise birthday present while they were away on a trip, but, having selected all their furniture, she'd little idea of his tastes. The decorator had nothing to go on except that Dobbs was some sort of writer, and he'd done up the room in its present Explorers' Club Rococo—the sort of rattan-and-hide stuff a set designer might've placed around Gregory Peck for "The Snows of Kilimanjaro." Barb must've hated it, but Steve had convinced her that he sort of liked it. Anyway, at least it was funny—he'd kept a papier-mâché cow head over the mantel till it scared Courtney—and at least the hides weren't real, but all he really needed was a table and chair, maybe just a pad of paper, a pencil, and a clean floor, and besides—. Cutting him off, Parker asked what he knew about Tolerance Management. As if on cue, Courtney knocked at the door. She was a cute kid with blond hair, blue eyes, and the habit of standing practically on your toes and gaping straight up like a tourist. Steve picked her up and brandished her to deflect further questions. "Here's Courtney's joke," he said. "Hey Courtney! Guess what!" "What!" she squealed, bug-eyed in anticipation. "That's what!" he shot back, and they both laughed raucously. Then

Parker had to tell her the joke; she enjoyed it so much he'd have felt like a cad if he didn't oblige her by repeating it fifty or sixty times. That killed another five minutes, and Steve suggested that they rejoin the women.

Parker reached over Dobbs's shoulder and held the door shut. "Has someone been threatening you?"

Dobbs asked Parker to suppose—hypothetically!—that someone was. Should he let someone maim Courtney—for example!—for the sake of Parker's rather abstract, amorphous problem? "What exactly makes your life more awful than anyone else's?" he asked Parker. "You don't look so bad off to me. How 'bout it, Courtney? I don't see a mark on 'im, do you? Oh, yeah, that teeny bump between the eyes. Parker thinks we should get maimed 'cause he got a boo-boo. Or because he hasn't lived up to his income-earning potential, is that it? He's funny!" "He funeeee!" Courtney beamed, and Parker followed them back to the living room.

He'd have liked to leave, but Fran was talking animatedly to Barb and luxuriating in the Eckhart couch, her hair spread over the back. He sat down next to her, keeping clear of her expansive gestures. Dobbs brought in a tray of margaritas and perched on the armrest of Barbara's chair, but despite this impersonation of a casual manner, he was starting to look as he had in Parker's office—hunched and hemmed in.

When Parker couldn't bear to watch him squirm any longer, he said, "John tells me you've acquired a following."

"Like you 'acquire' lice, and just as hard to get rid of. I was never sure what they wanted: rumors, tips, secrets, inside dope—religion, but hipper. Just a bunch of rich Republican assholes looking for a philosophy incoherent enough to justify their lives."

"You admit to being incoherent?"

"Of course! Like I told you, if you're going to tell the truth in this country, you need cover. Anyway, I'd say, 'You're wasting your time!' They'd say, 'Of course!'"

"Sounds like they were imitating the master."

"Exactly! But I hated being aped by dummies who didn't get the point. I'd say 'The magazine's garbage! I'm a liar! I contradict myself!' They'd say 'That's right.'"

"But of course *that* was a lie. *You* think your contradictions are really paradoxes and your lies protect some esoteric core of truth, right?"

"Exactly!"

Getting into the spirit, Fran said, "The last thing you said—that was a lie, too?"

"No," said Dobbs, affronted, "that was true."

But he didn't waste time sulking, still eager, Parker thought, to deliver his long-rehearsed anecdote to an audience.

"Finally I had my following whittled down to three or four incredibly tenacious people. I'd throw drinks in their faces; they thought it was some kind of Zen-master thing. I told one guy, 'Look, if you want genuine spiritual advice, go read Gurdjieff.' A few weeks later he comes back, says Gurdjieff taught him that he's been a self-centered, self-deceiving asshole. I say, good, now go away. But he won't shut up. He says that that morning he was about to give money to a homeless man—then he realized he'd only be doing it to aggrandize his self-image, so he didn't. I said 'You're still a self-centered, self-deceiving asshole.' He nods knowingly: 'Of course!' After that I decided that if they were going to pester me, I'd start asking for donations. Once a week I'd take their money and tell them to go away, until finally it occurred to them that they could go away for free."

Throughout this monologue Barb sagged in her chair, unable, Parker thought, to share Dobbs' professed satisfaction in the loss of all their friends. It must have been for her sake that Dobbs hadn't canceled the evening.

Fran asked about the story she'd read in Parker's *Exhibitionist*—"You know, the one about the woman who finds out her imaginary voices come from two guys in undershirts reading *Facts on File* into a microphone? How'd you dream that one up?"

"Oh, that was true," Dobbs said, folding his arms, impervious to the exertions of her brows and eyeballs to force his smile. Barb must have known from previous experience that the evening had entered its downward arc; Steve ignored her hand on his back, and, when she leaned forward to face him where he sat on her armrest, gazed over her head. He realized by then that Parker and Fran weren't about to fill the void in his wife's social life, and he was probably sick of behaving himself. "There's nothing fantastic about it," he said to Fran. "You've heard of people who pick up radio broadcasts with their fillings? Direct Neural Broadcasting applies the same principle. Of course you don't believe me."

"Steve, if you told me there's a law of gravity, I'd wear a ceiling protector on my head." She said it mock-hautily, brandishing an imaginary cigarette-holder, in her usual faith that people were rooting for her to assert herself. But Dobbs stood up, about-faced, and walked out of the room.

"Did I insult him?" Fran asked Barb. "Is he coming back?"

"Documentation." Barb was fussing with the barrette in Courtney's hair. She looked up and, flashing her brights, added, "More margarita?"

Dobbs returned with a journal-size publication and dropped it into Fran's lap. His back to his wife's glare, he stood over Fran while she found her place, scanned, and flipped pages.

She looked up. "This is all technical jargon. I guess I'll have to accept everything you say since I'm too stupid to understand your evidence, is that how it works?"

"If the evidence sprouted horns and butted you, would you believe it then?"

"Yes; in the meantime no."

"Look at Courtney!" Barb had covered her daughter's entire head with a sombrero. The diversion produced a half-minute of bristling silence punctuated by Courtney's muffled giggles.

Dobbs was still standing over Fran. "It's complaisance like yours that lets corporations and the military test DNB all over the world."

"If they're doing it all over the world," she said, "why doesn't *everyone* hear voices?"

"If *everyone* heard voices *all the time*," he said, "it would be like living in a boiler factory. They wouldn't know they're hearing anything. Kinda like *your* life, aye, Jeff?"

"So I've been told," Parker said agreeably. Fran wouldn't want him fighting her battles; the sooner the argument ran its course, the sooner they could leave Dobbs to his wife.

"Let's see what else you're afraid to believe," Dobbs said. "Three weeks ago Sam Markaris—male Caucasian, fifty years old, no fixed address—is standing in front of the Pacific Garden Mission talking to his buddies when he starts rubbing his scalp and complaining about a headache. A few seconds later he keels over dead, a plume of smoke spouting from a tiny hole in the top of his head."

"Did he whistle like a tea kettle?" Fran asked.

"According to the guy who drives the meat wagon for the morgue, this past year they've brought in over a dozen homeless people with quarter-inch- diameter holes burned deep through the tops of their heads. Of course you won't believe me when I tell you that the government's testing space-based laser weapons on the homeless, but I have the documents."

The evening creaked on, each topic taking the same course—Dobbs asserting, Fran negating; Dobbs documenting, Fran debunking. The stakes of this contest were unclear to Parker. Dobbs, he supposed, won either way: You either fed his Inside Tipster conceit or his Prophet-Crying-in-the-Wilderness conceit.

As for Fran—Parker wished she'd humor the guy. Whether or not Dobbs believed what he was saying, he was trying so hard to be *interesting*! But Fran had stopped joking; she looked angry and anxious. Eyes narrowed, lips compressed, she held her head up as if the pile of documents rising to meet it threatened to pull her under. Parker massaged her neck and shoulders, careful not to spill the last of the margaritas balanced on her pile of documents. He'd have to postpone the proposal. The only question he could ask her tonight was the same one he kept asking everybody: What was *that* all about?

* * *

A thunderbolt jerked Fran awake. "Enough," she mumbled into his neck.

A line of yellow blinkers closed off the two rightmost lanes. The rain pulsed with turnlights, but nothing moved.

He said, "What was all that about between you and Dobbs?"

"I'm a politician's daughter—okay?" The thought seemed to scald her wide awake. "That means I grew up thinking it's good manners to smile and nod while some man lies." She sat up, pushed back her hair, untwisted her shoulder harness. "My mom's been smiling and nodding at my dad for thirty years, thinking he's a lying sack of shit." She put her head back on his shoulder. "These days I smile and nod—or not!—and tell the guy he's a lying sack of shit. I could never have done that before I met—" Parker strained to hear the name as her voice trailed off.

"Who?"

Recalling her voice on the phone the other day when he thought there was someone else in the room, he pictured her making faces into the receiver to amuse her guest. Parker tried to laugh off the image. But lately the worst he could imagine kept proving true, as if his imagination were hemorrhaging into the world.

"Fran? … You awake?"

Her hair had closed over her face. He wanted to push it away and see what was going on in there, but traffic had started moving. Beyond the guardrail the lake blinked on and off.

* * *

He muscled the car half-blind into a space across from his building; unfolded Fran out of her seat and stood her beneath his umbrella; maneuvered her round an overflowing gutter, across the street, and through the entrance; dissuaded her from lying down on the stone table in the lobby and doing her impersonation of a mummy; and supported her weight up the steps. He was so pleased with himself that he practically had the key in before noticing that the door was a crack ajar and the light on.

Turning to Fran he put his finger to his lips and raised his palm. She held up her palm and scowled like a cigar store Indian.

He uncovered her ear and whispered, "Don't come in till I tell you it's okay."

Through the opening he caught a faint vinegary smell. What he could see of the living room—couch, end table, lamp, a segment of white wall—disclosed nothing. Inching the door open, he reached into his coat pocket and recalled that he didn't have Jack's gun. He was reconsidering tactics when Fran walked into his back and bumped him inside.

* * *

In order to keep her balance, control her articulation, maintain her dignity, and hold down her margaritas, Fran stood perfectly rigid in the center of the living room.

Observing this no-net performance from the couch, Parker knew better than to offer his help. "Would you like to sit down?"

"I intend to do that, yes." She was squinting at the glare off the white walls. "Meanwhile I still don't get it."

"Okay, I have a new security system. One of John Standell's people installed it this morning. While we were out tonight someone set it off. Need help with those buttons?"

Her overcoat was still buttoned to the neck. She quickly undid it and smirked triumphantly. "Correct me if I'm missing something. Your burglar alarm doesn't make noise and it doesn't bring the police. It makes the burglar smell bad."

"The stuff sprays out of those nozzles on the ceiling. It smells vinegary—smell it?—unless it makes skin contact. Then it's unbearable."

She batted a strand of hair out of her eyes. "What's wrong with an ordinary burglar alarm?"

"What I really need is information. When—"

"Higher-ups, powers-behind-the-scenes, Mr. Big?"

Ignoring her tone, Parker said yes. "When the system activates, John's voice comes out of that speaker. He tells the intruder that if he wants to get rid of the smell, he'll have to contact John's people. When the burglar comes in, we offer to neutralize the smell in exchange for information. That was the number I just called. Nothing yet."

"Maybe a panicky burglar isn't about to stand around taking down addresses or phone numbers."

"There may still be a few bugs in the system," Parker conceded.

Widening her squint to a childish gape, she whispered, "Oh, and tell me about the infrared dye and ooo! the magic glasses."

"I sense you're trying to make a point, my darling."

She lurched a step forward, causing the open umbrella at her feet to roll a quarter-turn. "When you and Dobbs went off to have your chat, Barb said, 'There they go! Off to the paranoid clubhouse!'"

She was starting to look wobbly; he reached her in two strides and, grasping her by the waist, guided her to the couch. She suffered herself to be helped off with her coat and they sat down. Knowing she was about to collapse, he glumly watched her black mini ride up her thighs. Legs crossed, back, neck and chin prepared to balance books, she seemed amused by her own poise, as if she were imitating someone else. "Off to the paranoid clubhouse!"

"Why don't you sleep this one off? I have Maalox, Excedrin…"

"The paranoid clubhouse!" She giggled.

"I take it you don't believe anything I told you about——"

"Jeffrey, I don't believe anything you say!"

Staggered, he tried to interpret her smile. He didn't think it meant she was kidding.

"I could never have said that six months ago!" she exulted.

"Maybe you weren't shit-faced six months ago. Oh, that must be when you met—what was his name?"

"You're changing the subject. Too many things happen to you that don't seem to happen to anyone else."

"If someone's controlling events, plausibility doesn't count."

"What about the five-inch cockroaches?"

"I can't change events to fit your restricted sense of possibility."

"What about the bee! That flew up your nose!"

"In, actually, not up," he said. "It was buzzing around under my nose, my nostrils flared, it flew in, flew out, it was a small bee, so what?"

"I suppose Mr. Big trained it!"

"I never said *everything's* a conspiracy. Why is it that last week you were willing to believe a man who claimed not to have a face?"

She tucked her hair behind her ears. "I didn't *believe* him, I just—"

"I'll bet you were a gullible kid, and you've been overcompensating ever since. Bet you used to fall for the how-fast-is-your-dad joke."

"Oh? What's that?"

"I say, 'Fran, next time you see John Standell, ask him how fast his dad can run the fifty-yard dash.' So you ask, and John, who's in on the gag, says, 'As you know, my father has no legs.'"

"Ohmygod! I didn't know!"

He tilted her chin up and kissed her, her margarita-flavored tongue darting against his till she drew back to look at him. "I just said I don't believe anything you say. Shouldn't we talk about it?"

"It's too depressing to take seriously. If you've never believed anything I said, you could never have been in love with me."

"I didn't say that, damnit!"

"Then I'm a pathological liar, but—I know!—I'm sensitive."

She put her hands around his neck and mimed strangulation. "God-damnit, Parker!" She cradled his face in her hands, attempting to beam a message through the lights welling up in her eyes. He was still trying to read it as the lights blurred, her lids dropped, and her head plopped onto his chest.

* * *

At breakfast he tried on the glasses. The view was no different than through red-tinted sunglasses. "What do you think?"

Fran was testing her ability to hold down a pill-size bite of toast. She looked down, smoothed a wrinkle in her skirt.

He said, "Well?"

She propped her chin on her hand. "What do you call those again? Detecto-glasses?"

Lifting the frames, he pronounced each syllable crisply and unflinchingly. "Infra-red-like-dye-detector."

"'Infra-red-like-dye-detector.'"

"That's a pretty lazy form of sarcasm—just repeating what I say."

"You're beyond embellishment."

"Maybe you'll be more creative when the Maalox kicks in." He stroked her cheek with the back of his hand. "How are you feeling?"

"I dunno. A little better."

"What about as a fashion accessory?" He flashed right and left profiles, then raised the frames an inch and peered out from beneath.

"I guess rose-colored glasses are better than the usual blinders. Remind me what happens when you spot your bad guy."

He lifted the frames again and, deadpan and unblinking, said, "When seen with the infra-red-dye-detecting glasses, the culprit emanates a purplish glow."

"'The culprit emanates a purplish glow.'"

"The system was John's idea. He's very successful at what he does. Do you think he's crazy, too?"

"I think this is some kind of guy thing—you and John and Dobbs in your treehouse. Will you take those *off?*"

Holding the frames in place, he wrestled her hand away. "You must be feeling better. But you see, these are no ordinary rose-colored glasses. They have special optical moral properties. The same technological breakthrough that lets me spot criminals lets me see into people's hearts. So—tell me about what's-his-name."

She closed her hair over her face and torso and drew her arms inside; he was looking at a hill of hair.

He said, "That won't do any good. Tell me about what's-his-name."

"You shit!" A few strands fluttered in the vicinity of her mouth. "You want to grill me and pretend it's a game."

"Coffee? I think I have a straw somewhere."

"Is there something you'd like to ask me?" She held open the wings of her hair, waited a moment, and let them fall back.

"I haven't had much luck with the truth lately," he said at last. "I don't know if I can take any more bad news." This blatant appeal for sympathy sank without a ripple into her hair.

He removed the frames and clattered them on the table. "All right?"

He uncovered her face with a curtain-parting motion, her hair draped over the backs of his hands. She watched him expressionlessly, eyes bloodshot and teared-up.

"Are you seeing someone else?" What he dreaded, he realized, wasn't that she'd say yes but that she'd say no and he wouldn't believe her. As far as he knew she'd never lied to him; there was no reason *not* to believe her, right?

She gathered her hair up and let it plunge down her back.

"No."

* * *

He found Fletcher leaning against a wall in the corridor, waiting with the noontime crowd for classes to change. He wasn't glowing.

"Rose-colored glasses, Jeff? Would that be a philosophical or a fashion statement?" The Styrofoam cup in Fletcher's hand burst in his grip, splattering coffee on his suit jacket, shirtfront, and briefcase. Dropping the case and the remnant of his cup, he made flicking motions with his hands and arms. A wisp of steam curled off his jacket; he removed a soaked handkerchief from his breast pocket and hopelessly began rubbing at his sleeve. "Thanks," he said, accepting Parker's handkerchief. "That's the great thing about tweed: It's absorbent and it hides strains. I wonder if that's why it caught on in academia—high coffee consumption, low motor skills?"

Parker laughed.

"See? I'm funny—that goes with the symptomatology. I'm only funny under stress. This weekend I found out I have an enemy." Unbuttoning his jacket and lifting his tie, Fletcher daubed at the brown transparency pasted to his chest.

"Why don't I get you some paper towels?"

"Tell me, Parker, how many people in the Chicago metro area do you think would be interested in a three-year-old Corvette for $5,000?"

"Nearly everyone, I guess."

"I can confirm your estimate. In yesterday's *Tribune* someone advertised that car at that price over my name and address. I took the phone off the hook, but the doorbell was still ringing after midnight. Around two this morning they started throwing pebbles at the windows. I know it sounds funny but, professionally speaking, a week of this could drive you nuts."

"Maybe some student you failed."

"You mean professors still fail students? I've never had the heart. I know, I'm contributing to grade inflation and the decline of the West, but unless there's a terrorist cell operating out of the Committee on Academic Standards, I don't think this is about grades. Last night I sat down and tried to make a list of my enemies. What enemies? I know, people think I'm pompous and boring, but as my ex-wife says, I'm not vivid enough to hate. Which leads me to conclude that someone picked my name at random."

"If that's so, maybe they'll move on to someone else."

"And maybe not. Anything follows from an illogical premise. My guess is now that he—sociopathic pranksters are nearly always male—now that he's found a vessel for his rage and paranoia, he's got a custom-made enemy for life. I spent five minutes in a gun shop this morning before I walked out in the middle of a sales pitch. I didn't care to hear the definition of 'stopping-power' just yet."

"Aren't you over-reacting?"

"Let me see. A stranger's trying to destroy me; next time he comes after me the kids might be over; why worry?" Maybe he was a terrific actor but his fear was reaching Parker like a bass chord vibrating the floor.

Clearly ashamed of his outburst, Fletcher hefted his briefcase, re-formed the ironic twist of his lips and the quizzical crease of his brow. "Ah, well! Neither rain nor sleet!"

Once again Parker tried to recall the super's description of his intruder. He wasn't certain of anything anymore except that he'd become Fletcher's personal demon. It was time to confess.

"Ken, we have to talk about this."

"Isn't that what we've been doing?" Fletcher checked his watch. "I appreciate the moral support."

"No, wait."

"Mr. Parker?" Stephanie Molnar was twisting her purse strap and running a hand through her perm. "I think you'd better come see this."

"What? See me in class."

"It's, like, an emergency?" She sucked back the corners of a smile, as if she were about to laugh at a funeral.

* * *

Parker's students had joined a crowd twenty yards down the hall from his classroom. Equidistant from the room in the opposite direction, a second crowd faced them across the deserted length of corridor.

"She's still in there," said Bob Vasquez. "We thought of dialing 911, but..." He looked to his classmates for a clue to the appropriate facial expression. "Man, somebody shoulda closed the door."

A whiff of perfumed rot tugged at Parker's gorge. "Wait here." He thought he was used to the stench, but a few yards closer it slammed into him. Breathing into his hand, he poked his head round the doorframe.

"Oh, Jeffrey, thank God, help me, please!"

Glowing purple, Mrs. Slansky sat trembling at the seminar table, motes of luminous face powder swirling about her head.

* * *

By the time John Standell's men arrived with the device, everyone had crowded behind Stephanie, who, staring through the pane in the door, was issuing an update: "Still trembling....I think she's crying. What?" She turned, blinked.

"Step aside, please." The men wore jumpsuits and spray-painter's masks. Their device resembled an exterminator's: metal cylinder, rubber tube, nozzle, trigger. They'd cleared a path through the crowd when Parker tapped the elbow of the man carrying the device.

"I'm Jeff Parker." He led the man a few yards down the hallway, the cylinder sloshing as they walked. "What happens now?"

The eyes above the mask squinted impatiently. The voice behind it came out muffled. "We make a deal—information for a spray-job."

"Forget dealing. She's an old woman; she's already had a stroke."

"The fuck's goin' on here?"

The other man had joined them. "All right, listen." The same muffled tone. "First we spray her."

"She's so frail," Parker said. "I'd hate to get her soaking wet."

"She'll be damp. Moist. Stuff comes out in a mist. If she looks to
be in bad shape, we take her to a hospital. She's okay, we take her to our
company doctor for a checkup. Then we have a chat. No third-degree,
they're usually glad to have someone to talk to."

"Should I go along?"

"This woman broke into your apartment. Maybe she don't trust you."

Parker followed them to the door and watched through the pane.
The man who had reassured Parker appeared to be explaining what
would happen next. Mrs. Slansky gripped her pearls as the man with the
device took aim, her cataract lenses caricaturing her fear.

Parker tapped the window and smiled at her. She smiled back,
waved.

* * *

Parker snatched up his office phone on the first ring. "John?"

"You ready? Here's what she told us. Last year Mrs. Slansky started
going to a rage clinic."

"What's that?"

"She gets into fights with store clerks and managers, right?"

"Yeah?"

"Thinks they're all disrespectful, trying to cheat her?"

"Mm-hmm."

"Okay, last year she flipped out at a Dominick's—something to do
with strawberries, I don't know the details. It must've been major because
the store called the police. She got a suspended sentence, but she had to

sign up for something called 'rage counseling.' According to Mrs. Slansky, the only thing the rage people wanted to talk about was you. They told her you were plotting to ruin her life. Jeff?"

"I'm here. I can't spend the rest of my life saying 'Huh?' What was she doing in my apartment?"

"I don't know. The clinic's run by a corporation called Tolerance Management. Heard of 'em?"

Parker checked the clock on his desk. "My appointment's in two hours."

* * *

Arriving early, he bought a pretzel from a vendor in front of Carson Pirie Scott and sat down on a planter. Before this part of State Street had become a "mall," there'd never been benches downtown, the city having no wish to make vagrants comfortable, and the hard cement planters seemed like a compromise: have a seat, move on! Still, it calmed him to sit watching the rush-hour crowd, the sunset hived in the windows above him.

The man John had described was coming up out of the subway, sprouting infinitely, it seemed, as his long legs continued to emerge.

Parker walked over to meet him. "Todd Woolcurt? Jeffrey Parker." John had told him to watch for a Michael Jordan look-alike, and Woolcurt resembled the basketball star down—up!—to the shaved head, the wedge-shaped nose, the head like a torpedo standing on its point, and the infectious grin.

He shook Parker's hand. "Let's get a few things straight, Jeffrey. I'm here as a favor to John. Nobody's paying me to stand between you and a beating, see what I'm saying? You do your thing, I'll stand there lookin' bad. I exist, that's usually enough."

"I just want to talk to these people."

"You do that, Jeffrey. My presence usually has a calming effect on the situation, understand what I'm saying? All I have to do is exist."

"You are; therefore they think."

"That's right."

Across the street a man in a porkpie hat and a sandwich board recited Bible passages through a bullhorn. The crackling, staticky voice reaching Parker sounded like a police dispatcher calling all cars: "The number of the beast is six-six-six."

"I like the suit."

Woolcurt flashed the lining of what looked like a powder-blue Armani suit. "Yeah? It's a knock-off—looks good, though, don't it?"

Parker was wearing a brown corduroy jacket, a beige shirt open at the collar, jeans and loafers. He'd pocketed the infrared glasses. "I was just thinking of the formidable entrance we could've made in matching Armani knock-offs."

"We'll be formidable enough, Jeffrey, long as you don't get stupid. What do I do?"

"You exist."

"That's right!"

"I assume that includes hulking, towering, and overshadowing?"

Woolcurt slapped him on the back. "Comes with the package!"

* * *

Maybe it was protective obtuseness; maybe his offended sense of reality had deleted part of the scene; but his first view of the outer office took in only eggshell walls, track lighting, green miracle-fiber carpet, a leather couch, a black mahogany desk, and a slim blond receptionist in a gray worsted suit and blue bow. It wasn't till he'd given his name to the receptionist and accounted for Todd Woolcurt—"Mr. Woolcurt is my associate," he said, paraphrasing some gangster movie—that Woolcurt nudged him and directed his attention to the framed photographs lining the walls. Blowups, their backgrounds cropped, they captured Parker in numerous variations of numbness, confusion, and stupefaction. The portrait above the desk mirrored his present transition, eyes focusing, smile flickering, a witticism dissolving on his tongue.

His amazement was reflected now by the receptionist, who'd just looked up from her appointment book—he teetered above a widening expanse of blue. Her eyes nearly closed when she smiled, as if self-bedazzled. "You're Parker! Nobody's gonna believe this!"

She wore her hair in a bun, a few wisps dangling over the ears, and as she continued smiling at him he half-expected her to unknot it and shake it loose. Instead she began rummaging through the papers on her desk. "I know it sounds stupid, but—"

"You'd like my autograph?"

"Would you mind?"

He might have asked her out, if not for Fran and his tenuous grasp of what was going on here.

Ignoring the blank sheet of typing paper she held out, Parker stepped behind the desk, took down his photo, and slid it out of its frame.

Behind him she stammered, "Maybe you shouldn't—oh, what the heck! Make it out to Joyce."

A headshot, the photo gave little evidence of time or place; the hair was a little longer than he'd worn it this decade. As for the expression, it had probably been passing across his face at least once a day for quite some time, and it occurred to him that one thing he'd failed to notice all these years was his own astonishment.

Fiddling with the picture had given him time to review his plan: Find the man in charge and beat him up. Check!

The door to the inner office was just to the right of where the picture had hung, an arm's-length away. Of course a sudden move might also surprise Woolcurt and prevent the man from doing whatever it was he did. Behind the door a chair creaked.

Holding the picture against the back of the frame, he wrote: "To Joyce, with intense admiration, Parker." He stepped back in front of the desk and handed her the portrait and the frame.

She laughed. "Everybody'll think I wrote this myself. Is Parker your real name? The secretaries think you're some kind of mascot. You know, like Mr. Clean?"

Woolcurt snorted. Since they'd walked in, he'd grown increasingly sullen, compact and alert. He kept his profile to the desk, eyes sweeping the glass doors they'd come through from the elevators, the empty corridor to the left of the desk, the inner office door to the right.

Parker assured Joyce that he was real. "Now, if you don't mind, Mr. Woolcurt and I are here on urgent business."

She announced them over the intercom.

"Send in Mr. Parker." It was the voice Parker had heard on the phone. "Mr. Woolcurt will have to take a seat out there."

"Tell him that's not acceptable," Parker said.

Woolcurt put a hand on his shoulder. "It's cool. I'll just do my thing out here."

Joyce smiled reassuringly. "I'm sure he's been looking forward to meeting you. Oh, he's a bit strange," she whispered, "but we like him. He cracks us up."

* * *

The door clicked shut behind him.

A bearded, burly man rose from behind the desk saying, "I suppose I ought to congratulate you on a triumph of the human spirit, hmm?" He cocked his head and a grin split his tangled black facial hair. The grin went on floating in the balding, beaked, horn-framed, tilted head—insisting, it seemed, that Parker was conspiring in the joke.

"Tolerance Management" conjured lab coats and clipboards, but, come to think of it, the personal-demon industry called for a more whimsical disposition. Refusing the hand extended across the desk—"Krell, Harry Krell"—Parker had a few seconds to take in the Mr. Potato Head perched on a heap of files; the yellow walls crammed with B-movie posters, spray-painted graffiti doodles, and more framed double-takes of himself; the wastebasket encircled by paper planes and crumpled near-misses; the diagonal-striped tie clashing calculatedly with the plaid flannel shirt. Together these symbols contrived to proclaim that here was the playpen of a very creative guy. Beneath that—Parker was certain—they asserted status and power: "You *still* have to take me seriously!"

Having withdrawn his hand and blotted his grin in his beard, Krell was absently fingering the drawstring of the ceiling-high purple curtains behind the desk.

"What now!" Parker blurted.

"What...oh." Krell let go of the cord. "It's just a window back there. Let's get started. I'll fill you in, and then let's see what we can do about repairing the damage and getting your life back up to speed." He sat down, waved the back of his hand at the chair next to Parker.

Parker continued to glare down at him.

Krell nodded. "I wouldn't blame you a bit for punching me out, but we've a lot of ground to cover and you won't have time. You *do* want to know what's going on, don't you? Sit down, you can always hit me later. Maybe I've got it coming."

Parker sat down and scooped up one of the crumpled papers at his feet.

"So tell me, Jeff. What do you know about Tolerance Management?"

"Only that you're trying to ruin my life."

Krell used a thumb and forefinger to push up his glasses and rub his eyelids, then folded his hands at the edge of the crowded blotter. "That's not how *we* think of what we're doing, but considering all you've suffered it's a valid point of view, and it makes me ashamed. For what it's worth, I'm sorry. But look—here's the sort of thing we think about at Tolerance Management. Notice something odd?"

"Compared to what?"

Krell chuckled appreciatively. "I see what you mean! But confine your observations to our chairs. Standing we're the same height."

At the back of his mind Parker had been aware that the desktop reached Krell's upper chest. "Your chair's too short for the desk. So?"

The scrawl on the crumpled sheet he'd opened read:

Swarm of flying ants!

Parker balled it up and dropped it back on the carpet.

Krell was saying, "It's a bit of one-upmanship. Ordinarily I'd try to gain power in our transaction by making you feel shorter, but this way you feel a vague sense of unease and you're not sure why."

"You just told me why."

"Yes! and here's where it gets interesting. Why am I telling you?"

"This is infantile." Parker wondered if he was stalling for reinforcements. Would Woolcurt standing by the door glowering do any good?

"Is my giving away the game part of some larger stratagem? Or—"

"I'm not interested."

"—is my hinting at the existence of a larger stratagem just a ruse to—"

"I said I'm not interested. What exactly do you people do?"

"I've always admired your ability to transcend problems other people feel obliged to solve. There's a faction here who think you're plain stupid, but I call it a triumph of the human spirit."

"Ever been in a headlock so painful you black out? Just wondering."

"I apologize for the sarcasm, but you hurt my feelings. And I don't think you're stupid. Anyone who's observed that wall of obliviousness as long as I have begins to suspect that *you're* toying with *us*. What do we do?" He crossed his feet on the desk, found he couldn't see Parker over his high-tops, and set them back down. "I suppose the most famous example of our work is the New York bank study. This was back in the late seventies, you might have heard of it. We determined how long people were willing to wait in bank lines, then the banks cut back on staff so customers had to wait exactly that long. Sound familiar? That's what we do."

"You figure out how much crap people will take?"

"Succinctly put. Our clients have a vested interest in quantifying the tolerance boundaries. As I was saying, the bank study was a typical assignment—establishing just how crummy, useless, dangerous, loud and stupid things could get. You must be wondering why I'm telling you this."

"We're back to the chairs?"

"Forget the chairs. The point I'm trying to stress is that my cards are on the table. I hope to convince you that we're really on the same side and we'd better trust each other. I anticipated that look—there's one just like it on the wall behind you. Bear with me.

"The bank study leaked to the press, and needless to say they played up the mad-scientist angle. We were contributing to the 'erosion of American life'! Conspiring with big institutions to hound people to their limits! But as I see it, we perform a valuable public service by setting those limits. By figuring out how much crap people will take, we force the client to adopt minimal standards of decency and civility." He tilted his head. "How does that sound?

"I don't buy it either," he continued. "In the early days we practically recited it in chorus at staff meetings, but no one really believed it. Even if we did act as a brake on the rapaciousness of our clients, there'd still be the Rebound Effect. In other words—I'm simplifying, but the more Tolerance Management you use, the more you need. The more you fiddle with people's sanity and patience, the less sane and patient they become, and the more Tolerance Management it requires to maintain equilibrium." Pleased with this formulation, he cracked his knuckles.

Parker's chair creaked as he forced himself out of a slouch. He reflected that despite his gun, his bodyguard, his home booby-trap, and his balled fists, he'd spent his "investigation" thumb-twiddling through a series of digressions. But he hesitated to interrupt, hearing something urgent beneath the snideness and mock candor: The man was striving to impress. It fit, Parker supposed, with the conspiratorial greeting, the garrulous manner, the snit at having his theory interrupted. For years these people had been staging a live spectacle for one man. They might not wish him well, but Parker was the audience—the only opinion that mattered. He decided to sit and wait for the truth to gush out with the rest.

Krell said, "Take your mother's friend Mrs. Slansky. She has this constant feeling she's being cheated, but most of the time she can't attach it to anything concrete. That's Tolerance Management at its best— the irritant widely dispersed, released gradually in discrete imperceptible doses. Everybody shares the burden, nobody suffers enough at any moment to notice. My Irish aunt used to say, 'In a lifetime, everyone eats one peck of dirt.' Not a bad way to organize things when you consider how other societies get things done— bread lines? dictatorships? all those

Japanese workers dying of stress at forty? Just one peck of dirt! That was the dream of Tolerance Management. I know, I'm getting sappy.

"Now when Mrs. Slansky can reduce this feeling of being cheated to a specifiable complaint, it always comes down to a matter of pennies, and she always seems to be at the front of a long line, imagining the groans, the pointed watch-checking, all those people wishing her dead. And what if she made a mistake?

"It comes to a head over strawberries. 'That's not the price you advertised,' she pipes up to the kid at the register. The kid says, 'It's the blabneeto, ma'am. It's that price causa the blabneeto.' Now she knows her hearing isn't very good, so maybe the kid didn't really say 'blabneeto.' But she thinks she hears snickering behind her, and she wonders if the kid's mocking her to entertain the folks in line. She considers turning around and looking into their faces, but instead she puts down her money. 'Oh, I see, thank you.'

"As she pulls into traffic she cranks up the Muzak station. She doesn't want to hear that whiny voice sneering, 'The blabneeto, ma'am. It's the blabneeto.' All this gets mixed up with the death of her husband, her stroke, the coldheartedness of her children, the withdrawal of her friends. A classic Rebound Effect. Then it hits her—she can't hold this one down. If she tries, she'll choke on the whole load. On Skokie Boulevard she makes a skidding U-turn across rush-hour traffic—doesn't care if the whole world comes screeching and blaring down on her 'cause she's *gonna do something about those strawberries, goddamnit!* You know the rest. Overturning strawberries, resisting arrest, confined for observation. I'm beginning to think that the next big upheaval won't come from the underclass. It'll be people who feel like they're being—what's the expression?—nibbled to death by minnows."

Parker said, "What was she doing in my apartment? No, save that. What does any of this have to do with me?"

"Right. Let's deal with you." Krell reached under the desk and the lights went out.

Resisting the impulse to spring to his feet and flail at the darkness—the anticipated response, he thought—Parker called out, "Mr. Woolcurt! Could you come in here!"

The curtains slid back from a window-wall. "Relax," Krell said, letting go of the cord. The dusk lit filaments in his beard and pooled in his bald spot. "It's my end-of-the-day ritual." He swiveled to face the engorged buildings, the Sears Tower beacon flickering at his ear. "As you can imagine, the bank study generated some carcinogenic PR for this firm. It got so bad I'd start my end-of-the-day ritual at two, one in the afternoon. One night everyone else had gone home and I was still here at the window trying to take the philosophical view that I'd gotten what I deserved. And just as I started thinking of all the *murderers* who get away with it and wondering why *I* had to get what *I* deserved—it hardly seemed fair!—just then someone cleared his throat behind me."

Pausing for narrative effect, Krell snuck a peek over his shoulder. "And that's how I met Hank Monroe, Junior," he said, turning back to the window. "Makes quite a first impression, doesn't he? That night he was wearing a black leisure suit, chosen, I'll bet, to make his pallor more sickening. And I'm sure you've noticed the dullness of the eyes and that—he's not fat, but that pudgy softness of the face. You're in a pugnacious mood this evening so maybe you'll appreciate my image: If you punched him in the face, you wouldn't hit bone—he'd squish. I was about to ask him how he'd gotten into the office when he opened the suitcase on his lap. It was stuffed with fifties and hundreds, new bills, still in the bank bands. He told me, and I verified a few weeks later, that the case contained three hundred and fifty thousand dollars."

"He gave me the capsule vita—you've probably heard this much of it. The crank calls—how he'd impersonate a public health official and trick women into shaving their heads and leaving the hair in a bag on the doorstep? How the FBI recruited him to make your life unpleasant. By the way, I asked him once what he did with all that hair. He says he kept it. What do you suppose he *does* with it?

"You know, I don't think he was always so decrepit-looking, but by 1979 he'd been on your case for nearly a decade, and it was already clear that you'd won. You'd squashed him, and your complete obliviousness to the contest, let alone the victory, was, I think, the greatest victory of all.

"He told me that even though the FBI had supposedly called off its dirty tricks, his checks—huge amounts!—kept coming. Maybe it was one of those legendary bureaucratic accounting errors—in which case he could've kept the money and done nothing—but he claimed to believe that if he didn't keep it up, certain people...he was vague about it, but these people would come after him.

"Think about it from his point of view. What would it do to a sadist's one pleasure if it became an eternal, inescapable duty? And if his victim hadn't the least inkling that something out of the ordinary was going on? To protect the program, you understand, he was required to keep out of sight and make the gags look like random events. And to insure that the program continued in perpetuity, he was severely restricted in how much damage he could do." Krell folded his hands behind his neck. "By the way, I have two theories of what this is all about. The first—you have this secret, self-perpetuating program tucked away in some dark nook of the federal budget, right? Suppose no one knows the program still exists except for a few middle-level bureaucrats skimming money off it. They keep sending our friend his checks to keep him quiet. Or maybe they keep sending him his checks because the scam has worked so well up to now, they're superstitious about tinkering with it. I'll save the other theory for later.

"Getting back to our friend—he kept hoping that as time passed you'd gradually piece together what was happening to you. Or better yet, that some day you'd be contemplating your latest pink slip or the ashes of your possessions or the death-rattle of your latest car, and the connectedness of everything would hit you all at once. But he hadn't counted on your invincible stupidity. I call it stupidity, but is that the right word for a trait with such high survival value? What should we call it?"

"Protective obtuseness," Parker said to keep him talking.

"Protective obtuseness!" Krell slapped the desk. "I like it! You've heard the saying, 'Lord, give me the strength to change what I can, the patience to bear what I can't change, and the wisdom to know the difference.' Well, maybe 'protective obtuseness' is just another name for that wisdom... But as I say, think of it from Monroe, Junior's point of view. I don't think he cares about the money. As far as I can tell, he's practically an ascetic—outside of his 'job,' he's got nothing happening but junk food and late-night TV."

"Then you know where he lives?" None of the addresses and phone numbers on Monroe, Jr.'s IDs had panned out.

"No. Sorry, just a professional guess. But imagine how he feels about his assignment, the crushing sense of futility, the sense that he's Sisyphus endlessly rolling his boulder back up the hill."

"You're kidding."

Krell swiveled to face him. "Now, there's a proposition we could analyze all day."

"Let's not."

"When you've been a professional prankster as long as I have, and—cards on the table?—I hardly have the right to go on calling myself a clinical psychologist; when you've been at it this long, your sense of irony becomes either completely coarsened or incredibly heightened, I'm never sure which. Am I kidding?"—he tilted his head and pressed his fingertips together in front of his beard—"I don't know. But let's not dwell on *my* little problems. Where was I? The suitcase with three hundred and fifty thousand dollars.

"Our friend had read about this firm when the scandal broke, and he thought he saw a way out of his problem. If he couldn't escape his obligation, he'd subcontract it to us. I was incensed—no, really! I told him that while our work raised a need to clarify some of the ethical canons of the behavioral sciences, we weren't just a bunch of thugs. You can smirk, but that night—August Eighth, 1979—I wasn't just a thug *yet*. You should have seen me! I kicked him out of this office, I threatened to call the police. And this was after he told me that the three hundred and fifty thousand would be just a down payment.

"Then the calls started coming in. Important people in the social sciences—a member of a peer-review panel, a journal editor, someone from the President's Council on Mental Health—all these people telling us that there was a good deal of interest 'in the field' in our accepting the 'research grant' we'd been offered. I don't know if the interest was official or whether Monroe, Junior had bribed or coerced a few individuals. But anyway—some of us were hoping to return to academic life someday, and it was implied that if we accepted the offer, we wouldn't be stigmatized by our recent notoriety. And by then we'd developed our own professional interest in you. For years we'd been studying the side effects of Tolerance Management—watching average people degenerate into seething, short-fused hotheads. Then along comes a guy who can take an infinite amount of crap and *not even know it's happening*! You've found an inner calm the rest of us desperately need. Think of the good we could all do if we could share your secret with others. So we took the money." He shrugged. "I know, I know.

"To allow us to maintain the pretense that we were still scientists, we were told to keep records of our 'experiments' and to generate scholarly papers on the findings. We kept that up for about a year; once a month a courier picked up the latest 'research.' I don't know where it went—maybe into the garbage, who knows? But in those early days we did everything under a veneer of professionalism. We'd discuss the work in terms of stress, anomie, reaction-formation. Of course we didn't get much in the way of findings, since your reaction to everything was momentary puzzlement or astonishment followed by no reaction whatsover. What were you thinking, for example, the day you woke up to find yourself standing fully dressed standing in front of your class?"

"I—" Parker rubbed his palms on the arms of his chair while the rest of his sentence failed to arrive.

"Look out there, it might help you remember." Krell swept a hand over the violet-blue buildings, lit windows deepening as the night confected. "They used to think cities were incompatible with a rich inner life, but look at those colors! Are you remembering anything?"

"I somehow know it happened, but it's not like remembering."

"So you keep a covert record of events separate from the sequence you think of as your memory—like two sets of books. See if this rings a bell: work work work work work work work work work."

Parker fought back the sensation that lights from the Outer Drive were swarming up at his head. "Yes!"

"As I said, everyone here was trying to stake out a respectable-sounding area of research. One industrial psychologist thought it might be interesting to get the words 'work work work' running through your head. We used miniature pillow speakers, videotape subliminals, a nightclub hypnotist. The point, as I recall, was to see if it increased your productivity. No detectable result.

"Then there was the graduate student who tried to structure the gags into what she called 'interactive fables.' She was hoping to turn your suffering into some kind of learning experience—hoped you'd distill a few Aesop-like morals out of it. Well, how about it? Do you recall learning anything from your experience?"

"Nope!"

"I thought not. Okay, remember this? There's a bad smell in your car. It gets worse as the weeks go by, till you can barely make short trips with all the windows down. You look under the seats, between the seats, in the glove compartment, under the hood, in the trunk, under the chassis. You take it to the garage, they can never find anything, they sell you a can of 'new car aerosol.' You know how we did the smell?"

"How."

Krell slapped the desk. "Flank steaks in the hubcaps! As you can see, we were degenerating from scientists into a bunch of frat kids playing pranks. You might think it was all a lark for us, sitting around our offices thinking up jokes. But there was the loss of professional identity and self-esteem, the immorality and overwhelming pointlessness of the work. There were nervous breakdowns, a lot of drugs and alcohol. I'm not claiming that the torturer deserves as much sympathy as his victim, but how about a tenth as much? Can you spare that? Okay—forget it! Anyway, some days morale was so low we'd play just one prank and go home. For instance, the day you walked out of the shoe store wearing a new pair of Florsheims, guy bumps into you, scuffs your shoes? That was a day's work.

"Things turned really ugly four years ago. Till then we hadn't heard much from our friend Monroe except for the few occasions when we slacked off completely—then there'd be death threats. But one day four years ago he sent us a note. It said 'Poison his dog.' We decided immediately not to do it, but we were scared. We sent our families out of town, and for the next two days we holed up in the conference room bouncing rimshots off the wastebasket. Finally our observer phoned—in those days he lived in the apartment across from yours—he told us that Monroe, Junior had poisoned the dog himself." A yacht like a miniature pastry gleamed on the dim lake.

"So after that, a division of labor was established. A few times a year a note would arrive, saying, for example, 'Arrange a little accident for his mom—flight of steps, broken bones.' We'd sweat it out till he pushed her down the steps himself. Hey, we'd have loved to warn you, but we have families, too."

"Fuck you."

"Just before the first 'accident,' we'd been thinking of dividing up the money and leaving the country, but now we were too scared. What next! we kept asking, and shortly after your mother's fall we found out. He sent us Ziploc. According to the note that came with him, Ziploc was to function as a sort of consultant or oracle. By structuring our work on his random associations, we'd insure that none of it has the taint of human intention. We'd assure—what?—the continued appearance of randomness. Something like that—who knows? Incidentally, you were wondering the other day whether Ziploc can grant wishes. Yes. Ziploc is empowered to grant your wish. I hope you'll choose wisely.

"Where was I? Oh. As our sense of entrapment grew, so did the number of theories of what was really going on. Inevitably the theory arose that *we* were the real test subjects, and you were in league with the experimenters. I'm sure you've heard of the experiment in which the 're-searcher' is asked to deliver a series of increasingly painful electric shocks to a test subject. The 'subject,' though, is really an actor, and what's really being tested are the moral bearings of the 'researcher.'

"Paranoid sophistry, of course. My own theory—theory number two—finally jelled shortly after Ziploc arrived. Why, I asked myself, were the government, the intelligence community, and the psychiatric establishment all so interested in you? Why was there so much money available? The answer, I thought, was in the kind of experience we were constructing for you—fragmentary, discontinuous, frightening, absurd, random. What is it but a condensed version of the twentieth century?

What you've discovered, apparently, is nothing less than the antidote to the twentieth century."

Parker laughed. "You're making this up as you go along, aren't you ?"

"Granted: I'm improvising. What else can we do, given the vaporousness of our circumstances? Anyway, that's pretty much all I know. Before I suggest a way out of our mutual predicament, are there any questions? No? Then—"

"Mrs. Slansky—why did you involve her in this? What was she doing in my apartment?"

"The idea was that, being your mom's friend, she could help us compile a psychological profile. An occasional innocuous question at a mah-jongg game, and we'd have all sorts of invaluable data: Was he bottle-fed or breast-fed? Afraid of the dark? What about toilet training? We recruited her at one of the anger clinics we run—she was sent there after the strawberry incident and unfortunately we had to increase her paranoia. The story we told her was basically yours, except in this version *you're* doing to *her* what *we're* doing to *you*. Things got out of control. We didn't send her to your apartment, you know; she stole your mom's spare keys. I feel terrible about what's happened to her. But she's not much crazier now than when she came to us, and our lawyers are about to offer a handsome settlement. Any other questions?"

What about Fletcher? "Is anyone else I know working for you?"

"You mean like Fran?"

Parker managed a laugh. "You've been associating with paranoids and liars for so long, you've forgotten how to lie convincingly." He thought of his own suspicions, but he'd never suspected this. No, it was out of the question. No need to think about it.

"That's right. I'm making it all up. Not a grain of truth in it, nosiree! Fabrication out of whole cloth. Imagine me thinking I could put one over on you!"

"This is dumber than the chairs," Parker said.

"I sincerely apologize. It's that irony problem I mentioned. It's become a sort of tic; I just can't resist getting in one more dig." He removed his glasses and looked Parker in the eye. "She's a good woman, Jeff, and I swear she has nothing to do with this."

"You won't make your lie more convincing by sounding unctuous and smarmy when you take it back."

Krell spread his upturned palms. "You're right, of course. Please accept my apology."

Lunging, Parker slid over the desktop debris. He held onto Krell's shirt as the swivel chair toppled beneath them and the force of Krell's head rattled the plate glass wall. Sitting up he found Krell sprawled on his back. He was kneeling for a closer look when someone wrenched his arm behind his back and pressed a huge forearm against his windpipe.

Hauled to his feet, wriggling against the unseen man's grip, Parker recognized his assailant by the jumpsuit sleeve and the size of his forearm.

"Whoa! Relax, champ!" Parker recognized the voice as the big despairman's. "I'm stopping the fight and declaring you the winner." He led Parker around the desk and squashed him back into his chair. "You okay, Mr. Krell?"

Seated, his glasses replaced, Krell was rubbing the back of his head. "I'll live. You interrupted me, Jeff, before I got to the part about solving our mutual problems. But first, what can I do to make you a little less quarrelsome? I know." He opened a desk drawer. "This should help pacify your miserable temper."

The despairman pressed down on Parker's shoulders as he struggled to rise from his chair.

"Woolcurt! Get the hell in here!"

Parker heard a knock and the door opening. Craning his neck he saw Joyce in the doorway.

"Are you looking for your friend? I went to the Xerox room a while ago and when I got back he wasn't here. There. Hi, Bob!"

"Joyce." The despairman turned to face her, exerting enough pressure with one hand to keep Parker in his chair.

"I'm being held here against my will," Parker said. In the ensuing pause he failed to think up a less quaint, stilted way to put it. Was it kidnapping if they didn't take you anywhere? "I'm being kidnapped. Call the police."

She glanced from face to face, then laughed politely.

"Be sure the handouts are ready for the staff meeting," Krell said.

"I swear this is no joke!"

"Hey, love the suit," said the despairman as she disappeared behind the door.

The despairman applied his two-handed grip as Krell came around the desk and Parker thrashed in his chair.

Krell held what looked like a hundred-dollar bill in Parker's face and snapped it by the edges.

It was a hundred-dollar bill.

Krell folded the bill in half, opened Parker's corduroy jacket, and slid it into the inside pocket. "He still looks pissed off. What do you think, Bob?"

Bob's meaty face looming upside down eclipsed Parker's view. "Still pissed, Mr. Krell."

Parker struggled experimentally.

"You might as well sit still," Krell said, "I'm out of petty cash. But I hope you're beginning to entertain the idea that our working together could be advantageous." He walked back behind the desk and sat down. "Our mutual interest should be obvious. We'd prefer not to make you miserable. You'd prefer not to *be* miserable. We can't just close down operations, though, we're too scared, and we're afraid to go to the police. The FBI's involved in this, don't forget, or at least they started the whole thing.

"My idea's this. We retain the old setup, the structure, to placate Hank Monroe, Junior and whoever else is watching us. But what if we used that structure for a new purpose? In other words, we'd still be controlling your life, but suddenly it'd be *good* things happening to you seemingly at random. If these fortuitous effects were subtle enough, I'll bet the people observing us wouldn't know the difference."

"Would I?"

"To pull this off we'll need your cooperation. For starters, don't flash that money around. And don't act cocky. And for Chrissake don't ever look too damn happy. That's it, go on looking confused and suspicious, perfect! By the way, you *do* want to be happy? There's a faction here who think we've given you exactly what you want, but I find that kind of blame-the-victim psychology despicable. How about it: happy or unhappy?"

"You're taking my order?"

"That's what I'm doing."

"I prefer to be left alone."

Krell repeated his palms-up gesture. "Sorry."

Parker felt compelled to answer. "All right, happy."

"Done! But there's more at stake than your happiness. I hate to be theatrical, but our lives might be in danger. We've been nervous here ever since our friend started visiting you. That's against the rules, and the rules, vague as they are, are the only thing that reins him in. I propose an exchange of intelligence. If you learn anything about what he's up to, share it with us; we'll do the same. If he's completely out of control, we'll all have to protect ourselves.

"Well, I guess that covers it. You don't have to do a thing. Just go home, sit back, and await the new order. Will you shake my hand now?

"Still pissed?" Krell withdrew his hand. "Oh, that's right, we ruined your life. We aborted your promising academic career. Never mind the tight job market, never mind that you had one slightly original idea in your life back when you wrote your dissertation. Isn't it a tiny bit conceited to assume you'd have been a success without us? Sorry—our studies prove you'd have failed anyway. *I* think we did you a favor—we created the one environment where you could thrive. In fact, what really has you upset lately isn't the stuff we've been doing to you all these years—it's the break in your routine! You don't cope very well when you're forced to pop out of your hole, do you? Look at how you've behaved this past week: the test of your life, and all you can do is fly into a useless rage or sit passively listening to bullshit. Look at you now...Jeff? Oh Je-eff! Jeff!"

Parker stood up, casting a sidelong glance at Bob. "I think I'll go home and await the new order."

"Hey, sorry I flew off the handle." Krell started to extend his hand and, catching himself, fingered his shirt where he'd lost the top button. "You hurt my feelings, that's all. I didn't mean any of that about your character. You've prevailed where a lesser man—or a more observant one—would've packed it in. I wish you luck. Wish? I'll do better than that! Bob, drive him home. Take the limo. Oh, Jeff? I'm truly sorry for that crack about Fran."

* * *

Three more secretaries had gathered near Joyce's desk to await a glimpse of Parker. None of these fans, if that's what they were, would admit to having seen Todd Woolcurt.

"We iced 'im, right, girls?" The despairman perched on the desk and lit a cigarette while Joyce phoned Security in the lobby. No one had seen Woolcurt leave the building. Parker used the phone to call John Standell, who hadn't heard from the "bodyguard," and who, more puzzled than alarmed, quipped that Todd was too proud of "existing" to stop doing it voluntarily.

Parker said that if there were no objections he'd have a look around, and with an after-you-Alphonse flourish of his cigarette, Bob followed him into the corridor. Parker walked down the hallway opening doors, the offices darkened, webbed by lighted windows. Passing another row of his stunned images, he imagined that if he walked fast enough his clueless face might be animated into wisdom.

SIX

The next morning he knocked at Fletcher's office door and waited, relieved that no one was answering, his relief already waning at the thought that he'd have to come back. A chair creaked; it might have been the office next door. He stood listening, hearing only distant noises, heels reverberating, a door shutting.

He'd been up all night, shuffling the same few thoughts. 1) Judging by the evidence, his suspicions of Fletcher were almost certainly true. 2) There was still room for doubt, and he couldn't bear the thought of tormenting an innocent man. 3) His instincts told him that Fletcher was a nice guy. 4) His instincts had proved worthless lately, except when he'd suspected the worst. By morning he'd decided to tell Fletcher everything. He'd reminded himself that if his suspicions were correct, Fletcher already knew. Still, confessing would be handing him a new weapon. And what if Fletcher called the police?

As two students walked by, he pretended to study Fletcher's office hours, feeling more and more like a criminal. There was a sharp metallic click inside the office; he knocked again.

Behind the door Fletcher cleared his throat. "It isn't locked."

Parker opened the door, then froze in the doorway.

"Parker! Come on in!" Fletcher was blotchy and red-eyed, his smile a mismatch. Alerted by Parker's stare that the gun he held in both hands was pointed at Parker, he set it on the desk.

"So Parker! What's new!" Except for the drawn face and the gun, he'd managed to keep up appearances—combed and clean-shaved, the axiomatic tweeds fresh-pressed. "You don't think I was aiming at *you* " he protested without discernible irony. He folded his hands near the gun. The desk was otherwise bare, the blinds drawn. "Oh. I wasn't about to turn it the other way either, if that's what you're thinking. I'm simply getting used to holding the damn thing.

"Though I'll admit," he added, "to fantasizing that my enemy has just walked through that door." He seemed to be confiding in a friend, not needling an enemy, and Parker resisted the prudent impulse to back into the hallway.

"Why don't I take the gun," he said.

Fletcher picked it up by the barrel. "If it makes you feel better, why don't you take charge of it while you visit? Oh, come on in!"

Parker stepped up to the desk, gripped the gun by the handle, and sat down, releasing his breath.

It looked identical to the small blue-black automatic he'd surrendered to Jan Cohen. "Where'd you get this?"

Glancing over Parker's shoulder, Fletcher said, "If we're having a guns- and-ammo show, hadn't we better...?"

Parker slid the gun into his jacket pocket. "Oh, you mean the door." He reached back and closed it.

"I don't suppose"— Fletcher arched an eyebrow—"you're hoping I'll forget about the gun?"

"Where'd you get it?"

"It's a gift from my new friend," Fletcher said. "I still don't know his name, but two days ago he sat down across from me at lunch and in lieu of introductions sweepingly deplored the state of things in general."

Parker groaned. "John Connor Murray!"

"Heavyset? White beard, dapper dresser?"

"MM-hmm!"

"Anyway, the standard curmudgeon act, but he does it well, and it's rather infectious. Pretty soon *he's* railing against Lionel Trilling, *I'm* cursing *my* enemy, and we've worked ourselves into a fine rage—'Fuck 'em, fuck 'em all!'" Fletcher swearing was nearly as startling as the gun. "He's come back the past two days, and we've formed our own little lunchtime bile club. Today I was describing my enemy's latest attack; he excused himself and a few minutes later he came back with the gun."

Parker's stomach tightened. "Your enemy...."

"He's got my name circulating in the most esoteric reaches of the porno scene. I'm a psychologist, and I can't figure out what the callers want or how they might react to not getting it."

Parker hadn't been sure that the perversion he'd dreamed up existed. But even before there'd been time for the ad to appear, word of it was drumming through the underground.

Fletcher was saying, "I changed my number to an unlisted one but they keep calling. They probably have connections in the phone company or the police. It's the first time I'm grateful for the divorce—at least my kids won't be put through this."

Parker couldn't confess from a standing start. "Someone's been playing dirty tricks on me, too."

"Then it *is* a student!" Fletcher set his briefcase on the desk. "I'll show you my roster."

"It's not a student."

Fletcher was shuffling through his briefcase. "Here it is." He tried to hand Parker the printout.

"I said neither of us is being harassed by a student."

Fletcher put the roster back in his case, set the case back on the floor, replaced his folded hands on the desk, and awaited whatever was coming.

"I can't think of a way to gradually lead up to this," Parker said, "so here it is. I ran those ads." He wanted to rush into the pause that followed, blurting explanations, rationalizations, abject apologies, but he found himself watching Fletcher's reaction.

His eyes on Parker, Fletcher reached into the flap pocket of his tweed jacket—the unlikely thought of a second weapon crossed Parker's mind—and set his pipe on the desk. He reached in three more times, lining up a tobacco pouch, a tamper, and a lighter in a straight row next to the pipe. He continued to watch Parker while methodically loading and tamping and sucking in flame with a pa-pa-pa sound. He was looking at Parker with puzzled concentration, as if he couldn't quite place the face. Not wanting to lose sight for an instant of the curiosity in front of him, he expelled smoke through the side of his mouth. "Why?"

"I know how worthless it is to say I'm sorry, but—"

"Yes, but I won't know *how* worthless till I hear your story."

Beginning with the faceless man, Parker made an effort to point out that *he* knew how ridiculous it all sounded, and to stress how skeptical, how reasonable he'd been, accepting Dobbs's explanations only when more plausible hypotheses proved untenable, and even then—. But Fletcher was tapping the flat end of his tamper on the desk, and Parker speeded up his narrative—the drop of blood, the burning hair, the talking Coke machine, the despairmen, the women paid to almost go to bed with him...

The hand holding Fletcher's pipe had frozen, the stem hovering just beyond his slightly parted lips.

"I must have looked that way myself when I heard Dobbs's story," Parker said.

"Let's not pretend we're both in this together, shall we?" Fletcher looked hurt. It occurred to Parker that during the time they'd seemingly pretended to be friendly, they'd actually become friends.

He went on with his story—Ziploc, Mrs. Slansky, Tolerance Management, raw steaks in the hubcaps—his listener's expression flickering from anger to incredulity to pity before hardening into clinical neutrality.

Parker rubbed his palms on the armrests; Fletcher relit his pipe.

"And how do I fit into the grand design?" Fletcher asked.

"On three or four occasions my super saw you letting yourself in and out of my apartment."

"And you're certain it was me?"

"It was a detailed description. And let's face it—anachronistic Oxbridge tweeds aren't standard issue for break-ins."

Fletcher chuckled and cleared his throat. "This is some kind of record. You've known me over a week, and this is the first crack you've made about how I dress. My ex-wife bought the original tweeds at a secondhand store; we were celebrating my first university post. It was just a joke—and why does everyone assume that I don't know they're funny?—but she said they made me look handsome, so I searched the antique clothing stores and bought five more sets." He lowered his eyes and minutely realigned the tamper, the pouch and the lighter. "After the divorce I thought of donating them all to Goodwill, but..." Looking up he seemed to have recalled that he wasn't speaking to a friend. "So. Your burglar wore tweed and that was reason enough to ruin my life."

"As I said, it was a detailed description."

"Not detailed enough, apparently, because here you are trying to apologize."

"That's right. But I'm trying to point out that I had reasons for what I believed."

"Any other reasons? Not that you don't have an airtight case already!"

"Well, I still might not have connected you with my intruder if I hadn't been seeing you everywhere—bars, theater lobbies, Wrigley Field. And the El—for months I'd been seeing you on the train twice each day, regardless of how I changed my schedule or which car I rode."

"You're sure it was twice every day? There couldn't have been one day when you didn't see me? Not one ride?"

"Suppose you missed a day. What would that prove?"

"Were you even looking for me before you heard your conspiracy story? Were you paying close attention? I'll bet you didn't give a second thought to whether I was on the El or not. Let's grant that you saw me on the train regularly, even frequently—we do work at the same place. But once you started looking for patterns, you convinced yourself you'd been seeing me twice each day without fail. And then if you saw me in a theater lobby or at the ballpark, it was easy to believe you'd been seeing me 'everywhere.'"

Pat, but couldn't it be true?

"You live in Hyde Park, Ken. What were you doing at the Granville El every day? Excuse me—nearly every day?"

"It's none of your business, but I'm seeing a woman in your neighborhood. Would you like to call her?"

What would that prove? "That won't be necessary."

"She teaches at Loyola; you can contact her through the sociology department. Babe C. Tuttle."

"That's all right, I....You call your girlfriend Babe *C.* Tuttle?"

"To distinguish her from a colleague in the department."

"Babe A. Tuttle?"

"Professor Barbara Tuttle," Fletcher enunciated in a display of strained patience. "Known to her friends as 'Babbs' Tuttle."

"Why not?"

"My phone's in the drawer. Why don't you call?"

Parker couldn't shake off the image of Fletcher shut up in his office, the blinds drawn, the phone in a drawer, a gun in both hands. "I believe you."

"Go on, ask her about her private life and laugh at her name while you're at it."

"I said I believe you."

"You believe everything I'm saying."

"Yes. I do," Parker said. And he supposed he did.

"Positive? I wouldn't want to find a bomb in my car because you awoke in the night with a nagging doubt."

Parker waited for him to get off it.

"So I don't seem demonic to you?" Fletcher took the pipe out of his mouth and leaned on his forearms.

"No, Ken, you seem like a nice guy."

"Why, thank you."

"On the other hand, *I'm* a nice guy and look what *I'm* doing."

Fletcher allowed the remark to hang there—as if for Parker's inspection—while he knocked the pipe against the side of the wastebasket and pocketed his things.

"Here are my conditions," he said at last. "I'll give you two weeks to get into therapy. Otherwise I'll call the police."

"And what if I lie to the police?"

"I don't think you will."

"No, but—look. You saw the guy in the trenchcoat and the fake beard."

"Let's stipulate that there might be something to your conspiracy. Believe me, I've learned that having an enemy changes how you view the world, but—"

"Even people with real enemies can be paranoid?"

"Yesterday I walked out to the parking lot and saw that my car had a flat. There was a kid standing there with what I took to be a taunting little smile on his face. He said, 'Looks like you got a flat tire, man.' I read his license number aloud and told him I'd remember him. There was no real reason to suspect him, of course, and after we cleared up my misunderstanding he even helped me change the tire. Tell me, Jeff, what would you have done in my place? Torched his house? Oh, by the way—you wouldn't know anything about that tire, would you?"

"No," Parker said truthfully.

"No, of course not! Another thing: I can't buy your scenario about Tolerance Management. I know those people; they've helped fund my research."

Parker all but slapped his forehead.

Fletcher irritably gusted smoke and said, "I seem to have revived your suspicions. Would I be telling you this if I had something to hide?" Crowd noise swelled in the hallway; he glanced at his watch.

"Tolerance Management is the largest private funder of research in the field of stress," Fletcher added.

"Okay."

"Nearly all the major work is undertaken with their backing."

"Well then. Okay."

Parker thought back to their first conversations—Fletcher droning jargon; himself nodding politely and gazing at the vicinity of Fletcher's hairline. "Anomic stress formation," "social shock absorbers": He'd been talking about tolerance management! Then again, didn't all social scientists talk about stress?

Parker was back where he'd started: morally obligated to beg forgiveness for acts that were almost certainly justified. "I'm truly sorry," he said rising from his chair and extending his hand.

Fletcher stood up and shook it. A close-up view confirmed only that he hadn't been sleeping. The redness mottling his face and rimming his eyes flared against his pallor.

He was observing Parker with what might have been genuine concern. "I know you are. Get therapy!"

Parker mumbled equivocally. As he turned, the gun in his jacket pocket bumped against his hip. He opened the door and pressed into the crowd.

* * *

"Yes, Jack," Parker told John Connor Murray, "that *is* a gun in my pocket, and yes I'm glad to see you because you're going to help me put it back." He didn't stop to consider the prudence of this public announcement until well into the silence that followed it.

The students who'd stayed behind after Jack's class had joined their teacher in staring at Parker's jacket pocket. Jack was doing his usual caricature of astonishment, even the huge white carnation in his navy blue blazer gaping.

"I'm kidding, of course," Parker told the students.

Jack was breathing noisily through his open mouth; agitated bare branches in the window diced up the light.

"I don't really have a gun in there," Parker went on gamely. "Would I announce it if I did?"

Uncertain, they affected a smirky nonchalance.

"It must be the gun," Jack said, "because regrettably you don't look glad to see me." His students laughed.

"Janet's at lunch. Let's go to her office and put the item back where you found it."

It was beginning to seem like a *Guns of Navarone*-size mission, and Parker wondered if his friend was actually drunk. He'd long ago realized that Jack thought it gave him an edge if no one could be sure—cover when he was, license when he wasn't—so he consistently acted half-crocked. The flushed face—given high contrast by the white beard—and the slurred speech and watery eyes were chronic. He was grinning hugely and indiscriminately, but it could have meant anything.

"What about our tweedy pal?" Jack wondered.

"He was sitting in his office drawing a bead on anything that came through the door. I nearly made his day—thanks!" Parker tugged him by the arm to the doorway, where Jack turned to face his students, his grin brimming with some anecdote or aphorism.

"It'll keep!" Parker snapped.

As they passed through the crowd in the hallway, Parker marveled, as he always did, at his friend's ability to convey the breadth of human emotion with one basic expression: pop eyes and a dropped jaw. Fine-tuning it with twists of his lips and eyebrows, he was greeting passersby with leers, double-takes, stylized wonder, mock horror. All in all Parker preferred Jack's usual barely suppressed rage to these "good" moods, which hummed along at far too many RPMs to be mistaken for ordinary happiness.

Turning to watch a woman pass by, Jack did a head-snapping goggle-eyed double-take, as if the very concept of a woman in tight jeans had only just dawned on him. He turned to Parker. "I'm enjoying your little caper, young Parker, but it's completely unnecessary."

"I know you think you've got nothing to lose, but if you think *teaching* here is humiliating, imagine getting fired."

"'No worst, there is none!' What I mean, kiddo, is that you're in for a pleasant surprise."

Parker halted. "There's no such thing."

"Then it will be even more of a surprise."

"Not that I don't wish you the best, Jack, but seeing you this happy makes me very nervous." They backed against a wall to let people by. "What's up?"

"Shall we scrub the mission, Cap?"

Parker gave up. "No. Just...just don't horse around."

A few yards from Jan's office Parker lowered his voice. "All right, do whatever you've been doing to get in there." The outer door was open, a typewriter clacking out of view beyond it.

"There's no trick involved. All it takes is a kind word and a warm smile." Jack strode into the outer office.

Jan's secretary Judy was a pale skinny redhead with round gold wire-rims and an oversize perm. Faced with the full expanse of Jack's eyeballs and teeth, she snatched back her hands from the typewriter.

"Ah, the numinous Judy!" he said breezing past her. "I'll just go in there and consult the master syllabi."

"He's not supposed to go in there," she said hopelessly to Parker.

"I'll take the blame if there's any trouble," said Parker, validating all her anxieties. He shrugged commiseratingly. "I'd better go in there and keep an eye on him."

In Jan's office Parker closed the door and locked it.

With a panoramic sweep of the back of his hand, Jack slathered contempt on everything that represented Jan Cohen: the wallfull of books on the science of writing, the cluttered desk and bulletin board; even the green metal filing cabinet seemed to piss him off.

"Where'd you find it?" Parker asked.

"Same place she always puts it—bottom-right desk drawer, under the two file folders. The woman has no imagination."

Parker stepped behind the desk. Between the phone and a pile of mimeographed journal articles—"The Etiology of Pauses in Student Writing"—an old framed graduation photo showed her redheaded son squinting into the light. A static of crunched leaves drew Parker's attention to the cracked-open window behind him, where thunderheads were stacking up over the parking lot. He decided against drawing the blinds; unless he waved the gun in the window he'd be visible but not noticeable to the crowd filing between the cars. He sat down and gripped the drawer handle. "What do we have here? Some sort of booby-trap?"

"Nope."

"Just a pleasant surprise."

"The fear of surprises is a character flaw," Jack observed, "especially in a critic."

Parker opened the drawer and, lifting the file folders, found a small blue-black automatic identical to the one in his pocket. "Not pleasant so far."

"Go on, kiddo, take a good look."

Reluctantly Parker picked the thing up.

"Not very observant, are you?"

Parker had just noticed the tiny hole in the top of the barrel. "Oh, a lighter."

"You see, Parker, the whole caper was redundant. As far as Genghis Cohen is concerned, the gun never left her desk. Hand it over, I want to show you something.... It's a *lighter*, kiddo!"

Parker handed him the lighter.

"Except for the hole and the little flame regulator on the handle, it's a perfect replica. Look, there's even a safety. Banned in twenty states.

You see, young Parker, even Philistines acknowledge the ineffable power of the image."

"Either that or some kid got shot by the police while he waved around Dad's lighter."

Jack stepped around to Parker's side of the desk. Holding the lighter behind his back, he seemed to be making an adjustment. "Stand up, I want to show you something."

Parker rose to his feet and, anticipating what was coming, jumped back an instant before a foot-high yellow jet blazed up an inch, Parker estimated, in front of where his nose had just been. He snatched at the blind-cord, the slats fanning sideways before crashing shut.

"Has it ever occurred to you, Jack, that it might not require the existence of a black-listing academic cabal to explain why people act as if they find you annoying?"

Beneath his doe-eyed caricature of hurt feelings, Jack looked hurt.

"Just kidding," Parker relented. "All right, I'm sorry. But you're supposed to be this curmudgeonly humanist shoring up the Western tradition. Where do guns—oh, I get it. The Western tradition."

Jack perked up. "I'm restoring the place of the cannon." To illustrate he crouched over the open drawer and replaced the lighter under the file folders.

"Hold on! I want the real thing in there!"

The doorknob jiggled; springing up, Jack closed the drawer with the tip of his shoe. They'd just stepped round to the front of the desk when Jan's key turned in the lock.

As usual she was dressed and groomed casually: bulky white turtleneck, denim skirt, pink-tinted glasses, longish gray hair worn loose. But the look she was giving them made Parker feel as if adult life were a dream he'd had during a never-ending visit to the principal's office.

"Gird yourself, young Parker, she's about to raise the glasses!"

Letting go of the frames, she brushed past them to the desk and sat down. She opened the drawer, felt around, and seemed surprised to find what she was looking for. "What are you doing here?"

"We're the grievance committee," Parker said—anything to pre-empt Jack.

"Oh, really?" she said in her Alice-in-Wonderland voice. "Dean Grover is the person to see about grievances, as I'm sure you know. Why was the door locked?"

"You saw that guy in my office. Locking doors has become a habit." He shrugged apologetically and smiled, as if the lameness of his lies were a joke between them.

She smiled back sourly. "If you'll excuse me—"

"And why were the blinds drawn?" Jack asked mischievously.

She glanced at Jack for the first time, then returned her gaze to Parker. "Tell me, Jeffrey, do you have any qualms about being gun-buddies with a borderline personality?"

"I promise we'll have that talk soon," Parker said.

"Whatever." She opened her top drawer, set a pile of student essays on the desk, and leaned over the top paper. "Play outside, boys," she said without looking up.

Jan's habit of mothering "her" faculty had always struck Parker as slightly comical, but her giving up on him added to his sense of drift. He looked down at the crooked part in her hair, thinking, Come on, Jan, say something common-sensical. Just one platitude and I'll go.

She looked up, expressing exaggerated surprise that he was still there.

* * *

A few yards down the hallway Jack placed a hand on Parker's shoulder and addressed him in a valedictory tone. "You are now armed and dangerous."

"I don't know about dangerous. The first two people I pointed it at sort of shrugged it off."

For once Jack looked genuinely surprised. He removed his hand.

"It's done nothing for my sense of security," Parker went on, "let alone my actual safety, and it'll probably just escalate the—"

"Ah, Chekhov's third-act rule. If you introduce a gun in the first act, someone has to fire it in the last."

"Not only can't I get *rid* of the damn thing, it's *multiplying*!"

"Would you like me to take it off your hands?"

"NO!" Smiling blandly at the heads turning in his direction, Parker lowered his voice. "Until a few days ago I didn't see myself as the sort of guy who grabs people by the lapels and points guns. I mean, I was an antiwar activist. I hadn't been in a fight since seventh grade. I was so quick to see other people's points of view, they got confused. I don't want to end up as some rage-filled old crank living off his old grudges. Oh."

But Jack didn't seem to take it personally. "Nothing wrong with hatred—there's no such thing as a wrong emotion—but hate wisely. Don't go around pointing that thing like a magic wand expecting your enemies to disappear. Come to think of it, young Parker, you might be the guilt-ridden sort who always hates badly. Maybe you'd better take Nixon's advice. Remember? He said your enemies can't destroy you unless they make you hate them, and then you destroy yourself. I always wondered if he knew he was talking about himself."

Parker was wondering the same thing about Jack, so he changed the subject. "What about the flamethrower in Jan's desk?"

"What about it?" Jack let his mouth hang open to indicate incomprehension.

"I don't know. Lately I've had the feeling that the worst I can imagine is bound to happen."

"'No worst, there is none!' Do you imagine a fireball in sensible shoes roaring out of the office?" From where they stood the office doorway disclosed a segment of white wall and the jaunty rattle of typing. "A pleasant thought, but she thinks it's a gun—remember?—and I doubt if the occasion arises for Jan to shoot people in her office."

"Still—"

"Let's consider the matter actuarially," said Jack, clearly relishing the experience of being the reasonable one.

Parker had just decided that tonight he'd drop the gun off the Pratt Avenue pier. Tomorrow he'd sneak back into the office and turn down the flame on the lighter. But already he was having second thoughts about the gun, having just recalled that according to Harry Krell he was in for a series of pleasant surprises.

"The odds are greater," Jack was saying, the reasonable man to the hilt, "of her being struck by lightning in the next five minutes."

Parker nodded and they stood there, two reasonable men, watching the office doorway.

* * *

The next morning Parker was stirring a batch of eggs, watching Oprah on the black-and-white portable he'd wheeled in from the bedroom, when he looked down. A white sphere about three-fifths the size of a golf ball floated in the eggs. It turned languidly with the swirling liquid, its smooth surface dribbling egg. He extended a hand to pluck it out, changed his mind and spooned it onto the drainboard, where it rolled to the middle and stopped. He was about to probe it with a fork when the phone rang.

A continuous high-pitched tone on the line nearly drowned out the voice of Harry Krell. "The new order," he was saying, "will commence momentarily."

"We have a bad connection," Parker yelled. "Call me back." Watching the thing glisten on the drainboard, he felt a sudden reluctance to touch it even with a fork.

"That isn't the line," Krell said raising his voice. "It's an anti-bugging tone. By the way, how annoying *is* it?"

"Do your research on your own time."

Gingerly Parker prodded the thing with his fork tines. It shuddered. "Jesus Christ!"

"I suppose I *could* turn it down a bit," Krell said. The noise screeched on at the same pitch and volume.

Rolling the thing around the drainboard with his fork (it seemed to have the consistency of a hardboiled egg), Parker assured himself that it hadn't moved. He glanced up at the fluorescent tube flickering on the kitchenette ceiling.

"I want to prepare you for the new order," Krell was saying.

"What'll it be—party hats or armbands?"

"Good—that's just the right note of skepticism and dread. Remember, we don't want you looking too damn happy. We'll have to satisfy the people watching us that any improvements we make in your life are just wallpaper for the rat cage. Well, Jeff, that's all for now!"

"Wait! I feel like a sucker asking this, but..."

"Skepticism and and dread—that's the ticket!"

"...what, specifically, is going to happen?"

"Oh, I wish I could *be* specific, but then your reactions would seem rehearsed. Suffice it to say that the good life will arrive on the sly. Be prepared for luck in small undetectable doses or with all the outward signs of *bad* luck. Or maybe your good luck will be so breathtaking and immediate, it'll look fishy. Remember—it's *supposed* to look fishy. We have to make those bastards think we're diddling with your head."

"If the point of this call is to diddle with my head..."

"That's the ticket!"

"...your efforts seem laughably inept."

"Bravo! Stay where you are, Jeff. The new order will begin any minute."

Parker hung up the phone; it rang before he'd let go.

"Jeffrey Parker?"

"Mm-hmm."

"This is Bill Hungerford. I'm Vice-Chair of English at the University of Illinois at Chicago...Circle Campus?" he added after a long pause.

"Yes."

"I wonder," Bill Hungerford said delicately, "if you're still in the job market."

"Yes I am."

"Well, I don't know if you've heard, but Huntley Crane died last week."

"I'm sorry to hear that," Parker said warily and a moment later remembered that he'd met Huntley Crane two years earlier while interviewing for a job at Circle. Parker recalled a snappily dressed, moist-eyed, wispy man. He wasn't senile, as Parker had first thought, just a slow talker, and the ends of his sentences had proved worth waiting for. Parker wondered if he should be reassured by the caller's knowing that he'd applied to Circle two years ago and that he'd met Huntley Crane. Probably not.

"I suppose I should get to the point. If we followed the usual procedure we'd distribute Huntley's course load among our current faculty and advertise for an opening in the fall. But...I don't know if he told you this...Huntley was a great admirer of your work, and..."

"He willed me his job?"

The intake of breath at the other end made Parker wonder if he'd just blown a real job prospect. "Sorry," he said, "a friend of mine likes to play practical jokes."

"How can I convince you? Would you like to...ah...grill me?"

"No, please, I'm very sorry."

"Truly, this is no joke. We'd like to talk to you about the position again. Look, I was on sabbatical when you applied. Perhaps you've heard of me through my book?"

"Oh, yes," said Parker, clueless. "The..."

Hungerford let him squirm a while before bailing him out. "*The Elizabethan Mind*," he said a trifle sullenly, perking up as he continued. "I was about to say that Huntley used to pass around your book, and as a result you've quite a few admirers in the department, myself included. I don't think I'm revealing state secrets when I tell you that you came very close the last time you applied."

Circle Campus had been Parker's last interview before he gave up applying. His prospects there had followed the usual arc: interview, shortlist, unofficial assurances, verbal offer, abrupt kiss-off, evasive explanation. "Toward the end I couldn't get my phone calls returned. Maybe you people were holding me in awe."

"There *was* a bit of a cloud. Nothing we couldn't—"

"What are you talking about?"

"I'd prefer not to discuss it over the phone, but..."

"No, I want to hear about this cloud."

"I'm sure," Hungerford soothed, "the committee will be eager to accept your explanation. Let's focus on the present, shall we? Frankly, the department was weak in twentieth-century studies even before Huntley's death, and a number of us think you'd fill the void nicely, possibly as early as spring quarter if it suits your plans. We'll have to consider other people, obviously, but you're the favorite."

"I'm flattered."

"I just had an idea. This is rather abrupt, but the search committee holds its weekly meeting tonight, and I wonder if you might be free to drop by for a chat? We meet at eight o'clock in the basement lounge in Stevenson Hall. Of course if you have plans..."

"No, I'm free." Parker had never heard of a university department hiring in this fashion, but if the point was to lead him into some sort of—what?—setup?—wouldn't it make more sense to have everything appear normal? And then there was the possibility that all possibilities were true: that Hungerford worked for Harry Krell *and* the Circle English department *and* —in accord with the new order—was trying to give Parker a job. At eight o'clock, Parker thought, the campus would be nearly deserted.

"As you know," Hungerford was saying, "the applicant usually gives a paper, but since we have your last one on file, I think we can skip that step. Would you mind taking a few questions on your paper tonight?"

"Sure. I'll look it over."

"You sound guarded. Do you still think this might be a joke? Is there anything you'd like to ask me, just to satisfy yourself?"

"All right, what was Spenser's wife's name?"

Hungerford released a shrill skull-rattling laugh. "Spenser's wife's name! I should have braced myself for the Parker wit. See you tonight. Spenser's wife—oh dear."

"Good-bye, Bill."

Hungerford was still on the line, chuckling. Confused about the etiquette of hanging up on him, Parker held the receiver a moment then replaced it, gently, on its cradle.

He looked up the Circle English department and was relieved to hear a dial-tone when he picked up the receiver. His call was answered by a woman's recorded, rather nasal voice announcing that the twentieth floor was closed for repainting and that urgent messages should be left at the main switchboard. So much for verification!

He emptied the bowl of egg in the sink, used a spoon to nudge the thing into the garbage, stared at it among the coffee grounds and cartons, and closed the bag.

To distract his mind from its flying turns, he focused on the television; he liked to watch Oprah with the sound off, trying to guess the day's topic. Today's panel consisted of four women and a man—a fat guy with combed-back white hair, tinted aviator glasses, and a cheap suit whose shoulders settled slowly back into place when he shrugged. The women had big hair: polygamy, Parker guessed. He was about to open the bag and take a quick look at the thing when the phone rang.

"Yeah," he answered.

The woman's thick accent and his own difficulty concentrating kept him from grasping anything, at first, beyond the fact that he'd won.

"Won? Won what?" Was it possible that Harry Krell, with his huge funding and shadowy connections...?

It gradually penetrated that that he was speaking to Sylvia Chen of the Broadway Bank and that he'd won a GE clock radio in their raffle.

He wondered if *this* was Harry Krell's surprise and if the timing of the previous call was mere coincidence. Or if Krell had engineered both calls to make him wonder.

Thanking Ms. Chen, he hung up and stared at the phone. Well? It rang.

"Jeff! We're going to press with your story and—"

"Steve?"

"Oh, sorry," said Steve Dobbs, sounding even more agitated than Parker. "Hi! We're going to press with your story and I thought I should warn you not to get your hopes up. It won't be as detailed as we planned."

"So they've been threatening you...Steve?"

"I feel like I let you down."

It had been a morning of strange perceptions, and here was another one: He liked Dobbs. "You have to protect your family," Parker said. "It would be immoral to put them in jeopardy just to keep these guys from... what?...interfering with my breakfast. So, how general is it going to be?"

"'Midwest Man Beset by Vague Forces,'" Dobbs said sheepishly. "That sort of thing."

Parker couldn't stifle his laugh and Dobbs joined in with a brief rueful burst of his own.

"They get vaguer by the minute," Parker said and described that morning's calls.

"Of course you're not going!"

"Actually, I am."

"What is it? Some sorta man's-gotta-do-what-a-man's-gotta-do thing?"

"No, I'm imagining dinner with Fran at La Perroquet. She's wearing something black and strapless, maybe those turquoise earrings with the cows."

"What?"

"Anyway, I announce that I've just been offered a professorship at Circle and propose. *She* doesn't care about the money, but I see now that proposing with no money and no prospects would've..."

"Look—there's no job!"

"How do *you* know? I have a Ph.D. from Cornell, a book from Columbia University Press. Why *shouldn't* there be a job?"

"That's just the way they want you to think."

"And what do *you* think will happen?"

"For a while I've had a hunch those people are sick of you and they're looking for some kind of wrapup."

"And?"

"I'm thinking ritual sacrifice, theater of cruelty, that sort of thing."

"I hear the dental plan's good," Parker said.

"Let me have the time and place—in case the police want your last known destination."

Parker gave him the details. "I have a gun. Should I take it?"

"Yes!"

That pretty much killed the conversation, but Parker was in no rush to get off and spend time thinking in his empty apartment. "I'm sorry you and Fran didn't hit it off. I'm sure you two—"

"My fault. We haven't had company for a while. Guess I'm out of practice."

"Well, let's try again soon—we might even have something to celebrate."

"Maybe we will," Dobbs said doubtfully. "Good luck, Parker."

"Thanks. Bye." Breaking the connection, Parker shut the receiver in the silverware drawer. He opened the bag, took a long look at the thing, and having satisfied himself that it wasn't looking back, carried the bag to the garbage.

* * *

Parker narrowed his eyes against a damp gritty wind. The dirt lot between the El station and Circle Campus was lit by banked white lights that made the surrounding darkness blacker and ran together wetly behind his squint. A woman approached and rushed past him, mouth set in the I'm-not-a-victim scowl, blown hair flaring in the lights.

Waiting to cross Harrison, he gazed up at University Hall on the other side, which—wider at the upper stories, as if balanced on its head—perfectly expressed his disquiet. He hefted his briefcase and heard the gun clunk against his books and papers. He reached into his inside suit-coat pocket and switched on the voice-activated microcassette recorder he'd borrowed from John Standell, hoping the conspirators would adhere to their penchant for confessional monologues. And, just in case it was a real job interview, he adjusted his tie and smoothed down his hair.

He crossed the street and followed in the band of shadow cast by the overhead walkway through the orange halogen lights. If the point was to raise his hopes, why lure him here? With its moon-colored pillars and walkways, its identical facades of opaque brown windows in cubby-holes of gray girders, and its desolate sunken stone amphitheater, Circle Campus resembled something the Aztecs might have built if they'd had pre-stressed concrete.

The place was deserted; he nearly walked past the shadowed figure leaning against a pillar and facing Stevenson Hall. His back was turned to Parker, but there was no mistaking the hunched narrow shoulders and balding red frizz.

"Steve?"

The shoulders flinched and Dobbs spun round to face him. "I think they're all in there," he said.

"What are you doing here?"

"Good question!"

"I appreciate your worrying about me, but—"

"Thought you might need backup."

"Okay, I'm glad you're here. What do they look like?"

"Like professors," Dobbs said.

"Maybe *too much* like professors?"

"Too much?" Dobbs grinned. "I like the concept! I can't answer that. You've taken precautionary measures?"

Parker tapped the briefcase.

"Me, too." Dobbs unzipped his black leather jacket and disclosed the gun handle protruding from his waistband.

Parker paced to keep warm as the wind rose. "Any last-minute advice?"

"Let's get outta here."

"And barring that?"

Zipping up his jacket Dobbs said, "Figure your escape routes and your lines of fire as soon as you walk in. Keep the briefcase in reach and unlatched."

"And if it's a real interview?"

"I hear it's bad form to bring up salary," Dobbs said.

* * *

The hum of fluorescent lights and vending machines resounded through the deserted ground floor. He was heading down a cinderblock hallway past rows of doors with darkened windows when a gravelly voice called his name.

Parker turned. "Yes?" A man in a brown topcoat was coming up behind him—short, trim, sixtyish, curly brown hair, wind-reddened nose, round steel-frame glasses, cocky walk, mournful smile.

"Tom Grand," he said solemnly and shook Parker's hand. The lugubrious sheen of his watery blue eyes gave a note of deadpan humor to anything he said. "I suppose you want to know what's in store for you."

"Yes!" Parker said, so urgently he felt obliged to laugh.

"Nothing to get rattled about, but you hurt Bill's feelings. He thinks you insulted him on the phone—I know, I know." He flicked away Parker's effort to object. "It's Bill. We're all bulls in his china shop. You'll like him when you get to know him."

"If I ever get the chance. Maybe I should take him aside and—"

"I wouldn't advise it. Let him give you crap for half an hour and he'll come round. No one else is opposed but Marty Applebaum, who's opposed on principle as always. He and Bill might form a tag-team for a while, but maintain your equanimity. I'm only telling you this so you don't get discouraged if things seem a bit frosty at the outset. As for the rest of us," he added mock-obsequiously, "we are gripped by Parkermania." His misty eyes and the quaver in his gravelly voice made the line truly funny.

"Relax!" he said, responding to Parker's nervous laugh. "This isn't your orals—think of it as a chat among colleagues."

"That's what they said at my orals."

"And here you are, cock of the walk, leading candidate for a plum job at a fine state university. Of course you've done this before."

"Interviewing? Not for a while. I suppose it's like falling off a bicycle. You never forget."

"At this level," said Tom Grand as they started down the hallway, "we don't even call it an interview. Just a get-acquainted session, a chat. You know how to chat, don't you?"

"I think I—"

"Nice weather!"

"Oh. Yeah. They're predicting rain."

"There ya go!"

At the head of the steps Parker heard cups and plates rattling. If they were speaking down there, they were whispering. "Of course," he said, "with that cold front coming down from Canada—"

"Don't show off. We know you're a smart guy!"

* * *

Except for his uneasy sense that the people in the room had lurched into sound and motion the instant before he walked in, Parker was reassured by what he saw. They'd entered a large, blue-carpeted, brightly lit space with a couch, leather armchairs, a long walnut seminar table in the middle, and a buffet near the door. Reconnoitering, he counted seven people: three on the couch, two standing near the walnut table, one filling a plate at the buffet, and Tom Grand at Parker's side. They looked like professors: faces that betrayed years of displaying attention and suppressing boredom. Okay, he was spinning his wheels about the faces, but anyway most of them looked harmless. Just one tweed suit in the room, too wormy to look like a prop.

"I don't recall meeting any of these people last time," he said, trying to make it sound like a casual observation.

"We're all impostures," said the man at the buffet. Parker recognized the voice as Bill Hungerford's. "Or we're the search committee—take your pick. Spenser's wife's name was Elizabeth."

Did you look it up? Parker nearly asked. But a close look at Bill persuaded him that he might as well save his teasing for a swarm of Africanized bees. With his short stature, tiny perfect features, wraparound glasses, tailored suit, and perfectly trained brown hair, Bill ought to have looked elegant. He looked like a kid who'd been dressed up and forced to behave all day and who was gathering his energies for a tantrum.

They exchanged tense pleasantries while Tom Grand, standing behind Bill, warned Parker off certain topics—sports, the Renaissance, the weather—gesturing like a flight-deck officer in choppy seas.

"Why don't you circulate and introduce yourself?" Tom said to Parker. "I'll catch up after Bill and I talk business."

Circulating, Parker intercepted Esther, an athletic redhead in a calf-length charcoal suit, on her way to refill her wineglass. She looked down at the briefcase, then returned her eventful brown eyes to Parker. "You could set it by the coatrack if you like, or don't you trust us?"

"Oh. My notes are in there," Parker said vaguely.

"Well if you brought *notes*, I feel obliged to discuss something esoteric, but I was going to ask if you play racquetball. Do you need to check your notes?" She smoothed down her attractively chaotic perm and it sprang back up.

"Hey, can't a guy like his briefcase?"

"What *do* you have in there? You're literally clutching the handle. Have you considered handcuffs?"

He was searching for a mildly flirtatious retort about handcuffs that wouldn't offend a total stranger with a say in determining his future, when a man came up and introduced himself. He bore such a strong resemblance to the TV astronomer Carl Sagan that Parker had already forgotten his name. Judging by his grim expression and businesslike handshake, this had to be the second no vote—the man who according to Tom Grand was always opposed on principle.

"I want you to know," said Carl Sagan—his deep unctuous voice also recalled the tele-scientist—"that my opposition to you isn't personal." Behind him Esther did a Tallulah Bankhead eye-roll. "It's a matter of principle," Carl Sagan asserted, "of sticking to our own procedures. But I want you to remember that if you end up joining us—and I'm sure you will—I'm not your enemy." He nodded to Esther and strode off.

"I need that refill," Esther said. "See you later."

Parker walked over to the couch, where a tiny woman with white bangs and big glasses was complaining about the rabbits in her garden. Parker introduced himself to the rabbit woman (he'd already given up trying to remember names) and her companions. The black-clad woman on her left, who claimed to be a graduate student, had a nervous habit of wiggling the fingers of her right hand and staring at the glints off her long black nails. The man to the right of the rabbit woman was a pinstripe-suited bruiser with slicked-back salt-and-pepper hair and a neat mustache. He emanated a powerful aftershave and reminded Parker of those well-groomed movie gangsters who get shot in barber chairs. It was possible to see him as undermining the authenticity of the occasion or—Parker seized the second possibility—as someone no one trying to impersonate a professor would look like.

"Jeff, have you met Delbert Zontar?" Tom Grand had brought over the man in the one tweed suit—a balding dewlapped man whose bulging eyes made Parker think of Graves' disease and Warner Brothers cartoons. It occurred to Parker that his heightened concern with reality and unreality was lending everything the grotesqueness of Warner animation. Perhaps that accounted for his impression that Carl Sagan and Bill Hungerford, conferring in an isolated corner across the room, were staring at him while speaking from the sides of their mouths.

The bug-eyed man was droning an anecdote having something to do with the elevators in University Hall, and Parker was trying to look interested without making his own eyes bug, when Bill called the meeting to order.

"I trust you've all read the paper Jeff submitted for his previous interview. Shall we take our seats?" He placed a hand on the chair at the head of the table. "Jeff," he said over the groans of his colleagues, "why don't you sit here?"

"That's overly formal, isn't it, Bill?" said Tom Grand from one of the leather armchairs, where he'd just settled with a plate of appetizers. "I thought this was more of a get-acquainted session."

"I told Jeff there'd be a few minutes of Q-and-A on his paper."

"Sure, but why turn it into colloquium? I just finished reassuring the poor guy that this isn't going to be like his orals. Why the *basso profundo* big deal? Let's just get comfortable and ask a few questions."

Carl Sagan had walked over to Bill's side. "Normally Jeff would deliver his paper *at the table* and remain *at the table* for the Q-and-A."

"Well then. Q.E.D.," Tom said sweetly.

"I only meant," said Bill, "that we ought to treat Jeff with the same seriousness—"

Tom turned to Parker. "Jeff, Bill feels that the full seriousness to which you are due inheres in that table."

"I've no objection to tables," Parker said.

Esther rose from the armchair next to Tom's. "Why don't we sit at the table and each of us can be as serious or as casual as he or she likes. Tom, you can slouch in your chair."

Parker took his assigned place at the table—avoiding eye contact with Bill and Carl Sagan, who sat to his right and left—while the others took their sweet time gathering up purses, cigarettes, plates and cups.

When they were settled in, Bill addressed Parker. "Before we get started, I have some concerns about your publications. There hasn't been a second book?"

"No. There were three articles in the PMLA."

"All published within three years of your dissertation. The work I've seen is all fine, but it seems to me you haven't done much lately."

Parker was thinking that maybe he had a point. At moments he thought of the conspiracy as a necessary adjustment in the order of things to keep him from getting breaks he didn't deserve. But Tom Grand came to his defense.

"Is that fair, Bill? First time out of the box he writes one of the most cogent, original works of recent criticism, and you're asking, 'What have you done for me lately?' You've all read Jeff's book—is there anyone who'd deny it's the work of a first-rank critical intelligence?"

There were murmurs of agreement. "First-rank," the bug-eyed man echoed, "and I'm grateful to see a young critic who doesn't parrot the party line from Paris or Yale. Have you published at all lately?" he asked Parker.

"In film journals and *Down Beat*. And I've nearly completed a collection of literary criticism for a second book manuscript."

The pinstripe man had begun to drum his fingers on the table.

"Are any of those essays published?" Carl Sagan asked.

The literary criticism journals had started giving him the cold shoulder at the same time as the English departments.

"No," Parker said, "but I'd be happy to send you a copy of the manuscript."

"Oh dear," the rabbit woman mumbled under her breath.

Bill tented his fingertips in front of his face and began kneading his lower lip with his forefingers. "Here's our problem. You haven't published any literary criticism for nearly a decade and you teach at Skokie Valley College. Why don't you contact us when you're further along in your career?"

The group began stirring, preparatory, it seemed, to rising from the table, when Tom Grand intervened. "Now, wait a minute, Bill. You knew all this when you invited him here and and all but promised him a job. I'll defend you against the inevitable charge that you've lost your mind, but how are you going to live this down?"

"I'm willing to hear—"

"He's thirty-five, thirty-six? Plenty of people are just getting their Ph.Ds at his age. Jeff got his Ph.D. at twenty-five with a work that established his reputation. So what if he can't repeat that trick every year or two? He's regrouping, that's all. It happens to a lot of people who have early successes."

"Why *are* you teaching at Skokie Valley?" Esther wondered.

Carl Sagan seized the topic. "Esther is too polite to say so, but Skokie Valley has a reputation as a refuge for burn-outs."

"Is that a question?" Parker asked.

"Do you know John Connor Murray?" Carl Sagan asked accusingly. "Several years ago he was with a group of us who went out to dinner after a session of the MLA. I made an innocuous remark about the late Lionel Trilling, and the man pulled a gun on me! He said—quote!— 'Maybe it's time to air out the stuffed shirts.'"

Good for you, Jack! Parker thought.

At the mention of guns the nervous woman opened her purse and took out a revolver. She gave it a smart sideways flip to make the chamber fall open, checked the rounds, flipped it shut and replaced it. The others at the table reacted with bemusement or mild embarrassment, as if to a mere breach of etiquette. Parker had let his right hand dangle above the unlatched briefcase at his feet; he replaced his hand on the table.

"Sorry if I scared you," she said to Parker, leaning forward on her arms to see past her colleagues. "I have to walk to the parking lot. I had a problem there last year." She retrieved her cigarette from the ashtray and, tapping it with a black nail, took a long noisy drag.

Tom said, "I thought we were at the table for purposes of high seriousness, and here we are gossiping. Wouldn't anyone like to ask Jeff a question about his paper?"

"One minute, Tom." Bill fidgeted with his cuff. "I agree with everything you said about Jeff's work, and I must admit to letting personal resentments cloud my professional judgment." He turned to Parker. "Jeff, I apologize, but you seemed to be baiting me on the phone this morning and I was insulted, frankly, by your seeming to doubt that I was a real professor."

"I apologize for giving you that impression. I do have an acquaintance who plays elaborate practical jokes."

"William James said there are two ways to be fooled," Bill said. "Dupery through hope or dupery through fear."

Hearing his remark of the other day quoted back word for word, Parker gasped. John Standell's people hadn't found any bugging devices in his apartment, which only meant, they'd warned, that they hadn't found any. Smiling blandly at the glitter off Bill's glasses, he reminded himself that there was a sort of communal telepathy in academia: It was common for a lot of people to have the same thought at practically the same moment, and lately William James had been in the air—especially his passage on dupery.

Still turned toward Parker, Bill said, "Before we go on to the Q-and-A, I think we should address the primary obstacle. Last time you applied—"

Esther leaned past Tom Grand to face Bill. "Really, Bill, you're not going to bring *that* up!"

"Last time you applied we received a letter making certain allegations..."

"It's outrageous to bring this up." Tom Grand's furious gravelly whisper filled the room. "Bill, you're out of line."

"Nobody is claiming the allegations are true," said Carl Sagan. "But frankly they're too serious to ignore. I'm sure we'll all be eager to accept Jeff's explanation."

"Can I know what I'm charged with first?" Parker snapped. "Or doesn't it matter?"

"I'm sure you realize," Bill said, "how uncomfortable it would make any of us to describe them. I hope you're not planning to use our understandable reticence as a means of evading the issue."

"I know there's some kind of rumor," Parker said. "But everyone's as squeamish as you are when it comes to telling me what it is."

"You know there's a rumor," said the pinstripe man, "it's kept you from finding work for most of your professional life, and you don't know what it is."

"I don't know what it is," Parker insisted, and everyone at the table except Tom groaned.

"The rumor will never be discussed in our deliberations," Bill warned, "but I'm afraid that if you don't take this opportunity to address it, it will be on everyone's mind, and you might be rejected on some pretext."

"It's like trying not to think of elephants," said the rabbit woman.

Parker was thinking no real search committee would behave in this manner, when it hit him. Maybe these people *weren't* part of an obscure psychodrama staged by an immense conspiracy for its own impenetrable reasons. Maybe they were just jerks. He could deal with that. After all, it was a commuter university; he could teach his classes and leave. Aside from the odd unavoidable meeting and an occasional wave, he'd never have to see these people again. If he had to put up with their bloodsport to get the job and marry Fran, he'd clench his teeth and smile. He'd think of it as a trial—a kangaroo trial—of his devotion.

"I agree with Tom," said Esther, "it's outrageous to force you to answer rumors. But by not answering, you're giving Bill a power he wouldn't have otherwise. You're giving specious importance to his specious issue. Why don't you offer your side of things—of course you've every right not to!—and we can move on."

"Let me put it this way," Parker said. "Whatever the rumor is, I can assure you unequivocally it's false."

"It's reassuring to hear you deny it," said the rabbit lady, "but couldn't you be a bit more specific? Can't you offer anything beyond the bare denial? We *want* to be convinced. We're *begging* you to convince us. Give us just a *little* more than 'it's false.'"

"Something's puzzling me," Parker said to Tom Grand. "Your colleagues profess their willingness to believe anything I might say about the rumor except that I've never heard it."

"I was about to point out that very contradiction." Tom was polishing his spectacles with his tie. "But I'm afraid we're outnumbered, Jeff," he said rubbing the pouches under his eyes. "Why don't you just give them what they want?"

Things had progressed beyond the bounds of the jerk theory. "This isn't a job interview, is it?" Parker asked Tom Grand.

"No, it's not," Tom said brusquely, replacing his glasses. "Let's get on with it."

Parker stuffed the unlatched briefcase under his arm and rose from his chair, then hesitated. For years he'd been the sole audience of this spectacle, and he felt an urge to sit through the ending. The point of it all, he couldn't help believing, was about to be disclosed.

The others were watching him, waiting to see what he'd do next. He headed for the door.

"I wouldn't do that if I were you," Tom said.

"I'd love to stay," Parker called over his shoulder, "but I'm scheduled for flogging at Loyola and cattle-prods at the U of C."

The pinstripe man, who'd been sitting at the end closest to the door, arrived there first and blocked Parker's way.

His name, Parker remembered suddenly and irrelevantly, was George. "Move, George."

"Why don't you sit down?"

George stumbled, struck from behind by the door as Steve Dobbs flung it open.

What followed seemed to happen in jump-cuts: George trying to pry loose Dobbs's gun; Parker and the nervous woman pointing guns at each other from across the room, each trying to outshout the other's terrified gibberish; Bill biting down on Parker's gun hand; Parker punching the top of Bill's head; Carl Sagan chocking Parker from behind; Parker clutching the gun under a pile-up, his face pressed to the carpet, the room constricted to punches, kicks, and breathing; the nervous woman yelling, "Get off him! I've got him covered!"; Dobbs firing into the air, shocking everyone stock-still while plaster dust drizzled from the ceiling. . .

They were running through the deserted campus between hives of darkened windows—Dobbs in the lead, bouncing off the balls of his feet, skinny arms pumping; Parker, still aching from the pile-up, still holding the gun and his briefcase, falling behind; the footfalls of the search committee coming up fast. Blood was dribbling into his open mouth. He tossed away the briefcase. A staticky blast of leaves made the lights strobe; the footfalls of the search committee reverberated off the walkway. By the time he reached Dobbs' BMW behind University Hall he was wheezing, his heart butting against his eyeballs. Dobbs was honking the horn. Parker just had time to get in and lock the door before Bill sprinted ahead of his colleagues and hammered his fist on the window.

The glass muffled his words, but his face was engorged and distorted. He jumped back when the tires screeched, waving his fist as he diminished in the rear window.

* * *

"You know what?" said Parker, pressing the stop button of the recorder, which had somehow survived the pile-up with nothing worse than a cracked tape window. "I think that may have been a real job interview."

The passenger window looked out over brick two-flats and empty lots and a horizon glittering with sulfurous factory lights.

"Are you nuts?" Removing a hand from the wheel, Dobbs picked up a wad of Kleenex from the holder between the bucket seats and pressed it to his bloody nose. "He *told* you it wasn't a job interview."

"I've been thinking about that," said Parker, using his handkerchief to mop at the cuts on his cheek and lower lip. "At that level they don't call it an interview. They're fastidious about distinctions—you're not being *fired*, you're just not being renewed."

"I'd say their trying to kill us is pretty suspicious," Dobbs said.

"*Were* they trying to kill us? You walked in there with a gun. They were pissed off—wouldn't you be?"

Dobbs looked him in the face, then turned back to the road. "I walked in with a gun," he enunciated, "because they weren't letting you walk out."

"Tom said 'I wouldn't do that if I were you.' Maybe his point was that I shouldn't give up. That I shouldn't walk out just because things had taken a bad turn."

Dobbs snorted. "Why don't you go back there and apologize?" He sounded even more like Bugs Bunny when he was mad.

"I'm not saying it *was* a job interview."

"Don't you see what they're doing? They've been screwing with you for so long you've developed defenses. So they've come up with a new plan of attack. Hope! You're not used to it—you're a pushover."

Parker was replaying the interview in his mind and turning over Dobbs's advice, when he realized that he should have been seeing the lake from his window, not high-rise projects. They were heading south on the Drive. "We're going the wrong way."

"As I tried to tell you while you were playing with that thing, we're being followed. I'm trying to lose 'em."

"White limo?" Parker asked without turning around.

"Yeah!"

"That's just Ziploc and his minders." Parker proceeded to give him the short version of Ziploc.

"He's going to *grant your wish*?" Dobbs searched his face for so long, Parker felt obliged to point at the road.

"I'm not saying I *believe* it."

Dobbs was watching the rearview mirror. "By the way, you're getting a shiner."

Parker lowered the mirrored sun visor and winced as he touched the shadow under his eye. Examining his cheek and glistening lip by the lights of traffic, he decided he wouldn't need an emergency room. He smiled just to see how it would look, and blood trickled onto his chin. Behind his reflection the white limo followed them into the exit lane.

"Let's pull off," Dobbs was saying, "get a drink, I'll phone some cops I know and find out if there's a warrant on us. You'd better hope those people *weren't* real professors."

* * *

They stopped at a dim New Wave bar near the U of C. Its black-clad patrons seemed torsoless—skinny necks and pale supercilious bulbs of faces blooming out of the darkness. They agreed that just in case Dobbs had saved Parker's life, Parker ought to get the first round; and just in case Dobbs had wrecked Parker's last chance at a career, Dobbs ought to get the second. While Dobbs went off to make his call, Parker ordered two Jack Daniel's and watched his raw face throb behind the bottles.

Something popped up behind his reflection and disappeared. He turned on his bar stool and saw a glimmering object bob up over the heads of the crowd. It bobbed up again. Transparent and filled with floating vaguely organic shapes, it reminded Parker of a drop of water shivering under a microscope. As he nudged his way toward it he began to hear a desolate male voice moaning "no no no" and recognized the voice as Ziploc's. He broke through to the head of the crowd, which had formed a circle around Ziploc and a group of drunken undergraduates who were playing Keep-Away with his Ziploc bag.

There were six of them, four men and two women. Parker looked around for the despairmen; where were they when you needed them? Probably waiting in the limo.

One of the guys held Ziploc back while a girl with purple lipstick held up the bag and shined a pocket flashlight through it.

"Open it."

"No!"—she wrinkled her nose—"there's some kind of gunk in there, honey or aspic or something, and there's, like, stuff floating in it."

The second girl peered in from the other side. "What's that? A sea-horse?"

"And that thing next to it," said the girl with the flashlight. "It's a picture of a baby! Half a locket with a picture of a baby! And what's that thing there?"

"Dump it out!" said the guy holding Ziploc, and the other guys took up the chant. "Dump it out! Dump it out! Dump it out!"

Ziploc's glasses flew off as his head whipped from side to side.

Some post-brawl adrenaline must have been coursing through Parker's system because he stepped into the circle having no idea what he was going to do next. He snatched the bag and the flashlight. "Let him go," he said, shining the light in their eyes and flipping open his wallet to give them a quick glimpse of his Skokie Valley ID. To discourage any expressions of skepticism, he opened his jacket and gave them a quick peek at the gun handle. The gun, presumably, was enough, but Parker was beginning to enjoy himself, and as a final touch he shined the light under his chin to make his face look scary.

Dobbs had stepped up to Parker's side. "I think they're ready to leave," he whispered, "if you stop entertaining them."

Parker traded the flashlight for Ziploc, and the students retreated to a table at the back. He was anxious about lingering in a place where he'd just flashed a gun, but Dobbs wanted to watch the ten o'clock news at the bar while he waited to try his call again, and the bullies, drunk and underage, were unlikely to call the police.

At the bar, Ziploc attempted to tuck a strip of torn shirttail into his pants or under his jacket. The stubble of his left cheek was empurpled with a recent bruise, and his glasses tilted at thirty degrees.

"We make quite a group," said Parker, pointing at the mirror. "The Three Stooges, with consequences." His own shiner was beginning to take on a russet hue. "So, Zip, can I get you a drink? Wait a minute. Are you on any medication?"

Ziploc began searching his pockets; Parker ordered him a Coke.

Leaning on the bar, Ziploc looked past Parker at Dobbs. "I like you, mister! You got *brain* energy! I can tell by the whaddayacallit—the emanations!"

"Oh, shut up!" Holding a ball of cocktail napkins to his nose, Dobbs stared hatefully at the TV screen, where Secretary of State George Shultz and Soviet Foreign Minister Eduard Shevardnadze stood together at a podium, their expressions signifying the usual cautious optimism. "Arms control is such a fucking fraud. We hold the summit so Reagan can go to Congress for *bigger* appropriations for *more* weapons so we can use them as bargaining chips at the summit."

Ziploc blinked and returned his attention to Parker. "So, Parker, whaddaya need!"

"Oh, my wish? I'm still thinking about it."

Dobbs was looking past Parker at Ziploc. He set down the balled-up napkins and ran a finger over his red-rimmed nostrils. "Here's the wish. End the Cold War."

"Okee-dokee!" Ziploc picked up his bag, slid off his stool, and strode purposefully to the door.

"Hey! That was *my* wish!" Parker yelled.

"Wait a minute!" Dobbs called to Ziploc. "Come back here."

Ziploc walked back and Parker grabbed his arm. "That was—"

Prying Parker's hand loose, Dobbs asked Ziploc, "How do you plan to do it?"

"Call some guys!"

"How long will it take?"

"Don't know!" Ziploc seemed eager to get on with it.

"Good-bye and good luck!" Dobbs laughed as Ziploc marched off.

"That was *my* wish," Parker muttered. He dabbed his cuts with a napkin and gulped down his Jack Daniel's, pushing out his lower lip so it wouldn't bloody the rim. Closing his eyes, he followed the whisky's warm descent. When he opened them the bartender was setting down Ziploc's Coke in front of his empty stool.

"You really believe it," Dobbs was saying.

"I don't *believe* it, I just—"

"Don't you see? They're using hope against you. It's worse than despair—it'll eat you alive. So I wished for something even you aren't gullible enough to hope for."

"Thanks, pal. When you pass the abandon-all-hope-ye-who-enter-here sign, remember how lucky you are." Parker stared gloomily at a commercial in which people smiled while shampooing their hair. He licked his lip and tasted blood. "We need first aid," he said, brightening at the thought. "Bandages, compresses, lots of sympathy. Fran lives two blocks away."

"I don't think she likes me."

"Nonsense!"

"Kinda late, isn't it?"

"Oh, she's still up. We're bleeding! I rest my case."

* * *

"I said I can't see you now, Jeff. I'll call you tomorrow."

Parker gaped at the speaker grill as if it, not Fran, had spoken.

Reading the mailboxes, tapping his foot on the earth-tone tiles, and fingering the caked blood under his nose, Dobbs was striving not to look at him.

Parker pushed the bell. "We're bleeding!" he shouted into the squawk-box, startled by his voice booming in the entryway. Licking his lip he discovered that he'd stopped bleeding. He was gazing into the copper mesh of the grill, watching his worst suspicions take shape, when the buzzer sounded and his hand shot out for the knob.

Fran, in the black mini she'd worn the other night, was leaning over the second-floor banister. "What happened?"

"Job interview!" Parker called up. As he reached the landing he asked, "Just get back from a party?"

She shook her head, dislodging a fat tear and a spoor of mascara.

"What's wrong?" He opened his arms, but she backed through the doorway and stepped aside from his view of Ken Fletcher rising from the couch.

Accustomed as he was growing to shocks, he couldn't quite take this one in. Fletcher seemed violently out of context, like Parker's first view of the gun when it was placed on his office desk. It required an act of will to place Fletcher in these surroundings—in front of the beige couch with its burnt-orange embroidered flowers; behind two half-empty wineglasses on Fran's Aunt Margaret's escalloped brass coffee table; among the refinished secondhand store chairs and bookcases; beneath the Chagall print of the bridegroom reaching up and gripping the bride's hand as she floats away; across from the tall windows where the room floated among other lighted rooms above Hyde Park Boulevard.

"Jeff—" Fran swallowed.

"We've met. Hi, Ken! Last time we spoke you were expounding the 'small world' theory. I guess tonight proves it."

"Hello, Jeff," said Fletcher, amiably impervious to the sarcasm. "How are you?" He was wearing his tweeds. Fran, Parker supposed, would find that sort of thing endearing.

Fletcher settled back on the couch, the only one in the room willing to look at Parker.

"Hi." Dobbs was standing in front of the door, hands in his pockets.

Fran dabbed the back of her wrist at the mess gathering under her eyes. "I have Band-Aids and mercurochrome in the bathroom," she said, her voice as drained and small as its reproduction in the speaker.

"Why don't you go first, Jeff?" said Dobbs, running a finger over the dried blood beneath his nose. "I'd like to try my call again."

When Parker returned from the bathroom, holding a box of cotton-balls and a bottle of mercurochrome, Dobbs was in the kitchen making his call; Fletcher was lining up his pipe and accessories on the coffee table; and Fran stood hugging herself, her back to the room.

Stepping in from the hallway, Dobbs said, "We're in the clear—at least for tonight." He shook his head at the mercurochrome and cotton-balls.

Parker walked to Fran's side and gave her a quick squeeze of the shoulders. "Anything you'd like to say to me before we go?"

She shrugged in her straitjacket of folded arms and hunched shoulders; he kissed the top of her head.

"Can we have a word in private?" he asked Fletcher.

"I don't want you guys fighting," Fran said wearily.

"Am I going to need first aid?" Fletcher was looking at the cotton-balls in Parker's hand.

"Oh. Look after these for me." Parker handed Fran the Mercuro-chrome and the box of cotton-balls, which she enfolded in her arms and grimly hugged.

* * *

Parker sat down on the bed—relieved, pointlessly, to find it made; Fletcher seated himself on the yellow armchair a few feet away and began patting himself down for the pipe he'd left on the coffee table. "So Jeff!" he began with the same eerie breeziness he'd affected since Parker arrived. "What would you like to talk about?"

Once more Fletcher seemed pasted into the foreground. Against the yellow armchair, Fran's white-painted childhood dresser, and the handmade quilted bedspread with its ranks of black and brown cows, he seemed like a badly done special effect.

"Does Fran know what you're up to?" Parker asked.

"Of course not."

"That was a bit too easy. Let's be sure we're talking about —"

"Does she know I'm trying to ruin your life? No." This blithely callous persona seemed to exist only while Fletcher was speaking. Between sentences the hapless awkward man Parker had known peeped out to gauge the effect. "Oddly enough, she thought *she* was deceiving *me*. She didn't tell me about you till after you phoned a few nights ago and I happened to be in the room. You might as well know that tonight I'm going to ask her to marry me. Fran hasn't quite resolved her feelings toward you, but we're working that out."

Like a bicyclist on a tightrope, whose survival depends on constant motion, Parker kept talking. "You got involved in this through Tolerance Management?"

"That's right. They were funding my work in anomic stress—"

"I suppose they've threatened your family?"

Fletcher's tightly wound smile came undone. "How did you know?"

"They threaten everyone. Except me, of course. Me they like."

"There's no 'they,'" said Fletcher. "It's Hank Monroe, Junior. The rest of us are terrified of him. Want to hear something funny?"

"Oh, why not!"

"Those ads you ran—at first I thought they were a hint from Monroe, Junior to speed up the courtship."

Glancing at the door, Parker said, "Aren't you afraid she might be listening?"

"With your friend watching? And be caught looking bad? Did you know she's never smoked pot because she's afraid she might look like a chipmunk holding in the smoke?"

Parker knew but wasn't about to exchange knowing smiles with Fletcher at her expense. "You're head over heels, aren't you? It won't take her long to figure out you don't love her."

"Eventually I'll tell her everything we've done to you, and I'll give her a divorce. You'll forgive her, she'll never want to look at you again. Tolerance Management has it all worked out. I'm truly sorry."

"Have you given any thought to what you're doing to *her*?"

"I promise I'll treat her kindly. That's about the only choice I have in the matter. I tried to back out once and Monroe, Junior sent me a present—night-vision photographs, taken in my ex-wife's house, of my kids sleeping. As for Fran, he let me know that if I backed out he'd 'handle the matter himself.' I don't even want to think about what that means." Fletcher tugged the knot in his tie and unbuttoned his collar. "I keep hoping I'll fall in love with her. I think that would be best for all of us. And why shouldn't I fall in love with her? She's beautiful, smart, compassionate—it's just that she can be a pain in the neck."

She could, but Parker stared down Fletcher's appeal for commiseration.

"Okay," Parker said. "You marry her, probably divorce her, she never wants to see me again. What then?"

"I think everyone involved in this business is sick of it—even Monroe, Junior. I think he'd be willing to call it off if you'd just fully experience your own suffering."

"Huh?"

"You're suffering, of course, but you don't seem to *notice* that you're suffering. I think he keeps it up because without your full awareness his work is aesthetically incomplete. It's like a tragedy—"

"Without a recognition scene?"

"That's it. Believe me, Jeff, you'll be better off. The only thing more wretched than despair is despairing and not knowing it."

"Okay, I'll despair."

"I hope that glibness is a sign that you're down to your last defenses. For all our sakes, I hope you crack soon."

"I guess the New Order's out," Parker said.

"Pardon?"

"Harry Krell told me he was going to use the same covert system to make *nice* things happen."

Fletcher tilted his head and chuckled appreciatively. "It would be like Harry to do something like that behind the rest of our backs. He's probably lying, of course, but with Harry you can never be sure. Listen to me—you'll only suffer more if you keep hoping."

"I'm getting the same advice from my friends and my enemies."

"I'm not your enemy," Fletcher said.

"What about the job interview?"

"Pardon?"

Parker described the melee at Circle Campus.

"I'd say you seriously jeopardized a job prospect," Fletcher said. "But don't waste your energy on ordinary disappointment."

"This idea that the whole business will end if I just face life squarely and despair—did someone tell you that or is it wishful thinking?"

"He doesn't seem to be trying to *kill* you. What else could he want?" Fletcher massaged his forehead. "I don't know. Maybe it *is* wishful thinking. Let's put it this way—you might as well despair. Either I'm right and it's hopeless, or I'm wrong—he won't stop even if you crack—and it's even more hopeless than I thought."

Parker stood up. "I suppose if I punched you out it would just suit your purposes?"

"It *would* confirm her notion that I'm the sensitive one."

"And if I start ranting about your part in a conspiracy, it would confirm Fran's disbelief in everything I say."

Fletcher shrugged sympathetically.

"Stand up," Parker said.

Fletcher rose from his chair and thrust out his chin. "As long as it's hopeless, you might as well hit me. Maybe we'll both feel better."

Parker had once seen a man do what he was about to try—a bar bet, the man so drunk he might not have felt it. He and Fletcher stood a few feet apart, wincing.

Parker made a fist and bringing up his arm in a drink-hoisting motion punched himself in the nose. His vision swarming, he found himself tilting backward with the dresser; it crashed into the wall. On his back now, he licked the blood running over his mouth and flashed a gory grin up at Fletcher.

Fletcher's habit of knitting his brow when puzzled was as genuine, apparently, as all the other traits Parker had thought fraudulent. The creases abruptly vanished, the skin between the eyes tightening as Fletcher looked up.

Stepping into Parker's view, Fran shoved the other man back. "You *hit* him?" she yelled, banging the heels of her hands against his chest. "You *hit* him?"

Having no doubt reviewed his options, Fletcher said, "I'll go make an ice pack."

"You do that."

She grabbed a handful of Kleenex and began cleaning up Parker's face. "Maybe we should get you to a hospital."

"No, nothing's broken."

"Tilt your head back—here," she said handing him the Kleenex. She turned away and left him facing her profile—lips compressed, chin trembling, the long throat swallowing.

While Fletcher banged and cracked an ice tray in the kitchen, they sat mutely posed on the blood-spotted floorboards—Parker with his head tilted back, holding the ball of Kleenex to his nose; Fran still in profile, staring concentratedly at nothing as if her thoughts crawled by on a Tele-PrompTer.

She faced him. "If I call you tomorrow, will you speak to me?"

"Of course. Fran, I—"

Her look alerted him that Fletcher was standing in the doorway behind him. Fletcher stepped between them and reached down to hand Parker some ice cubes knotted in a dish towel.

"I'm sorry, Jeff. I know you can understand how I felt because you love her, too." Clearly Fletcher had used his time in the kitchen to regroup. He held out his hand, and Parker—not to be outdone—set down the compress and grasped it in both his own.

"It never happened," Parker said.

Fran stood up. "You guys make me sick." Claiming the moral high ground seemed to energize her. She threw back her shoulders and glared spectacularly. "When you leave I'll be standing on the balcony and I'll expect to see you walking in opposite directions." She glowered at Parker, daring him, he thought, to ask what if they weren't parked in opposite directions?

They walked back to the living room, and Parker settled himself on the couch with his ice pack, grateful that the necessity to tilt back his head let him contemplate the white expanse of ceiling and ignore the tense silence in the room. Soon Fran went off to bang dishes in the kitchen, leaving the burden of sociability to Dobbs and Fletcher. Fragments of their dialogue washed through Parker's blankness (Fletcher: "No offense, but I find your argument fantastic." Dobbs: "That's my point!" Fletcher: "You're contradicting yourself. It has to be one or the other." Dobbs: "Exactly!") till Fran, her face washed, stood over him asking how he felt. Better, actually, the ice pack having stemmed the bleeding and numbed the pain.

"Well, guys," she said, "it's been a long day."

Fletcher stood up and touched her elbow. "Can we speak in private?"

"No!" she yelled and for the sake of impartiality shook her head at Parker.

"I'll go clean up," he said.

In the bathroom he locked the door, ran the tap, stuck some toilet paper to the blood under his nose, and removed the tape recorder from his inside suit pocket. He pressed REWIND and while the reels spun behind their cracked window opened the medicine cabinet. He didn't want to leave the recorder in plain sight, just in case Fletcher tried to out-stay him by asking to use the john as they were leaving. Parker couldn't help feeling a surge of jealousy at how thoroughly and atypically she'd scrubbed the bathroom.

He stopped the tape, pressed PLAY, held the speaker to his ear, and heard Dobbs saying "We're in the clear." He fast-forwarded: Fletcher was saying "So Jeff!" He pressed Stop.

He looked at the shelves: Band-Aids, Advil, sunscreen, a pink disc-shaped birth control pill dispenser. He set the dispenser on the rim of the sink, the recorder on the shelf, and closed the cabinet. In theory she'd open it to replace the pills, find the recorder and play it. But he couldn't just step out and press PLAY. She wouldn't listen. First because she'd be furious that he'd recorded Fletcher. Second because if she listened at all, she wasn't going to be bullied into doing it in front of everyone else. Or on Parker's schedule. She was the most stubborn woman he knew, he thought exasperatedly and a bit admiringly. He could leave a note: "Urgent! Please play at once." But if she felt pressured, she might keep it at the bottom of a drawer for months before she got around to it, as she'd done with letters. The shirt-pocket recorder with its tinny speaker wasn't powerful enough to force its contents through sheer volume into her well-defended brain. And if he started playing the tape, the inevitable screaming match, cathartic as it might be, would drown out everything else. The outcome would likely be himself and Dobbs on the street, and Fletcher still up here.

He washed his face and returned to the living room, where everyone else stood waiting.

"Good night, guys." Fran walked behind them to the door, keeping her distance, and stayed out of reach as they let themselves out.

"I feel like I'm back in high school," Parker said on the steps; Fletcher nodded in agreement, but they stopped in front of her building to wait for each other to walk away. Traffic was sparse on Hyde Park Boulevard, the court apartments and brownstones quiet. A cold mist blurred the streetlights. Nobody budged but Dobbs, pacing the mashed leaves: "C'mon, Jeff," he said compassionately. "Let's go."

Parker stood with his hands in his pockets, teeth set against the chill. Watching him, Fletcher patted himself down, brought out his pipe, clamped it in his teeth, patted himself down...

The annoying prospect of watching him complete the ritual strengthened Parker's resolve. He took a step closer and whispered, "They've threatened your family, for Chrissake. Shouldn't we be on the same side?"

Casting a quick glance upward, Fletcher said, "Are you threatening me?"

"Hey, are you threatening him?" Fran was leaning over her balcony, tucking her dangling hair behind her ears. "Let's go, guys. Opposite directions—hup two three!" She hugged herself, rubbing her hands over her sleeves. As the wind rose, her face seemed to gather light from her rush of black hair.

Gazing up at her on the balcony, Parker spread his arms in an actorly pose. It was supposed to be a joke, but she gleamed in soft focus as his eyes brimmed.

SEVEN

"My man! Hey!"

He usually gave money to panhandlers, but this one, too proud to beg, was trying to earn it through salesmanship and borderline extortion. Parker told himself that tact might not be a virtue for the homeless, but the brow-beating tone made him quicken his pace and avert his eyes. He hurried north, his stalker keeping pace, past the Evanston Kroch's and Bretano's, past Rose Records, eyes on the convergence of bare trees up Sherman Avenue. As he stepped off the curb at Emerson the stone clock tower and the streetlights lit up all at once.

"What's *wrong* with you, man?"

Parker still hadn't looked at the guy, whose disembodied words (Parker was barely listening) hovered over traffic and faces like voice-over narration.

"Hey, motherfucker! I'm *talkin'* to you!"

Here we go, Parker thought, his escape impeded by the rush hour crowd and by the three-foot-long white teddy bear under his right arm. He'd bought the bear at Marshall Field's a block south—where his unwanted companion had fallen in step as Parker duck-walked out the revolving doors with his burden—and was on his way to Evanston Hospital to deliver it to John and Peg Standell and their new baby.

Past Emerson the street turned residential; they were alone on a block of wood frame houses and apartment courts. Parker heard mouth-breathing and the crackling of leaves.

"Hey, mother! *Look* at me!"

It violated his ban on unnecessary eye contact, but if someone *asked* to be looked at, Parker owed him that much as a human being. He stopped, tightened his grip on the bear, and looked.

He walked several yards up Sherman before he stopped and looked again. The man was heading back toward Emerson. Parker had seen a short, skinny, crewcut black man in a tan trenchcoat, an ostentatiously fake red beard, and mirror sunglasses that displayed the latest version of Parker's dumbfounded stare.

Parker ran after him, nearly fumbling the bear, as the man crossed Emerson and blurred into a knot of shoppers. And here was the guy coming back. No, this one, similarly disguised, was taller, white, and adorned with a beard of pastel pink. Parker nearly walked into his own reflection in the mirror lenses of a third man.

Parker blocked his way. "What's going on?"

This one had a chestnut beard that contrasted handsomely with his white hair. "You been on Mars, bud? It's the convention!" He handed Parker a leaflet:

JOIN US IN SOLIDARITY!

ANNOUNCING THE CONVENTION OF THE LEGION OF FACELESS MEN AND WOMEN (Formerly the Legion of Faceless Men)

FACE US—IF YOU DARE!
ANTON J. CERMAK ARENA
FRIDAY-SUNDAY, 6:00-10:00

Two days away. Glancing at the reflection of his own black eyes, Parker decided not to grab the man by the lapels. "Solidarity in what?"

"The Legion started out as a group of Vietnam vets who couldn't get the V.A. to pay for all their plastic surgery." (Parker found himself staring at the last vestiges of personality in the disguised face—a beery nose and a row of small beige teeth.) "But we've moved on to the bigger picture."

"Championing the faceless everywhere?"

The row of teeth widened. "You wouldn't be making fun of us, would you, bud?"

An elderly woman whose heart-shaped face and round blue eyes reminded Parker of Lillian Gish said, "I understand perfectly. It's what happens to women when they turn fifty. People start to look through you."

"That's part of it, ma'am."

They stepped back from the entrance of Rose Records to let customers pass.

"I'm planning to attend," said the old woman. "Shall I bring my own beard?"

"We'll be handing 'em out at the door, ma'am."

"I *shan't* be attending," Parker informed the leafleter. "And now I'm leaving, and you'll have to carry on your street theater without me, if there's any point to that. Why don't you just save yourselves a lot of time and expense and call off whatever frat-boy prank you're planning for me at the Arena. I'm not even curious. I won't be there."

"That's tough talk for a guy with a teddy bear," the leafleter observed.

"Young man," the old woman said to Parker, "I'm seventy-eight years old, and you are the most self-important person I have met."

"Do what you like," Parker told the leafleter. His image in the mirror lenses was less adamant than he'd hoped, and already he was wondering if he could stay away. Mustering all his defiance, he threw down the gauntlet: "I won't be paying attention."

* * *

Peg's room was papered with sky-blue lambs leaping yellow fences and was divided by a plastic curtain behind which Parker heard the evening news and a languorous female voice drawling, "that's the *other* baby." From the doorway all he could see of the viewing annex was a wall to his left, but a baby was crying with the force of an El train screeching round a curve. It occurred to Parker that his bruised face or the enormous bear might scare the babies, and he paused in the doorway.

"No," Peg called wearily to the woman behind the curtain, "it's *your* baby." She was rolling her eyes at Parker in the doorway when she noticed his fat lip and black eyes. As he walked in with the bear, she straightened up against her pillows and pushed back her wire-rims. "What happened to *you*?"

Rejecting any number of jokes, he opted for an airy sweep of the arm implying "*c'est la vie.*"

"Someone was gesturing broadly and you got in the way?" Her voice was cracked and her face pale but her cheerful sarcasm unflagging.

Recalling the theatrics of his "job interview," Parker said, "It's true! So—let's see Kathryn!" But he hesitated to turn around and walk back to the glass behind him.

Stepping out of the bathroom, John shook Parker's free hand with both hands, exchanged thumps on the back, and leaned against his palms on the windowsill at the head of the bed. Branches cracked the cold lights of the hospital wing behind him.

There was none of the usual ironic distance between John and his Wonder Bread smile. It flickered momentarily at the sight of Parker's face but he said, "They make scale models, ya know. You didn't have to get a real bear."

"I hope it's not so big it'll scare her. Maybe I should—" As Parker searched for a place to set the thing down, the chairs and endtables seemed like miniatures in a Japanese monster movie. Stepping forward, John relieved him of his burden and held it up to the waist-high glass of the annex, where Kathryn Ann Standell, awakening in her bassinet, opened her mouth, widened her eyes, and bravely took in one more fact.

The fat dark-eyed baby to Kathryn's right, having stopped crying for an instant to consider the possibility that everything is funny, carried on. A fat unsteady woman in a blowsy hospital gown, her brown hair crushed to her cheeks and forehead, stepped into view behind the glass and, smiling at John and Peg, carried away her baby.

Peg tugged her own greasy bangs away from her forehead, whispering, "I swear, all women who go into labor come out with the same hairdo."

Parker squeezed her hand. The day after she'd flashed him the hate look, she'd called to apologize, and he'd accepted, but he couldn't help searching for its traces in her utterly uncomplicated smile.

John was waving the bear's arms at his daughter and for some reason giving it the voice—a baritone bellow—of talk-show host Larry King. "Bangor, Maine—Hello!"

Handing Parker the bear, he stepped behind the glass and held up his daughter, whose wide-open blue eyes gulped Parker whole.

"You're the most interesting thing she's seen so far," Peg said.

John leaned forward to see Kathryn's expression. "She's studying the Parker phenomenon!"

Parker shrugged at the goggling baby: *You* tell *me.* She reached for John's nose as he set her down in the bassinet.

When John stepped out, Parker clapped him on the shoulder. "She's beautiful."

"I didn't know how *breakable* new babies look. I keep thinking we'll never get her home."

"You'll do fine," Parker said.

"What is it, buddy?"

"No, I'm fine. Uhm, I have to make a call." Parker resumed his search for a place to put the bear till John took it out of his hand and turned it sideways to fit next to Peg.

"Your time will come, Jeff," she said. "Wistful perplexed little Parkers will roam the earth."

"Someone told me I'll die all alone in a room full of soup cans."

John cocked his head. "So ya like soup?"

* * *

In the deserted hospital lounge, shadowy volumes of furniture hulked beyond the light of two reading lamps. He was still having second thoughts as he punched Fran's number, and his stomach compressed as the line began ringing. He reminded himself that he wasn't just trying to save the relationship, he was trying to save *her;* imagining her shriek of hilarity if he put it that way.

She'd called a few hours after he got back from her apartment. There wasn't much conversation—mostly the breathing of two cagey people interpreting each other's pauses. Aside from their agreement to meet for lunch on Thursday (tomorrow), nothing was resolved, but right at the end she'd said, "Don't give up on me." He hadn't asked about the tape, but it would have been a different conversation if she'd played it.

He let the phone ring, waiting for her answering machine. Through the fluttering lights and branches in the window, he could just make out a pink strip of horizon and the bruise-colored sheen of the lake. Gazing damply at the hackneyed twilight, he tried to bear in mind that self-pity is comical. "Poor me!" he sighed, and as her machine came on he was emitting a grim powdery laugh that ended in a cough.

"You had to be there," he said. "See you tomorrow." But he was still on the line. When he was this unhappy, the silence of an answering machine—like the reticence of a great police interrogator—was a provocation to babble. He hung up just ahead of a mob of idiocies crowding into speech.

* * *

As he stepped back into the room he heard the same baby crying and the woman behind the curtain murmuring, "*That's* the other baby."

"No," Peg called sweetly, "that's *your* baby."

She smiled at Kathryn on the other side of the glass—sleeping through the din as imperturbably as a holy man lying on spikes—and at the sheepish wobbly mom retrieving her baby. She whispered, "See? Mothers instinctively recognize the cries of their young. That reminds me," she said at conversational volume, "there's a piece in today's *Times* about the Doomsday Baby. In case of nuclear war they're going to broadcast the cries of a baby over whatever frequencies the enemy are listening to. It's supposed to make them think twice about pushing the button."

"It's inserted subliminally under other sounds." John picked up the TV remote from the tray table by the bed and leaned back against the windowsill. "The theory is that the guys in the missile silos won't want to launch but they won't know why."

"Go on!" Parker snorted, perching on the sill next to John.

"*You're* talking about plausibility?" Peg dug out the front section of the *New York Times* from under the bear and handed it to John, who handed it to Parker.

The Doomsday Baby, according to the *Times* defense correspondent, was code-named Swee'pea. "Sorry," Parker said when he looked up. "I was trying to imagine that something implausible might not be true. Just an experiment!"

"Department stores are doing the same thing," John said. "They're running subliminals under their Muzak to hold down shoplifting."

"You mean all the people who think they hear voices are right?"

"Pretty soon! Anyway, the Doomsday Baby's just an upgrade of what the department stores are doing."

Parker said, "Isn't this kind of a morbid topic, considering?"

"It's hopeful if you think about it." Peg straightened up against her pillows. "Here are these guys trained to blow up the world without raising their pulse rates, and they can still be reached by a crying baby. It proves that people are basically sane. They know what's really important. Try to look a little *sadder*, Jeff."

If happy people ran the world there'd be fascism, he thought. He said, "It's the black eyes. They make me look like a soulful Disney raccoon...The doomsday people could use that Mark Strand poem. How does it go? 'Save the babies! Let us run downtown and save the babies!' Uh..."

"I like that! 'Let us save the babies!'" John recited in his Larry King voice. 'Let us run downtown and save the babies!'"

"By the way"— Peg rubbed the bear's head—"did we thank you for this guy? You really shouldn't have."

"I wouldn't have been able to afford it, but the other day a total stranger slipped a hundred dollars in my shirt pocket. So what else is new?"

She let the remark pass, it seemed to Parker, for the same reason John hadn't asked about his face: Whatever was following Parker, they didn't want it in this room.

John aimed the remote at a set mounted high on the wall. It brightened on a closeup of a trenchcoated man in mirror shades, his jet-black fake beard trimmed to a point and tilted rightward.

"Can anyone come?" asked the offscreen voice of the interviewer, his molten reflection floating in the lenses of the man's sunglasses. "And what about beards—is it BYOB?"

This sarcasm was met with the glitter of the lenses and a silence that, judging by its length, had spooked the interviewer and even the videotape editor. Parker was relieved when the answer came.

"Everyone's welcome," said the spokesman. "We'll be handing out beards at the door." Past his shoulder teenagers waved and made faces amid a silent, motionless phalanx of disguised men. It seemed to Parker that the pinpoints gleaming off all those mirror lenses were aimed at him.

From the corner of his eye he caught John studying his reaction. "Are those the guys?" John asked. "Jeez!"

They'd cut to the reporter, also in a trenchcoat, his sculpted hair windblown at the fringes, his composure not quite recovered. "The poet T.S. Eliot had a phrase for it: 'a face to meet the faces that you meet.'"

"He's winging it," Parker said. "He has no more idea of what this 'convention' is about than I do."

"Will you look," said the nervous reporter, filling, "when the faceless demand to be seen? Or will you look away? But isn't it *ourselves* in those reflecting lenses? Isn't their fight ours? In today's impersonal, digitized world, aren't we *all* faceless? The Legion of Faceless Men's Convention begins on Friday. From the Daley Center Plaza, I'm Chuck Vasquez. Back to you, Bill and Walter."

John switched off the set and reluctantly asked Parker what was going on.

"I think they're trying to get my attention. The joke has just about run its course and they're preparing the punch line, the recognition scene, whatever you want to call it. I think we'll know in two days because I'm sure it's connected with this convention."

"Do you have a plan?"

"Don't pay attention? I mean, it's worked pretty well so far. Is that contemptible? You wouldn't think much of Hamlet or Oedipus if the moment of recognition comes and he's thinking of something else."

"Can you do that—not pay attention?"

"I seem to be losing the knack. I wish I could remember how I managed not to when I didn't know I was trying. I don't suppose you've ever come up with the world's most sophisticated security system? Boy, could I use it."

"Ultimate security means something different for everyone, but, yeah, I could design the ultimate security for *you.*"

"Great! What is it?"

"I can't tell you."

"You're kidding."

"It'll only work if you don't know what it is. All I can say is I got the idea from the Doomsday Baby and 'Save the babies!'"

Parker was so used to seeing John smiling boyishly or impishly that even at his most serious, a phantom grin seemed to flit over his face.

Parker glanced at Peg for her reaction, but she was watching Kathryn sleep behind the glass.

"There'll be a button," John said. "When everything else fails, push it."

"What—nuclear war? John, you're one of the smartest people I know. You solve problems like a frog catching flies with its tongue—thhhhhp! Quick and focused and efficient. Except when you get whimsical. And especially when you start thinking about the world's most sophisticated security system. Then you start getting Baroque."

"I go for Baroque!"

Still, if there was anyone Parker trusted absolutely, and whose ingenuity he'd rely on a crisis, it was John. "I guess the situation calls for the services of a bent pragmatist. All right, pal, do what you have to do, and thanks. Say, what if I get curious and press the button?"

"You'll regret it," John said, and Parker had no doubt of his seriousness. "The button's a last resort. I'll lend you a burglar-alarm system that alerts the police, and I think I can get you a bodyguard. If none of that works, press the button. I'll send out an installer and a bodyguard as soon as I can make the arrangements. You might have to hold out till Friday. Okay?" he added, meaning, can we change the subject? "Do you think Kathryn looks like Peg or me?"

"Just one question. Does it still include my favorite part? 'You have just activated the world's most sophisticated security system. You have one minute.'"

"It couldn't work without it." John looked toward the glass and declaimed in the voice of Larry King, "Save the babies! Let us run downtown! Let us run downtown and save the babies!"

* * *

He was watching her cross the restaurant; Fran could truly be said to sashay across a room. It was, to be sure, a postmodern sashay: ironic, self-amused, filled with allusions to movie history, to the iconography of slinky dames, but confident, graceful, unselfconscious. Silhouetted by the dim light of Thompson's she approached his booth, a headtoss streaming hair off her shoulder. As usual she was late, and when she sat down across from him it seemed to Parker that he rose in the esteem of the waitresses and busboys, who'd been exchanging wised-up shakes of the head while he thumbed the menu and nursed his drink.

He'd thought it a good sign that she picked Thompson's, a piano-bar restaurant across Wabash from the Palmer House. In happier times they'd spent whole afternoons there drinking, flirting, scarfing down free appetizers, and laughing at the exuberantly maudlin jazz piano. But from her flurry of small talk—apologies for being late, war stories about traffic—and the slow, systematic way she folded her coat, he judged that she was trying to put off their conversation. The conversation she was trying to put off, he thought, wasn't the one they'd be having at all if she'd played the damn tape!

Fran shook her head at the bowl of mini-eggrolls he started to slide across the table. She was wearing a blue shoulder-padded power suit for her job interview; "very Joan Crawford," he said approvingly, straightening the blue bow at her neck. The pianist was tinkling "How My Heart Sings" with lugubrious Bill Evans licks.

"I'm so sorry I hurt you," she said miserably, still looking at the bow as if cribbing her apology, the candle on the table scooping hollows in her face. Having collected herself, she looked at him. "When you guys left I started wringing my hands—look!" She held up her chafed hands. "Like Lady Macbeth!" It wasn't clear that she wanted him to laugh, so he smiled.

"I know you didn't want to hurt me," he said, "and I forgive you, but you have to make a decision."

He guessed that if she'd put off playing the tape she had also put off deciding, and her oblique response seemed to confirm both assumptions. "The funny thing is," she said, "he reminds me of you."

He unbuttoned his balding corduroy jacket and, sneering like a model, showed off the lining.

She laughed. "I didn't mean you wear tweed." She picked a thread off his cuff. "Jerk. I mean you're both sensitive. I feel like you know me, when you're paying attention. And you both have a droll, ethereal sense of humor."

"I guess I never told you the one about the talking dog. And give me one example of Ken's sense of humor."

He had to wait for his example while the waitress took their order, and then Fran ignored the question. "You can both be incredibly empathetic one moment and the next you'll vanish from the conversation, swallowed up by your thoughts. Looking ragged and windblown when you finally stumble back into the world."

He put his thumbs under his armpits and wiggled his fingers. "Well if you're looking for an odd inattentive sensitive wimp, look no further. You've got the original right here. Accept no substitutes."

"If only the original weren't in such short supply!"

"What does that mean?"

"What I'm trying to say," she said, struggling to keep her voice down, "what I'm always trying to say is, *you're unobservant*!"

"Of course if Ken is unobservant, too—"

"By comparison Ken is merely absent-minded. I can put up with that. What I can't put up with is *your conspiracy*. That seems to be your name for the place you go to when you *stop being here*! At least Ken exists."

Suddenly—no, Parker thought, predictably, inevitably—a head popped up over her shoulder from the booth behind: a little face, mirror lenses, fake beard dangling half off.

Get used to it! he told himself. If you live in a theme park, things are going to pop up. What was called for now was an act of will. If he looked one more instant Fran would turn around, it would be the "burnt face" incident all over again, and he might lose his last chance to win her back. If he even allowed his attention to wander from her for a second, it might be all over. He forced his eyes back on Fran; her chin was crinkling as it sometimes did when she was holding back tears. He took her hand, aware of movement behind her. Apparently the man was tilting his head from side to side.

All right, he was unobservant. But was he unobservant *enough*? Could he, through an act of focused, intensive obtuseness, blot out the man's existence? It was his only chance. Yes, he could do it.

"Your hand is sweating," she said. "You're like a teenager, Parker; I suppose that's part of your charm."

He smiled at her, trying not to think of the candle flames like pupils in the mirror lenses.

He gripped her hand; exultantly he thought, I know how to do this! It was all very simple: an application of the mental processes he used when he walked through a dangerous neighborhood with his eyes straight ahead; turned on the TV because he didn't like where his thoughts were heading; looked away from an old friend crossing the street to avoid him; gave money to the first two homeless people he saw and then had to pass three more; insisted so energetically to his parents that he was fine, he began to think maybe he was; awoke with the terrors and, just as he remembered why, rolled over and fell back to sleep.

It was over; he knew he'd done it. What had happened, he believed, was that he'd rebuilt the world from the ground up with the annoying little face snipped out. He didn't try to look directly at the spot the man had occupied. The prospect of what remained was too frightening: a nothing, a negative hallucination. He was thinking metaphorically, of course—of course! of course!—but he believed he'd found an inner power that made him impervious to the little face. Parker recalled Harry Krell's snide comment that his obtuseness was a triumph of the human spirit and wondered if it might be true. He wondered if he was on the verge of some spiritual milestone or a run-of-the-mill breakdown.

"You see what I mean?" she said, tearing her hand from his grip. "You don't pay attention. I used to wonder how you could live with no hobbies, in an apartment with practically no furnishings and nothing on the walls. Then I realized: It doesn't matter what your apartment looks like because you're not there. *You're not here!* You don't exist."

Apparently his spiritual progress had a ways to go because now all he wanted to do was one-up her. "*I'm* unobservant? Tell me: You walked right past the booth behind us. Notice anything funny?" He pointed behind her at the man who wasn't, after all, a silhouette carved out of the void, but still a squirrely little guy whose dangling beard swung pendulously as he tilted his head from side to side, gawking at Parker. The pianist was noodling a glissando-filled "How High the Moon?"

To spite Parker Fran had taken her time turning around but now she emitted a brief shrieking laugh.

"Didn't I know you in high school?" the little man asked Parker. He'd lifted the frames and was squinting out beneath them. He took hold of his beard as if to pull it off, but whatever ritual he was enacting seemed to restrain him. "Lane Tech? Electric Shop? Mr. Krolowitz?"

" 'Electric Shop,'" Parker quoted Mr. Krolowitz, "'is like a game of football.'"

"'You've got to know the game—uh...'"

"'You've got to play the game before you know the rules?'"

"Jeffrey Parker, right? Ted Stevens."

Parker said, "The facelessness is familiar, but—I supposedly knew this guy in high school," he told Fran.

"I don't know what to say," she replied with undeniable sincerity.

Parker was trying to recall a Ted Stevens from high school but found himself distracted by the man's dark, expensively layered hair: Why bother if you're going to end up looking like a maniac anyway? The portion of the man's face from which the beard had worked loose was pink and clean-shaven. Parker wondered if it was a Faceless Man custom to eat with one's beard dangling out of the way.

Fran's sense of the absurd had overcome her squeamishness; she flashed her parade-float smile at the mirror lenses and in her brightest politician's-daughter voice said, "Hiiii!"

The greeting's volume and sheer force of vivacity made Ted shrink back a bit. "This is Bob," he said, moving aside to let Fran and Parker see the man rising from the seat behind him—expensively tailored, barrel-chested, mirror-lensed, his beard pointing rakishly to the left.

Bob nodded and sat down.

"I can't help noticing—" Parker said.

"No one can. That's the point of the Legion of Faceless Men."

"Were you injured in Vietnam?" Parker regretted the question even before Fran flashed him an anxious glance.

"No, those were the founders. But the Legion's expanding. It's for the little guy—every average guy who gets the shaft and you never hear about it. The disguise is because the elites in this country want us to shut up and stay invisible. They want us under wraps. We'll show 'em under wraps! They don't want to hear from the little guy." Fran flashed Parker a look that he thought took note of the fact that Ted really *was* a little guy—his mouth just reaching the top of the booth.

"It sounds kind of vague," Fran said.

"There's nothing vague about it. Little guys like us work hard and pay taxes so welfare cheats can sit on their stoops. I have property in upper Michigan and I can't chop down my own trees because some hoot owl might—"

"So you wear beards and mirror sunglasses because you're *Republicans?*" Fran marveled.

Ted observed her studiedly deadpan expression to see if he was being made fun of. "Some of us are Republicans, some are Democrats. Some are conservatives like me, some are liberals like Bob. Some—"

Parker hadn't come here to be edified in dimwit populism. "Nice seeing you again, Ted," he said tersely. He'd find out soon enough what these people had in mind: The convention started tomorrow.

As far as one could make out, Ted Stevens appeared to be glowering. "You know, I didn't like you in high school either."

"At least you remember who I am. You were saying," Parker said to Fran.

Her rounded eyes and mouth imitated a child who'd just been read a ghost story. Behind her Ted had turned back to his friend. For half a minute she leaned back against her seat, listening to the conversation behind her, eyes narrowed in concentration.

"All right," Parker whispered, giving in, "what are they talking about?"

"Real estate," she whispered. The waitress arrived with their plates; caught, Fran sprang forward and folded her hands at the edge of the table.

When they were alone Parker said, "I don't want to lose you. I'll observe you so closely, so continuously, so unblinkingly, so adoringly, so exclusively I'll bump into lampposts." With exaggerated scrutiny he watched the salad fork rise to her mouth.

"It's better than walking *me* into lampposts," she recalled, chewing. "Can't you observe me *and* the lamppost?"

"It can't be done." He sliced his roast beef. "Every time you open a door you close one someplace else, is that the cliché I'm looking for?"

The implication wasn't lost on her; she turned her splendid profile to him while she thought, compressing her lips and crinkling her chin.

He watched her Expressionist cheekbones flutter above the candle till she turned to face him, propped her chin on her hand, and said, "You're a great guy."

"Uh-oh."

"Let me finish. Maybe I'm still in love with you, but…for instance, where did you go when I lost you a few minutes ago? Sometimes talking to you is like talking to a rain check. "

Reluctantly Parker told her how for approximately ninety seconds he'd snipped Ted Stevens out of existence.

"You're weird!"

"You haven't asked," he noted, "why heavily disguised men keep turning up, their beards askew."

He waited; she methodically cut up her salad.

At last he said, "It's too threatening, isn't it? You're dealing with it by protective obtuseness. You close a door to open one someplace else."

She playfully tapped his shin with her toe. "So you think you've discovered a higher level of obtuseness?" she asked with a gee-whiz expression.

"Maybe what we call inattentiveness is just a weak, halfhearted version of something else. When a yogi walks on coals or lies on a bed of spikes without feeling pain, we don't say he's unobservant. We don't say he's in denial!"

"Let me get this straight. You're taking Attention Deficit Disorder to a higher plane." She ran her hand along his cheek. "Please tell me you're joking."

"Yes, I'm joking, but I can't help thinking there's something to it. There'd better be. These people have something planned for me, and so far the only defense they can't deal with is adamant rock-solid oblivious-ness. Maybe it's not just a character flaw." He took his first bite of the roast beef, whose gravy had begun to congeal. "I suspect, my darling, we're discussing my powers of observation because you're not going to make a decision today."

She set down her fork and leaned on her forearms. "No," she said running a thumb over the back of a chafed hand. "I have to leave in five minutes for my interview." She waited for him to say something. "If I leave a door open will one close someplace else? Don't give up on me, Parker."

* * *

When the doorbell rang at nine that night he fleetingly entertained the thought that Fran had played the tape and was waiting downstairs to beg his forgiveness. Far more likely, he'd find the entrance teeming with disguised men and his hapless reflected image. The super still hadn't fixed the inter-com, and Parker hated giving his enemies the satisfaction of making him come down to look. He could buzz the caller in and question him through the door, but the buzzer usually didn't work, either. He tried not to imag-ine Fran waiting for him on the stone table in the lobby, eyes closed, arms crossed, impersonating a mummy for old times' sake. Fat chance!

It seemed as good a time as any to abandon hope. He adjusted the neck of the fluorescent desk lamp and was about to return to the paper he'd been grading when the bell rang again. He cocked his head. The gun would have come in handy, but he'd put it in Dobbs's glove compart-ment before they visited Fran, and afterward, deciding it created more problems than it solved, he'd asked Dobbs to get rid of it.

Half a minute later his visitor rang again, but Parker forced his eyes back on the phrase, "Marriage is a valuable institution because it pre-pares children for the institution of marriage." He rubbed his eyes and reread the sentence. The blear of blue and red ink threatened to flow off the page.

When on a third reading the sentence still read "Marriage is a valuable institution because it prepares children for the institution of marriage," and the bell rang again, he decided to answer the goddamn door. Anyway, the lock on the entrance door was broken, too, come to think of it, and the bad people could walk right up. Perhaps no one but Fran awaiting the chance to impersonate a mummy would ring so persistently.

Unless someone was waiting for him to step out of his apartment. He inched open the door, found no one on the landing, and started down the steps. He met no one on the stairs, and though a distant stereo thrummed through his shoes he heard nothing but a repetitive squeak.

When he reached the lobby he saw that he'd been half-right about his visitor and that his prayers had been answered imprecisely. Two women lay on the huge stone table, arms crossed over their white blouses and shoulder-padded power suits, fists tightened around their purse straps. The stout blonde next to Fran, whom Parker recognized as her high school friend, law school classmate and drinking buddy Marcy Voglemann, was tittering rhythmically—three squeals alternating with a pause. He guessed they'd been taking turns running to the bell and back to the table. Their heads were pillowed on their folded coats. He crept up; Fran opened one eye, then closed it, reassuming her mask of impassive glamour, inviting him to notice that even drunk as a skunk she had poise and posture and cheekbones enough to rule the dead.

He sat down on the edge of the table between their heads, watching the rise and fall of Fran's chest and the thin bow of her mouth, hearing Marcy giggle behind him like some hazardous untended machine, and tried to use the moment before they opened their eyes to figure out why they were here. All he knew was that Fran wouldn't have brought Marcy if she'd played the tape. He assumed they'd met downtown for dinner after interviewing at law firms, and somewhere past the first drink they'd had a brainstorm. Whatever it was, it surely involved more than driving all the way up here for the pleasure of impersonating mummies. Still, it was cold in the lobby, and they'd gone to some trouble to make him laugh, so he laughed. Fran opened her eyes, and it seemed to Parker that in the next instant they completed a complex transaction—she searched his face for signs of resentment or hatred, he smiled and she relaxed, displaying her Queen of Egypt sneer.

"When I saw the two of you lying there, I thought, there must be a caption for this." He glanced over his shoulder to include Marcy, who'd sat up and was rubbing her lower back with both hands. The dampness of the lobby was unraveling her perm. With her round blue eyes and round face she reminded Parker of a gigantic Cabbage Patch Kid. He liked her but was always wary of her nervousness, her pained laugh, and her preemptive sarcasm.

"When I was a kid," he said turning back to Fran, "there was a guy who did a series of books—photographs with wacky captions. I can't remember his name but he's dead. I keep thinking everything would make sense if we had the wacky captions."

"I know," she said lugubriously, reaching up and mussing his hair, "there ought to be Cliff Notes." She sat up. "We have a surprise for you, Parker."

"Uh-huh," he said cautiously.

"Hellohhhh!" Marcy yelled, testing the reverb of the cavernous lobby, whose four archways led to stairwells. The expanse of stone tiles— dingy black-and-white—contributed to the bizarre acoustics, a dim subway roar in which no sound seemed to die. A fake chandelier missing half its glass and lights twinkled above them, and candelabra wall fixtures holding flame-shaped bulbs, most of which had been removed, threw splashes on the eggshell walls. It had been a while since he'd looked at this place—so awful it was cheering him up. And despite his disappointment at Marcy's presence he was grateful for the company and any diversion.

As the two women sat listening to the sourceless noise, he dreaded that Fran might give him her old pep talk, asking why he'd surrendered to his depression and sought out the most depressing place on earth. But aside from Marcy's "I love what you've done with the place!" when they stepped into his apartment, and the glance the two women exchanged in reaction to the bare bulbs, bare walls, and stick furniture, the subject didn't come up. The subject of his face didn't come up either, so evidently Marcy had been briefed.

"Can I get you anything?"

They shook their heads; Fran tossed her coat on the couch, plopped next to it, drew a deep breath and began. "So!" She drew the coat closer to make room for Marcy. "This evening we were having dinner at the Berghoff—"

"How did your interviews go?" He sat down on the folding card-table chair he'd brought over from the "dining table."

"Parker! I'm telling a *story*! Well!" she continued breathlessly, making her eyes big. "When we left we saw a crowd of men dressed like those men we've been seeing—the no-face club?"

Parker wasn't surprised; he'd resigned himself to the omnipresence of faceless men. In the course of the day his fear of them had waned to anxiety and now (maybe it was just exhaustion) to boredom—he wished he could change the channel.

"In disguise! Leafletting! They have megaphones! They're having a convention! It starts tomorrow!" In hilarity Fran's speech could turn songlike, a ringing mezzo-soprano that recalled her high school voice training. "Remember what you said, 'A convention of faceless men, oh sure!' So anyway—"

"Faceless!" Marcy shrieked, struggling with her coat till Fran helped with the sleeves. "Faceless guys in disguise! Oh, and what's their motto, 'face us!' *They* can't face *us*—they're faceless!" The two friends broke up with their ritual side-clutching and back-slapping.

Feeling like a party poop, he took their coats to the bedroom and draped them on the bed.

When he returned to his chair Marcy yelled, "Tell him about the badge!"

"So I have that toy FBI badge we found on the sidewalk, remember, Parker?" She was referring to the plastic badge Ziploc had dropped outside the disco. "It was sweet," she said to Marcy. "When I left the next morning Jeff pinned me with it."

"With something he found on the *street*? Frannie, you don't know where it's *been*!"

"Oh, he cleaned it up, but anyway, I have this *badge* in my purse."

Parker missed the next few sentences, distracted by the thought that he could measure Fran's ambivalence by the things she consigned to her purse. If they had an argument and he wrote her a letter, she'd carry it unread for weeks in her purse. Pinning her with the badge was just a joke, of course, but still, she'd put it in that damn purse! It occurred to him that the microcassette recorder and his tape were probably in there now. For her sake he'd have to make her listen to it tonight, even if she never spoke to him again.

"—so I remembered what you said about our faceless man being connected with guys who carry toy FBI badges that they got from the real FBI, is that how it works?"

"As I like to remind you, my darling, I'm impervious to sarcasm."

Marcy snorted.

Fran lifted her hair off her shoulders and let it fall down her back. "I'm not being sarcastic—listen. I put my badge on and we mingled, just to see what would happen? Oh, did I mention that their beards were all on lopsided and none was a plausible color? So this guy with a blond crewcut and a black beard comes up and opens his coat. I thought—oh, you know what I thought. I'm walking away with my eyes averted and Marcy yells stop! look at the coat!" Her voice had risen to its aria register, white teeth and eyeballs at full wattage. "He was wearing a badge just like mine! Pinned to the lining!"

Marcy said, "Frannie thought fast. Tell him what you did."

"I said, 'Take me to your leader!'" She folded her arms, dramatic pause.

Parker obliged. "And?"

"And he kinda did!" Fran whooped. She opened her purse and before Parker could catch a glimpse of the tape recorder she drew out a card and snapped the purse shut. "It looks fake, but that's part of the plan, right?" He wasn't sure now whether she was being sarcastic or accepting the absurd facts with Alice-like earnestness. "He said this was his FBI contact."

She handed him the card—it was old, smeared, and faded and appeared to have been crumpled, opened, folded, and smoothed-out for decades. On one side was a rubber-stamped impression of the FBI seal; on the other, in smeared and faded but legible handwriting, was the name "Ed Vishoolis," an address in Albany Park on the North Side, and a phone number.

"We tried asking questions, but he was incoherent. I think he had the impression, though, that if Marcy and I were part of the same conspiracy we had to date him. So we walked away and he followed us for two blocks. Every so often Marcy turned around and yelled, 'Will you *fuck off*?' and he'd freeze for a second looking hurt."

Marcy said, "Finally Frannie waited for him to catch up and said, 'Report back to headquarters at once.' And off he went! *Is* there a headquarters? Maybe *we* should have followed *him*." It was clear Marcy believed no such thing and that for her all this conspiracy talk was a lark.

"We found a phone booth and dialed the number." Fran tucked her hair behind her ears.

"And?" he prompted.

"The guy who answered sounded old. There was a TV on in the background. I asked if he was affiliated with the FBI, he said who wants to know? I said, can I take that as a yes, he asked for my name. I said Emma Bovary, he said he'd taken up literature in his retirement and *Madame Bovary* was one of his favorites. I said, so you're retired from the FBI? He said he liked my voice, would I like to drop by and discuss literature? Why are all these conspiracy people so horny? I asked if he was affiliated with the FBI or not. He said, come on over, we'll talk about it. He said that ever since his wife died he didn't have anyone to discuss books with. I knew he was trying to make me feel sorry for him, but it was *working*— and he sounded like he'd been drinking. I guess I looked uncomfortable because that's when Marcy grabbed the phone and said, 'Do you have Prince Albert in a can?' and hung up. So what do you think, Parker? Want to call him?"

"We need a plan. I'm grateful you did all that detective work for me, but I don't think you have any sense of how dangerous it could have been."

She blew a strand of hair out of her eyes.

Parker asked her, "Are you at least willing to concede that there might be something to what I've told you?"

Fran shrugged. She drew a shock of hair sideways to its full length and stared at it with distaste, as if wondering where all that *hair* came from. It was a mannerism he'd seen before, a sure sign she was fading fast.

Parker leaned sideways to catch her eye and stroked her cheek with the back of his hand. She did an antic imitation of a lovestruck smile, batting her reddened eyes.

"I'm sorry," he said. "You took a risk walking up to that guy, and you were doing it for me. Thanks, kiddo. Just promise me, no shootouts, no leaping onto the hoods of speeding cars."

"Well," she said thinking it over, "okay."

"So what do you say we call him and see what happens?"

Marcy clapped and shouted hooray.

"Hooray," Fran murmured, swatting her hair down her back.

Parker extended the phone's cord out of the bedroom, sat down on his card-table chair, and set the phone on his lap. "In around 1970 the FBI started farming out the harrasment of their victims to freelance nuts. Maybe they still reported once in a while to an FBI handler. I don't know how many victims there were, but the nut who followed you might not have been assigned to me. He's probably been 'retired' for decades. Let's hope your nut and mine were assigned to the same handler. . . I don't know. It's hard to figure out exactly who we're dealing with. The conspiracy gets pretty hazy around the edges, but I suspect there might be people behind that guy we met. He's still getting paid a tremendous amount of money, apparently. He has his own think tank!"

Fran ignored Marcy's sidelong glance. He punched the number. It rang five times before a man's voice mumbled a phlegmy hello.

"Is this Mr. Ed Vishoolis of the FBI?" Parker asked brightly. He winked. "This is Roland Batke in Pensions. I know it's unusual to be calling this late, but things are getting backed up—you know how it is at the Bureau!" Parker forced a stagy baritone laugh. He was trying to to entertain Fran, who seemed to be coming round. She knelt next to him and put her head to the back of the earpiece; he smelled cognac and herbal shampoo. "I just need to confirm your term of service."

"You're with those women, aren't you?" his listener asked cannily. "They as sexy as they sound?"

"As an FBI veteran, what do you deduce?"

"Oh, you're cute, sonny! Name!"—the voice suddenly official.

"Roland...Actually It's Jeffrey Parker. Sound familiar?"

Fran leaned forward to show him an anxious face.

"*The* Jeffrey Parker?" Ed Vishoolis sounded delighted at the prospect. Parker had forgotten that all these people seemed to like him.

"Yes."

"I should have known this was coming," Ed mused. "I just got a call from a guy who ran errands for me fifteen years ago—those damn *women* told him to report to headquarters." (Fran put her hand to her mouth. "*What?*" Marcy whispered. "*What?*") "You wouldn't be recording me, would you?"

Parker noisily slapped his forehead. "Darn, I didn't think of it. But of course an old FBI hand wouldn't get tricked into blurting things over the phone."

"We used to wonder whether you'd ever notice there was something wrong. You know what we called you? Mr. Magoo." (Fran started to smile, then swallowed. She gave Parker her Poor Baby look.) "I suppose you want to know the meaning of it all. Why you? Where does *Parker* fit in? Come on over."

"Now?"

"Of course if you're *afraid*...didn't *you* call *me?*"

Parker would have liked to put if off till tomorrow when he had John Standell's bodyguard, and it seemed idiotic to do otherwise just because his girl had her ear to the receiver. "Okay."

"Oh, and bring the ladies. I want to see if they're as charming in person." "They're not here," Parker said.

"You must think I'm stupid *and* deaf. Come on, I just want to be formally introduced."

Fran said, "We'll be there!"

"She's got a mouth on 'er," said Ed Vishoolis, "but I like that."

* * *

The house was one of a row of Georgians, distinguishable mostly by the color of their trim. Ed Vishoolis was a skinny man with caved-in cheeks—he looked like he'd been ill—but he stood in the doorway with his chest thrust out and his back stiff. Parker found his "hair" disturbing. Full-headed and interstellar black, it seemed another variation on a theme of recent days: designed not to look like hair but to call attention to itself as a toupee. Steady, boy, Parker told himself, just a bad toupee. Ed was probably wearing it to dress up for his guests, along with his light-blue dress shirt, black suit pants with creases, pointy black shoes, and plenty of Old Spice cologne. The man's smile—blatantly contemptuous and condescending—was harder to dismiss, and Parker wondered what "Mr. Magoo" stories he was recollecting. Ed stopped smiling when he realized Parker was alone on the front porch. "Where are the women?" he demanded.

"They fell asleep in the car." Parker pointed a thumb over his shoulder at the curb behind him, where Fran's blue Omni sat with the motor running and the heat on. He'd locked the car and activated the alarm, surprised he could set it with the motor running. "They've been drinking and they'd be hard to wake. I'm sorry."

"They *both* fell asleep?" Ed asked incredulously.

"Fran fell asleep and as usual Marcy tagged along."

Ed glared at him. "I'll have to verify that. Wait there." He walked through the living room into what sounded like the kitchen, opening and closing drawers. Judging by Parker's view from the front doorway, the house remained as the late Mrs. Vishoolis had decorated it: plastic covers, fake plants, wide-eyed animal figurines.

Ed returned carrying a jumbo flashlight. "Let's check it out," he said, brushing past Parker down the steps. He switched on the light and aimed it at a black mufflerless Firebird coming up the sidestreet, its stereo thumping. A middle finger rose from the passenger side as it sped past.

When they reached the curb Ed peered through the front window and aimed the flashlight; still asleep, Fran averted her face.

The light glided along her thighs.

Parker grabbed Ed's arm, their breaths swirling in the upturned beam. "All right, enough 'verification.' Will you talk to me or not?"

"I'm just trying not to shine it in her face is all." Ed shook loose, surprising Parker with his strength, and aimed at the back seat. "The fat one, she got a boyfriend?"

"Really, Ed, what would Mr. Hoover say?"

The light went out, the white disc imprinted on Parker's vision, Ed's hollow cheeks sucking up darkness. He started back toward the house. "You want to hear what Mr. Hoover thought about *you*? Let's go inside."

* * *

From what Parker had seen of the rest of the house, Ed's study was the only room that didn't show the dead hand of Mrs. Vishoolis. It contained an old walnut roll-top desk, a mahogany liquor cabinet, a leather armchair, a leather couch, bookshelves, a primitive watercolor of the Chicago skyline signed by Ed, and framed autographed photos crowding all four walls. Among the celebrities posing with Ed—who looked handsome with forty more pounds and straightforward hair—Parker recognized the late Mayor Daley, *Sun-Times* columnist Irv Kupcinet, sportscaster Jack Brickhouse, FBI number-two man Clyde Tolson, Fran Allison of the "Kukla, Fran and Ollie Show," and J. Edgar himself—looking, Parker thought, like Mayor Daley compacted to his mean jowly essence.

"Don't sit down yet. Before I tell you anything, I'll have to make sure you're not recording me."

Parker took a step back. "You think I'm 'wearing a wire'? Like on *Miami Vice?*"

"I'm not telling you anything till I frisk you. What's your problem?" Ed rolled his eyes. "Afraid you might like it?"

The search was quick and professional. Ed gestured for him to sit down on the couch and asked what he was drinking.

"Nothing for me, thanks." Parker crossed his ankles and drummed the armrest.

"You'll want a drink," Ed stated.

"All right, gin and tonic," but when his host curled his lip Parker said, "Why don't I have whatever you're having?"

Ed poured them both straight-up whisky, sat down on the armchair, and tapped a finger against his glass. "Where do I begin?"

Recalling Ed's behavior on the phone, Parker wondered whether the man had really brought him here to disclose secrets or whether he just wanted company. "I don't want to rush you, but my friends are outside, and when it comes to explaining things you guys tend to take the scenic route."

"You want the unvarnished truth." Ed smiled pityingly, the alcoholic moistness of his eyes adding to the effect. "Have you heard the expression 'Human kind cannot bear very much reality?' You know who said that, smart guy?"

"T.S. Eliot. You *have* been reading books. Can we get to the point?"

"Right between the eyes, huh?" Parker recalled a similar tone when he asked a Thai waiter for the hottest dish in the house.

He cocked his head, realizing that for the past half minute he'd been hearing the bleat of Fran's car alarm. "Excuse me." He rose from his chair and walked out of the study, heading through the living room for the front door.

"Cold feet?" Ed called after him.

* * *

Fran and Marcy stood a few yards off from the yipping car, hugging themselves and pacing to keep warm. Parker aimed the clicker from the front porch; the car beeped twice and shut up, succeeded by a rush of wind and leaves. The women turned to face him.

"Come on up!" Parker called, his voice unexpectedly loud. "The meaning of everything is about to be disclosed."

Fran and Marcy exchanged dubious glances.

"He's harmless, more or less. Come on," Parker urged, "where's your sense of adventure? Don't you owe it to me," he asked Fran, "to see whether I've been telling you the truth?"

She looked dubious on that count, too, but she started up the walk to the house, Marcy following.

* * *

While Marcy smirked at the living-room furnishings and Fran yawned shudderingly, Parker tried to reason with Ed about searching them. The women had underlined their refusal by standing at the opposite end of the room with their coats buttoned.

"Just put that back where you found it, Miss," Ed barked across the room at Marcy, who'd picked up a yellowing doily from the arm of the couch and was holding it fastidiously between her thumb and forefinger. She returned it to its place, gave it a pat, and slowly backed away from the couch.

Reengaging his host's attention, Parker said, "I don't blame you for trying to get a body search out of the deal, Ed—'a man's reach should exceed his grasp'—but they're not going to change their minds. Look, do you really think they're wearing microphones? Do you suppose they'd've shown up drunk if we knew what we were doing? If you can't be reasonable about this we'll have to leave."

"Tell you what, ladies." Ed feigned reluctance but could barely disguise his avidity. "I'll search your coats and purses." The women exchanged wry looks.

"Is this standard investigative procedure?" Fran wondered. "Do they teach it at the Academy along with panty-sniffing?"

Ed was undeterred. "Strangers see the insides of your purse every time you look for your credit card." Getting no response to that one, he played his strongest hand. "Come on, ladies, don't you want to help your friend?"

Fran unbuttoned her coat, coldly returning Ed's stare. She held out the coat and her purse, trying to make a ten-foot pole of her arm, and Marcy followed.

Ed tried to make a party game out of it. He patted down the women's coats, hung them up and seated his guests round the coffee table, where he did his best to look unmoved as he turned Fran's purse upside down and her things cascaded out—wadded Kleenex, a billfold, lipsticks, a pen, the toy badge, a change purse, a checkbook, a compact, a datebook, and plopping onto the pile last, the microcassette recorder.

"Well well well," clucked Ed, picking it up. "What do we have here? Very clever, except you forgot to turn it on."

"It wasn't on," Fran said slowly and anxiously, "because it wasn't *supposed* to be on. It has nothing to do with you." She rose from her chair; Ed stood up from the couch and held the recorder over his head.

Parker stood up. "Just give it back and let's call it a night."

"People usually use these babies for surveillance," Ed told Fran. "So either you're lying, Missy, or you lead an interesting life."

"It's none of your business, asshole," she said trying to grab it. "It's personal."

That was all Ed needed to hear. Still holding it over his head he switched it on.

Parker stepped between Ed and Fran. "She said it's personal."

"So Jeff!" Fletcher was saying.

"Turn it off." Parker snatched at the recorder.

Ed stepped back and turned up the volume.

"Does Fran know what you're up to?" Parker was asking on the tape. Ed was doing a jig step on tiptoe, waving the machine over his head.

"That I'm trying to ruin your life?" Fletcher's tone was as bland as Parker recalled it. "No."

Parker tugged at the machine, causing Ed to stumble forward, and pulled it free. Fletcher was saying, "Oddly enough, she thought *she* was deceiving *me*," when he pressed stop.

He turned his back on Ed, who was muttering "Okay, sonny boy, let's finish this," and held out the recorder to Fran. She stood rigid in a paralysis of self-control, freckles vivid against her drained face. She stared at the recorder, then took it, never looking at Parker. He extended his arms to hold her and still without meeting his eye she shook her head. It seemed within the realm of possibility that she'd never want to look at him again.

"I'm going out to the car to play the rest of this," she said addressing no one in particular, her voice small. "Please give me a few minutes."

Parker handed her the ring with the car-door key and the clicker. She shook her head at Marcy's offer to come with her. Holding the purse open, she swept her things into it with her flattened palm. Ed brought her her coat and was no doubt trying to think of something to say as she put it on. "I'm sorry," he said, watching her open the door. The wind and the rasping leaves made him raise his voice. "I didn't know it was—'

"Personal?" She gathered the mass of her black hair from beneath her collar and released it to the wind as she brushed past him.

Ed looked pathetically at Marcy. "Tell her I was just teasing."

"I'll wait outside," she said tersely. "Can I have my coat?"

Through the door pane, Parker watched Fran open the passenger side, tilt the seat forward, and stoop into the back. The interior went dark when she closed the door, and he tried to see her face behind a blob of reflected streetlight. "You might as well get mine, too, he said to Ed. "I guess those secrets were so much hot air."

"Think so? Well look at me, smartass. I want to see your face when you hear this hot air. So you want it straight, huh?"

Parker turned to meet Ed's reddening face and malicious grin. "Spit it out, Ed. And the secret is—well, come on!"

"You stand right there, sonny boy. I want to see your face." Ed held up both hands, thumbs extended, and framed Parker's face.

"Here we go round again—except I'm getting off. Just get our coats." Fran was a smudge in the back seat.

"J. Edgar Hoover—" Ed began portentously.

Parker turned from the door pane and put his face close enough to Ed's to see the cracks and stringy veins beneath his eyes. "Yeah? J. Edgar Hoover what?"

Ed stood his ground, exhaling fumes. "You're here, so you must know about the Breather Program, but I'll bet you don't know how you were picked. The Director was looking for some nobody in the antiwar movement."

"I know that."

"*And so,*" Ed continued, "he went through the files looking at photos. I wasn't there—I worked out of the Chicago field office—but I have it on good authority that the director didn't like your face."

Marcy giggled; Ed folded his arms awaiting Parker's reaction.

"So—go on."

"That's it. I guess it hasn't sunk in, aye, sonny boy? Your life was ruined because someone didn't like your face."

Parker let it sink in. "So?"

Ed looked stunned.

"I'm sorry," Parker continued, "but I don't see how that's any worse than if he picked my name at random. What's your point?" He'd come here prepared to face the worst—almost looking forward to it—and he couldn't help feeling disappointed.

"The point is, 'as flies to wanton boys are we to the gods.'"

"Quit reading, Ed. You're going to hurt yourself."

Crestfallen, Ed gave it one last shot. "Don't you understand?" He repeated his secret slowly and emphatically, hoping, perhaps, that italics would drive the point home: "Your whole life *ruined* because *someone didn't like your face.*"

Parker turned to Marcy. "Would you feel worse if you were picked for no reason or because J. Edgar Hoover didn't like your face?"

She shrugged. "Six of one."

Suddenly Parker was slack-limbed with relief: If this is the worst, he thought, I'll have seconds. He was lightheaded enough to feel magnanimous toward Ed, who'd only wanted to be the life of the party. "I'm sure it's a good story, and if I hadn't rushed you—."

"Don't patronize me, sonny boy."

Marcy said, "So the FBI really ruined Jeff's life?"

Ed, who must have decided that the night held no further enticements, was opening the coat closet. He stuck his head around the door. "Yup."

"Um, what didn't he like about Jeff's face?"

"Oh, yeah. He said he looked smug. He looks smug now, wouldn't you say?"

Parker tried to compose his features into perfect neutrality as Marcy studied him. "Not smug, really. A combination of baffled and amused." (Parker knew what was coming next and strove to freeze his face.) "Fran says he looks like a guy who's forgotten the punch line in the middle of a joke."

Ed gave a hacking laugh and brought out their coats, Marcy declining his offer to help her with her sleeves.

Fran's name had brought Parker down to earth and farther. He was anxious to get out to the car, but he paused with his hand on the knob. "One more thing. Why is it still going on?"

Ed blinked and smiled tentatively. "What do you mean?"

"You do know, don't you, that your guy is still on the job?"

"You're pulling my leg!" Ed didn't seem to be feigning his surprise. "The Bureau stopped doing that stuff fifteen years ago."

"Well you'd better get word to your guy. A lot of people know about this, he's calling more and more attention to himself, and it's going to be an embarrassment for all of you. You don't have much time. I don't know what he's planning but it's connected with a convention at the Cermak Arena tomorrow evening."

"I'm retired, you know," Ed said defensively. "Well, okay, I'll talk to some people. See if we can keep Mr. Monroe from making a nuisance of himself. He's kind of a nut, you know."

He shook Parker's hand. "It's the dream of a lifetime to finally meet Mr. Magoo."

"Glad to oblige, I guess."

"I'm sorry we didn't have a chance to get acquainted," Ed Vishoolis said to Marcy; she tightened her grip on her purse strap.

* * *

Parker tilted the rearview mirror till he saw Fran, her face turned to the window, the lights of the Drive streaming up her profile. "How ya doin' back there?" They'd found her stretched out in the back, pretending, he was certain, to be asleep.

Still facing the window she said wearily, "Aside from that, Mrs. Kennedy, how was the ride through Dallas?" Her cheekbones seemed to have come unmoored, tugged by the run of lights and shadows.

Marcy giggled, struggling against her shoulder harness as she turned in her seat. "I always thought he was an asshole," she said.

Sickened at the thought of Fran introducing Ken Fletcher to her friends, Parker tried to put it out of his mind; he wanted to help her get through this.

Marcy said, "Those jackets he wore? Not even real tweed."

Facing her, Fran widened her eyes. "Go on!"

"Fifty-percent polyester."

"If only I'd known!" Fran wailed. They all laughed.

"The pipe?" said Parker, touching the brake to let a van merge. "Bubble!"

"Go on!"

He made an O of his mouth and smacked it with his palm to imitate a bubble popping.

A pause settled in, and Fran returned to the window. Parker followed her gaze across oncoming traffic to the arc-lit deserted beach. She turned from the window and studied the back of his head till she was able to meet his eyes in the mirror. "I'm so sorry, Jeff. Can you forgive me?"

"I forgive you. But I've got to ask—what did you see in that guy?"

"I don't know. I thought he was this wistful, shy…gentle man. He seemed a little lost—"

A catch in her breath made him think she was editing. "Like me?"

She shrugged.

"You thought with the right woman…"

"Uh-huh. My mother said 'never get involved with a man to improve him!'"

"Yeah, but keep working on me."

"You take a lot of shit from me, Parker. That's one thing we'd have to work on. Say, I nearly forgot—what *is* the meaning of everything?"

"J. Edgar Hoover didn't like my face."

"So?"

"Exactly! I'm beginning to think the ultimate metaphysical question isn't 'Why?,' it's 'So?'"

"I see no reason why Ken should sleep peacefully tonight," she said. "I'm going over there. I want to make him look me in the eye and justify what he did."

"Maybe you should think this through."

"All right. I show up. I ring the bell. I keep ringing till he turns up in the doorway in his monogrammed pajamas—"

Marcy sniggered. "Monogrammed pajamas? *Really?*"

"Stitched over the pocket in scroll."

While the women laughed, Parker was distracted by jealousy and by a fleeting sympathy for Fletcher in his silly pajamas.

"So there he is," Fran was saying, "looking sleepy, sensitive, ridiculous, baffled, hopeful, and imperviously innocent. That's when I grab him by the lapels." She seemed to have completed her thought.

"Speaking from experience," Parker observed, "grabbing people by the lapels doesn't do much good. But okay, you've got him by the lapels. *Now* the plan kicks in." The skyline's blinking beacons and levitating windows seemed to wall off the road just ahead.

"What's *your* plan?" she demanded.

"I don't think you should go over there. They've threatened Ken's ex-wife and kids. It's hard to think of him as a violent man, but he'll do anything to protect them. And the people who are trying to hurt me are obviously willing to hurt you to do it. I think whatever they're planning will happen during this convention. It starts tomorrow—why don't you stay at Marcy's for a few days?"

"What good would that do? I still have to go to classes and more interviews tomorrow. Anyway, from what you've told me, these people wouldn't do anything as obvious and comprehensible as attacking me. There's no cause and-effect. They're just as likely to send a pizza to your aunt. And *your* plan is..."

"My plan is to ignore them."

"*Ignore* them?" Marcy snorted.

"Exactly!" he said, realizing he'd acquired this verbal tic from Steve Dobbs.

"I've heard of people dodging a bullet," said Marcy, "but ignoring it?"

"Don't get him started," Fran warned.

He said, "I don't think their plan is all that diabolically complicated. Everything they do is a show staged for my benefit. This whole faceless man campaign is just hype for the finale. They've done all these assessments of my character, and they think they can count on me showing up at the convention out of sheer curiosity—to see how it all turns out. And to tell you the truth..."

"Well, what happens when you get there?" Fran asked impatiently.

"See? They've got you wondering. Do you remember that tablecloth at the seafood restaurant? 'How to catch a lobster?' Or was it a crab? Remember? Basically you set a cage down on the seabed and prop it open with a stick. The lobster or the crab sees the cage, thinks 'Hey, what's that?,' walks in, knocks over the stick, bam! caught!...So: I ignore them."

"What you have isn't a plan, it's denial."

"Exactly! If it'll make you feel less anxious, John Standell...say, did I mention that John and Peg just had a baby? A little girl, Kathryn."

"That's terrific! Give them my best. Let's hope sarcasm isn't inheritable." Fran had never quite forgiven John's crack that she was "merely perfect."

"Anyway, John is sending someone over tomorrow to install the world's most sophisticated security system in my apartment."

"Oh, great! John and his world's most sophisticated security system. He has a little too much fun thinking about it, wouldn't you say? What does it do?"

"It's supposed to work better if I don't know."

Fran groaned. "Don't you worry that your life will depend on it and it'll turn out to be flashing lights and a noise like a whoopee cushion?"

"He has a sense of humor, but he's good at his job," Parker said, beginning to share her doubts. "And he's going to send over a bodyguard tomorrow afternoon. All I have to do is get through the next fifteen hours or so and I'm in the clear...and what's *your* plan?"

Her wet eyes gave her a glint of determination. "My plan: Grab him by the lapels, make him look me in the eye."

* * *

As Parker picked up the phone the next morning he wondered if he'd already lost her. He'd forgiven her—that was the easy part!—*she* had the thankless role of being forgiven. Tolerance Management thought they had it all worked out: He'd forgive her, she'd never want to look at him again.

But he was calling because he'd thought of something worse: Why *wouldn't* his enemies hurt her to get at him? After tense negotiations last night, it was agreed that Marcy would go over to Fletcher's with Fran and wait on the landing in front of his apartment door. After five minutes Marcy would start screaming. In return for that modicum of reassurance, Parker agreed to be dropped off first and butt out. It was the best he could get, and even if he'd physically restrained her that night, what could he do then? Maybe he still hadn't *really* believed Fletcher was capable of violence.

He pictured her furious march up Fletcher's sidewalk at one in the morning, eyes narrowed, lips compressed, hair flying, a burst of heels ricocheting off the darkened brownstones.

"Hi, it's me," he said breezily when her answering machine came on. The prospect of confiding his fears to her machine suddenly made them seem ridiculous. "Could you call me? So...how 'bout those Bears!"

He ate a bowl of Cheerios as he thumbed through the *Tribune*, looking for anything on the convention. It would be easier to ignore, he reasoned, if he had a clearer idea of what it was. He found the disguised men on page one of the Metro section—a crowd of them in full hardboiled glory, the flashbulb twinkling in their mirror lenses. The story was headlined FACE US! and subheaded, ANONYMOUS AND IN-YOUR-FACE: THE LEGION OF FACELESS MEN CONVENES IN CHICAGO TODAY.

The only facts he could gather were that the convention would commence at six today, that all members of the public who shared the Legion's goals were invited, that Chicago merchants were running out of trenchcoats and mirror sunglasses, and that the Legion's cause was sweeping the nation. The writer was as clueless about that cause as Parker, and so most of the article played variations on "They represent the little guy." The participants seemed equally incapable of articulating why they were there. From their quotes it was hard to discern their common grievance, if they had one, but mainly they didn't sound like the traditional victims—the poor, the persecuted, the dispossessed. They sounded, Parker thought, like the nebulously peeved. They'd awakened one fine morning to find that they were disappointed. It had something to do with feeling shut out, ignored, thwarted, rendered invisible by the... what?...by those pointyhead bureaucrats, those big-shots up there in their big...and so forth.

He was wondering what any of this had to do with him, suspecting that that was what his enemies wanted, and vowing that any minute he'd stop thinking about it, when the installer arrived lugging two huge cases. A fat young bearded guy with scant hair combed like guitar strings, the installer plunked down the cases and identified himself. The beard made Parker uneasy, but it was the same black as the hair, anchored firmly to the face, and didn't point at an experimental angle.

"I'll have a look around," said the installer, heading toward the back door. Unzipping his jacket he tapped the right-hand wall a few feet from the door, where a vertical rectangular outline could be made out beneath the white paint.

"I think that used to be a fuse box," said Parker, who'd tagged along hoping to strike up a conversation and glean something about the world's most sophisticated security system. "I guess these old buildings..."

The man's glare let Parker know that his assistance was not required, so he returned to his Cheerios and his article. A spokesman for the Legion wished to stress that people of all races, religions, ideologies, and genders were invited, and that the first order of business would be ratifying the new name, The Legion of Faceless Men and Women. Parker skipped back to interviews with participants—more about the little guy. The little fella was taking it on the chin, all right, but he wasn't down for the count: He was fighting back, sending a message to the elites with their giant desks and their sissy dogs and...and...

Parker wondered if this could be the start of an actual mass movement and recalled Harry Krell's prediction: "The next upheaval won't be the underclass; it'll be the people who feel like they're being nibbled to death by minnows."

But a few of the subjects interviewed brought something extra to the party. In a paragraph headed, "The convention truly attracts all kinds," the writer quoted those populists who wore tinfoil hats to evade thought control; who spoke of Them with a looming capital "T." Parker thought of the guy who'd shown Fran his toy badge. The convention seemed shapeless enough to accommodate every kind of free-floating grudge.

From the back he could hear a hammer-and-chisel and falling paint chips. He finished the article and read through the rest of the paper, then cleared the dishes and replaced them with his students' essays. As his pen hovered over the sentence, "Divorce has many causes; therefore this problem cannot be solved," a teeth-drilling screech of feedback made him sit up straight. He continued to grade through pounding, clanking, and bursts of feedback.

When he tried to sneak a peek on his way to the bathroom, the installer, crunching newspaper and paint chips as he moved, positioned himself to block the view. The guy had taken off his jacket, and white dust sprinkled his jeans and denim shirt. He jumped back into place as Parker came out, blocking a glimpse of littered wires and springs and the dark interior of the open panel.

"Would you like a sandwich? a beer?" Parker leaned to one side, mirrored by the installer, who was trying to fill his sight. (The man shook his head.) "I don't suppose I could—"

"John thinks it'll work better if you don't know what it does." The installer wiped his hands on a rag. "But okay, if you've got a minute you can help me test one thing. You go in there," he pointed to the living room, "I'll be right out."

Parker went to the couch and sat down. He placed his right ankle on his left thigh, clamped his folded hands over his knee, and drew a breath. "Whenever you're ready."

The installer came out carrying a speaker the size of a tabletop radio's; a cord attached to the speaker played out till he stopped in front of the couch. "I'm going to test the subliminals."

"Did you say subliminals?" Parker recalled the Doomsday Baby and thought his worst fears were being realized: John had contrived something whimsical and complicated. "I always thought that stuff didn't work. I heard that scientists..."

Grinning, the installer began to recite the words in unison with Parker: "...tested subliminal advertising back in the fifties and the early sixties."

Parker stopped and stared. "And..." He waited for the installer to provide the next word.

"it's..."

They completed the sentence together: "...all bunk!"

"Wow!" Parker laughed. "You mean *that* was subliminal advertising?"

"Yup. They've been running that one on TV and radio for years."

The installer set the speaker on the floor and returned to the back. A few seconds later the speaker emitted a scratchy rendition of Glen Miller's "In the Mood."

The installer poked his head round the corner. "What are you feeling?"

"Thirsty," Parker said.

"Great. Test completed."

"Wait!"

The installer's head reappeared.

Ignoring an expression he'd seen countless times before—the look that means, "This job would be great if I wasn't for the damn *people*"— Parker said, "I'm going to hear the same subliminal message as my intruder...should I be wearing earplugs or something?"

The installer ran a hand over his skull, smoothing down his hairs. "No."

Parker tried to think it through. "I suppose it could still work if the message was something like 'go to sleep.'"

"You're thinking of hypnosis. Subliminals don't work that way."

"Let's see. It could still get the job done if it says 'run away' and we both run away, or 'turn yourself in to the police' and we both—"

"Specific subliminal commands are hit-and-miss; they don't *work* that *precisely*. The subliminals here aren't that kind, and they're only a small part of the system. Okay?"

"Something along the lines of 'Save the babies'?"

The installer's face disclosed nothing but his impatience. "Look. If you're having second thoughts, I could still pack it up."

"Wait! Just answer this." Parker stood up. "If your life depended on having the world's ultimate security system, would you trust this one?"

"Ultimate security," said the installer, "means something different for everyone. John thinks this is the ultimate security for you. Of course if you don't trust John..."

"John's a genius and my best friend. There's no one I'd trust more to get me through this." Hearing himself make the choice calmed Parker down. The installer went back to work. Parker went back to grading with his faith restored, except for one bad moment when what sounded like a giant spring uncoiled with a cartoonish BOING!

* * *

When he'd finished grading he decided to go teach his class as usual. In part it was an act of defiance—"You know where to find me, bastards!," etc.—but the installer wouldn't be done for hours, the bodyguard wasn't due till five, and he'd probably be just as safe at work. He could have hidden out for a while but thought the best survival tactic might be mindless adherence to routine.

Looking out the window of the El, he worked on his protective obtuseness. The train made it easier, the crush of strangers and the rhythm of the ride creating a near-trance state of their own. He tried to fix on the bright vacancy beyond his smeared reflection and the blinking rush of trees.

As usual he had the feeling people were staring, and he concentrated, if that was the word, on ignoring it, until a shape in his peripheral vision leaned across the shape on the seat next to him, and a woman's voice asked if he was Jeffrey Parker. He couldn't manage to snip her out of the world, as he had the man in the restaurant, and he felt like he was merely being rude as he continued to stare out the window. After she'd gone the feeling of people staring remained. He tried to recall a time when he could count on reassuring himself by having a look.

The prospect that what he'd see would not be reassuring finally made it impossible not to look. He saw his own face on the front page of a newspaper held open above the first of the backward-moving seats.

It was Steve Dobbs' tabloid, *The Exhibitionist*. The headline read, PROFESSOR PLAGUED BY VAGUE FORCES. He and his image on the front page regarded each other with mutual puzzlement. He couldn't tell when the photo had been taken but made a note that if he lived through the day he'd shave off the damn mustache. For decades he'd barely noticed it—shaved around it, flicked off crumbs, and otherwise forgot it was there. At the time he'd grown it, he'd supposed it made him look like a gloomily sensitive Eastern European intellectual; he looked like the last man in the disco.

He wondered what else he'd missed during all the years he hadn't been paying attention and realized that today might be his last chance to find out. But he couldn't afford to be the sort of doomed man who sees things as if for the first time. He believed that all the while he'd been missing everything, he'd been learning precisely how to survive this day.

A woman's face appeared over the top of *The Exhibitionist* and caught him looking. He turned back to the window after noting she was more presentable than he expected Steve's readers to be—stratospheric eyes behind big designer frames, short springy blond hairdo. He supposed this was the one he'd snubbed, and here she was coming up the aisle, probably to call him an asshole. He had it coming, so he resisted taking refuge in the window. She was turning sideways to squeeze through the crowd, grabbing a pole as the train lurched.

She carried a briefcase and had on an expensive tan overcoat unbuttoned over the sort of navy-blue power suit Fran wore. He tried to account for the intensity of her smile and didn't rule out the possibility that she was insane. "You *are* Jeffrey Parker!"

The guy next to him—a skinny black teenager in a Cubs cap—drew back his head to check out this Jeffrey Parker: Big deal.

"My name is Natalie Westerman. I was just reading about you!" They shook hands over Parker's seatmate. "When I think of everything you've faced…I don't think I'd have had the courage."

He thought of replying, "It doesn't take courage to 'face' a pie when there's no time to duck. Anyway, I wasn't paying attention." But, susceptible to the praise of attractive women, he allowed his silence to be taken for modesty.

"I suppose they say 'vague forces' because it involves powerful people behind the scenes?" The breathlessness in her voice was suddenly familiar. She was a fan. He recalled the fawning secretary at Tolerance Management and wondered if he was about to become the latest celebrity-victim. There'd been a good deal written lately about the blurring of victims and heroes; if pressed by Natalie Westerman he thought he might observe that a victim is just a hero without means.

"May I see that?" he asked, and she handed across the paper.

The threats against Steve Dobbs and his family had served their purpose; the article contained not one detail. Its impenetrable style veered between pseudoscientific abstraction ("Parker lives in a realm between causality and casualty") and Celtic Twilight lyricism ("his leaden, dove-gray days"). Poor Steve!

"I suppose you'd like me to sign that?"

"Oh yes, please!"

He signed "Vaguely, Jeff Parker" and handed back the paper. A dozen more people pressed around him, some holding copies of *The Exhibitionist.*

"I couldn't help feeling a connection as I read your story," said Natalie Westerman. "I know this sounds odd but I kept thinking—"

"—the same thing happened to you?"

"Why yes!"

"Me too!" said an old man in a leather cap with dangling chinstraps. There were murmurs of assent.

"Not exactly the *same* thing." Natalie Westerman narrowed her eyes in the effort to express her meaning. "But I kept thinking there was a connection...that what happened to you somehow..." People around her said "Yeah!" and "Me too!"

He'd thought his story would be greeted a tad more skeptically. People seemed eager to believe it—believed it, considering that the article was hopelessly obscure, without knowing what it was. Perhaps it confirmed something they'd always suspected and had only been waiting for permission to express: They, too, had been forced to eat a peck of dirt.

"Do you believe everything you read in *The Exhibitionist*?" Parker asked Natalie.

"Of course not! We pass it around the office for laughs, but then you start thinking. Of course some of it is just too dreadful to—"

"The dreadful has already happened," said a voice behind Parker, so deep it seemed to come up from the rumbling floor of the car. The voice-of-doom delivery left no doubt what he'd find in the seat behind him, but he couldn't resist the impulse to show off for his fans.

He turned to face the usual props in the latest incarnation. "Ah, there you are!" he said to the faceless man and smoothed down his hair in the mirror lenses. "At least you're quoting Heidegger. Classing up the act?"

"No, man, it's the Legion." This one had long greasy pale-blond hair and a brown beard; he reached into his trenchcoat pocket and unfolded a yellow flyer, which he held up for Parker and the crowd.

**The Dreadful Has Already
Happened!**

What are you going to do about it?
Come to the Legion of Faceless Men Convention
Today! 6 P.M., Anton J. Cermak Arena

Addressing the crowd, the disguised man said, "It's today at six o'clock, folks, and you're all welcome. What you people are talking about—that's just the sorta thing we're fighting."

In the mirror lenses Parker watched himself run a thumb over his mustache. "What do you think, Natalie? Deep-six the mustache?"

"Jeff, it's an honor," said the faceless man. "Your fight is ours, man. It would be righteous if you'd come speak to us tonight."

"And what if I don't? What if I just don't go?" It was the question Parker had been asking himself for days. He gave his mirrored face a sardonic expression, hardening every feature, but his fear seemed to leak out of the cracks. "Let me put it this way. I'm not going."

"Then we'll all fight the good fight in our separate ways, but I just want you to know, man, we're with you."

"You certainly are with me—every time I turn around."

"Yeah!" said the people in the aisle, cheering whatever they thought he'd said. "Right!" "Damn straight!" They looked angry and mildly disoriented; it was only just dawning on them that the dreadful had already happened.

* * *

As they pulled into the terminal he wondered what his mom would say if he told her about the vague forces and the faceless men. Perhaps she'd say, "The world doesn't revolve around you, Mr. Bigshot." *The world doesn't revolve around you, Mr. Bigshot.* It seemed a perfect mantra to keep his mind constricted, and he recited it under his breath as he stepped off the train.

* * *

He arrived for class early, but most of his students were already there, copies of *The Exhibitionist* in hand, each no doubt awaiting a chance to confide, "The same thing happened to me!" Adele Slansky had been given a wide berth at the seminar table. It was the first time he'd seen her since the bad-smell incident, and her glittering furious eyes, tremendous behind their cataract lenses, reminded him of those rogue comets which, according to a recent *Nova*, periodically destroy all life on earth. He'd phoned her after the incident and tried to convince her that he wasn't the enemy, but her perfectly civil replies were delivered in the tone of someone who says "Have a nice day!" in lieu of throwing a punch.

"Mrs. Slansky," he'd reminded her that night on the phone, "I've known you my whole life."

"Yes, dear, and *I know you.*"

"Surely you don't think—"

"Of course not, Jeffrey. Now why would I believe any such thing, hmmm?"

"The same people who hurt you are trying to hurt me. I think we ought to share what we know."

"Yes, Jeffrey, I'm sure you know my enemies quite well. I'd love to go on chatting, but I'm in the middle of dinner, and you wouldn't want to interrupt my meal, *would you*? Say hello to your mother, dear!"

Taking his place at the head of the seminar table, he braced himself to try again. "How are you feeling today, Mrs. Slansky?"

"How do I feel? Why thank you for asking, dear. I feel just fine." The magnified ice balls blazed toward collision with the earth.

Just before class began, John Connor Murray walked in and seated himself next to Mrs. Slansky. "I hope you don't mind my sitting in. Adele and I are going to the convention today." Instead of the usual white carnation, he was wearing a red rose in his buttonhole. "We have a rendezvous with destiny, young Parker. Shall we split a cab?" Jack expressed destiny with pop eyes and a dropped jaw. And when Parker shook his head dismissively, he goggled his disappointment. Jack turned to Mrs. Slansky, and the two paranoids whispered in the manner of conspirators: nudges, chuckles, sideways glances.

Was it possible that these two were an item? Mrs. Slansky was in her seventies, more than ten years older than Jack, and she'd been weakened by her stroke, while Jack seemed in furiously good health. The last time Parker had seen them together they'd been agreeing that the manager of the Oakton Theater would, if he could, have made Mrs. Slansky dig her own grave. Could mutual paranoia be the basis for romance? It would confirm certain clichés, Parker thought: Love as a conspiracy of two, the purest form of Us Against Them. Parker was jealous, recalling the disdain with which Fran said, "Your conspiracy." The thought of these two as a couple seemed endearing, though he was doing his best not to picture it too clearly.

He knew he was focusing on gossipy speculation to keep his fears at bay. But if he was hoping to change the subject when class began, his students were having none of it. His complainers wanted to talk about vague forces and faceless men and the little guy. He forbade several students from donning the fake beards and mirror sunglasses that 7-Eleven was handing out free with a ten-dollar purchase. But when Steve Margolis suggested that Parker, having fought the vague forces, was just the sort of role model the Legion was looking for, Parker blew up. "Haven't I taught you people anything?"

Continuing in a gentler tone, he urged his complainers to check their sources, define their terms. He warned them against mistaking slogans for arguments, spite for grievance, cattle prods for the still small voice. He reminded them what they ought to have learned after nine weeks of listening to one another's complaints: that self-pity is funny. That from the moment they slap your ass in the delivery room you have your complaint, and it was easy to mistake it for your cause. He'd been hoping—just in case this proved to be his last class—to leave his students with a Mr. Chips valedictory, but judging by the expressions of puzzlement around the table, he wasn't carrying it off. He knew that his arguments for logic, empiricism, and common sense were coming out in a giddy adrenaline rush. But he couldn't stop now, he was on a roll, and he went on to analyze the phrases of the Legion and the *Exhibition-ist*. Vague forces—what were *those*? The little guy—who was *he*? The elites—who were *they*, and why couldn't some of them be little? As for this plot against him—if there was such a plot, why did the article name no other names, no dates, no sources? He attacked the article so exuberantly that it was only at the end of class that he remembered it was true. Turning down offers to carpool to the convention, he shot out the door. All he wanted now was to pick up his mail, go home, watch TV with his bodyguard, and if necessary watch the world's most sophisticated security system do its stuff.

"The world doesn't revolve around you, Mr. Bigshot," he recited under his breath, buoyed through the crowd in the hall on waves of protective obtuseness. "Hello, Andrea!" he sang to the receptionist as he picked up his mail, and Andrea—a tiny brunette with a ponytail and purple fingernails—handed him a phone message. He read it and stepped back toward the mailboxes, trying to slow down his thoughts. He reread it as people brushed past him reaching for their mail. The worst he could imagine had happened, and all he could do was pay attention. He kept rereading the message, filling himself to the brim. He got to his office somehow, locked the door, and went on rereading the message.

* * *

Compulsively he lowered his eyes to his desk blotter and reread the note he knew by heart. "Hank Monroe, Jr. and Fran will meet you at the opening of the convention at 6. They'll have you paged. Fran would prefer that you don't bring anyone else." The implications—I have Fran, don't bring the police—were clear enough to Parker, but phrased euphemistically enough to inspire no sense of urgency if he did involve the police. And if he didn't come up with a severely edited version of what was going on, it might be impossible to involve the police at all. He checked his clock radio: ten to four; he'd leave himself a full ninety minutes to get there. The best thing to do, he decided, was go there alone and phone 911 just before he went in—a bomb threat if he couldn't think of anything else.

He stared as if to unravel more from the bunched narrow loops of the receptionist, who couldn't remember whether the caller (a man) had a Southern drawl—let alone a fake Southern drawl. He closed his eyes, the vibration of a mufflerless car in the lot passing through him like a mild electric shock.

For the second time in five minutes he called Fran. He'd been holding down his panic with the thought that she wasn't really a hostage—that Monroe, Jr. knew her schedule and knew she'd be unreachable by phone all afternoon. Her machine came on; he said, "Call me at my office—urgent," broke the connection, got Marcy's number from directory assistance, punched it. While it rang he looked at his briefcase, his books, the collapsing heaps of papers on his desk, cars in the lot glistening under a drizzle—all of it so prosaic, so authentically dull he'd mistaken it for his real life.

Marcy wasn't answering, so he called the law school. By pretending to be Fran's brother and referring vaguely to a family emergency, he managed to get her schedule: Her last class of the day had ended at two, an hour ago. On a long shot he asked the secretary if she could tell him where Fran was interviewing that day. For some reason she couldn't grasp the question and he had to keep rephrasing it. "You mean, you'd like a list of all the firms who interview our students?" she asked on his third attempt. Perhaps he was more distraught than he realized. He managed to get the idea across on his next try. She summed up: "You want to know *if we keep a schedule of Fran's interviews?*" "Yes!" he exclaimed, relieved that he was still capable of communicating even a stupid question. "Now why would we do that?" she asked, her drawl and her temper intensifying as she told Parker that she and Fran had discussed their families and she recalled now that Fran had mentioned three sisters but never a brother. He hung up and phoned Fran again.

"If you can't reach me, get out of there," he said at the beep. "Go stay with a friend. They sent me a threatening note, and I think they might be coming after you. And don't tell me there's no Them!" It occurred to him that he couldn't help arguing even with her answering machine, and that he was anticipating objections she was past making. He thought of adding, "I just hope there's an Us," but it didn't seem like the moment. A new scenario occurred to him. "If you got a phone message from the law school receptionist about meeting me at the convention, ignore it, it wasn't from me. And for Godsake don't go!"

The phone rang as he set it on its cradle. To his shouted "Yes!" John Standell replied, "Jeez. The world's most sophisticated security system," he announced with a flourish, "is now operational. If you're desperate, press the red button under the light switch in the living room or the bedroom. Say, buddy—don't get curious. Uh, the bodyguard will be at your place between five and six. Stay on your toes till then and the two of you can crack open some beers, put on the news, and laugh at the guys in the funny beards."

Parker filled him in.

John thought about it. "Oh, shit. Do you have a picture of Fran?"

"Yeah, but—"

"Fax it. They've got a fax there, right?" (Parker said yes and wrote down the number John dictated.) "Okay, the bodyguard will meet you at the convention. There won't be time for him to get to Skokie and then for the two of you to get downtown by six. I'll have him leave as soon as your fax comes in." Some people display their sensitivities in a crisis; John went to the War Room. "Maybe he can find Fran and your pal before you get there. Fran's pretty noticeable—hope she has her hair down. So anyway, page Todd when you get there."

"This is Todd Woolcurt who went with me to Tolerance Management? Who was so proud of existing and then didn't?"

"Todd told me about what happened last time, and he's sorry. He was watching the door of that room you were in when a guy walked up and asked him if he'd mind answering a few questions— market research, the guy said. Todd said he didn't care, as long as he could keep watching the door."

"Okay. Could we—"

"So the guy's asking Todd about his car, his clothes, his hobbies, favorite movies, and suddenly Todd's nervous. I mean, Todd doesn't *get* nervous, and he's scared of a guy with a clipboard. He ran out of there— still gets headaches and ringing in his ears. I don't know what they did to him, but you said these guys study how much crap people can take. I guess they have ways we've never heard of to dish it out. So, anyhow, Todd's a good guy and he wants to make it up to you."

"He'll have to do more than exist this time—though he even flubbed that."

"This time it's the whole package. Like I said, he wants to make it up to you. The fact that he fucked up last time makes him even more reliable this time."

"I dunno, John. I wouldn't try that one on a résumé."

John laughed. "To tell you the truth, I didn't have much time to line this up and Todd's the only one available...You know what? I think I'll come down with Todd."

"I appreciate that, but I'm supposed to go alone. How will it look if I've got a Michael Jordan lookalike *and* the Wonder Bread Boy for bookends?" Parker had decided that if there were no other way to keep his enemies from killing Fran, he'd force them to kill him instead. He didn't want to have to figure *John's* life into the calculus. "Thanks, pal, but go home. Some guys'll do anything to avoid changing diapers. Oh, uh—"

Parker stood up. Ken Fletcher was walking briskly between parked cars toward the building, briefcase stuffed under the arm of his raincoat, jaw bulging around his pipe, smoke like a frazzled thought balloon scattering round his head. He caught sight of Parker, averted his eyes and increased his stride.

"Call you back!" Parker made it out the door and round the turn in the hallway in time to spot Fletcher's retreating back.

* * *

"Ken!"

Fletcher stopped, turned, waved, pointed to his watch, and bolted. Parker ran after him, dodging through the crowd coming out of the classrooms. Ken had a quick, surprisingly graceful stride—prep school track, Parker recalled—and would have had time to lock himself in his office if he didn't have to pat himself down for his keys. Parker just managed to block the closing door and pushing against it gasped, "C'mon, Ken,

I just..." He gave it his shoulder, and to his surprise Fletcher stumbled backward.

Backed up against his desk, Ken reached into his raincoat pocket and aimed a small blue-black barrel which in a moment of utter confusion Parker recognized as the lighter he'd seen in Jan Cohen's office.

"Well, as long as you're here, Jeff, have a seat." Keeping the thing aimed, Fletcher picked his pipe off the floor, set it on the blotter, stamped out some live ashes on the linoleum, backed around the desk, pushed a shock of damp hair off his forehead, and sat down. "We've got to stop meeting like this," he quipped nervously, his smile waning. He held the grip with both hands as he had the last time, but this time he didn't put it down. He was probably doing what Parker had done in his position—frantically reviewing his cop shows. It was out of the question that this doofus with a lighter trembling in his fists had anything to do with kidnapping Fran.

"That's not a gun, it's a lighter," Parker said. "So be careful."

"If that's a witticism, I'll have to analyze it later." Fletcher looked awful—eyeballs blood-rimmed and -splintered, the lines in his brow gouging deeper. "Will you kindly sit down?" He gestured with the barrel at the chair in front of his desk.

Parker had remained standing. "There's a flame regulator on the handle and a hole on top of the barrel."

"That's the oldest trick in the..." Fletcher nonetheless glanced down. "Oh." Failing to elicit any sympathy with his sheepish look, he clamped the dead pipe in his mouth. "Last time—was that—?"

"Last time was a gun. Where'd you get the lighter?"

Fletcher unbuttoned his raincoat, shrugged it onto the back of his chair, and tugged at the sleeve of his tweed jacket, aligning it with his cuff. "When my angry friend—John Connor Murray?—gave me the gun last time he said something about 'keeping a spare' under some file folders in Jan Cohen's desk. The nuts you turned loose on me keep calling, so yesterday I snuck in there and took it. And when I saw you coming with that agitated look, I thought...I thought some firepower might keep things collegial. Sorry. Why did he keep a lighter there? Forget it, I don't want to know." He turned the "gun" sideways and held it over the remains in his pipe.

"Hold it!" Parker yelled; Ken froze. "Jack had it turned up to the Jerry Lewis setting. Just put the thing down, okay?" While Ken knit his eyebrows at the lighter, and placed it, slowly, next to the phone, Parker sat down, leaning his forearms on the desk. "Where's Fran?"

Fletcher was hauling out his other lighter, his tobacco, his tamper. "The last time I saw Frances was at one this morning." He kept his eyes on the filling of his pipe. "I answered the doorbell and she grabbed me—not a word, just stood there for a full minute with my pajama front in her fists, glowering, then walked away." He actually winced at the recollection—whether out of shame or because Fran had scared him wasn't clear. "I gather you found some way to make her believe you?" Fletcher sucked in the flame of his lighter and expelled smoke through a bleary close-lipped smile. "I don't suppose she'll let me speak to her again, but tell her I've never been so ashamed of anything I've done. I do care about her, you know."

"Swell. Where is she?"

"I don't know. If she's done with classes maybe the library. I think she might be interviewing this week. Why?"

Parker told him about the note, and, watching the space between his eyes tighten, thought this was the first he'd heard of it.

"Oh, God," Fletcher whispered.

"You can help her," Parker said, "by telling me everything you know about this convention. I'm going to assume that you're a decent guy who was just trying to protect his family and that you'll tell me the truth. I might as well—I doubt if I can scare you more than they can."

"All right." Fletcher set his pipe on the ashtray, touched his palms together and picked it up. "I suppose *you* got a call last night, too?"

"What are you talking about?"

"Mr. Hank Monroe, Junior is on the warpath. Someone's been speaking to the FBI about him. They paid him a visit last night, and now *he's* threatening *us*. Even Harry Krell's plain scared—I mean scared without seven kinds of ambiguity and nine kinds of irony." He'd been holding the pipestem in front of his mouth; he emptied the bowl, clanging it against the ashtray, and dropped the pipe into his side pocket.

"What about the convention?" Parker asked. There was no time to be paralyzed by the thought that his own actions—the visit to Ed Vishoolis, the threat to embarrass the FBI—might have driven Fran's kidnapper into a rage. "What's the point?"

"I don't know. Maybe Hank Monroe, Junior has nothing to do with it."

"Maybe pigs fly!"

"He's made use of it, of course, starting with the night he improvised that story about his face. But if he's behind the convention, I've heard nothing about it."

"I've been seeing these men everywhere I go."

"Everyone sees them everywhere; they're all over town."

Hadn't they already had this discussion?

"Then why," Parker asked, "is he so anxious to get me there?"

"From what I know about him I can make an informed guess. Jeff, I'm so sorry I had any part in this. I think of you and Fran as my friends. I've concentrated on my work since the divorce, and you're really the only—"

"If my family was being threatened," said Parker, conscious that this might be his last opportunity for an act of charity, "I might have done the same thing. I don't think you're a bad man. What," he added immediately, embarrassed to see to the other man gulping tears, "is your educated guess?"

Fletcher tried to cover with another of his wan smiles. Looking at him for what was probably the last time, Parker noticed that whenever Ken smiled he looked ill at ease, as if trying to get across in barely recollected scraps of a foreign language.

Fletcher said, "Our man likes to put on a show. I think it appeals to his sense of humor to commit a murder whose only witnesses are the thousands of identically disguised suspects."

* * *

In his office he buttoned up Fletcher's raincoat and checked himself out in the closet mirror. The lighter-gun in the flap pocket, the next-best thing to the real gun he'd left in Steve Dobbs' glove compartment, didn't present a conspicuous outline. Considering that all he'd done with the real thing was point it at people who didn't take him seriously anyway, the lighter would probably serve just as well. He believed it would look convincing to anyone who didn't examine it closely or wasn't expecting a fake. And it might make an actual weapon if the enemy were sporting enough to stand still and be ignited. He supposed this breezy interior monologue was another form of protective obtuseness; well, it seemed to be keeping his dread manageable, like not looking down from a height.

Fastidious about his clothes, Ken had given up the coat without protest but with obvious distaste. He'd thought it over just long enough to avoid being reminded that he'd ruined Parker's life and at the very least owed him a fucking *raincoat*. He'd looked equally pained in turn as he squirmed into Parker's coat.

Ken's raincoat—a pricey tan Thornhill & Thornhill—was a bit roomy in the shoulders, but Parker was conscious of coming out ahead in the trade. He tried to recall the distinction between a raincoat and a trenchcoat. A trenchcoat, he believed, was a baggy raincoat. The Thornhill & Thornhill looked a bit upscale compared to the grungy trenchcoats he'd been seeing. The important thing, he supposed, was to look like a man in disguise; he'd fit right in once he had his beard and sunglasses. Shut up, he thought, stop prattling.

He pushed the closet door till the room in the mirror was empty and tried to assure himself that not existing would be as easy as that.

There was a knock at the office door; he gripped the lighter in his coat pocket as he turned the knob.

"It's time for us so-called paranoids to stand together," said John Connor Murray. "Let's prove that even a paranoid's enemies can have real enemies." He wore his own Thornhill & Thornhill unbuttoned over his blue blazer. At his side, Mrs. Slansky wore a baggy discount-store knockoff. She stared at Parker voraciously, determined to let nothing he did escape her.

Parker decided to split a cab with them—he wasn't going to stake Fran's life on the CTA—and lose them at the convention. "Okay. Let's go."

Jack looked disappointed, gassed up with arguments he couldn't use now.

Parker had always suspected that Jack didn't truly believe his own paranoia; that his rants about Lionel Trilling were just a way to let off steam, Jack having stored up more rancor than the real world had provocations. Then why was he going to the convention? Even if he *were* nuts, he was still a snob, and he surely found the Legion's populism offensive. So he must have been accommodating Mrs. Slansky's genuine paranoia—letting his date pick reality.

Outside it was still drizzling. As Mrs. Slansky unfolded her plastic rain hat, Jack produced a collapsible umbrella from his briefcase and snapped it open smartly above her head.

She put up her collar. "Is this how they wear it? Like in the movies?" The coat was too big; she must have bought it before her illness. If you squinted, Mrs. Slansky—with her moist inflated eyes, her blazing make-up, her slack hollow face looking tiny in the coat and collar—resembled a child playing dress-up. "What do you think, Jeffrey?"

"I think up," he said, raising his own collar. He still had no plan.

Jack transferred the umbrella to his other hand while he straight-ened out her collar. "There. Now we're cool." Bound by iron laws of nattiness, he kept his own collar down.

They cut across the lot toward Oakton, the plinked cars sounding like a glum steel band. Wondering if Jack was sane and sober enough to be of help, Parker ventured, "Lionel Trilling's dead, you know."

"Stipulated," Jack sang merrily and smiled at his friend. She gave his arm a squeeze; they were headed for their Woodstock.

Mrs. Slansky lowered her voice confidingly. "You know who looked good in a trenchcoat? Lawrence Tierney."

"Toughest guy in the movies," Jack recalled.

"Gable? You can have him. My friends and I all thought Lawrence Tierney was so handsome." She might have been blushing if her cheeks weren't already bright orange. "You know who looked like Lawrence Tierny? My Harry. Don't you think so, Jeffrey?"

The late Harry Slansky was a short round Jewish guy who smoked nox-ious cheap cigars and bore as much resemblance to Lawrence Tierney as he did to, oh, fill in the blank. But she was looking up at Parker with a girlish smile he found both scary and touching. "Now that you mention it."

"Jeff!"

A few yards ahead Steve Dobbs was getting out of his BMW. No sissy Thornhill & Thornhill for Steve; he wore a real trenchcoat, the funky kind Mike Hammer would surely get up from the gutter in after a beating. His two shiners from the brawl at Circle Campus were the same shade as Parker's. He grinned as Parker came closer, touching the discoloration under one eye. "You and I could be a rock act." The frizz on his head was strung with glittering drops.

He nodded at Jack and Mrs. Slansky. Jack was too self-absorbed, apparently, to note the coincidence of the black eyes. But Mrs. Slansky looked cannily from Parker to Steve and back to Parker; she was onto his little tricks.

"What are you doing here?" Parker didn't wait for an answer. "I see you're dressed for the convention. What do you know?"

"I'm covering it for *The Exhibitionist.* That reminds me. I'm sorry the article..."

"The convention, Steve?"

"All I know about the convention is that they dress like your guy—so there must be a connection—and that people like these..." He searched for a phrase adequate to his contempt.

"...give the paranoid community a bad name," Parker said to get him off it.

"Yeah. Anyway, I was visiting my dad and my stepmother and I thought I'd see how you're doing—thought maybe you'd have some idea what's going on. Don't tell me *you're* going? You couldn't be that..."

Parker led him by the arm down the row of cars and when they were out of earshot filled him in.

"Well, let's go!" Dobbs said without skipping a beat, propelled by all his hunched-up energy, and they were in the car—Mrs. Slansky in front, Jack and Parker in the back—before Parker thought to ask about the gun.

As they pulled onto Oakton Dobbs held up his middle finger, parrying the horn-blast behind them. "Let's see if we can get something on the convention." He turned on the radio and stabbed buttons.

Mrs. Slansky covered her ears at the detonations of music and speech. "Would you please?" she shouted.

"Steve," said Parker when Dobbs had turned down the news station, "remember that item I asked you to get rid of?"

"Oh, shit. It's still in the glove compartment. Guess I was a little slap-happy that night."

Parker thought it wise to say no more about it till Jack and Mrs. Slansky were out of the car.

Mrs. Slansky turned in her seat and regarded him; he endured her stare till he felt compelled to speak.

"Shouldn't you have your belt on?"

She said, "I was just remembering how you were as a little boy. I used to give him a quarter," she told Jack, "for knowing all the state capitals. Your mother was always showing you off. She'd say, 'Jeffrey, where's Alaska? What's an electron?' Oh, and you'd look so serious answering. A real little man. Your mother was so proud. You know, I'll bet that was the problem. She spoiled you."

Inhaling a compound of damp coats and makeup, he waited for her to commence bouncing off the roof. He couldn't afford to squander energy on this.

"My doctors told me what you did." She pushed up her glasses to wipe away tears, her voice cracking. "Do you hate me that much?"

"I don't hate you, Adele."

"I keep trying to remember something I did. When you were little you couldn't say 'nuclear.' I remember I corrected you and, boy, did you make a face at me."

"The doctors were lying. The rage clinic is run by a firm called Tolerance Management and... "

"Oh, that's right, everyone's conspiring against *you*. The doctors are lying because Anne Parker's little Jeffrey is so important."

"Parker's a standup guy," Jack said. "Let's give him the benefit of the doubt. To the casual observer it might seem improbable that all those clerks have it in for you. Why, some people might even doubt that Lionel Trilling ruined my life." It was tempting to hear irony and self-mockery in these remarks, but with Jack it was hard to be sure. "These matters call for something like professional courtesy. I believe you, you believe me, why shouldn't we believe Parker? Without some solidarity the bastards win."

She looked uncertain. "But if you don't believe your own doctors... isn't that a sign you're not getting better?"

"To the uninformed," said Dobbs facing the road, "it might seem hard to believe that the government's testing space-based weapons on the homeless."

In the protracted silence that followed, Mrs. Slansky appeared to lose her train of thought; she turned back to the road.

The streetlights came on. He watched Skokie pass by like a film loop—a reiteration of houses, franchises, powerlines, and scant scrawny trees—hoping the view might narcotize his fear.

They were approaching the closest thing in Skokie to a landmark: In front of Besnick Ford a red Thunderbird, a new model every year, turned on a platform at the top of a thirty-foot pole, and he'd never heard a satisfactory explanation of how they got it up there. This year's Thunderbird glistened above them. It was undermining his efforts not to panic, and he focused on his plan.

If he was lucky, Todd Woolcurt would turn up when paged. Todd could follow discreetly—as discreetly as a 6'7" Michael Jordan lookalike could be—choose his moment, and do whatever it was he did. Or he might choose that moment not to exist.

What about 911? Locate Fran (he hoped her hair was down!), clear the place out with a bomb threat or a fire alarm, grab her in the confusion.

Was it too late to call the police? He'd have to simplify the story. No. There wasn't time. What if he tried to involve some cops when he got there? The sight of uniforms dispersing among the crowd would certainly get her killed. Even disguised cops...

How about this? It appeared that Hank Monroe, Jr. was hoping to use the hallfull of identically disguised men to his advantage. It could work the other way. Presumably there'd be uniformed ushers; bribe one and change into his uniform. Send Dobbs—in the ubiquitous beard, shades, and trenchcoat—to the rendezvous, and when Monroe, Jr. approached Dobbs, thinking him Parker, come up behind and get the drop on him. Well, couldn't it work? Maybe, if the guy was really acting alone. But the enemy had the advantage of dictating where they'd meet, and he'd be expecting some kind of bonehead cowboys-and-Indians ploy. And Dobbs was short, red-headed, and practically bald. The most likely outcome was that Steve, or whoever Parker sent, would get killed.

Which left him with his original plan—the least desirable, most workable: Get killed. If there was no other way to save her, he'd force them to kill him instead. He hoped she'd use the chaos to get away—hoped that once he was dead, his enemies would lose all interest in her. Well *that* was easy, he thought. Determined as he was to do it, he couldn't quite picture it happening. But surely the reason people could throw themselves on hand grenades, say, was that they didn't imagine it first.

But what was he missing? He went back over his plans, all scenarios ending in shots, screams, trampling, a crush of beards and mirror images.

By the time he found it necessary to crack open his window, the skyline was massed across the expressway, the Sears Tower silvered with the rain's last light. Jack was speaking to the back of Dobbs's head, his words lost in the uproar of clammy wind, his profile flickering as an El sparked past on the median.

Parker closed the window; Dobbs was saying, "Exactly!"

Jack leaned close to the back of Dobbs's neck. "James Joyce once said, 'I appreciate that there are two sides to this issue. But I cannot be on both sides at the same time.' But you—."

"Hold on." Dobbs turned up the radio.

"...the most stringent security measures this town has seen since the infamous Sixty-eight Democratic Convention: Metal detectors at all entrances, emergency exits guarded, and no one, and I mean no one, admitted inside without submitting to a weapons search. After a half-hour delay for a bomb search, the doors..."

So much for bomb threats. So much for the gun. So much for getting the drop.

What was he missing?

How could Hank Monroe, Jr.—working alone, if Fletcher was to be believed, and under scrutiny by the FBI—kidnap Fran, then smuggle his victim and a gun into a tightly guarded convention? Maybe he couldn't!

"Hear that?" Dobbs was saying. "Overturned sixteen-wheeler about a half- mile ahead. I'm gonna shoot over to Lake Shore Drive."

"Steve, let me have the phone."

Dobbs took it off its bracket and handed it over his shoulder; it looked like a TV remote with illuminated buttons. Parker dialed, hoping she'd at least left a new recording. But it was still the old one, Fran doing her tough-cookie impersonation: "This is Frances Anne. Don't waste my time," and he thought she'd better *be* that tough.

If he truly believed she wasn't there, it was time to bail out. But *what was he missing*? He made his mind a blank, then turned on the thing and seized it. Wait...

Mrs. Slansky was staring at him again, her rouged face a non-color in the sodium vapor lights. "Did you know I could have been killed when that stuff sprayed on me? The doctor says I could have had another stroke. You didn't *want* that, did you, dear?" She was trembling, perhaps with the effort to keep her voice down and her smile affixed.

Whatever he thought he'd grasped was leaking away like a dream riddled with daylight. He let it go for now, alarmed at Mrs. Slansky's trembling and rigidity. She winced from the exertion of her smile, and he wondered if all her mannerly passive-agressive wrath might kill her right here.

"Do you really think I'd try to hurt you, Adele?" He was floundering. Perhaps she needed a little good-natured teasing to remind her he was still young Jeffrey Parker. "If I gave you a stroke, do you know how mad my mom would be?" He spread his arms palms up. "If I knew it was you I'd have set out candles and caviar."

She gripped the top of her seat. His attempt at a reassuring smile had gone badly wrong.

He turned to John Connor Murray. "Help me out here, Jack."

Jack undid his seat belt and leaning in front of Parker placed a hand on her arm. "Adele and I have a surprise, don't we, dear?" Hearing Parker's intake of breath he added, "It's a *good* surprise, isn't it, dear?"

She appeared to have no idea what he was talking about and after a moment returned her attention to Parker, the expressway lights rippling across her glasses and distorted wet eyes. "Did you know that when I get nervous I have spasms? Usually it's my right leg. I'll be at the grocery store or at one of my meetings or even out on the street and I'll fall down and scream. Is that what you wanted?"

"Adele and I bought disguises," Jack persisted. "We picked up some beard-and-sunglasses kits at 7-Eleven. They'll be handing out beards at the door, but Adele thought these would be more sanitary, and I agree. We bought extras in case anyone joined us. I have three in my case and you have two in your purse, dear." He leaned back and picked up his case.

Opening her purse and gazing inside, she seemed to come upon herself. "Oh. Yes."

"Shall we hand them out now?" Jack still wasn't used to being the reasonable one and couldn't help overplaying. His false reassurance and protuberant eyes were alarming: he looked like he was about to read the funnies out loud. "Oh, let's!"

Mrs. Slansky handed Parker his package; the glasses and beard were encased in molded plastic and mounted on cardboard. He held it up to the window. Just under the punch-hole and the 7-Eleven logo was a drawing of a man's face wearing the disguise. The face—craggy and half-shadowed, white starbursts exploding off its mirror lenses—was centered against an American flag.

Parker reached for his wallet. "How much do I owe you?"

"It's my treat, dear." It looked like a real smile this time, nothing caged behind her teeth, and for the moment she seemed her old self.

"Thank you...very much." He set the package on his lap and tried to be still, worried that any sound or movement might shake her fragments into their mad configuration.

Dreading eye contact, he slowly turned away. They'd just come off the ramp into stalled traffic on Lake Shore Drive, and ignoring her stare he looked up at glass-and-steel curtain walls and gapped rows of lights.

He brought his mind back to the question of Fran and her kidnapper, and there it was. "Step on it!" he yelled, causing Mrs. Slansky to flinch and Dobbs to sweep a hand across the panorama of taillights frozen in the windshield.

"If this was a monster truck I could drive over them," Dobbs said, "but no can do. What's up?"

"All this time I've been thinking either Fran's been kidnapped and she's at the arena, or she hasn't been kidnapped and she's someplace else. And the more I think about it, the more I think he couldn't get her in there. But what if she's there and she hasn't been kidnapped *yet?*"

"So she's..."

"Say someone phoned the law school and a left message with the receptionist for her, supposedly from me: big emergency, life-and-death, meet me at the convention, I'll page you when you get there. Something like that."

Dobbs scratched the back of his neck. "But what's the point, as long as he can get *you* there?"

"Before he kills me, I think he wants to kill her in front of me. The point is to make me despair. I know it sounds arty, but that's what I've been told."

"She's pretty smart. Wouldn't she see through it?"

"She's smart, but she's never gotten over growing up in Schuyler, Minnesota where people don't lock their doors. It's an anti-trauma. For example, she's finally accepted the idea that there's a conspiracy against me, but at the same time she finds the whole thing silly. She can't help expecting the world to be sane, orderly, and decent. And I doubt she'll even consider the possibility that one of my phone messages might really be from someone else."

Mrs. Slansky had fixed on him again. "Kidnapped? *Killed?*" The last word came out in a screech.

"It's nothing you have to worry about," Parker said. "Steve, we can talk about this later."

"That's right," Mrs. Slansky said bitterly. "Better not talk about it. We don't want to make the old lady nervous. Let's everybody smile and smile and say stupid things because we have to humor the old lady." Her grotesque smile was back, caricaturing an eternity of false cheer. "Why don't you just say it's the blabneeto? Everybody *else* says it's the blabneeto."

Turning off Lake Shore Drive at Chicago Avenue, they were gridlocked among the clubs and singles bars. Usually on a Friday night the after-work crowd would be packing the entrances of O'Halloran's, Rogue

Moon, the Hardy Har, and Mr. Silky's. Tonight Mr. Silky's animated neon top hat tipped above an empty doorstep. The singles had either stayed away or were hiding indoors; he saw no one on foot but the huge crowds of disguised men heading west for the Arena, moving in a lightning of mirrored lights.

He opened his window. The Cermak Arena was a mile away, but the rain had stopped, cars glittered, mirror lenses flashed, the wind carried the smell of the lake, and no one was waiting for the shuttle buses. Except for the darkness and disguises, it might have been opening day at the ball park.

"The blabneeto, dear?" Jack said conversationally.

"It started when I had that trouble with the strawberries at Dominick's. I told you about the smart-aleck kid at the register who answered everything with, 'It's the blabneeto, ma'am.' I thought, it's got to be my hearing, he can't really be saying, 'it's the blabneeto.'" Parker was glad to have her looking at someone else. Jack nodded, pop-eyed with empathy.

"Well, I told you what happened then—knocking over the strawberries and getting arrested and having to go to therapy and so on. And I was never sure. Did the kid really say 'blabneeto'? But two weeks ago I'm at Save-Rite. I hand the kid at the register a coupon—Ocean Spray Cranberry Juice, $2.75. He rings up 3.09! I say, excuse me, it's 2.75, that's what it says on the coupon! He says it's 3.09... and then he lowers his voice and it's hard to make out the rest, but it sounds like he's saying, 'because of the blabneeto'!" And I swear he looks over at the girl at the next register and smirks. And I ask him, *what* did you say? And he looks at the girl again and then at me. Needless to say, there's a long line behind me, and people are making those *asthma* sounds they make when you're holding up the line. The kid says, 'It's 3.09,' and then he lowers his voice again, but I'm ready this time, and I lean in when he speaks, and I swear it sounds like he's saying 'it's the blabneeto.' And then he tells me if I don't want to buy it, I should step aside! And I think, maybe I'll just go *berserk*. But after the strawberries I knew better. Let me give you boys some advice. If you're going to go berserk, do it while you're young. If it happens when you're old, you can't *break* anything, and people think it's funny. And the kid? Can't hurt *him*. He's big and he's got a big greasy black ponytail and he looks like he lifts dumbbells. He *is* dumbbells." She laughed; Jack chuckled warily. "And then I started thinking."

"You're still in line?" Dobbs wondered.

"I'm still in line, and the kid's looking at the people behind me. He gives everyone a look, like, *I know she's an idiot, and I'll have her out of the way in a second.* Well that's when I started thinking. Do all these smart-aleck clerks have some kind of *club*? Why would the kid at Dominick's and the kid at Save-Rite both be saying 'blabneeto?' And why don't they say 'blabneeto' to anyone else? And I thought, maybe I'm just crazy, and you know, it was a relief."

Parker wondered if Fran was being paged right now.

"The only trouble was, I was sure he'd said, 'blabneeto.' So I said, 'Young man, will you please write down what you said about why the price is 3.09?' Well he looks right over me like I don't exist: 'Next!' But I wouldn't let the next person past me and I put my face right in front of that kid's. He said he'd call the manager. I said, if you want me to have one of my spasms, fine, clear the floor, but all you have to do is write down one short sentence. Well, he says he doesn't have a pen, but all the people in line are taking out pens and scraps of paper. So he writes it down. The writing is very tiny and it looks like it's just scribble. I say, 'I can't read this,' and that's when the people in line started yelling at me. I tried to show it to the people behind me and they wouldn't even look. So I told the kid I was going to take that scrap of paper and have it analyzed, and it better mean something. When I got home I turned on the lamp and found a magnifying glass, and I thought, At last the truth. I was hoping for the best. I thought maybe I'll take a good look and it will say, 'You had to buy two bottles to get the lower price.' But I opened my purse and the paper was gone! I took everything out—it was definitely gone. I figured that kid must have palmed it, like a magician? Then I told myself, come on, Adele, you're old, you don't hear so good, and you lose things. Those kids in the stores don't have a club where they decide to say 'blabneeto.' So you're cracked, Adele. Big deal."

They'd reached the outer ring of parking lots and sports bars surrounding the arena. The crowd was immense now, spilling onto the street, flashing and rumbling like a strolling storm. Parker thought of putting on his disguise and walking the remaining blocks, but there was still the matter of the gun. He hoped Dobbs had a sufficiently devious mind to figure out how to get it past security.

"But then three days ago," she continued, "I found a coupon in the paper. Baked Chicken Dinner at the Country Crock, half price." There was a careful exhalation of suppressed groans. "So I have dinner there and then when the check comes..."

"You're not insane." Dobbs glanced at Mrs. Slansky, then turned back to the road. Somewhere nearby glass broke and a cheer went up.

"I'm not?"

"Steve..." Parker warned.

"It's all right," Dobbs said. "That blabneeto business is a classic bit of retail psychology. Tolerance Management thought it up. You overcharge maybe every third old person. It's especially effective if there's a long line. The elderly are terrified of being humiliated in public, so if the customer complains you start speaking in a very low voice. Every time the mark asks for an explanation, you say, 'blabneeto.' After a minute you tell the mark to either pay or step aside. They usually pay."

"I knew it!" she shouted. "There's a Jewish saying. Do any of you boys know Yiddish? Well, in English it means, 'They'll make you eat a peck of dirt.'"

Deciding there wasn't time to wait till Jack and Mrs. Slansky were out of the car, Parker said, "Steve, about the item."

"There's no way you'll get it past security."

In what seemed like one second Mrs. Slansky pressed the button on the glove compartment, the lid flopped down, and she scooped up the gun. She turned in her seat, holding the gun in a two-hand grip, the barrel not quite pointing at Parker. "'The item!'" she mimicked contemptuously. "You must think I'm stupid." He thought of making a grab for it, but—remembering her cop shows, apparently—she released the safety.

Dobbs kept his foot on the brake as traffic opened ahead and horns bore down behind; Parker decided that jumping out might provoke her into shooting; and then they were moving.

"I suppose I should have locked it up," Dobbs said. No one thought this worth a reply. "I was pretty woozy that night," he added.

Jack said, "Adele, what are your intentions?"

"I'm not going to *shoot* anyone, if that's what you're worried about. I just don't want to be tricked."

Jack leaned close but this time avoided touching her. "Remember what the doctor said? Do your breathing."

"Fuck breathing!" she screamed, looking shocked and pleased at her obscenity. The window was still open; a voice in the crowd roared, "Fuck breathing!"

"You'll never get it past security," Jack warned her.

"Security?" She chortled. "You think they're going to take me that seriously? 'You go right on in, Grandma!'"

"Have you ever in your life—"

"Fired a gun? No, why? Do you think I should practice?" She giggled. "It's getting chilly in here, don't you think? Jeffrey, could you put up your window? That is, if you don't mind."

Traffic had slowed again, and a bald fat guy was walking alongside the car—trenchcoat unbuttoned over a black T-shirt, shiny black beard tied in a braid, mirror lenses filled with Mrs. Slansky and her gun. He cocked his head and gave her a two-finger salute. "Stylin', Moms! Don't take no shit, hear?"

Parker raised the window. "If you don't keep the gun down, we'll *all* get arrested."

She lowered it behind her seat.

"I'm going to get out of the car now." He gripped the door handle; he thought it best to do this slowly so she wouldn't feel tricked.

She glanced down at the gun as if to remind him it was still there.

"This isn't a trick. A friend of mine is in trouble and I think I can get to her faster if I walk the rest of the way."

"Jeffrey has to get there first," she summarized, "because he's very very important."

"I have to say something to Jack and Steve before I go. Do you mind?"

She said nothing, keeping her options open.

"Jack, you remember Fran, don't you?"

"Indeed." Even at this tense moment, Jack couldn't resist raising an eyebrow over a bulging eye—his "Oo-la-la!" expression.

"Yeah, well, I have to get to her before my enemy does. Steve will fill you in. Could you guys search the crowd? If she's with someone, don't get brave, page me. I'll page you if I need you. Let's think of a code name for the public address."

Mrs. Slansky's snort was reminiscent of Fran's in these matters.

"How about Victor Bravo?" Dobbs yelled as stalled traffic began honking in unison.

"Victor Bravo it is." Parker tore open the plastic bubble on the disguise package, took out the sunglasses first, and rested the frames on top of his head. It might be politic, he thought, to let Mrs. Slansky feel included. "Adele, I'd be grateful if you'd help out, too."

"That's right. Let's make Adele feel useful."

The beard was wiry and irritated his skin; he got a foul taste of adhesive before positioning the beard-and-mustache combo around his mouth. Looking away from Mrs. Slansky—he didn't want her to take it as a challenge—he pulled the door handle, and, careful not to hit men walking in the gutter, set down one foot, then the other, and eased the door shut.

* * *

The foot traffic was as static as the cars. He was hemmed in next to Mrs. Slansky's window, his face averted, his back rigid in anticipation of her decision, getting elbowed each time he tried to push up onto the sidewalk. He stifled a cry as someone bumped him from behind, then the crowd lurched forward, moving at an avid clip that he dreaded might become a trampling run. As they approached the bright lights ahead, the mirror-lightning off all the sunglasses grew disorienting—light and shadows smashed to bits and blowing about like confetti. He set the mirror lenses on his nose and tried to keep his footing in the mobbed strobe-lit darkness. Dobbs's car was out of view, but he remained tensed for the bullet.

Three blocks ahead, floodlights ignited the white walls and turrets of the Anton J. Cermak Arena—not too shabby for a structure that began its life as a notorious Virginia Civil War prison. To hold back the images his panic was disgorging, he recalled that in the 1890s a consortium of Chicago millionaires had it disassembled and shipped north, where it was rebuilt as a Civil War museum. It wasn't till the thing was put back together, apparently, that they realized how depressing it was and surrounded it with a facade in the style of a medieval castle. The venture failed anyway; for the next few years the building took in livestock shows and the orgiastic "fundraisers" of certain ward bosses till it was remodeled for the 1904 Republican convention. In its heyday it brought in another Republican convention, women's suffrage rallies, a Democratic convention, the first public demonstration of television, War Bond rallies, hockey, the Ringling Brothers Circus, and Billy Graham. It was at the Arena that the great aerialist Gilbert Brazzo, despondent over a lovers' quarrel, attempted a suicide leap from his trapeze, did what some call recorded history's only quintuple-flip on the way down, lived (though paralyzed below the neck), and spawned decades of litigation against the record books, Brazzo arguing that it was a successful quintuple-flip because he was *trying* to hit the ground. Deteriorating in the late fifties, the Arena was demoted to roller derbies and pro wrestling. McCormick Place was under construction, and no one thought it profitable to refurbish a competing venue. In the late sixties and early seventies promoters booked a few rock acts, but engineers worried about the building's structural integrity, and it had been closed for two years by the time the night watchman fell through a rotting balcony in 1975. A few years ago a new group of investors fixed it up, and now the gleaming faux fairy-tale castle, grand with pretension, floated on the darkness as if entitled.

A block from the arena he began to feel it in his groin, soles, and spine—a rumble deeper than the mere noise of thousands. It was the Arena's famous Roar, an acoustical oddity that trapped the noise of the crowd till it swelled and burst and came crashing down. At sports events the opposing team must have been terrified as the ordinary hoots of morons became something immense, God in the whirlwind. Parker had seen the Doors perform there, the music carried off on all that noise like smithereens on a flood. At last Jim Morrison gave up trying to sing and with Faustian audacity began to conduct the Roar. The higher he raised his arms the louder it got. When he lifted his arms above his head, Parker's ears seemed to close up entirely and fill with the rush of blood.

Morrison stood there like that for a good five minutes, powerful as Jaweh, helpless as the Sorcerer's Apprentice, the Roar cresting above him.

If Fran thought she was there to meet him, she'd make herself easier to find by wearing her hair down. But finding anyone out here was impossible; the flashing lenses and near-identical disguises were making him dizzy. He tried to look for her without provoking any staring contests, but he'd already set off one spiky-haired citizen who went on muttering and balling his fists as the crowd bore them off now on separate currents.

He hadn't quite ruled out the possibility that the crowd was there to kill him, and he tried to get a sense of who they were. He couldn't follow more than fragments of conversations. The phrase "the little guy" kept cropping up, but so did plans for late suppers, news of old acquaintances, and Legion business: the Cedar Rapids Bi-Metalists, he learned, were sending a delegation. Variations of the standard costume included a sprinkling of Cubs and Bears caps and the occasional spy-movie slouch hat. The few women he saw were beardless. Glass kept breaking; bullhorn-amplified commands broke up under their own echoes. A boy in a Cubs cap rode his father's shoulders, but it seemed less like a baseball crowd by the minute; Parker thought it likely that the festive atmosphere was the joy of vengeful people about to get their due.

As they approached the castle gateway—stadium gates took the place of a drawbridge—mounted cops with bullhorns warned them to stay on the sidewalk. Parker couldn't help looking up, searching the facade's fake tower for signs of life. An area in front of the castle wall was enclosed by police and blue barricades. Inside the barricades, a photographer held up a light meter, a crew positioned light poles and a wind machine, and on cue three male models in faceless-man gear crowded behind a woman, raised their sunglasses, and leered. She was wearing a fedora, mirror sunglasses, and a form-fitting black vinyl raincoat; she took off the hat and shook out her long black hair. Thinking of Fran, Parker groaned with dread and longing. Now she lifted the sunglasses to expose her eyes. Her face was clown-white except for her mascaraed silver-gray eyes and a red-lipsticked bow. Rubbery shadows on the wall mimed the poses. The crew stepped back against the barricades; the wind machine came on, growling like a wounded Harley; her hair exploded around her face, erupting behind her up the phosphorescent wall.

* * *

At the top of the ramp people halted, staggered, turned their faces, grabbed posts and the backs of seats. No one had reckoned on the solar flare of television lights off thousands of mirrors, and at first nothing was visible beyond white-hot blobs of dazzle, intervals of blackness, and a blizzard of after-images. No one was shouting or applauding— the first speaker wasn't up yet—but already the Roar hummed through the crowd; feeling its juice, he thought of that toy football game whose vibrations sent plastic men reeling jerkily over a tin field. As the phantom discs faded, he took his bearings. He was standing at the back of the second balcony, the highest point in the house; convulsive blasts of white light shot up from the main floor as if a meteorite had just crash-landed there.

Across the bowl-shaped arena the empty podium rose from the box seats. The floor space had been filled in with folding chairs. The permanent seating—padded blue chairs on concrete risers—was interrupted by the platform and the ten-foot-high podium draped with bunting. Ten minutes remained before the scheduled Opening Address, and already the place was nearly full. The member delegations occupied the third of the floor closest to the podium, their placards and banners unreadable from here except for one huge banner unfurled across an entire row: THE DREADFUL HAS ALREADY HAPPENED!

Parker was picking up one of the house phones when, bland as an airline pilot announcing the loss of all engines, the P.A. announcer read, "Frances Girard, please come to the information desk. Will Frances Girard please come to the information desk."

He pressed "Operator," hoping to put up his own message and warn her away, but the line was busy. The solid crowd coming up the ramp would be impassable; he decided to make his way to the exit at the front of the balcony, and as he shoved and pleaded and elbowed down the stepped aisle, the tightly packed, tightly wound crowd shoved and elbowed back. He bumped the pony-tailed man in front of him and apologized as the guy turned and swore, pink lips writhing in their nest of hair, and for one instant Parker was ready to forget everything else and smash him. Instead he squeezed by and caught a punch to the ear; it set off a feedback screech in his skull that made him want to close his eyes, but he pressed forward.

Ushers—they wore sunglasses along with the standard Andy Frain uniform—pleaded with the schmoozers blocking the aisle, but more and more people were getting out of their seats, too jazzed to sit still. Cries, calls, bursts of energy spread through these clumps and networks and swirled round the arena; the crowd, newly born, was exploring itself, trying to determine what it was. As he pressed ahead, all space filled with bellies, necks, backs, pores, tops of heads; waves of body heat, breath, and aftershave. He fought to control his breathing among thickets of damp fake whiskers and swarms of his own crazed reflection. Shutting out the howl in his battered ear, he listened for the P.A.; when he heard himself paged he'd be too late.

* * *

The crowd on the exit ramp was sparse enough for Parker to run, his running shoes skidding on the turns. The momentum of a turn flung him out to his left, and as he sidestepped a man walking up with two large Cokes, he caught sight of Fran rounding the turn ahead. Even in heels she was a fast runner, already rounding the next turn, the telegraphy of her progress fading. He yelled her name, so winded he could hardly draw the breath back. The heels slowed down, then grew louder.

"Jeff?" she called up, still out of view.

"Yeah!" He gripped the handrail, catching his breath, and as the heels approached he asked himself how he'd known it was her. He'd glimpsed the back of a trim woman in a raincoat...long dark hair...Fran's height, but he'd seen a dozen others. He didn't recall anything unique about the way Frances ran, but maybe he'd recognized it even if he couldn't name it. Was there something irreducibly *Fran-like* in everything she did? Some little idiosyncrasy, some tic? Was that what we fall in love with?

She came up the last turn and, seeing that he wasn't hurt, slowed to a walk. She must have been having an anxiety attack—he could imagine the sort of message that had brought her here—so she was putting on a massive display of poise: hips turning, a flick of the head spilling hair off her shoulder. Mirror sunglasses only enhanced the effect. For a moment they both enjoyed the show—she didn't take it the wrong way when he burst out laughing—then they closed in a fierce hug, kissing through his badly aligned whiskers.

She drew back her head and grabbed him by the lapels. "Parker, you had me so worried! I thought..."

"I'll tell you all about it when we're out of here. Right now we have to stay alert."

She let out a nervous hoot of a laugh. "I'm sorry. Well, *you* were laughing at *me*."

"My darling, I'm much too happy to be offended." The man with the boy riding piggyback walked past. The kid was still wearing his Cubs cap and had added a pair of child-size mirror sunglasses; the sight was unnerving enough to focus Parker's mind on the danger at hand. Better not run, he thought. He put his arm round her waist and they started down the ramp. "Let's just get out of here. Blend in."

"I'm still not clear on who these people are."

He lowered his voice. "For the most part these are reasonably well-off white guys who look at the poor, the persecuted, oh, starving people in Africa, and think: 'Why do *they* get to be the victims?'"

"Why are we leaving? Your message at the law school said you were in trouble and you needed me here."

"That wasn't *my* message. Mine said stay away. I got one saying *you* were in trouble. Say, didn't you check your answering machine?"

"Two hours ago, no messages. Why?"

Recalling something John Standell had told him, Parker said, "There are just a few codes that control all the major brands. Anyone who has those codes could erase your messages over the phone."

She planted her heels. "Goddamnit, what's going on!"

"All right. My enemy wants us both here. We could stand here speculating why, but then we might find out." He nudged her into motion. "Here we go, just a coupla populists walking briskly, not running, eyes straight ahead." A rumble emanated from the auditorium; for a moment he thought the event might be starting, but it was just the mysterious tectonics of the crowd. "So, anyway, you know who's getting the shaft? It's the little guy. That's right, the little guy." Talking this drivel was kind of fun. "And you know who's giving the little guy the shaft?"

She glittered at him through a long pause; this wasn't the subject she wanted to discuss. "The big guy?"

"Exactly!" He gave her a squeeze. "Almost there," he said through the side of his mouth. They rounded the last turn and started down the incline to the rear exit. "Remember Fred Harris? Populist democrat? Ran in the primaries a few years ago?"

"Yes! It's my dad's favorite political joke! 'The little people would've voted for me but their tiny arms couldn't reach the levers.' What is it?" He'd stopped so abruptly she teetered on her heels and grasped his shoulder for support.

They were halfway down the incline; through the gate's turnstiles he could see Adele Slansky pacing a tight circle on the sidewalk, her face submerged in her collar up to her cataract glasses. He tried to make sense of her being there. Maybe she'd failed to get past the metal detector, or maybe she'd chickened out. Maybe she was still armed, completely out of her mind, and trying to decide what to do next. If she was waiting for him, wanting to be sure he didn't sneak out early, that would be the place to stand.

He led Fran a few yards back up the ramp and gave her the abbreviated version. He didn't have time to make it sound plausible. "You believe everything else," he concluded. "You might as well believe this."

She shrugged. "Might as well. Couldn't she be waiting for a cab?"

"She hasn't looked at the street once."

He led her back down to the place where he'd first stopped. "I don't think she can see us." Behind Mrs. Slansky he saw a double-parked van from Channel 7 News; stragglers heading for the entrance at the opposite end of the arena; traffic getting back to normal. The cops were on the other side of the building.

She indicated the Andy Frain usher blowing cigarette smoke out the turnstiles. "He could get a cop."

"I hate to think what that might set off. Her hands are in her pockets." "Maybe she's cold?"

"I don't think she'll do anything if she's not provoked—whatever *that* means. I'm afraid she'll recognize me. She's seen the raincoat and she gave me the beard. Would you be able to spot me like this?"

"The hair. Nobody has hair like that."

The voice of the P.A. announcer ping-ponged through the lobby. "Jeffrey Parker, please come to the information desk. Will Jeffrey Parker please come to the information desk."

"He couldn't get hold of you," Parker said, "but he's hoping I'll think he did. Look—*you* can get out this way. Go. Stay with Marcy tonight. I'll call you when I get home."

"I'm not leaving."

"Don't be an idiot. There's nothing you can do."

"For all you know we're being followed. He could stab me when I get to the parking lot. Don't pretend you know the safe thing to do. You don't *really* know what's going on here, do you? We might as well stick together."

"If we were being followed, why would he have to call us to the information desk? Your argument is too dumb to take seriously, so I'll assume you're being loyal. Ya numbskull." He squeezed her shoulders and kissed the top of her head. "Okay, here are our options. One. We go back upstairs, enjoy the show, leave with the crowd." He was tempted to see if they *were* being followed but thought it wise to keep looking straight ahead, without, of course, looking directly at Mrs. Slansky.

"Uh-uh. It hasn't even started yet and I'm sick of it."

"I don't think we should decide this on aesthetic grounds."

"Two?"

"Two—we walk through the lobby and leave by another gate. That's chancy because we'd have to walk past the information desk. Three—we walk through the auditorium to the other side of the building and leave through the main entrance."

Fran was watching Mrs. Slansky, who'd stepped back to lean against a car.

"Auditorium," Fran said. Like her poise, this terseness kept her from losing control—parsing her confusion into tiny certainties.

"Or we could cut over by way of the balcony." He was having a hard time shutting up. "Cutting across the main floor is faster and riskier. When our friend sees we're not coming to the information desk, he'll probably..."

"Right," she said, her profile a bulwark of cheekbones, "main floor."

"If we keep the usher between us and Adele, I don't think we'll have any problem. Her eyes aren't very good."

The lobby grew quiet; men carrying soft drinks or popcorn rushed past them up the ramp.

"I think it's about to start," he whispered. "Whatever *it* is."

* * *

The tiny man had almost disappeared behind the podium, his beard, his upturned collar, and the twin bursts of radiance that covered his eyes. "The fire marshall has asked us to clear the aisles. Will you please take your seats!" He was met with a detonation of hoots and applause. This was hardly the Roar in full cry—it was barely clearing its throat—but he shrank further into his trenchcoat.

They'd just come in through the back of the auditorium. Parker had worried that the ushers might send them back upstairs and had instructed Fran that in the event of their being asked for their stubs, she was to wear down the usher's resolve by laboriously rummaging through her purse—an old trick for upgrading seats at rock concerts. But security was busy elsewhere, passing latecomers through the metal detectors, pleading with the people in the aisles, and forming a Maginot Line in front of the podium.

The aisles were all packed, so they started up the closest—up the center aisle toward the podium and the main entrance. In the stands above them thousands of mirrors bore down like a smashed sun.

"Tonight I have the pleasure," said the tiny emcee; he broke off in mid-sentence and held onto the podium. The crowd in the stands had begun doing the Wave. From where Parker stood the effect was of riding a merry-go-round spinning loose of its underpinnings. Fran leaned against him; he closed his eyes against the cyclone of peristaltic brightness, whirling now in opposite directions.

The man at the podium was mouthing into a rising wind. "Without further ado!" he screamed and stepped down.

The wind and the waves died, the brightness settled, and while everyone watched the empty podium, the arena grew quiet as a bomb that stops ticking.

It occurred to Parker that there'd been no printed programs, no advance word of topics or speakers. He thought of the famous hoax in which the British comedian Spike Milligan advertised a mystery event at the Royal Albert Hall; when the long-anticipated moment arrived and the curtain rose, the audience was facing a second audience. The two audiences gave each other a standing ovation and went home. Parker doubted that this crowd would be as sporting. If the podium were still empty in another minute, the place would be dismantled for the second time.

"Come on," he whispered to Fran, who'd stopped to wait.

The man rising behind the microphone drew scattered applause. He didn't appear to be what the crowd had envisioned as they stared at the empty podium. Beneath his unbuttoned trenchcoat he wore a check flannel shirt and a striped tie. He cocked his head, and Parker recognized the sharp-boned nose, the grin opening like a seam in the real beard. It was Harry Krell.

Parker frantically reassessed their predicament. He'd accepted Fletcher's theory that the convention was the gathering of demagogues and boneheads it appeared to be, that Hank Monroe, Jr. was acting alone, and that he was planning to use the camouflage of "thousands of identically-disguised suspects" to kill Fran and Parker. Now it seemed like the optimistic view.

He reached behind him and tugged Fran past two beer bellies closing between them. The sight of Harry Krell had brought back his worst fears: that the convention was a ruse, that the crowd was about to turn on them. Did it know where they were?

Krell took a sip of water, adjusted the mike stand, and looked out on the audience, the blasts off his sunglasses intensifying the merriment of his smile.

They squeezed ahead at the pace of fleeing dreamers. He reminded himself that the crowd, according to the news, was mostly non-members; they couldn't *all* be in on it. Fran was nudging him to point out a guy with flag pins in his beard.

"I hate to kick off the proceedings on a somber note," Krell began, "but it's likely that within the next ten minutes someone in this hall will die." The last of the crowd noise withdrew from the arena in one great inhalation. Parker turned his head—no room to get out the way they'd come in. His hand going numb in Fran's knotted fingers, he pulled her forward.

"I won't keep you in suspense about the identity of the victim, and yes it will be murder," Krell said and took another drink of water. He set down the glass. "It's me."

The queasy laughs and fainthearted boos fell away as he continued. "And I won't be coy about the identity of the murderer, excuse me, murderers. It's you." Above the rising murmur he said, "That's right. Discuss the matter among yourselves." Fran tilted her head at Parker, mouth agape. He shrugged.

"We've progressed," Krell resumed, "to the stage where you can't imagine *why* you'd kill me, but already you don't like me very much." He chuckled and nodded through the brief loud round of applause. "But that's beside the point, you think, because *you have no intention of killing me.* So what do I know that you don't? Let's take a survey. Come on, let's see what kind of populists you are. Fill in the blank: This would be a great country if it wasn't for the goddamn_____."

To Parker the cacophonous response sounded like "HUBBA-YALE!" Not even his paranoia could suggest what the man was up to.

Krell nodded. "We've established two points. You're angry. And practically none of you are angry about the same thing.

"A few minutes ago, some of our lab people showed me the latest readings. If you're a specialist in human disgruntlement—and I am!—the findings are unmistakable. In a few minutes you boys will reach reach critical mass...you will, you know, flip out. Lose it. Go nuts. Revert to savagery. Bust up the joint. My colleagues warned me that if I got up on the podium, the odds didn't favor my coming down. Well, that's like telling a surfer don't go out today, the waves are too big." He cocked his head. "Stay away from the cage, Mr. Lion Tamer: those critters look mean!

"I take if from your silence that that's not how you see yourselves. I'll bet reaching critical mass was the last thing on your minds when you brushed your teeth this morning. It's probably way at the bottom of your list even now. That's the funny thing about people in a bunch—crowds, audiences, mobs, nations. It's been demonstrated that entire nations can have nervous breakdowns while their individual people go on working, falling in love, meeting with their brokers, having babies, or planning dinner."

"Is this all bullshit?" Fran whispered.

"Maybe. I think he wants you to ask that question."

"Why?"

"See? You're looking for the point. Now he can play with you like a ball of yarn."

"No he can't. If he thinks so he's crazy. *Is* he crazy?"

"See?"

"We're back where we started: it's bullshit. . . But there has to be more to it."

"Ah!" But Parker took another look at Harry Krell—the snow-dazzle smile still fixed among his whiskers—and added, "I think he's scared. Maybe he believes what he said."

"Right at this moment," Krell was saying, "one of you is working up the nerve to yell, 'what makes *you* such an expert, you condescending prick?' Frankly, that 'condescending prick' part hurt my feelings, but let me tell you how I came to be a scholar of discontent. I invented Tolerance Management—which a friend of mine succinctly described as the study of how much crap people will take—twenty-three years ago this month. I remember it was a rainy November afternoon. There was a wind in the eaves."

He leaned his elbows on the podium and cracked his knuckles. "'There was a wind in the eaves'—you like that, don't you? It sounds like the beginning of a story, and you like stories, don't you? You're thinking something is about to happen. Things are about to *mean* something. You'll wait a few minutes and see. Meanwhile I'm trying to postpone the inevitable blowout by precisely controlling your boredom, your curiosity, your hope, your rage, and your impatience. *That's* Tolerance Management, and it's how we preserve the social order. I'm sure you'll agree it's more humane than the alternative." He pointed a thumb over his shoulder at the Chicago cops massed in the lobby.

Halfway up the aisle now, Parker and Fran were passing the official delegations, becalmed banners sagging across the rows.

The audience had been silent, but Krell cupped his ear in a stylized pose of listening. Now Parker heard it, faintly, mistaking it at first for his own anxious breathing—the Roar was singing, like a seashell at his ear. It didn't seem to be coming from any particular place; people everywhere were looking around for its source. Fran tilted her head back and gazed up into the lights.

Krell smiled exultantly. "It's coming." He leaned against the podium. "I don't think we'll have time for that story after all. Let's get down to basics. Why are you angry? And just what *is* this convention about anyway?

"Why are you angry? That's an easy one. Society is a complicated, inefficient machine, and it produces unhappiness as inevitably as any complex machine generates waste. In other words, you have to take a certain amount of crap. Think of the crap you take just living with your family. No wonder a network of relationships among thousands and millions of strangers creates whole new magnitudes of crap. In other societies crap can take the form of famines, death squads, and gulags. So why is it that you guys are angrier than the people who live in most of *those* places? I think I can answer that.

"I'm afraid it might be all my fault. You see, at Tolerance Management we consult with big institutions to make sure that people take only as much crap as they can bear. To make life as happy—as bearable—as possible, we try to assure that the inefficiencies of society are distributed imperceptibly, minutely, and—within the limits of a free market—fairly. Unfortunately, all that fairness never quite reaches the underclass, but you populists don't want to talk about *them*, do you? Let 'em stop whining, right?

"Anyway, to make sure that you don't even *notice* these discrete doses of crap, we distract you. And to be sure that you don't even feel *distracted*, we distract you from your distractedness. It's a benign shell game, really: sadness reduced to the size of a pea and never under the shell when you look. Better than a cattle prod to the genitals I'm sure you'll agree.

"So think of it this way: Everyone sleeps with a pea under the mattress. The trouble is, eventually you feel it. You might not know what's bothering you, but you feel tricked. Fucked with. Conspired against. And that's why you guys think this event is about the Little Guy and the Elites, when it's really about the Princess and the Pea. And that's why you're angrier than the billions of people in the world who have something real to complain about."

A man shouted, "My wife and I have four part-time jobs and no health insurance!"

"And that's true, too," Krell said magnanimously, conceding and dismissing the point. "At the moment, fortunately, most people don't even realize how angry they are; we're trying to corral all that rage while there's still time. The latest thing we tell our clients is, 'Agree with it.' Here's how it works. First, we agree with you: feed you back your half-baked notions through the polls, the politicians, and the TV. Then these lookalike opinions become your own, 'opinion makers' echo *those*, and *you* mimic *them*. It's a feedback loop—each time your opinions come back to you they've lost a little more coherence, until finally they degenerate into noise. That's why you're reduced to this vacant ranting about the little guy. What we hoped was that as your anger grew more and more thin, nonspecific, and hazy, it would disperse like mist. Well, it doesn't seem to be working. The less you mean, the madder you get.

"I first heard of the Legion a few weeks ago, when my dear friend Hank Monroe, Junior played one of those little pranks that...By the way, I believe that Hank, Junior might be in our audience tonight. *He's* threatened to kill me, too. Good luck, pal, the line forms behind all these little guys. Where are you, buddy? Let's hear it for him!" He lifted his up-turned palms to milk the faint, befuddled applause. "Stand up, Hank, Junior. Let's make him feel at home, folks!" No one stood up. Krell looked out on his audience, assessing its murderousness as applause fell away to coughs, creaks, and that sound of a distant sea.

"Uh, as I said, I first heard of the Legion a few weeks ago. That's when I learned of an incident that occurred while Hank was tailing my dear friend Jeffrey Parker...that's right, Jeff Parker the famous victim, you saw the magazine." Fran gave Parker an elbow nudge. "Never mind who Hank is or why he was following Jeff. But Hank wanted his victim to know he was being followed, and what could make that point more forcefully than a beard, a trenchcoat, and mirror sunglasses? Hank knows how scary an out-of-context cliché can be." Krell chuckled softly. "Funny guy, Hank. Seems to me he's always seen himself as the Kafka character. Oppressed by the eerie denseness of his victim, the unfathomable designs of his masters. Uncertain of the role required of him—faking it, constructing it out of pop-culture static, the dank routines of dimly recollected villains."

The audience was mumbling, chairs emitting rack-like squeaks. Krell seemed to be veering off the topic. Was he panicking? Had he detected some ominous new harmonic in the crowd? Or was this a tactic—a precisely measured droplet of boredom to sedate their rage?

"But I digress. When confronted, Hank improvised: He claimed to be a member of your organization. The next day word of the incident reached me. It was the first I'd heard of the Legion, as I said, and I was enraptured. I was especially struck by the symbolism of the outfits. I thought they expressed everything we deal with at Tolerance Management—isolation, alienation, the rage of the underground man. I was so impressed, I bought the franchise. I thought this convention would make an ideal laboratory. We could measure your anger, tweak it, feed it. With luck we might even start a mass movement—channel all that wasted energy right back into the system. But until I walked into the Arena tonight, it somehow hadn't dawned on me just how pissed-off you guys are."

Krell's story about the convention rang true. Which meant that Parker had just one enemy to evade instead of the entire crowd—two, if you counted Mrs. Slansky. Now if Krell could keep everyone confused and distracted a few more minutes...

He was feeling hopeful enough to return Fran's nudge in the ribs. As she turned her head she pursed her mouth and absently lifted a hand to her hair. Standing beside her, he needed a second to grasp what he was seeing in the crush of heads and bodies behind her. A black skein, glittering in the lights, arced upward from the back of her head: a man was chewing on her hair.

* * *

Before Parker could raise his arm the man pressed something in his coat pocket against her back; she gasped and tried to look over her shoulder.

Blowing out hair and spittle, Hank Monroe, Jr. said, "Yep, that's a gun. Eyes front!" He'd given her a half-turn so that her body stood between him and Parker. He was wearing a black toupee instead of his bald wig, but even behind his sunglasses and beard there was no mistaking the round doughy drowned-corpse face.

Parker had a hand on the lighter in his pocket; crouched behind Fran, Monroe, Jr. said, "I'll take that. You don't have a line of fire, genius, don't piss me off. Lookit that, ma'am, that thing he's doin' with his mouth. I do believe that's a look of grim determination." The act was disintegrating—the accent so phony it was hard to recall what it pretended to be. "All tensed for his sudden move. Comin' up any minute now, Parker's sudden move. I'll grease her first, dickhead. Come on, Ace, let's see that move."

"Let her go."

"Sorry, bud. I need her to keep you *focused*. Goddamnit, *you don't pay attention!*"

Fran bit her lip.

"You just don't get the point, do you?" Monroe, Jr. squeezed his exasperation into clipped syllables. "I been tryin' to make my *point* for fifteen years. Can I make my goddamn *point?*"

Their conversation was sealed in a bubble; people inches away were focused on Harry Krell, who was saying, "You must be wondering: *Why am I telling you this?* Is it the desperate improvisation of a man on a sinking boat, tossing out everything in reach? But if that were true, why am I telling you *that?*"

All Parker had to do was call out and he'd be the center of attention. But he doubted it would stop this man from killing them. Still, there was time: He was required to get the point.

Monroe, Jr. held out his left hand. "First gimme the gun. Come on, for Chrissake, it's been a long day. Still thinkin' up his move—you gotta love the guy! Are we gonna have to do a countdown here, Slim?"

Fran cringed as Parker held it out by the barrel. The reaction of the people near them was unexpectedly quiet; they crammed out of its way, opening a space around Parker, Fran and Hank Monroe, Jr.

With military crispness and speed, Monroe, Jr. grabbed it with his left hand, transferred it to his right, and put the right hand back into his pocket, the barrel pressed against Fran's back. Parker was baffled by this maneuver, but suddenly things were looking up.

He said, "Now here's my plan: We ignore him." She gave him a tight, closed, agonized smile that roughly translated as, your joke is noted.

He tried to reach her through both their mirror lenses: Trust me. Icebound, she fought the pull of his hand as he yanked her forward, nearly toppling her off her heels, and they pushed up against the people in front of them. The way ahead was blocked.

Monroe, Jr. was laughing. "That's just pitiful. I'm right behind you, asshole. You think if you're pathetic enough I'll throw you back like a minnow?"

Perhaps the man had never had a gun in his coat— couldn't get it past the weapons check, maybe, had to leave it in his car. Or maybe he'd made the substitution because he thought it was more humiliating to kill them with Parker's gun.

The lighter was still turned up to the Jerry Lewis setting. "Don't turn around," Parker warned her, pushing her in front of him, and then there was heat at his back; Monroe, Jr. was screaming; a twist of dirty smoke made the lights smear.

* * *

Krell had gone rigid at the podium. The screams broke off; flocks of reverberations reeled off the walls and ceiling. Parker looked back, but all he could see were the bodies pressed up against him, lights exploding among their heads like the bulbs of mad ideas. He locked his fingers in Fran's. "What...!" she gasped, the rest drowned out by people shouting "Don't run!" The smoke had cleared, but the crowd was moving at a forced-march pace, the impulse to run a gale at their backs. His arm ached as he strained to keep her fingers in his grip. A man snared in their outstretched arms was yelling in Parker's face, the words lost, gathered into the Roar. Up front the cops were moving now, helmet shields down, hands on their holstered clubs.

The Roar, when it builds, has been compared to a subway train descending into the tunnel, gathering speed. Blasted by damp breath and nullified curses, Parker felt like he was clattering into the yelling man's mouth.

He couldn't be certain that he wasn't screaming himself.

* * *

He turned on the lights and tried to make sense of his disappointment. At some level he'd believed that the death of his enemy had changed everything; that he'd arrive home to something other than the old stick furniture, bare bulbs and bare white walls.

A whiff of the raincoat as he took it off brought on an olfactory hal-lucination; he could smell the man burning. He tossed it on the couch and headed for the Johnny Walker Black Label in the kitchenette cupboard. He took a gulp from the bottle, waves of horror and relief spreading with its warmth, and asked himself why he was sure the man was dead. He hadn't *seen* anything, but what about the smell, the screams?

Wasn't it just as likely that Monroe, Jr. was in a burn unit some-where? Well, he wouldn't be leaving anytime soon; there'd be time to deal with him. Regardless of how preposterous the story sounded, Parker would go to the police. If that didn't work, he'd go back to his FBI pal Ed Vishoolis, who seemed as eager as he was to make Monroe, Jr. go away.

Inevitably his imagination served it up: Monroe, Jr.'s disguised face thrust in his, shades of red, purple, and black detectable between the whiskers and the mirror lenses, Parker's hand drawn irresistibly to the fake beard. "Go on, amigo, give it a shot!"

Still, he thought, I'm taking it pretty well. He would have expected to be puking by now. Hasn't sunk in yet, has it, Ace? Nope! Protective obtuseness? You bet!

He squirted Joy onto his breakfast dishes and ran the tap. The Hank Monroe, Jr. of his imagined scene was still hanging about, camping it up now in the role of some silent looming accusing shade. Parker tried to form an impression of the man he'd...possibly, arguably...killed. He thought of how frightened his enemy must have been to efface himself behind that act; how vulnerable he must have felt to leave not one atom of a real self exposed. The obtrusively fake accent, the bad-guy clichés, the latex makeup, the beard, the sunglasses, the bald wig, the other wig: It wasn't a disguise or an impersonation; it was the debris that gathers around a black hole. Monroe, Jr. was frightening because there'd never been a person there to contend, plead, or reason with—he'd made him-self as unassailable as a recorded message. And before we do a telethon for the poor man, Parker added, let's remember him coming home at the end of a long day, going to his closet shelf and taking down a big bag of hair. He tried to think of one other thing he knew about the real guy. Oh, yeah: he'd been trying to make a point.

He assured himself there was nothing to feel guilty about, even if his brain seethed with a sort of atrocity minstrel show, teeth and eyeballs twinkling in charred faces. He reminded himself that the man might have had a real gun! The pocket was big enough for the lighter *and* a real gun. And if he'd warned him...!

It occurred to Parker that he was standing at the sink with the sleeves of his sport jacket plunged into soapsuds, and as if this were the last straw his legs gave way. He sat up. You could mop it with anything, the damn linoleum always looked dingy. He would have liked to close his eyes and listen to the refrigerator hum, but he had to call Fran.

Standing up? No problem. He filled half a glass with Johnny Walker, then carried it with him while he brought the phone out of the bedroom, turned on the TV—the 10 o'clock news was coming up, there'd be something on the convention—and plopped onto the couch as if from a height. It was the station break before the news, the set brightening on dust, cattle, a mini-van. He placed the phone on his lap, the receiver between his ear and shoulder, the drink in his left hand, and pressed her number. While it rang he set the drink on the floor and wriggled out of his wet jacket.

They'd gotten separated as the mob advanced on Harry Krell. Like the lone machine-gunner holding off the enemy in *Back to Bataan*, the grudgeologist held fast at the microphone, discharging bullshit till the last instant, when he escaped through a door in the podium. By the time the crowd kicked it down, he'd disappeared.

Weightless with shock, Parker was carried along with the crowd as it vainly scanned the parking lots, taverns, and Italian beef stands for an object commensurate with its rage. The cops were on their best post-

1968 behavior, allowing the feckless march to advance as long as it didn't block the street. But somewhere around Dearborn the marchers halted. It seemed to Parker that whatever had animated them this far was trying to form an intention. The cops mistook paralysis for civil disobedience and ordered the crowd to disperse. From somewhere in the middle he looked back at the throng behind him, a river of frozen lights. Then word spread down the line: The cops were negotiating to avert a riot; what were the crowd's demands? The effect was of startling a sleeper awake and asking him to recall his dream. The crowd began pocketing their beards and sunglasses, scratching at the adhesive residue on their faces, hailing cabs, walking toward parking lots or the El.

He took the subway to Hyde Park and, when no one answered Fran's bell, waited at Andre's, the same bar where he'd fought for Ziploc's bag. His tan raincoat an explosion of color among the funereally hip attire, he tried the pay phone every few minutes for the next hour till it occurred to him that while he waited, Fran might be impersonating a mummy on the table in his lobby.

So here he was, sitting by himself studying the damp stains on his bare walls while her phone rang. If I feel this lousy, he's still alive, Parker thought only half-jokingly.

Her recording came on. "If this is Jeff, I've been sitting in a restaurant till I calmed down enough to drive. I couldn't reach you, but I got your messages—the last one said you were leaving Andre's, so you must be on the way home. Wait there, I'm leaving now." Only her slightly parched voice betrayed her effort to soldier on. "Hey, my knight in shining blinders!"

Before he could savor those words, the news led with footage from the convention: Hank Monroe, Jr.—in longshot from above—trying to strip off his burning trenchcoat, the circle around him bulging outward each time he staggered in a new direction.

He tried to slow down his whirl enough to follow the story. "... this violent good Samaritan," the anchor was saying. A second figure entered the circle, threw a raincoat over the burning man and tackled him. The camera zoomed down, and Parker recognized the bald crew-cut and the Armani-knockoff-clad back. It was Todd Woolcurt, his bodyguard. Woolcurt removed his coat from the dazed man, carefully peeled off the burnt coat beneath, hoisted the guy to his feet—flinging out an arm to keep his balance, Monroe, Jr. displayed a blackened shirt sleeve—and proceed to beat the crap out of him. "...no word yet as to what motivated this..." Monroe, Jr. staggered backward with the punches like a windblown scrap, too crazed and disoriented to fall down. Each blow raised a small puff of smoke or ash. It seemed to Parker that after the fiasco at Tolerance Management Woolcurt was trying to redeem himself: Tonight he was leaving nothing undone. "For more we go live..."

Chips sprayed from a blow to the front door; Parker just had time to register his utter lack of surprise.

* * *

He was sprinting for the back door. "Who is it?" he called over his shoulder, hoping his enemy might waste a second fashioning a sardonic reply. He ran past the bedroom doorway, backed up and slapped the bedroom wall till his hand found the panic button beneath the light switch.

"You have activated the world's ultimate security system," announced the recorded voice of John Standell, sounding pleased with itself. "You have two minutes." The second blow to the door loosed a xylophonic clatter of wood and plaster.

Parker had the back-door key off the nail and into the deadbolt when the third impact sounded, followed instantly by the front doorknob banging against the wall, then shoes on the floorboards. He couldn't get the key to turn.

"Now *this*," said Hank Monroe, Jr. behind him, "is a real gun. Go on—ignore it!"

Parker stood with his face to the door's pane and hoping to attract the attention of the man climbing the steps—it looked like Mr. Vasquez from the third floor—raised his hands above his head.

"You have one hundred seconds," John Standell proclaimed. Mr. Vasquez, it was too dark to be sure, passed the window and started up the next flight, no change in his pace or his slouch. The TV in the living-room was still mumbling importantly.

"I didn't really mean you could ignore it." Monroe, Jr.'s tone of voice seemed weary and familial—they way you speak to a stupid relative you can't just stop talking to. "Turn around."

He looked about the same. If the horrors Parker had dreaded were there (how could they be? He couldn't be walking around, could he?), they were concealed. Monroe, Jr. was wearing his faceless-man disguise and a new trenchcoat, and he gave off a vaguely medicinal odor—something applied to his burns. The dark discolorations between his beard and sunglasses were probably just bruises. It was impossible to tell how badly he'd been hurt, but the gun was in his left hand. The right—the one he'd held the lighter in—was in his pocket, the arm held against his side. Parker didn't place much hope in his incapacity; he'd just broken down a door.

"Raised hands strictly optional, amigo."

He dropped his hands. Distract him, he thought, keep him rattled till the time runs out. Parker's reflection in the mirror lenses was that of a man thinking, Well, here goes. "What could happen if you dropped the act? Come on, what are you afraid of? You've got the gun." As far as he could tell with a heavily disguised man, it was having no effect.

"You have eighty seconds."

"The fuck *is* that?" Monroe, Jr. shook the gun in the direction of the nearest speaker. "Turn that fucker off."

"It's the world's ultimate security system. I'm afraid it's unstoppable." Parker had struck a temporary accommodation with his fear, channeling it all into a delirium of hope. "You know, the accent just isn't happening. Why don't you—"

"Security system! You gonna kid yourself right to the end, Ace? I guess that takes a certain kind of integrity. So what's it gonna do? Call the police? They'll be too late. Anything else, the death rays or whatever, you're gonna get it, too. A nap—that's the ultimate security for you, boy... I was tryin'—"

"You have one minute."

"—I was *tryin'* to make my *point*. You don't wanna die without knowin' the big picture! 'The meaning of it all!' This is sittin' *down* truth, boy." Monroe, Jr. gestured with the gun and they started toward the living room.

When they got there, they both remained standing. Parker switched off the TV. "Come on," he said mock-chummily, "drop the act. Just a peep of the real guy. Are you that ashamed?"

"I'm goin' out with the same act I came in with. That's what a man does."

"Forty seconds, chump," John Standell taunted.

They both looked up at the speaker mounted on the wall above the couch, dropping all pretense that they could focus on anything else.

It wasn't till Monroe, Jr. extended his gun arm, held the muzzle a foot from Parker's head, and snarled, "Please—share!" that he realized he'd been laughing. Parker chocked it back, and it burst from his nose and clenched teeth. "It's not you. No, really." He coughed, shrugged, turned up his palms.

"You ain't gonna go batshit on me, are you, Ace?"

"Not a chance." The truth was, he was feeling pretty good, his hope and terror having negotiated a sort of euphoria. He believed that only a gun at his head prevented him from running up the wall and and back-flipping onto his feet.

"Gas." Monroe, Jr. appeared to be thinking out loud. "First sign of gas I'll shoot you, I don't care if the building goes up."

"You have twenty seconds."

"If you're nervous," Parker said solicitously, "we could wait outside."

"I'm fine, thanks."

"Ten. Nine..."

One way or another, the life he hated was counting down. He smiled back at his goofball smile in the mirror lenses: See you on the other side.

Monroe, Jr. was right-handed. He was holding the gun with the left; his right hand, maybe the entire arm, was useless. The gun was a foot away. Soon as all hell breaks loose, go for it with both hands.

"Five. Four. Three. Two. One. Zero."

Nothing happened.

It went on happening. The gun was still a foot from his head. The two men went on facing each other, sneaking glances to the left and right. The seconds went on arriving, each with its freight of nothing.

Indicating all that nothing with a wave of his gun, Monroe, Jr. observed, "Your cavalry has arrived, such as it is."

There might have been a trace of compassion in Monroe, Jr.'s needling as he said, "Okay, hope didn't work. Settle for truth. And a chair, maybe—no kiddin', better get your ass secured."

Parker remained standing just to spite him. "Skip the drumroll." He glanced ruefully at his reflection: Here we are, still.

"My high school English teacher use to say, 'Man is the creature who asks "why?" ' Ever wonder—"

There was a crackling noise, then elevator music, heavy on the strings, began piping from the speakers.

"Jesus H. Christ!" Monroe, Jr. sighed. "What now! And where do you think *you're* goin'?"

* * *

The babies! Parker was heading for the place where the installer had been working, the old fuse box near the back door. He had to get there to save the babies.

In one part of his mind he knew that this business with the babies was subliminal trickery—its purpose beyond him—and that if he kept walking he was likely to get shot. But it didn't matter. It didn't matter because...because of the babies! He had to save the babies!

He was halfway down the hall when Monroe, Jr. shouted, "Forget the story, I'll kill you now!"

The part of his mind that thought it knew what was going on saw two choices: He was dead either way. Either face the truth and get shot, or turn your back on it and get shot in the back. He stopped, turned to face his enemy. He was ready for his recognition scene.

"This better be good," he said. He didn't know if he could stand there another second; things were looking bad for the babies. "What's the point!" Situation with the babies: critical.

Monroe, Jr. tilted his head to the left, then slowly cocked it to the right. "Not *now!*" he screamed. "Save the goddamn babies!"

Let us run! Let us run downtown and save the babies! He skidded into the back door and turned to the old fuse box on his right. Lift the latch and save the babies. From some old, irrelevant universe Hank Monroe, Jr. was calling, "If your hand comes outta there with any kinda weapon..."

He released the latch. Most of what followed came too fast, too bunched together for comprehension. At the time he was aware only of something hurtling toward him out of the dark; of Monroe, Jr. screaming "No!" and managing to shove him partly out of its way. It wasn't till long afterward that he could recall the moment clearly. In dreams, in random turns of thought, he'd see the thing coming in inexorable slo-mo, frame-by-frame, as if it had been heading for him his whole life.

* * *

A weighted slap of water shocked him awake. The eyewash of Parker's vision gave Hank Monroe, Jr., standing over him with the mop bucket, the gleam of a welcoming angel. He gagged up water and thought he tasted blood in the mix.

He closed his eyes; Monroe, Jr. poked his ribs with his shoe. "How—?" Parker exhaled. He'd been thinking "What?" and "Why?" but this was the easiest syllable to form, not much more than a sigh or a moan. He heard the hiss of water seeping into his clothes. It smelled like the Y.

"How long? Not long." Monroe, Jr.'s shoes squished when he shifted position. "You been out round a minute."

The sound Parker had been trying to place was his teeth chattering. "How—?"

"How'd you get knocked out? Don't you know?" Monroe, Jr. set down the bucket and loomed back into Parker's vision. By way of an answer, he jerked his thumb to Parker's right.

The slight turn of the neck required to look set off his pain. The blast of it threatened to push out the sides of his head; it left no room to take in the sight above him, a giant boxing glove at the end of a thick stiff spring.

Monroe, Jr. held the glove down and released it; with a muted *Boing*! it commenced bouncing up and down. "It's heavy. You'd be out colder than a tater if I didn't push you. Can't say I get the setup, Ace."

Parker refused to believe that the world's ultimate security system was nothing but a sadistic prank by his best friend. But whatever it was supposed to do, it clearly had failed. Unless it *had* worked and Parker was just too groggy to see how. Maybe things were going splendidly. No, he was fairly certain they were not.

Monroe, Jr. leaned against the wall opposite the glove. "So, anyway, man is the creature who asks 'Why?' Joe says the meaning of life is to work out your karma, Jane says it's to do God's will, and there's always the guy who says it's all in your head. Who knows, huh? 'Cept in your case. In your case we know. In a minute you might be the first guy who knows what his life means. Say, I bet that's the deal with the glove. You knew this was comin', you can't take it."

Suddenly Parker knew what it was. He released his breath, already thinking big deal.

"In 1970, J. Edgar Hoover had to pick the first target for the Breather Program. You know why he picked you?" Monroe, Jr. leaned close to watch his reaction. "He didn't like your face. That's right. He didn't like your face."

* * *

"So?"

"I knew you'd fight it , amigo, but the truth's gonna get in there. Nothin' can keep it out. Oh, you're gonna feel it. I won't think you're less of a man if you wanna cry."

"Actually," Parker was having trouble with his "l"s, "I've heard this before."

Monroe, Jr. sputtered, "Yeah but—"

"SO?"

Flustered, Monroe, Jr. went on trying to make the sale. "Most folks have days when they think their life's absurd." He faltered a bit on "absurd," uncertain, it appeared, whether Hank Monroe, Jr. would *say* that. "But they cheer themselves up by thinkin', 'There must be a good reason why my life's shit—'"

"Your life's shit?"

Before replying Monroe, Jr. gave Parker a good half-minute to contemplate his speck-size reflections. "They think," he amended, "there must be a good reason why their life's shit, even if they'll never know what it is. But you—"

"Yeah, sure, the despair."

The mirrors were trembling; Parker wished he'd let the guy have his moment.

"Okay, philosophy ain't your mode. Tell you what. I'll crack your goddamn pinhead."

He was dangling his heel above Parker's face when the doorbell rang. There was a splash as he set his foot back on the floor. "Now who do you suppose that is?" As if picturing what was about to happen he smiled into the distance, his sunglasses catching the light.

"The police," Parker answered.

"Nice try. It ain't a real party till the women show up. And I bet you thought *you* were stallin' *me!*" As he stepped over, Parker rolled onto his stomach and grabbed the man's ankle. Monroe, Jr. laughed, dragging him. Parker slid along the floorboards in his wet clothes.

They'd stopped moving. "You know, Ace, sometimes it's just more *dignified* to do nothing."

Parker slid the sock down, locked his arms round the shin, turned his head sideways and bit into the Achilles tendon. The real guy tasted of sweat, dirt, ash, dirty socks, old shoes, a scab or maybe a patch of psoriasis, and, at last, blood. Monroe, Jr. didn't scream; he might have been on painkillers. He was trying to shake Parker off, but this was his injured side. He dragged his foot forward—Parker was still clamped on—kneeled, and placed the muzzle against the back of Parker's head. Its cold spread down his neck and spine. The bell rang again.

Parker had decided he might as well die like those lizards that go on biting even with the head decapitated. His mouth was filling with blood—any second now he'd start choking—when the butt slammed the back of his head.

It hadn't quite knocked him out. He was curled up on his side gagging blood; through his squint everything looked wet and smeared together, rippling with the pulse in his skull. His intentions, having no workable body to enact them, went charging off like ghosts—to tackle Monroe, Jr., to knock him out with the baseball bat in the coat closet, to stab him with a knife from the kitchenette, to yell down the steps for Fran to run away. Maybe she was downstairs impersonating a mummy; maybe he didn't know the buzzer didn't work. Maybe by the time they found each other, the police really *would* be there.

Monroe, Jr. walked past the buzzer at the end of the hall; he was heading for the front door.

No sound. Parker fought to keep his eyes open. Blood or water or sweat trickled under his collar and across his back.

Then Monroe, Jr.'s voice bubbled up from the bottom of the steps. "Why Grandma!"

Grandma?

"Why Grandma, what a big gun you have! Give it here. . . So what you gonna do with it, shoot me?" Hank Monroe, Jr. chose that moment to try out a new fake laugh. He enunciated, "Hee! hee! hee!"

They proved to be his last words.

EIGHT

He'd hoped to wrap up his case with a party. Warming up the guests with
the classic "I suppose you're wondering why I've called you all together,"
he'd reach into the formless void of his case and pull out something like
a sentence diagram.

By the end he'd have settled for a party at which the guests explained
it all to him. He never gave a party, telling himself it was the practical dif-
ficulties of getting them all into a room: Fran hated Dobbs and wouldn't
speak to Ken Fletcher and still hadn't forgiven John Standell for calling
her "merely perfect"; John had told him that Todd Woolcurt, the bodyguard, thought Parker insufficiently grateful for his heroism the night
of the convention, when atoning for past inaction he'd beaten up and
rescued Hank Monroe, Jr.; Parker was reluctant to socialize with Mrs.
Slansky, who'd shot and killed Monroe, Jr., true, but had probably come
to shoot *him*; Harry Krell was unreachable, the offices of Tolerance Man-

agement having closed down, the phone been disconnected, the convention canceled after the first night; and Hank Monroe, Jr. was dead.

But the truth was, he was tired of his case. By now—it was early December—the topic of Jeffrey Parker seemed as used up as the light and the pulped leaves. He'd thought about little else since the day he learned he *had* a case, but lately he tried to focus on other people, leaning into conversation with a pouncing empathy that made them shrink back a bit.

At the moment his full attention had lit on Kathryn Ann Standell, who sat propped against her father's chest staring back. She didn't appear frightened by his swollen lips or the greenish shiners encircling his eyes like a superhero's mask; she seemed confounded by him—as if everything else had made sense.

"Babies always look so surprised," Parker observed. "What were you expecting?" he asked Kathryn. "Hmmm?"

Seated on the couch next to John, Peg leaned forward to study her daughter's face. "She's thinking about the old philosophical problem," she said, rubbing a cloth over the wet spot on Kathryn's Bugs Bunny T-shirt. "'Why is everything *out there* instead of in my mouth?'"

Parker laughed. "What I've been pondering is, what's the connection between security and getting punched in the face with a giant boxing glove? Sorry. I can't help wondering."

John looked down at Kathryn on his lap and tried to entertain her with his exaggerated sigh, going slack and deflated, but she was still watching Parker.

John's display of weariness was a reminder that he'd already tried to explain the boxing glove when he visited Parker in the hospital (where Parker had been given stitches for his head wound, held a day for observation, and released when they found no brain damage). He'd been contrite about what happened, of course, wincing so fiercely the tendons bulged in his neck, but as soon as he began explaining the system he was carried away by its conceptual elegance and literal brute logic. It had mostly whizzed past Parker.

"Forgive me if I wasn't more attentive in the hospital," Parker said. "I'd been hit in the face with a giant boxing glove."

"Yeah, well." John's sweep of the arm indicated life's infinite variety and surprise . His happiness still bore the gloss of a lotto winner surprised by flashbulbs.

"Jeff?" Peg held up the bottle and he extended his glass across the coffee table.

"I keep thinking," Parker said, "the whole point of the system... you were more interested in protecting me from the truth than from, ah, death?"

John did a fair imitation of Steve Dobbs's "Exactly!"

Peg poured the wine and looked as baffled as Parker. "When," he said as the wine reached the rim.

"Am I to understand that we're marketing a new kind of home security?" Peg wondered. "'Die happy'? Comparatively happy in Jeff's case. 'Die with your illusions intact'?"

"Protecting Parker from the truth was cheaper and easier than protecting him from his enemy."

Parker and Peg exchanged looks. "John's tweaking us a little," she said. "He hates having to repeat himself."

"You said the guy had an unlimited expense account," John began. He spoke with the terse grudging matter-of-factness of a man compelled to state the obvious. "Suppose we'd gone high-tech. He buys countersecurity, no way we can compete. Not with *his* resources."

Parker leaned forward to sip the top off his wine. "I'd've settled for four or five off-duty cops hanging around."

"Think so? You've heard the cliché 'anyone can kill the president if he's smart enough and willing to get killed himself'?" John made his daughter smile by lowering his face over hers and doing a loud wet Bronx cheer, then resumed, "You think a resourceful assassin can get past the Secret Service but not Todd Woolcurt's knockoff Armani suit? Face it, the guy could buy more gadgets, he could hire more gunmen. If that's your field of combat, you're dead."

"Speaking of Todd."

"He was detained for questioning after the incident. And he figured your guy wouldn't be in any shape to bother you that night."

"You talk about Monroe, Junior's resources. I don't know how 're-sourceful' the guy was. Maybe not even smart enough to get a gun past the security check. It was just him that night."

"Sure, it was a game to him, and he wanted to keep it close. Your chances would've been a lot less if you escalated."

"And of course the system was there to assure that in the event of a crisis my ignorance if nothing else would be preserved. Shouldn't I have had a vote on what I got protected *from?*"

"You said you wished you could go on ignoring the guy. You said obtuseness was the only thing that worked against these people." John kept talking as Parker opened his mouth. "Anyway, I didn't really mean that I was going to let you get killed, ya numbskull. Protecting you from the truth was the only way we could save your life."

Kathryn upstaged her father's dramatic pause with a yawn that scrunched up her nose and eyes. He continued, "You said your enemy was putting on a show. You're the star and the audience, and it was all leading up to whaddayacallit. The recognition scene. But if you were out cold..."

"I see, you were playing to my strengths." Parker had intended mild sarcasm but couldn't keep out a trace of self-pity. "Unconsciousness is my field of combat."

"Don't take it personally, buddy. I didn't think he'd shoot you before he made his point. And if he couldn't make his point," John raised an eyebrow, "hmmm? Meanwhile the system alerted the police."

"He *did* seem eager to make his point.... Why did we need the subliminal message? Why couldn't..."

"Because you might've hesitated to walk away from a man with a gun. Or get in the way of a giant boxing glove."

"I don't know, John, there was so much that could go wrong. And did! The system was based on so many blithe assumptions."

"Without the blithe assumptions, we had nothing but awful certainties."

"For instance, we both heard the same subliminal message. What if he'd gotten to the panel and opened it before I did?"

"You're not that lucky."

"Oh...right."

"He probably wouldn't have gotten there first anyway. My Subliminals guy says sociopaths are less susceptible."

"Well, what if Fran was over and *she* got punched in the face? What if he'd gotten scared when the countdown started and taken me outside? But I guess your point is that if we tried to anticipate everything that could go wrong, we'd've been paralyzed. And I have to admit that having the world's ultimate security system gave me courage. Without my false hope and your false assurances, I probably wouldn't have survived the night."

John chose to take these mixed thanks straight: "Glad to help out."

Parker said, "I've always thought that John's ability to act in a crisis is tied to his short-term capacity for regret. If he's made a mistake, he'll apologize, he'll do whatever it takes to make amends. But bring it up a second time and it's, 'John, you killed my mother.' 'And?'"

Wine spurted out of Peg's nose; she held her fist to her lips till she managed to swallow. "Warn me when you're going to say stuff like that. It's true, it's no fun arguing with him."

"Come to think of it, if you'd installed a perfect system, then I'd have been the one who answered the doorbell and gotten killed in the lobby. I guess it really did save my life."

Bored with the subject, John held up Kathryn for his wife's inspection. "Want me to give her her bath?"

"I should be going," Parker said.

"Stick around. We have ice cream. Anybody want ice cream? So what happened to the old lady?"

"Don't you read the papers? She's a hero. There's no real proof she came over to shoot me. In fact I thanked her—over the phone!—for saving my life. It seemed rude not to. She graciously accepted my thanks. She has a court date coming up for the unregistered handgun, but I'm sure they'll drop the charges, and everyone agrees she killed Monroe, Junior in self-defense. She's seeing a therapist, and I have assurances from her lawyer that...what?...next time she wants to come over armed, she'll call first."

"What was the damn point!" Peg demanded. "What's the big ultimate..."

"J. Edgar Hoover didn't like my face."

"So?"

"Exactly!"

"I don't like your face either," John said. "Did you feel a little let down?"

"I keep thinking there has to be something else. What am I still missing?"

"Is that why you look so down-at-the-mouth?" Peg asked. "There's something else and you don't know what it is?"

"People say I'm unobservant, but is that true? Don't smirk. I know that sometimes I'll be walking along thinking and I'll miss some acquaintance passing on the street. And I missed the whole conspiracy because when things go wrong, sane people resist the notion that it's a plot by enemies they've never heard of. But what do people *mean* when they say I'm unobservant? I'm a pretty good critic—could I do that if I didn't notice details? I could close my eyes and describe the furniture, your faces, your clothes, but...I don't know how to put this. Is there something everybody *else* sees?"

John shrugged. Peg said, "What? Like a kick-me sign?"

"I've always imagined it as a giant parrot perched on my head."

Without any noticeable cue passing between them, John and Peg focused a few inches above his hair.

"Yeah. That's the feeling. Okay, funny. Cut it out."

* * *

He hadn't exactly been missing anything—just thinking about something else each time the thing he knew came to mind. Having shouted it down, as it were, he knew only that it had to do with Fran.

For days he'd been waiting, studying her face, hoping, when he got caught, that she mistook his watchfulness for simple adoration. Not quite knowing how to react, she pretended not to notice or made a face like a movie star smiling for her public. Sometimes they'd be alone in her apartment or his, and she'd turn to look behind her, scanning the room for the deserving party.

Whatever it was that he thought he knew, he told himself he had to be wrong. After all, they'd never been closer. Take the night after he got out of the hospital, when she'd bought him a late dinner at Isabella's. Even before the drinks arrived she was referring to him as her hero. By the time dessert came he felt obliged to remind her, "All I did was ignore him."

They'd both paused to admire the elegance with which Fran dispatched her martini olive. "Maybe not noticing is what bravery is all about," she observed. "'All I did was not look down,' hmmm?"

"Then I guess a knockout blow to the head would improve us all," he teased, still feeling the heat of her praises on his face. He figured she'd see through this hero stuff any day, and at least he'd be able to say I told you so. "How are the interviews going?"

"Oh, you know." She watched herself rub a wet spot on the table with her napkin. Recalling the moment days later, he thought he'd had his first twinge right there.

"What, not going well?" Not likely!

"You're so deft at changing the subject," she said deflecting the conversation back to him. "All I was saying was, you don't give yourself enough credit." He watched her slide the wadded napkin back and forth with her finger.

But as they started up Rush Street to her car she locked her arm around his, her hip bumping against him. They were passing a row of singles bars when a voice behind them proclaimed her glories. "Ignore it," she whispered. Soon other voices joined in, rhapsodizing the joys that would be hers if she lay down right there, on the sidewalk in front of Halliday's. A man named Dick proclaimed that in honor of his erotic mastery, *the* dick had been renamed after him. Soon even that modicum of wit deserted the band of drunks following them.

"I think I'll have a word with the boys about their figures of speech." This was still the hold-me-back stage, but a return trip to the emergency ward was beginning to look unavoidable.

"Keep walking, Parker. If you get beat up 'defending my honor,' I'll beat you up, too."

She squeezed his arm and pulled him forward. "Ignore them," she whispered, "ignore them out of existence! Come on," she grabbed his chin to keep him from turning his head, "you can do it. Unobserve them." They walked double-time at Fran's urging, stepping onto the street to get around the line for the midnight set at Mallorin's. She leaned close; he smelled herbal shampoo and her martini. It was easy to believe that the fierce orange pinpoint at the center of each green eye was Fran, not just the sodium vapor lights. The air fizzed and it began to snow, inebriated mothlike flakes crowding the headlights and streetlamps. "Do it, Parker!" She was trying to keep him out of the emergency room and doing her best to make it all seem a lark, crossing her eyes now at a flake sparkling on the tip of her nose.

"All right," he said, getting into the spirit, "I'll do it. One two... three!"

They couldn't help stopping and turning around. They were alone on a block full of buzzing Christmas lights, the wet empty sidewalk radiant as an electric oven.

"Voilà!" he said.

"You zapped 'em!" She tucked the glittered streamers of her hair into her collar. "You know, we should make a list."

"In the interest of full disclosure I don't—boompf!" She'd mashed her wet face against his and plugged his mouth with her tongue.

So what was he missing, and why couldn't he go on missing it?

* * *

The evening she came over to make her announcement, he realized what he dreaded. That Tolerance Management had it right—"You'll forgive her, she'll never want to look at you again." Seeing him as her hero probably just made her feel guiltier. Knowing Fran, she'd avoid having it out. What she'd do was accept a job with an out-of-town firm. There are airplanes, she'd remind him, there are telephones. She needn't even admit to herself that she'd made a decision about anything but her job.

True, his suspicions were contradicted by every single thing—for example, here she was.

She sat facing him on his couch, curled up in her little black dress while he filled their champagne glasses from the bottle she'd brought over. The out-of-town-job theory had nothing going for it, really, except the usually sufficient reason that it was the worst he could imagine.

She'd brought candles, too, and when she held her head at a certain angle her face threatened to spiral down the darkness of her cheekbones. Preparatory to her announcement she adjusted the thrust of her chin, the hauteur of her eyebrow, and the sardonic tilt of her smile. He'd miss the private joke they shared in her glamour—as if she were simultaneously giving a performance and nudging him in the ribs backstage.

Things were looking up; he couldn't imagine her dumping him with quite this much ceremony. And she wouldn't be babbling, now, at this torrential cadence and aria pitch, nearly smacking him with an expansive gesture, champagne sloshing over the rim of her glass, candlelight amassed in her eyes and teeth. He'd been so busy analyzing portents that he'd missed the announcement itself; he tried to catch up, it wasn't hard.

"...Shakespeare in the Park! 'Meet me for lunch at the Guggenheim'—don't you love the sound of that? And you can stop being self-conscious about your dancing—spaz attacks are in out there. You can fly out weekends, or I'll fly here, money's no problem. Oh, and did I mention that Merlon and Cameron represent some of the big publishing houses? Finish that manuscript because someday you could be wearing that air of distant abstraction on public television. Goddamnit, Parker!" She grabbed his shirtfront with her free hand. "You'd better be happy for me!"

She was taking a job with Merlon & Cameron in New York. A long time ago she'd mentioned entertainment law as something she might want to pursue, and they were one of the best in the field. He needed a moment to get his breath back and another to recall whether he was one of those boyfriends who put themselves in the way of the girlfriend's career. He was not.

Her chin was crinkling as it did when she was about to cry.

He tried to head it off. "I'm happy, I'm just trying to take it all in. If this is what makes you happy I'm happy. No 'if'— just happy! Ow! Don't hit, I'm happy! I'll miss you, that's all, but it's *great* that—"

"If we see each other weekends, that's more than we could sometimes when I was in law school."

"Absolutely. We can make it there, we'll it make anywhere."

He was about to bravely propose a toast when it hit him. Here she was in her little black dress celebrating. If she was trying to get away from him, she didn't know it. And that led to the following hopeful thought. She didn't know what she wanted, if she wanted anything; he didn't want to think about what he knew, if he really knew it. It seemed within the realm of possibility that they could stay together out of sheer obtuseness.

"There are airplanes," he added, "there are telephones."

She was wearing her cartoon-cow earrings; he gave one a tap, watching it swing and turn.

"Look." She put her palm under his chin and squeezed his cheeks with her thumb and fingers. "If I was planning to dump you, would I do it this way?"

She was still squeezing, but he got out an approximation of "Absolutely not!"

"I have a year and a half more of law school. I won't be leaving Chicago for longer than that. Not the most efficient plan for getting away from you, if that's what I wanted. Do you think I'm leaving you in slow motion?"

It brought him up short. What if this was real happiness, and he was too busy feigning happiness to notice? "No," he conceded, "I don't" ("buy dough").

"Don't you see what they've done to you? They can leave you alone now because they've taught you to believe that everything's a trick. What did William James say—there's dupery through hope and dupery through fear, and they win if—"

He removed her hand from his face, kissing and nibbling her fingers. "You and I," she was saying, "never walk out of a movie. Why is that?"

He tilted her chin up. "Because," he replied, her good pupil, "we have to see how it ends."

"And do you think I'd walk out before—"

As he kissed her he wished this movie would end by freezing on the love scene. Freeze frame on the love scene before his next doubt came to mind.

He was unzipping her little black dress; she was running her nails up his back as she pulled up his shirt. "Jeff, do me a favor."

"Anything!"

"Starting tomorrow go out and look at things. Things that have nothing to do with you. My poor dear baby, if you just pay attention to what's actually out there—out here!—you'll be less scared."

"You—"

"Something besides me. You more or less notice me."

"Deal."

"Not *now!*" she laughed, pulling him back into the kiss. An earring clanked on the floorboards. They stood up sloughing off dangling, un-zipped, and unbuttoned clothing.

He made it to the bedroom, entwingled with her tongue, thinking, freeze frame on the love scene.

She grabbed his face again, wrestling him into an eyelock: "Here!"

Yes. Freeze it here. Before the next thing occurred to him.

* * *

One evening in January it occurred to Parker that nothing had been settled. He was still too uneasy to bring up marriage or even the possibility of his moving to New York, preferring, for now, to let the egg stay miraculously balanced on its tip.

He was walking home hugging his groceries (for some vaguely ecological bonehead reason he'd asked for one big paper bag), watching the sidewalk for patches of ice. Of course his living arrangements would depend on the results of the job search; nothing had panned out yet, but he'd only been looking since December. Anyway, he thought they'd never been more in love. Still, he never found the right moment to bring up Fletcher's prediction ("you'll forgive her, she'll never want to look at you again") and share a good laugh at how wrong it had been.

If things seemed a bit unsettled and indeterminate, he told himself this was ordinary life. Of *course* it seemed indistinct compared to the shrieking gaudiness of the conspiracy; it required some readjustment, that was all. He imagined how Steve Dobbs might put it. *Ordinary life: you're not used to it. It'll eat you alive!*

He paused under the El tracks to admire the broken glass. There was always more glass trimming the sidewalks of the neighborhood than his theories could account for. It twinkled back at the streetlamps like a remnant of the holidays, clear, red, green, and brown fragments shivering with flame-shaped glints. Its tiny scraping broken bells resounded in the lull of a passing train.

He knew that a man standing and staring at the pavement on that nearly deserted sidewalk would be a dear sight to muggers, plus his ears ached, he was blinking away wind-blear, and soon his arms would go numb around the bag. Nonetheless he kept looking. He'd promised Fran that each day he'd pick out something to observe and really *really* pay attention.

"'The glass is falling hour by hour,'" a lugubrious voice recited.

Tom Grand, Parker's "ally" on the "search committee"—perhaps he was exactly what he claimed to be—must have sidled up while he was contemplating the shards. Again Tom conveyed a deadpan mirth whose signs remained elusive. It had something to do with the quaver in his gravelly voice and the bright moist lights in his doleful eyes; it might have been doodled on his face and camouflaged among the solemn lines. Giving Parker a moment to collect himself, he removed his steel-rimmed glasses and wiped them with a handkerchief.

"Louis MacNeice," said Parker, chagrined that he still felt the need to impress Tom Grand. He thought he made out other faces from the search committee in the black Cadillac idling at the curb.

He hadn't run, first because of the groceries, and then, as seconds passed, out of the untested assumption that if they were here to do something violent they'd have already done it.

Half the businesses around here were boarded up and most of the others closed early. There was no one else out but a couple leaving Standee's a half-block up Granville and heading in the opposite direction. In the bright liquor store across the street the clerk was razoring open a box while he talked on the phone, the receiver gripped between his shoulder and his splotched bald head.

Tom Grand had replaced his glasses. "Don't panic.," he said gently, his breath unraveling on the wind. "This isn't your orals."

Parker laughed and started walking away, raising and lowering the bag to keep the blood circulating in his arms. He nearly lost his footing on the icy incline where the pavement sloped for handicapped access; Tom Grand righted him by the elbow.

He was crossing the street at Parker's side. "You know how it is with academic committees. Unspoken agreements, private jokes, ancient resentments, fragile detentes. It never makes sense to an outsider." They halted to let a car pass. "We don't usually have guests at those Wednesday-night meetings, and we must have seemed bewildering...maybe even threatening."

"So your trying to kill me—that was just a committee thing."

"You can understand how your friend bursting in and waving a gun might have given *us* pause. Let's call it a series of interpretive gaffes." The Caddy made a left off Granville and cruised alongside as they started up Winthrop.

Stereos thumped among the dingy apartment courts like a cardiac upheaval. Parker had forgotten how dark it was here; he thought of turning back to Granville, maybe ducking into Standee's. Instead he kept walking home, hoping to preserve for as long as possible the illusion of his free will. Toward that end, he decided to play his role to the hilt—a man living an ordinary life. The groceries, he thought, made a nice prop.

"So Tom!" he barked, imitating the unalloyed good cheer with which he imagined a man leading an ordinary life might greet an acquaintance. "What brings you out to this neck of the woods on such a cold night?" Not a smart question; he'd invited the committee to declare its intentions. He anticipated guns coming out, the Cadillac bouncing over the curb across his path.

"That position we discussed? It's yours. There wasn't time to mail a letter of acceptance, and we've been having trouble reaching you by phone." To get Parker past standing and staring, he added, "You remember—this is Huntley Crane's course load. Delbert Zontar was set to postpone his sabbatical and take the winter courses, but Del has infectious hepatitis."

Parker had gotten two calls that week from Bill Hungerford of the committee; each time he'd hung up as soon as the man identified himself.

"We were just at your building." To fill the long pause Tom added, deadpan, "You weren't home."

If this were ordinary life, one might ask questions. "Um, what would I be teaching?" Parker had decided that instead of dropping the groceries when he bolted, he'd hand them to Tom. It might give him an extra second or two if the guy was armed. The thought of Tom as a hitman was incongruous, but that hardly counted against it.

"Modern British and American Poetry and Intro to Criticism. I know this seems very odd. Till the last minute we thought Del would be back in time, and then we...why bore you with this? Tonight we decided to give it one last try before taping the dreaded note to the door. Your Modern Poetry section starts in less than an hour."

Parker resisted the urge to laugh in his face. Tom, would you mind holding this? No, just push the bag on him; he'd take it out of sheer reflex. Run back toward Granville—if there was traffic, the Caddy might have have a hard time pursuing the wrong way up the narrow street.

"We don't usually act this spontaneously," said Tom Grand, "and it's true that the idea of our driving up here came while the committee was deliberating at Little Joe's Bar and Grill. Someone joked that if you thought your all-powerful enemies had come to take you away, you might go quietly, like a Kafka character." Realizing that his joshing—if that's what it was—had failed to inspire confidence, he got down to business. "Tonight just show up. Write your name on the board, give your class some notion of the reading and the requirements. You'd be on an accelerated tenure track. I don't foresee any problem there, but get serious *fast* about updating your bibliography. Frankly, that's the only thing that could hold you back."

Update your bibliography: Nice touch. Behind the tinted rear passenger window he thought he saw a hand raised in a wave.

"When I was a kid," said Tom Grand, "we used to play a game called Cap. One guy holds his hand out, knuckles up, while the other guy holds his fists behind his back. The object for this second guy—the hitter—is to try to punch the hand. If the one with his hand out—the mark—pulls it away before the punch comes, he has to keep it out while the hitter gives him three of his best. But if the mark sees the punch coming and draws back his hand in time, then it's the hitter who gets the penalty. In both cases the trick," he said gliding back deftly as Parker thrust out the bag, "is to watch the eyes."

Disoriented by this feat of perfect timing, Parker hadn't bolted. He pulled the groceries back to his chest.

"Don't run off and waste all this good..." Tom bridged the distance he'd just opened and reaching into the bag held up a can of Beefaroni as if it were Yorick's skull. Putting it back, he gave Parker what appeared to be a look of commiseration.

"I know," said Parker. "It's sad-guy food. I'm over that." It was idiotic to confide in him, but then, why not? "Tonight was going to be my last can—I'd planned a little ceremony." It looked like there'd be no post-Beefaroni days after all.

"Think of it this way. If we were really...never did know who you think we really are. The Mafia?"

"Whatever." There was a clattering noise; a couple with a bundled toddler in a stroller steered around them. The kid had a wet mouth, a wind-reddened face, eyes straining toward perfect roundness, and a green stocking cap topped by a fuzz-ball. "EEE!" he proclaimed, raising his arms like a conductor. Ordinary life: Parker turned to watch it pass.

"—then I wouldn't be standing here trying to persuade you," Tom Grand was saying. "We'd be already be 'taking you for a ride.'"

"Things like this don't happen in ordinary life," Parker insisted.

Tom Grand had a robust and gravelly laugh. "Clearly you haven't had much experience with ordinary life!"

"Got me there," Parker conceded. As they approached his building he decided to test the scope of his freedom. "All right, what the heck! Count me in."

Tom Grand gripped his shoulder and shook his hand. "You've done the right thing. You have to move forward in your life, enemies or not."

As casually as he could, Parker said, "I'll just drop off my groceries and pick up my notes. Wait here, I'll be right out."

Surprisingly, Tom found that acceptable. "Don't worry if you can't find the notes." He looked at his watch. "Tonight it's especially true that 'Ninety percent of greatness is showing up.'"

Parker took the steps two at a time to his floor, and before he had the key in, the thought he'd been suppressing forced itself upon him. What if this were a real job offer? What if pigs flew! He unlocked the door and slammed it behind him, turned the two locks, set the groceries on the card table, and sprinted for the back door.

The key stuck in the bolt; you had to turn it slowly!; he turned the key and yanked open the door. He was startled by the full moon and the crisply focused sky. Panting, he forced himself to breathe deeply—it felt like he was inhaling the cold, sharp stars. There was no one in view from the porch but the familiar stocking-cap guy going through the trash bin in the alley. No sign of the Caddy. He stood with his hand on the half-closed door; a job at Circle would be a boost to eventually getting a job in New York. The fact that this wasn't exactly the job he wanted—did that make it more plausible? He'd begun applying in December after Hank Monroe, Jr. died: too late for even the fall term at many universities. He'd despaired of proposing on his Skokie Valley salary, but now. . .*there's no job, dipstick!*

The bell rang; to buy another minute, he came back in and pressed the intercom button, which tonight proved to be working. "Yeah, what?"

"If we were the Mafia"—Tom Grand sounded like Lamont Cranston on the tinny speaker— "would we be leaving you to your own devices up there? Free to sneak out the back?"

"If you were an academic committee, why would you hire a guy you believe to be a paranoid nutcase?"

"We never believed any such thing. Now can we please shake a leg?"

"You obviously— "

"We know you have enemies because of the letter. I'm referring, of course, to the infamous rumor letter. It was so over-the-top no one ever believed it. Bill was just looking for an issue."

It seemed like such a prime example of academic spitefulness, Parker was nearly convinced. A new thought occurred to him. "Maybe you're *not* going to kill me. Maybe I'm just back in the old slow-roast hell."

He regretted the outburst—it was unseemly to let your enemies *or* your colleagues hear you whine—but it didn't deter Tom Grand: "Look. This isn't just a decision about a job. It's about how you're going to live your life. In a minute we'll give up and drive away. You'll sit up there thinking it's some kind of trick. Maybe in a few hours you'll start prowling around the building until you've convinced yourself we're really gone. You might be relieved at first. Pleased with yourself—nobody takes Jeffrey Parker for a sucker! You'll be less self-delighted when it finally sinks in. Is that how you want to live?"

The prophecy was weirdly compelling in his crackling old-time-radio voice. But Parker had already decided: If there *was* a job, and he took it, he thought he could marry Fran.

"I'll be right down."

* * *

By the time he came out he was thinking, might as well. If the worst were true he'd never get away; he could only escape if he ought to have stayed. And why concoct so elaborate and unconvincing a ruse just to kill him? But as Tom Grand, playing chauffeur, snapped to attention and opened the car's rear door, it occurred to Parker that if you looked for the point you were playing their game. The interior radiated heat, booze, and perfume. Peering inside he recognized a bright burst of hair: it was Esther, the redhead he'd flirted with at the interview, and on her other side was George, the hulking man who'd blocked his way. The driver was the white-haired woman with the bangs and the big glasses—the one who'd complained about rabbits in her garden. Parker thought of Tom Grand's warning: He didn't want to look back in twenty years and think, I could have changed my life but I was scared of the rabbit woman. He ducked under the doorframe and sat down exchanging hellos. Next to the rabbit woman, Bill Hungerford turned around and glared unabashedly: "Hello." There was something reassuring in the thought that regardless of which scenario was true—the conspiracy *or* the job—this man was his enemy. When Tom Grand had closed the back door, walked around to the passenger side, sat down next to Bill and closed the front door, the locks came down with a *Chunk!*

Experimentally Parker raised and lowered his button.

"Please don't play with the buttons," said the rabbit woman as they pulled out.

"Sorry."

Tom Grand said, "You'll have to come down some day before five this week to fill out your W-4 form, sign your contract, and so forth. The department's on the twentieth floor of University Hall. Stop in and say hello to the chairman, Bob Overby. We couldn't have got this through without Bob's support."

"All right." It was beginning to seem awfully like a job, though in one part of his mind Parker was thinking, W-4 form: Nice touch.

Bill was still turned around giving Parker the look. There was a passive-aggressive bully like this in every university department, always on a committee. Their very presence was a silent dare to name anything they'd done to give offense. After all, they observed every legalism and made sure that everybody else behaved with equal circumspection—what was wrong with that? And if Bill's tiny pouty face seemed to be glaring, well, define glare. He was just looking at you, and what was the rule against that? And he *had* said hello—so how was he being rude? And his hair was impeccably combed. Guys like Bill were the reason civilization had never worked out. Parker had been planning to use his last seconds on earth—if that's what he was heading for—to reflect on his life. But he thought the time might be better spent planting a fist beneath those tinted aviator glasses. If the job was a ruse, was this guy just *pretending* to be an asshole?

Bill said, "I want my opposition on the record. What are we saying to future applicants with this appointment? 'If you want a position at the University of Illinois at Chicago, the best interview strategy is *a gun-toting brawl.*'"

"Bill's sore that you hung up on him," Tom Grand explained. "I'm sure it was just a misunderstanding." Parker grasped the implication that he could smooth things over with an apology, but he wasn't in the mood.

"Tom thinks you're a brilliant intellect"—Bill's sarcasm edged on hysteria now— "who 'took a wrong turn in his life,' whatever that means, and all you need is a second chance. I never thought it was the department's mission to be Boy's Town for troubled academics, especially when the ragamuffins instigate *gun-toting brawls.*"

"You've made your position clear." Esther uncrossed her legs and leaned toward Bill. "You're not advancing an argument any more, you're having a tantrum."

"I just think we should be honest and straightforward about our requirements. Next time we advertise in the PMLA—"

"Bill," she warned, "if you use the phrase 'gun-toting brawl' one more time—"

"She can do it," murmured George looking out his window. "Better shut up." They were turning off Bryn Mawr onto Lake Shore Drive.

"This evening," Tom said cheerily, "George and I were discussing some esoteric points of golf. Do you play, Jeff?"

"A few times. I don't really—"

"It's more a philosophical problem than a golfing one. Our dispute was on the matter of gross interference. Suppose, for example, that as your ball is rolling to a stop, some passerby kicks it in another direction."

The subject was of no interest to Parker, and he was tempted to go into his nod and stare routine, but there was something urgent in Tom's voice.

"None of the PGA rules seems like a fair remedy," Tom was saying. "You could, for example, invoke the 'free drop' rule: You measure the distance of your longest club, usually the driver, stand at that spot, and then drop the ball at arm's length over that new spot. You play it from the position to which it rolls after it's dropped. But what if the interfering kick rolled the ball downhill? It could go dozens of yards off course, and the free drop rule doesn't redress that injustice. And why shouldn't justice apply in the game of golf? Another possibility is to retake the shot, but the rules call for the addition of penalty strokes, and so we still have the problem of fairness." He was getting at something besides golf, Parker thought, what the hell was it?

"The PGA rule book," Tom continued, "has an entire section on 'Acts of God,' but frankly those remedies also seem...I'm sorry to keep coming back to this...unjust."

It's a parable, Parker thought. He's giving me the truth in a parable, and I'm too goddamn dense to get it.

"Now sometimes in a friendly game the players apply more informal 'winter rules.' A few years ago I was visiting my in-laws in Peru, Indiana, and my father-in-law and I played a round at a course there. A local screwball teenager ran onto the links, grabbed my ball, and disappeared with it into the woods, later to sell it to another golfer. Invoking 'winter rules,' my father-in-law allowed me a 'free drop at the point of injury.' Now George here is a golfer of the old school, and when I told him that story he was overwhelmed with disgust. But my own solution to the problem of gross interference would go even *beyond* 'free drop at the point of injury': I believe that to restore justice, you sometimes have to pick up the ball and set it down exactly where it belongs."

Suddenly it made sense, and the force of revelation, combined with the soporific heat in the car and Esther's hard-sell perfume, made him lower his head and inhale. He fought off wooziness as she leaned close.

"Are you all right?"

"Fine, thanks." His head began to clear as she drew away. Bill went on giving him the evil eye, his frozen smirk threatening to crack. Tom Grand also remained turned in his seat, waiting, it seemed, for Parker to indicate that he understood the parable.

"You're speaking," Parker began, "of the conspiracy of good. What Harry Krell called the new order. I've been so...so sad these last weeks; I didn't realize it till now. I just knew I was waiting. I kept telling myself my enemy's dead, the conspiracy's over, what could I be waiting for? And now I see. I was waiting to get everything back. I want everything that was taken from me, though I'm not sure I could tell you what that is. I lost *something*, I want it back. I want the life I would have had *restored*, if you can restore something you've never had. I've been waiting—and I love the way you put it, Tom—to be picked up and *inserted* into that life. So that's what this job is all about: 'Winter rules!'"

Tom Grand had listened to this outpouring with his usual deadpan alertness. He regarded Parker for one more beat, then turned to George. "Ever played Augusta?"

"Never made it down there. A friend of mine has a membership at Pebble Beach, and I've played a few rounds there. Best course I've ever played. Can't say it was the best golf." He laughed.

As they went on discussing golf, Parker's belief in the new order waned.

* * *

Esther, Tom, and George were escorting him to his building. Conspirators or colleagues, they must have been worried that he'd run.

They were following in the shadow of the overhead walkway, and as Parker surveyed the deserted campus he nearly laughed out loud. The concrete pillars, the stone amphitheater, the infernal orange lights, the sparse tortured dwarf trees, the dim glow behind opaque windows slotted in gray girders: it was all a bad movie of his dread. By the next time, he hoped, it wouldn't be an image of anything—it would just be another evening at work.

"What do you have planned for tonight?" Tom asked.

To run? Now? "I couldn't find my notes, but I remember my old Intro to Modernism lecture. Oh, I usually start with Virginia Woolf's idea that everything changed 'in or about December, 1910.'" He tried to recall the distant moment in his own life when everything changed. He wanted to believe that tonight would be the night everything changed *back*.

As they stepped from the darkness beneath the walkway, Esther did a childish twirl, her face raised to the sky. A languorous snowfall was crowding the air, blossoming around the lights. The stark gray-slab campus looked a tiny bit whimsical among the suspended flakes.

"Listen." She put a finger to his lips. "What do you hear?"

The shock of her touch was one more thing fizzing through his nerves. She might have been flirting, but her watchful smile made him think she was trying to calm him down.

"I have a girlfriend who does this, and I hate it. Oh, all right." The closest other people were coming out of a classroom building a hundred yards away. "I hear our footsteps. My breathing. That breeze sound distant traffic makes. Distant shouts. What did Joyce call history? A cry in the street."

"Never mind Joyce, you've already got the job." She squeezed his arm, snowflakes blinking in the riotous circuitry of her hair. "What else? What's *under* all that?"

"The lights on the light posts are buzzing."

"Good. And beneath that?"

"The snow. Poets call it a hiss, but it's more like a flick. Phht. Something brushing past you."

She raised an eyebrow. "Stop trying to impress me—you're missing the central thing. Don't tell me you don't hear it. Stop thinking."

And immediately he heard it. "There's this hum." He stopped walking and listened. It was hard to believe he'd missed it, but he must have been hearing it all along: a deep electrical hum, such as a generator might make. George looked back and pointed to his wrist.

"Keep walking," Esther said.

"The sound—what is it?"

"Who knows?"

"It's like Paul Robeson holding the last baritone note of a lullaby," said Parker. "Soothing...but it gets a little scary as it goes on."

"I use it for meditation because you have to empty your mind of other things to hear it. It *does* get scary after a while, and then you have to think of something else. But it's always there." They'd stopped in front of a hive of cubbyholed girders and brown windows, identical to most of the other classroom buildings. "And *you* are *here*."

"You look," said Tom Grand, "like the guy who gets the white robe at the ritual sacrifice. It's opening night, that's all. You'll feel better as soon as you realize your class isn't going to rush the podium."

"I'm sure I will." Ritual sacrifice—the phrase had been running through Parker's head since Steve Dobbs used it.

Tom shook his hand. "Professor Parker, I think you can take it from here." He was looking sentimental, though his eyes were always misty. What if Parker "escaped"—how stupid would he feel when he got home?

Parker slowed his breathing and tried to quiet his thoughts, which just made him aware of the hum.

George pointed to his wrist again. "They're waiting in there."

That decided it. It came down to a matter of professionalism: "They" were waiting, and they might be students. Parker shook hands all around and headed for the entrance.

* * *

He walked straight to the board, determined not to obsess about whether they looked like students—or too much like students. They looked real enough In his one hasty glance before he turned to the board. He'd hoped to look away before that impression changed. But even while he faced the board and picked up the chalk, it was dawning on him that they'd looked too old—like the college students in '50s movies, always played by over-age actors. He reminded himself that this was an eight o'clock class, and night students tended to be older. All right, then: No problem!

"Let's be sure we're all in the right place." He wrote down the course title and still facing the board said, "Does anyone know the section number?" Nothing. He didn't recall hearing the usual murmurings when he walked in. Since he'd turned his back, he'd heard nothing but the clack of his chalk and the buzz of a fluorescent tube.

"Doesn't anyone have a catalog?" Nothing.

"And my name," he said as he wrote, "is Jeffrey Parker." Nothing but a cough, but no answer was required.

A new possibility occurred to him. What if this was ordinary life? He'd been waiting to see how it ended, but there was one ending he hadn't foreseen: the crane shot where the camera pulls back skyward and the top of our hero's head merges into the crowd. It wasn't the end of our hero, just a sign that from here on, nothing special would happen to him—the rest was ordinary life. Not a *bad* thing, he assured himself, it would just take some getting used to. He took a step back from his writing on the board. Jeffrey Parker: What an utterly unremarkable name.

He turned to face them.

Acknowledgments and Notes

Thanks to all those who read the novel in manuscript, offered criticism, or otherwise helped, or tried, to make it a good and published book: Charlie Bass, Barbara Eaton, Jeanne Farrar, Richard Friedman, Dennis Loy Johnson, Larry Kart, Mike Keller, Peter Kostakis, Mary Ellen McManus, Phyllis Moore, Darlene Pearlstein, Matthew Sharpe, Sharon Solwitz, Doris Stockwell, Elizabeth Stockwell, Jim Stockwell, Beth Svendsen, and Jianying Zha. Thanks above all to Lore Segal.

Paul Hoover helped me understand golf's "free drop rule." I use a few phrases from his e-mail on the subject. Any inaccuracies on the topic are mine.

Philistine that he is, the movie theater manager is nonetheless discerning enough to lift from America's best and most under-utilized movie critic, Dave Kehr. The phrase "the cold vaults of technology" comes from Kehr's old capsule review of a James Bond movie (I forget which) in the Chicago *Reader*.

"Situation with the babies: critical" comes from John Woo's *Hard Boiled*. Parker could not have seen the movie in 1985.

The University of Illinois at Chicago has undergone a beautification program in the past decade or so and may not be recognizable from the earlier, brutalist image I present. No one recalls my description of klieg lights outside the El station there; I believe they were doing construction at the time.

COINTELPRO was a real FBI program that ran from sometime in the '50s to 1971. As far as I know, the FBI did not try to extend the life of the program by farming out the work to freelance cranks.

Clarification

In Chapter Three the Skokie Swift makes local stops in Skokie. The Skokie Swift does not make local stops in Skokie; the novel takes place in a world where it does. I regret the confusion.

BARRY SCHECHTER is a life-long resident of Chicago. His fiction, poetry, and criticism have appeared in the *Paris Review*, the *Chicago Tribune*, and the *Chicago Review*. This is his first novel.

Author photo by Darlene Pearlstein